# Between Two Moons
Cait Ness

Book Cover by Brian Roberts (@br.dsgn)

Map created by Ashley Jürgens (@wolfandbearr)

PAPERBACK ISBN: 979-8-9886812-0-5
eBOOK ISBN: 979-8-9886812-1-2

*For the wanderers, the lost, the displaced.*

# BETWEEN TWO MOONS

## Cait Ness

# PLAYLIST

Impossible – James Arthur

Power Over Me – Dermot Kennedy

The Killing Kind – Mariana's Trench

Broken Crown – Mumford & Sons

Tell Me I Matter – Point Blank Society

The Definition of Not Leaving – Hands like Houses

Starving for Friends – SLAVES, Vic Fuentes

THE VALE

THE ROE

HAVRIEL

# CHAPTER 1

## AZRAEL

Beyond the cicadas, Azrael Hikaim thought he could hear screaming. His name called out—breaking through the trees like the early morning sunshine currently blinding him—rang in his ears and, deep within his soul, he knew something had happened. He laced the front of his pants, picked his sword up from the rock he had it resting on, and ran back towards the makeshift camp his unit had settled in before they continued to track the rebellion further into the mountains. A crack resounded through the trees, rattling Azrael's bones, and the sickening crunch that followed increased his speed. His head began to swim as his body went on high alert. Something was very, *very* wrong.

Azrael broke through the tree line into the small clearing they had claimed in time to see a mallet of stone, seeped in blood, come down on Rayna's hands, her wrists bound tightly while her body was crushed beneath a second, larger man. Her scream snapped the tether on Azrael's fury, his sight reduced to the vulnerable opening in the armor of the man holding the mallet, between his chest and helmet. Without thinking, Azrael slipped the dagger he kept strapped on his thigh and hurled it through the air, sliding with ease in that small opening. The man's body dropped to his knees, mallet falling uselessly in the grass. The man holding Rayna down shot to his feet, black eyes promising a fight. Azrael didn't waste the momentum he had built. Angling his sword just so, he launched himself off the dead man's back and onto the one over Rayna. His sword sunk without struggle beneath the man's chin. The force of his jump sent him and the now dying man into the dirt behind Rayna. Azrael braced himself, rolling off the body, and leapt back to his feet. He took a breath, surveying the wreck of the camp.

His fellow soldiers were tied up at the feet of rebels, their misshapen and worn armor glinting in the sunrise, with all eyes on him. Twelve men stood behind his eight. He could do this. He would have to do this, to save them from what Rayna was still screaming from, and worse. He didn't know how his camp had been taken so easily, nor how twelve men had snuck up on them, past those on watch, but it didn't matter now. Azrael flexed his hand around the hilt before running at the closest rebel, but he didn't make two steps before the crack of a skull shattered his focus. *No.* Red hair and blood mixed together, pooling in the dirt.

His heart hardened with wrath as he kept moving, sword slicing through the first rebel, but met the second's with steel. The rebels, in Azrael's interactions, hadn't been trained as thoroughly as he was, and only a fraction as long, but their determination always surprised him. Determination to survive only took one so far. With a duck, a spin on his heels, and another scream striking the air, Azrael gutted the man before him.

It became a pattern before the others abandoned their screaming, pleading, victims and advanced on him. Step, duck, step, parry, lunge. Seven men surrounded him, overwhelming his senses and focus, but Azrael didn't stop swinging his sword until a blade graced his throat and hands secured his wrists. He should move—damn death—but another blood curdling scream wrenched out of one of his soldiers.

"Are you the captain?" A rough voice asked, but Azrael couldn't tell who it was that spoke.

"I am," he said at the same time as another voice replied, "I am."

The men parted before him, blade still pressing into his throat. Azrael looked at Jade, whose face was hardened and bloody and stared with a ferocity that Azrael couldn't condemn him for. He didn't know if keeping Rayna's title secret would keep her alive, but he would risk it for her. If all she had was two broken hands, it meant Azrael would take her consequences. It warmed a small part of his heart knowing that Jade had the same thought.

"Two captains?" The same rough voice *tsk*ed. The rebel at the far end of the clearing poised his mallet above a pair of legs and came down as laughter rippled through the others. "Never mind it. We've known you've been following us, and we don't appreciate it. Captain or not, tie him up too."

Azrael's sword was ripped from his hand and thrown across the clearing. Shoulders wrenched behind him, he was forced to his knees as rope looped around his hands, intertwining tightly through his wrists with no room for slipping out. He thrashed against the binds and the hands touching him to no avail. A hilt hit hard against his shoulder and a hand shoved him face down into the dirt. Azrael sputtered, spitting dirt and anger, and rolled onto his back to face his captors. A darkness surrounded each face he looked to, an evil that he vowed to snuff out like a trick candle.

A boot pressed against his cheek, turning his head towards his soldiers, his not-quite-friends-but-something-like-it. Azrael couldn't do anything but watch as bones broke, limbs were mangled, one by one. Azrael didn't fear death, not after all this time, but he didn't accept it. This wouldn't be where he died, left to rot by rebels that had to have been tipped off. He imagined his death would be on the battlefield, grand and bloody, not somewhere where his body wouldn't be put to rest.

Laughter above him drew his thoughts away from the bloody mess bloom-ing beside him. Jade's ribs had been smashed, his breath wheezing out of him, but he kept his face neutral, even as the rebel lifted the mallet again—this time aiming for his skull. Azrael didn't give himself time to second guess or calculate differently. He wrenched his head free from beneath the boot and thrashed until he kicked Jade out of the way in time for the stone head to collide into Azrael's foot.

Blinding, brilliant pain shone through him. The stars he saw were perfect diamonds glittering against a stark black. Laughter erupted again as the mallet raised, then fell on his other foot. Azrael felt each shard of bone splinter into his skin. His boots provided no buffer, no protection against the stone—he might as well be barefoot. Darkness threatened to claim him, but Azrael fought against it. There had to be something he could do, something he could say to make them quit, to leave. For the first time in ten years, Azrael felt powerless. He hated it. Through the agony, he hated himself for not being able to do anything.

Voices spoke over him, but he could not decipher what they were saying, or even if they spoke the same language. Stone broke bone again, this time in his kneecaps. Each blow, bone shattered to dust. Azrael was aware of nothing beyond the heart wrenching agony ripping through him. He swam in a sea of brambles, thorns puncturing his skin. In a flash of clarity, he realized it was bone breaking through skin, and he fell back into drowning again. Azrael struggled to breathe, to keep conscious, but he was dragged into the darkness.

# CHAPTER 2

## AZRAEL

Azrael knew he was dreaming, but the fact did nothing to dispel the warning that clanged through him at the sight of the Moor in flames.

Billowing black smoke came before the men who wore all black and stood taller than the houses. Holding the swords twice the size of a normal man's, they marched down the street. In this dream of a memory, Azrael watched from the side of the dirt road as the men moved like ghosts. With the sluggish movement of dreams, Azrael struggled to run towards his house, where he knew his mother was dying.

He felt the same fear, worry, and smelled the same blood as he did as that terrified eight-year-old. Azrael traced the steps he knew by heart—the dream was always the same as the memory and neither seemed to leave him to peace. In his old house, his mother's cup of tea and his father's favorite book were left untouched at the table. Step by step, the wood creaked, just as loudly, as he walked to the front of the house. This was where the hurt sharpened, no matter how many times he had seen it. His mother was on her knees with her hands out before her as if to cup the rain but caught the spray of her blood instead. The sword that had stolen his mother's life touched the earth and the hand that held belonged to a being that seemed to touch the sky.

Azrael brought himself out of the dream, calmly as he had learned to do when he dreamt. It had been a very long time since he woke up from his dreams sweating and bleary eyed when he couldn't decipher reality from memory. The pain had dulled into a story that he didn't care for anymore. Azrael woke to pink sunlight cast across the infirmary ceiling and the quiet singing that had greeted him from every dream for the past month.

"Az, are you awake?" Hanna padded over to his bed, a folded blanket in her arms. She sat carefully on the edge, resting her blanket in her lap, and pressed her fingertips to Azrael's forehead. Hanna, with her vibrant dark skin and hair she could never tame and the way her eyes glowed when she spoke to him, had easily become his favorite thing to wake up to. She was so very alive. Azrael had grown tired of chasing dead women in his dreams. "How are you feeling?"

Every day she asked him this and every day he could hardly answer. He felt every splinter that used to be his kneecaps and feet throbbing beneath the casts Hanna had created for him. He waded through guilt, hate, and depression every day, but he was thankful that the rest of his unit was not in the same room as him.

"I'm fine," he gritted out as calmly as he could.

Hanna sighed, took herbs out of her apron pocket, and sprinkled them into the water that sat on the table beside his bed. She pressed two fingers against his wrist and shot him a disapproving glance before handing him the glass. "You slept through dinner. I'll bring you something in."

"The Greater will heal you, son," Raphael mumbled from his bed beside Azrael's. He stretched out on his back and swatted his hand toward Azrael. "The Greater always heals."

Raphael prayed in his sleep, a habit that Azrael had learned to tune out. When Raphael was younger, he had belonged to the Tiras, the king's small group of exceptional soldiers—long before King Nekoda grew sick and died, eleven years ago now. Azrael had lost count of the stories Raphael told him of his time in the king's court and how he had found the Greater when he was lying in a field with his stomach sliced open. The other men who shared the room groaned, knowing this same story was coming. Azrael closed his eyes.

"The Greater took care of me in the Roen field, everyone thought I was dead and left me. It was raining that day. The rain washed the blood away, and I remember the air was vibrating, and it healed me. The Greater touched me through the rain, I had been found," Raphael told this story every day for the past month and told Azrael as if it were the first time. Though his memory faded there, Azrael knew that Raphael woke up each morning and knew who he was, and the thought made Azrael's heart ache. "The Greater heals."

Raphael's condition made him mobile but kept to the grounds of the infirmary. He brought Azrael news of current events surrounding the rebellion, which is all Azrael cared for anymore. King Melech avi-Predae held onto his throne as rebellions sparked throughout the kingdom, despite anything and everything the king did. For the past few years, it was Azrael's job to follow the trail of sparks and keep the wildfire from spreading. Logic told him that he hadn't failed, but Azrael couldn't help but feeling as though he did. The Greater was missing that day. The Greater has been missing every day since.

"Azrael, do you want to go for a walk?" Raphael said suddenly, sitting up on the edge of his bed, his fingers twitching like autumn leaves. "It's a beautiful evening."

"Not until he's eaten dinner," Hanna said as she walked back into the room. She set a plate of fruit and a pile of herbs on the table beside Azrael. He ignored the grumble of the others as they complained about preferential treatment. "You too, for that matter Raphael. I noticed how you picked at your food. You won't die of starvation on my watch."

Hanna helped Azrael sit, her gentle hands a welcoming touch as she fussed about him and stuck a pillow behind his back. She rested on the very edge of the cot and handed him a small glass. "For the nightmares," she said quietly enough that Raphael, distracted by the fruit, didn't hear.

Azrael drank the wine quickly and felt the warmth spread through his chest. The darkness of his dreams receded into the back of his mind, leaving only an echo. Hanna smiled, perfectly and brightly with her white teeth stark against her dark skin, and took the plate from Raphael's picky fingers. He disappeared through the door only to return minutes later with a wheeled chair.

"Alright, he's eaten, and so have I," Raphael said as he moved closer to the bed. "He can finish the rest on our walk. You want to come too, darling?"

Hanna began to protest, but she had learned to pick her battles. She grabbed a blanket for Azrael and a coat for Raphael, but he was already heaving Azrael into the chair. Ignoring the small bumps that jostled every splintered bone in his legs, Azrael gritted his teeth and breathed through the pain that threatened to empty his stomach before he attempted to continue eating.

This infirmary was the largest in Havriel and neutral in times of war. It was settled inside the mountain range that bordered the entire west side of the kingdom, which kept it safe and out of the way of warfare. A waterfall fell from the high peaks behind the building and ran into the river that lined the northern end and down through the mountains. Trees were sparse this high in the peaks, but a small, condensed wood grew along the river until it leapt off the cliffside. It was surreal, situated with the Vale's forest stretching out on one side and the bounding fields and plains of the Roe on the other, and a small valley expanding below it. The sky was soft with the pinks and purples of twilight and a gentle breeze swayed between the trees as the three of them moved. Raphael murmured something about the Greater as he pushed Azrael along. The ground was even enough that he didn't struggle, but he stopped when they got close to the wood.

"This is a good place to turn back," Hanna said as she stumbled to a stop beside them.

Azrael had almost forgotten that she had gone with them. It was usually the guards running after them, trying to get Raphael to go back. They didn't like how far Raphael would push their boundaries. Azrael rarely had a say in the matter. Only yesterday, Raphael had convinced Azrael to go on a walk that ended with the man being chased around the back of the infirmary because he tried climbing the boulders, while Azrael was useless in watching and trying to hide his laughter.

This time, Azrael wasn't laughing as he noted the fierce determination in Raphael's face as he turned to face Hanna.

"Let the poor kid see some nature, feel the moon on his skin!" Raphael let go of the chair but kicked rocks in front of the wheels to keep it in place.

"And I agree with that, but you will go no further this way. We can rest, let him enjoy the view, but we will turn back and walk the opposite direction."

Azrael grew tired of their conversations like this but didn't care enough to volunteer his opinion or tell them both to shove it. The sky was better than the stone ceiling and four walls pressing in on him every day.

He hadn't wanted to die a month ago when the rebels took the use of his legs, and he didn't regret saving Jade's life, but the monotony of his life now made him begin to think his decisions that brought him here. If he fought a little harder, a little longer, a little smarter, maybe he could have saved more than Jade's life.

It was an endless thought spiral that brought him in circles. If he hadn't woken up as early, if he hadn't gone to piss in the woods, would that have made a difference? If he ran faster, maybe Rayna would have use of her hands. If he killed faster, maybe the three soldiers would have lived. If he hadn't surrendered when the blade was at his neck, maybe the two that died in the infirmary because of their injuries wouldn't have been wounded so grievously.

Azrael was learning to tuck the feelings—the guilt, the hate, the rage—away within himself so deep that numbness was the only thing left. It was easier to feel nothing at all.

Dusk fell, darkness blanketing the Vale first as light strained to remain in the Roe. Stars began to wink in the darkening sky and Azrael let himself breathe easier. The other two were quiet until Raphael moved to stand in front of Azrael, the side of his face lit by the first moonlight.

"Are you ready to go in? I don't know what is out here after dark," Hanna said, letting out a small sigh as she shifted from her spot beside Azrael.

Raphael tilted his head, as though listening to something Azrael couldn't hear.

One moment, he was standing with his arms crossed. The next he swooped them around Azrael's waist and hauled him over his shoulder. Before Hanna could do anything, Raphael sprinted faster than Azrael thought possible of the aged man, heading towards the copse of trees.

Azrael's broken knees knocked against Raphael's ribcage, and he bit his lip to keep from vomiting from the pain that lit his entire body on fire. Every instinct told him to jab, poke, fight back, but the pain in his legs was too great to do anything but struggle to stay awake. His eyesight grew fuzzy. The sound of the river grew louder than the soft babble and the distant rumble of the waterfall etched fear into Azrael. There was no sense in anything.

Raphael had lost his mind—

Azrael didn't have a warning before the two of them plunged into the river, tearing them apart. Pulled below, the water pushed, pulled, and yanked Azrael in a hundred directions. It dragged him along the riverbed until it pitched him against a rock.

For a moment, everything was clear. Calm. The river stopped running and moonlight swam down to him. Time itself seemed to slow for Azrael, each bubble slowly drifting past him as the air slipped from his lips. The water's surface distorted the dim light, warping it as though it were a hand reaching to him. He felt nothing beyond the stillness. It was peaceful, serene.

So this was death.

Something tugged at him, deep within his body, and Azrael felt himself gliding to the surface. He broke through, the river calmer now, sputtering and spitting as water crashed into his face. Using his arms, he weakly swam to the bank, where he saw Raphael standing a good distance away like a proud, wet dog. Shouts behind him erupted before guards tackled him to the ground. Azrael dug his fingers into the earth, heaved himself out of the water, and flopped onto his back. Any moment now the pain from his legs would drag him unconscious and, after the shock of being thrown into the river, the darkness would be welcome.

Hanna flew over him, her hands on his pale face as she checked for damage. She was yelling, but Azrael couldn't understand what she was saying. He thought he may still be at the bottom of the river. Where he wanted to be—everything made sense, there was no feeling.

"The Greater heals," Raphael said before his face was squished into the mud on the bank. His eyes were wild and bright, a brilliant smile on his face.

Azrael shifted out from beneath Hanna and tentatively sat up, his body groaning at the effort, only to stare at his toes twitching.

His head emptied of everything, a bone chilling cold settling in.

Hanna spoke again, but Azrael wasn't listening. *How?* He focused on nothing but moving a toe, gooseflesh spreading across his body. He flexed his foot forward, bracing himself for the onslaught of agony, but it did not come.

This was a dream. There was no possible explanation for him to go into the water with broken legs, only to come out with healed bones. He pushed off the ground to his feet, knees sturdy beneath him.

Impossible.

Hanna threw herself at him, wrapping her arms around his waist in expectation of him collapsing, but he wiggled his toes in the mud. His legs ached, as though he had run up and down endless stairs, but the sting of a thousand shards of bone buried into muscle was not present. The air around him was tangible, like the heaviness of an oncoming storm, and simmered against his skin. He stared down at his thin body, at his crooked legs that weren't so crooked anymore.

# CHAPTER 3

## AZRAEL

Azrael tracked the first moon as it climbed the velvet sky from a solitary room in the far end of the infirmary. The privacy felt like isolation, but he didn't mind the silence. After the flurry of guards asking a hundred questions, then half a dozen healers looking over him, and his own thoughts rattling in his head, the silence was welcome. Hanna knocked, hours after her last visit, but Azrael didn't answer it. She let herself in anyway.

She had tended to a sedated Raphael, moving him to his own solitary room—locked and guarded. Azrael sat on the cot with his legs outstretched, knocking his toes together for no other reason than he could. He had been trying to come up with a logical explanation other than a god he didn't believe in healing him. A man had thrown him into a river and that's where he kept drawing a blank. He wondered if he had hallucinated it all—the breaking, the travelling, the healing, the river. Nothing made sense.

"Are you in pain?" Hanna asked after the door clicked closed behind her. She was a Lesser; she believed in the Greater and whatever powers the name carried.

"No."

"Were you?"

"No."

"Will you tell me what happened?"

Azrael opened his mouth but closed it. There was nothing he could say. He didn't know what she was searching for, what answer she wanted to hear. He hadn't seen her god. The world had stopped for him, just for a moment, and it was the only moment in his life he had known peace. He couldn't shake the feeling of the air buzzing around him like cicadas and swore that the very edge of his skin was still humming. Azrael sighed, exhaustion wearing at him, but he was afraid to go to sleep. What if he woke up to find that this had been a strange dream and his body would still be mangled, swimming in pain?

Even so, he didn't stop Hanna as she gently pushed him backwards into the soft bed and pulled a blanket over him, despite the warmth of the night. He fell asleep listening to her singing an old ballad quietly beside him.

†

The whispers started again, as they had when Azrael first arrived. The men he had shared a room with, whose names he had struggled to learn and remember, whose children he asked after, whose wives wrote letters that they all listened to, averted their eyes as if he had two heads. When he was in his therapy, regaining the confidence in moving and walking, the men ignored him wholly. He was no longer broken as they were. His days were quiet and lonely again. He kept to his solitary room when he wasn't in therapy or walking the grounds while a guard trailed him. Hanna stayed with him when she could. His mornings started with her singing and his nights ended with it, lullabies of her childhood in the Roe and stories of Telaanan pirates.

A week had passed when a knock pulled him from sleep. Azrael jolted, still terrified to find debilitating pain, but he opened his eyes to bright sunshine slipping under the door and the normal, quiet peace in the room. He wiggled his toes, as he did every morning, to make sure the healing hadn't disappeared.

The door opened and Hanna rushed in, moving to his side in an instant. The scuff of boots followed her, grabbing Azrael's attention enough to sit up.

Two Tiras soldiers in their black as night uniforms stood at the door, their blood red cuffs stark around their wrists. Their faces stared straight ahead, over him, as the king shouldered past them. Dressed in all black as well, the symbol of the Vale was stitched onto his chest—a crescent and a full moon side by side. His black eyes burned into Azrael's as he strode to the end of the bed. Azrael felt suddenly very small, completely and utterly unfit to be in front of the king.

"Azrael Hikaim?"

King Melech avi-Predae was someone Azrael had served under for the past ten years, accepting and following his orders without ever having met him. Here he was, after a ridiculous and inexplicable event.

"Yes, my king," Azrael focused his eyes on the moons on the king's chest, away from his dark gaze. His heart was loud enough for both guards to hear it.

"Word has carried of your talent with a sword and your recent victories. You are to join the Tiras." Melech straightened his shoulders, his presence taking up the entire room. Azrael tried wrapping his head around what the king had said, but it simply rattled nosily. The Tiras were his personal guards and, long ago under King Nekoda, it was an honor you had to fight and kill for. Melech chose his own guards, instead of hosting the tournament and making men and women fight to the death for a spot, and he only kept twenty with him. This was not the king asking Azrael, this was an order. To become a Tiras.

"My king," Hanna's voice faltered, though she tried to hide it, "As his healer, he should not travel anywhere at this moment."

"The boy walks?" Melech's stare did not break from Azrael's.

"Yes—"

"His legs were broken not a month ago?"

"Yes."

"Yet he walks." Each word was pronounced carefully, curtly.

"Yes, sir."

Melech took a step closer to Azrael, his head tilting. Azrael felt the weight of his attention, a mouse caught in the eyesight of a hawk. The king's eyes bore into his as though he was searching for an answer to a question he could not voice. Before Azrael could respond, Melech turned to his guard.

"The Greater has chosen him, and as do I. Gather his things. We ride within the hour."

He glanced back at Azrael, eyes dark and burning, before he strode out the door. One Tiras came to the side of the bed with a dark bundle in his hands and set it beside Azrael. He searched the Roen man's face for something, anything, but the Tiras left quietly after his king.

"You can't leave," Hanna said after she had returned from following them out. She paced the room with arms crossed and fingers drumming against her sides. Azrael sat on the foot of the bed, watching her, and ran his thumb along the cuff of the Tiras sleeve. His name had been stitched in the red fabric, worn and frayed at the end, as though it had been there a while. Perhaps that was his imagination playing tricks on him once more.

"I have no choice, Hanna," Azrael replied, not looking up from the stitching. There were a thousand reasons he couldn't say no to the king—the largest being he was the king, and the second being it was the most he could have ever hoped for in his life.

Azrael thought he would come undone the same way these letters began to. Another change to uproot his world, another event to set him apart from everything he knew. He glanced at the bag Hanna had packed for him—it wasn't much, there wasn't much of anything to his name these days, but he was sure there was something in there to remind him of her. It was also strange knowing this would be their last time seeing each other and, despite never voicing her feelings, he knew how she felt about him. He cared for her too, so much of his time had been spent with her beside him and under her hands, but he had to admit she had been a crutch, and nothing more.

The air around him hummed again, a hundred insects buzzing against him. He changed into the black uniform and felt the weight of the red cuff at his wrists and his fading name. He knew the sun would be rising now, with the light filtering in the room and hall. King Melech strode into the room then, cloak sweeping behind him, with his face unreadable.

"Come, son. The ride is long."

"Az," Hanna pleaded quietly, her finger closing around my wrist. He straightened.

"The Greater calls for him." Melech closed the space between the three of them and set his hand on Azrael's shoulder, eyes harsh as he looked at her. She took a step away, releasing Azrael's wrist.

It was strange, knowing this in-between was ending. Life as Azrael had known it ended when he was ambushed. His life as a talented, molded soldier had slipped away after the first break. He had stared down a void, his life missing everything that made him happy. In a month and a half, his life turned backwards and upside down. It didn't hit him that the pieces were falling back into place—nor that he was part of the Tiras—until Melech led him outside to his group of soldiers.

Azrael knew his Tiras was comprised of two healers, now eight swordsman, two spearmen, five archers, two horsemen, and a captain. Only eight of them were with him, including Azrael, but the sight of them stalled his heart. Despite the warmth, chills pricked at his skin. It had to be all one long dream. Melech led Azrael to a dark brown horse and ran spidery fingers through its mane.

"There will be time for introductions later. It is a week's ride to Vale City. We ride until we cannot. You are a Tiras now, and you will be expected to fight as such." Melech took a sword from a holster attached to the horse's saddle. "I've heard of your renowned skills with a blade, and I look forward to seeing it."

Melech set a hand on Azrael's shoulder, lightly squeezed it, and disappeared into the group. Azrael took the sword from its sheathe and felt the final piece click into place. Not only was it an incredible feeling finally having a sword back in his hands, but a Tiras sword, nonetheless. Old Havrien was etched into the blade, running down the center, and the steel shone brightly in the morning sun. The hilt was smooth in his grip and he knew it to be made from the white stone from inside the King's Mountain, with a crescent moon on one side and a full moon on the opposite. It was a masterpiece he never thought he would wield. He sheathed it, hoisted himself on the horse, and joined the Tiras with a heart ready to take flight.

# CHAPTER 4

## LARK

Lark Areeta didn't take her eyes off the man walking with Melech. There was something strange about him, though nothing in his outward appearance gave her anything to go off. Moonlight was in his eyes, despite the bright morning sun. He was pale and lanky, but it was obvious he was a ghost of his former self, whoever he may have been.

Worth setting off in the middle of the night for.

Melech had been fervent in coming himself to fetch the man. Lark couldn't forget the ripple of power she had felt that night sitting at dinner with the king. She didn't know how Melech had felt it too, and she knew better than to ask, but they rode within the hour. It had called to her—to them, apparently—beckoning like a stray cat who wanted a home again. A breath of power still lingered on the man, nothing more than a dusting of magic. Lark couldn't discern *why*. Why the god of night chose this man...and why he chose someone at all.

She wasn't jealous, she realized as she studied the swordsman. Apprehensive fit better. The god of night hardly deigned to include her in his plans, despite their close relationship, and this addition felt as though it played into something a lot bigger. Something that she felt as though she should have been informed of.

Melech caught her stare and gave her the slightest of nods before he swung onto his horse. Lark stretched her legs once more before climbing onto her horse. They fell into formation—Melech and Brannon, the captain, were in the

center, in front of Lark while the archers rode behind her, save for Kal who
floated around all of them. The new swordsman rode in front of them all, with
Ahmi a few paces in front of him. Lark noted how the man situated himself
behind the Roen, as if hesitant.

The ride down through the mountain proved trickier than riding up and
Lark had to wonder why the infirmary was built so high, if it had been necessary
to be hidden in the past. None of them spoke as they descended, save for the
captain offering the king some history of the land that Melech no doubt already
knew.

Lark caught Meir's eyes. The horseman's eyes were exhausted, and Lark knew
they shared the same thought: this excursion was an unnecessary risk for all of
them. A letter to the infirmary would have sufficed to send the man to the city,
but she hadn't been able to persuade the king.

The second moon was already high above them when Melech decided to stop
for camp. Kal had gone ahead to scout for a spot and found an alcove tucked
within the rocks. The relief rippled through the group as they filed in, leaving
their horses tied up at the opening.

The hour reprieve at the infirmary hadn't been enough. Lark's ass was sore
from riding the past week and she knew it would be even worse by the time they
finally reached the city. She had been steadily using her healing magic, soothing
the muscles in her back, but it did nothing to aid the stiffness she felt. A soreness
had long settled into her bones. She longed for her bed, laughing late into the
night with Hadri, the Tiras's second healer, and she longed for a proper bath.

None of them bothered to light a fire, but instead lined their bedrolls out
beside each other, with the exception of Brannon and Melech. Lark tore her
boots off, curling her toes in her stiff socks, and stretched out on her even
stiffer bedroll. She listened to Meir tease Asenneth about being a princess when
she grumbled about the unevenness of her bedroll, to which she responded by
hurling a chunk of rock at his chest. Lark stifled her laugh. She stared up at the
black sky, tracing designs amongst the stars, until she heard Melech's voice and
propped up on her forearms.

"My captain, Brannon," he said as he leaned against a boulder, his cloak off and teeth glinting in the moonlight. Brannon stood beside the king and new swordsman, his arms crossed and looking ever the serious captain.

"Azrael," the swordsman offered, putting out his hand, but Brannon only smirked and nodded. The ass.

One of the horses chuffed as Asenneth fed an apple to another, pulling her attention away from the men briefly. Lark hadn't noticed she had left her bedroll beside her, but offered Asenneth a small smile once she returned. Lark absentmindedly watched Asenneth rake her fingers through her knotted blonde hair, wind whipped from the afternoon gusts. Lark knew she should have done the same, but her braid was still tight against her hair and a small part of her was hesitant to undo it and tackle the knots.

"Hollis," Melech said, pointing to the Areenian perched high above us on watch. Lark had volunteered to be first watch, knowing Hollis needed the rest more than she did, but he declined, as always. "Skilled with the bow. And Asenneth, also an archer."

In response to her name, Asenneth lifted a limp hand and waved it in a different direction than the king. Lark fought a smile.

"Meir is a master horseman, and Kal over there is a spearman. And that one is Ahmi, one of your fellow swordsmen."

As if summoned, Ahmi strolled past, giving them both a wide grin, before he sat beside Lark. She breathed a sigh of relief. At least she had him with her on this ride. Her friend of many years, Ahmi was sunshine after a hurricane. He dropped some herbs into her lap as he settled down, groaning like an old man.

"They'll help you sleep," he said, nodding to the leaves. Lark's heart tightened at the gesture.

"I wouldn't be able to fight if I'm groggy."

"You'd be fine. Rather have you groggy than grumpy." Ahmi winked and tucked his hands behind his head as he stared up at the sky.

"That's Lark," she heard Melech say, his voice deeper and restrained as he spoke her name. She wondered if the swordsman noticed. The king offered no title for her, as if she were no one special. For those that didn't know of her magic, she was one of the remarkable healers of the Tiras. For those who did know of her magic and her past, she was Siena Hostien, forgotten princess of King Nekoda Hostien, the accompanying title long since stripped from her name in the fifteen years since she had last borne it. Her magic purred within her skin, as though asking for a reason to show off—to prove her worth amongst the talented people surrounding her. For Melech, she was the bane of his existence.

Lark focused on the swordsman's face, as much as she could in the moonlight. Boyish features lingered in his curls and his dark eyes, but the stark cheekbones and straight nose spoke to his manhood. He stood half a head shorter than the king, and looked as though a strong wind would topple him. His body had deteriorated in his time with the healers, but there was a vibrancy to him that Lark couldn't help but study. His gaze was on her as well, and she wondered if he saw her as clearly as she saw him.

"What do you think?" Ahmi asked quietly beside her. His eyes were closed when Lark looked at him and she sighed.

"I try not to," she replied as she flopped backwards onto the bedroll. Despite the warmth of the night, she fluffed a saddle blanket over her body and gazed up once more at the stars. She distinctly picked out the flowing darkness around the second moon and listened to its song instead of the swordsman's voice as he settled into the group.

Eventually, even the horses slumbered, and the only sound was Hollis above them, humming quietly the songs of his people.

<br>

T he golden sun brought better spirits as it rose. Lark had taken the herbs Ahmi had given her, dropping her softly into a soothing sleep she hadn't endured in a while. Her body felt flexible and molded to the saddle. She stroked her mare's mane as they kept a steady trot out of the lower part of the mountain and into the small valley.

They kept the same riding pattern, but Lark's heart plummeted when she met the king's eyes as he glanced over his shoulder. He had braided his black curls on either side of his head, looking ever like the warrior he had been—back before he was her father's heir, when he was only the captain of the Tiras, and not the usurper to her throne. Dark smudges lined his eyes, and Lark knew he hadn't slept. She made a mental note to give him something to sleep too; she'd rather have a groggy king than a grumpy one. Gods knew how he would get when he had gone too long without sleep. Melech's attention flickered to his captain before he fell back the paces she kept between them.

"Anything?" he quietly asked once Meir, who had kept steady beside her, moved away. The king's eyes searched her face, looking for an answer, a question, anything that she could give him. His eyes were as black as his hair and unreadable as his emotions shifted. His moods were as swift as the wind, here and gone in a breath. Lark supposed he was lucky the kingdom didn't know him as she did.

Lark, remembering he had asked her a question, shook her head, wisps of her braided hair tickling the back of her neck. The king's jaw tightened, but he nodded. Before he had gathered the Tiras, the king had spoken to her about what to expect, if anything, upon finding the man. The kingdom worshipped the Greater and spread the glory of the fictional deity high and low, but Lark knew better. Even still, there hadn't been anything close to the power surge she had felt the night Azrael had been healed. The last time she had experienced anything close was when she was a child, and it had been her own power that resonated through the palace. Lark always wondered who else had felt it that fateful night.

"Keep your eyes on him. If there's a whisper, I want to know." Melech glanced at her hands, the very ones he knew were the most powerful in the kingdom—the only hands who held magic.

Her father had destroyed himself over the fact that his useless, brat of a daughter had received the magic he hungered for. She had caught Melech reading through the same texts her father had, searching for answers that no longer lied in written word. Lark herself had given up finding an answer on *how* after she realized the bigger question was *why*. The god of night never deigned to answer that one, and Lark knew better than to hope for an answer one day. She figured she would find out whenever he led her to her fate.

Lark still said nothing to her king but nodded. His eyes were soft, smiling, while his face remained neutral to his guards surrounding them. He returned to his place beside his captain and her lungs relaxed. She was grateful he couldn't hear the thundering in her chest, and grateful that, though he was attentive to her, his gaze seemed to pass over the fact that she was always on edge around him. Lark stared at his back. It was a cruel game they played, one that did not have any rules, and always ended up with hearts cracking. She was too valuable to let drift away, and he was the only way she could reclaim the forgotten title of princess, knowing damn well that she wasn't strong enough to do anything else.

Indignant, Lark glared past the king, at the swordsman. Azrael spoke to Ahmi, each man offering small bits of conversation. A tendril of magic, invisible and light as smoke on the wind, reached out from Lark's chest, down her fingertips, and, as an extension of her, she felt the air around Azrael. It hummed, greeting her. Her hands tightened on the reins, knuckles white as her focus did not waiver. The god of night's magic still surrounded him, bracing his body like a cast. It only confirmed her assumption, but she yet wondered if any of that magic seeped into him, gifting him in a gentler way than it had gifted her.

Either sensing her stare—or, was it possible he could feel her curious wisps at his back?—Azrael turned, his dark eyes instantly finding hers. Lark shifted her face into neutrality, gently pulling back the extension of her magic, and met his stare with cool indifference.

Lark didn't have the faintest idea of his role, why he was chosen, and the silence of when she asked Iah, the god of night, grew frustrating. She couldn't shake the feeling that he had been dropped in their lives at a precise moment. The god of night steps outside his boundaries just as Lark makes tentative plans to do the very same. She gritted her teeth at the idea, her knuckles aching.

Brannon raised his hand, halting them behind him, and whistled lowly so those in front paused as well. Lark's shoulders sagged in relief when she heard a stream nearby. Even if it were only for a moment, she was ready to be off her horse. She watched Kal and Meir set off to scout ahead. The minutes they were gone felt like hours. Once they returned, Kal led the group through a thicket of trees, the stream growing louder with each step.

It wasn't much, the water looking only as though it would reach halfway up her shin, but it was crystal clear and inviting. Free from their burdens, the horses moved to the stream while the Tiras moved to the shade of the trees.

Lark sat against a tree, stretching her legs out in the grass. She noted the small mushrooms that grew beside the trunk, the ants that crawled within the bark, and sighed facing the sunlight streaming from the between the leaves. If she thought about it, they were mere days away from the city, being home. She was ready for the tiny cottage she called hers with Hadri, the smell of linen, salve, and lavender she grew in her windowsill.

The groan of a bow snapped her from her daydreams. She was on her feet before Hollis released the arrow, whizzing straight ahead to the form lurking in the shadows.

# CHAPTER 5
## AZRAEL

A zrael had his sword in his hand as the shadow thudded on the forest floor. He calculated where they were and wondered how they had strayed towards a rebel camp, how the men who had found this hadn't noticed their neighbors. Unless this camp was new. They sprouted up as soon as the old camp had been discovered.

Skin prickling with the promise of his first fight in over a month, Azrael didn't give pause to think if his body was ready before crossing the stream. Eyes scanning for signs of movement, he sensed the other Tiras shifting behind him.

*There*, hovering ten paces behind the fallen body.

Then a yell that scattered the birds from the trees and sent half a dozen bodies flying from the shadows. Azrael didn't hesitate, launching himself towards them. There was no fear of broken bones, only the promise of death. He savored the weight of the Tiras sword in his hands as he caught the blow of the first man who raced towards him, eyes burning with hatred and mouth mid-yell.

Azrael easily evaded the man's second blow, seeing only black and white, and buried the blade in the man's chest. As it slid out and the rebel fell to his knees, Azrael lifted the sword again in a wide arc to slash the throat of the man who had run up behind him.

He was aware of the other Tiras yelling from somewhere near him, their voices a familiar din amongst the rage swelling in his head. It had been so easy to fall back into the soldier he had been, violence brimming in his blood, as much a part of him as his breath.

The moss beneath his feet bloomed red as another body dropped before him, blood spraying the front of his shirt. This is what he had been molded into, an effective killer who didn't analyze the threat, but destroyed it.

A branch snapped to his right. Azrael's head snapped in the direction, but found Ahmi staring with admiration. He jerked his head and Azrael knew what it meant: circle, find more. He flexed his fingers around his sword and set off.

†

## LARK

"Fuck," Hollis breathed, fingers wrapping around the shaft of the arrow embedded in his bicep. Lark had watched the king disappear into the shadows of her own making when the last of the arrows found its home within her friend.

With half her mind occupied, she was slow to move to him. He had fired an arrow to claim the life of the one who shot him, and Lark heard him swear again. He held the arrow in his hand, blooding covering his fingers. She moved to his side, his upper arm level with her eyes.

"Sit," she snapped at him. She was angry with herself, Kal and Meir, and Melech, all for a hundred reasons, but their own stupidity for taking a reprieve in the forest. Hollis didn't deserve her wrath, but it flowed as easily as her magic did.

Hollis knew of her power, so she made no move to pretend to tend to his wound. The others, dispersed within the forest, wouldn't be able to see, and part of her didn't really care if they saw—it would only kickstart her plans early. Anyway, Hadri, his wife, would never let it go if Lark didn't do what she could, especially as she noted how close the arrow had been to nicking his artery. Lark

34CAIT NESS

closed her hand around his arm, her fingers unable to wrap entirely around the muscle. She placed her other hand where her fingers fell short and breathed slowly.

The threads of her healing magic unspooled in her chest, looping in ways only she could see, until the strands floated around her fingertips. She focused them, her intent, and sent thread by thread into his arm, rooting out the wound and slowly stitching it as if there had been no arrow at all. Time slowed around her, but she knew it was only for her. As if her magic gave her peace to use it.

She pulled, and pulled, and pulled the ivory healing fibers until she felt the blood stop flowing beneath her fingers and Hollis shifted his shoulders. It hadn't even taken more than five of his breaths, but, to Lark, it might as well have been hours. She lifted her hands from him and was about to step away from him when he caught her hand. He squeezed once and rocked to his feet.

The cost of her magic varied. Healing took less from her, but she felt as though she had surrendered a piece of her soul, a tiny sliver. Lark teetered on her feet, a sudden rush enveloping her head, but steadied herself as her eyes focused and Azrael appeared with Ahmi, Kal, and Meir behind him. His dark eyes were focused on her hands, the blood that covered them, and then flickered to the discarded arrow. There was almost something like distrust that flashed across his faces, the boyish features disappearing for that moment as the hardness of a solider slipped into place.

†

## AZRAEL

Azrael felt alive again. The anger he had felt honed into a weapon to fight the small voice that always whispered to him as he killed, the small slice of his conscious he couldn't kill. The sound of his bones breaking had echoed in his ears as he eliminated each threat that moved towards his king. His mercy slipped farther and farther from reach as his hands became darker with blood.

The vibrancy of the Vale around him was a stark contrast to the darkness in the king's face when he returned to the Tiras. Azrael noted the healer—Lark, out of all their names, hers was the only he could remember—with blood on her hands beside the Areenian, an arrow at his feet and his sleeve torn. He didn't have a wound, but they were both bearing his blood. Azrael glanced at Lark's ashen face, her freckles prominent beneath the gray eyes that studied him just as equally.

Melech paced as he spoke to his Tiras, but Azrael could not focus on his king, on the words he was slinging in an accusatory tone about the route they'd taken. Azrael instead did not take his eyes from the healer and the faraway look in her eyes. Had she been the one injured? Maybe she had torn the Areenian's shirt accidentally?

"We ride until we reached Vale City. We do not stop," Melech said, snagging Azrael's attention. They had ridden close to the hovel where bandits collected like roaches in their ramshackle village, and the road they had passed not long ago branched off to two rebel camps. He was not surprised that they had been attacked, but it had shaken his king. Azrael wondered the last time he had left the walls of his city, and felt a rush of heat roll through his body.

His king had dared venture out to find him and bring Azrael to the city while a force struggled to rise in the shadows to bring him down. As Azrael mounted his horse again, savoring the feeling of his legs against the animal's warm body, he wondered what it would mean for him—to be hand chosen by the king, and whatever force it was that had healed him. He still did not believe it was a god, but he came short on other answers. As much as Azrael wanted to know, a small part of him didn't care—the same part of him that felt most himself in the midst of fighting. The part of him that belonged to the darkness. He knew, though, that it couldn't have been magic. After his mother had died, he blamed demons, he blamed magic, he blamed anything but the hearts of men, until he learned magic had never existed on this continent. He refused to give a momentary thought to the notion that it had been magic to heal him. As the group broke into a gallop to follow the storm that was their king, Azrael let go. Let go of everything except for the feeling of the wind in his face, the sturdiness of the horse beneath him, and the feeling that his life was changing for the better.

# CHAPTER 6

## AZRAEL

The road leading from the Vale to the Roe was smooth from the thousand years of feet and hooves and grew populated the closer to the city. Merchants braving bandits took their goods along the dirt road, armed guards walking beside their carts if they could afford them. Tourists from the two other continents came through Westwick, the main port the Vale used to trade goods and welcome visitors, and converged on the path.

Days and nights blurred together until Azrael realized he had dozed off in the saddle a few times, his eyes too heavy to hold open. His body had grown used to a month-long infirmary stay where sleep was his constant companion. The late nights on horseback caught up to him easily. In the few and far between moments when they stopped, he didn't have much time from when his feet touched the earth until he collapsed onto his bedroll. He was thankful the archers tended to keep first watch. The horseman had argued with the captain about stopping at an inn, at the very least switching out the horses before they were no use to any of them, but neither the captain nor king wanted to take the risk, lest it snuff out unsavory camp guests.

Eventually, the forest terrain gave way to farms and orchards that bordered the outskirts of the city. The first moon fell as they encroached on the wall rising over the trees, doused in the light from the second moon that climbed the sky. White stone glinted in the silver light and Azrael knew it to be the palace towers rising against the black sky. It had been years since Azrael had been to the city, he'd almost forgotten what it looked like. It hadn't occurred to him, until then, that this jungle of crooked buildings and stone streets would be his home again—after years of living in small towns for weeks at a time, tents in the middle of the forest, the barracks in mountain camps. He would have a permanent home again, and he didn't know if he dreaded or enjoyed the idea.

Rows of tents for the homeless, miscreants, and wanderers—a temporary town that had become permanent—rose around them as the group meandered the crowded road as they trotted as one toward the gate. Between moonlight and firelight, Azrael noticed the Old Havrien that decorated the stone gate and the walls on either side of it, the letters scratched and hard to decipher. Plain, impenetrable, and with aged battlements along the top, the wall had been one of the first things built for the city. At the sound of a low whistle from the king, the gate opened enough for them to slip through. As Azrael passed through, a wave of familiarity passed over him. The city stretched out before them, and it felt as though he were meeting an old friend. Shops, taverns, and inns filled the entrance to the city, enticing visitors and travelers to stay. Azrael remembered the tight roads that led to the small homes, the small parks. The overwhelming but exciting entrance into the chaos of Vale City.

The west side, where Azrael had never ventured, was the wealthiest, built beside the waterfall that fell from the mountains and into the river that wound through the heart of the city, cutting it in half. The homes were tall, made of stone, with large yards, and spotless streets. The Church stood tall beside the rocky mountainside, right next to the waterfall's pool. The east end was the poor end, where Azrael had first lived, with the poorest at the furthest point where the wall curves toward the ocean. The buildings looked as though a strong wind would topple them, shutters shaking and wood groaning in the breeze. The northern point was the palace and the keep, with the barracks beyond both against the cliffside.

The market district was quiet as the Tiras trotted through, lights on above the shops and the wooden signs swaying before the stores opened for business. Azrael thought of all the friends he had made in his years here, before the threat of war called him away, and if they were still skulking around in the alleys, or if life had taken them.

Vale City was the oldest and largest in Havriel. Settled first by Areenians, it became a powerful fortress and stayed that way for hundreds of years, despite the constant wars and changing borders. At the very tip of the continent, an unforgiving ocean lies on two sides and a massive mountain range that expands on the western coast. Azrael passed countless statues of the current and late king scattered throughout the city as they moved through. Nekoda, the late king his father had served and died under, had a looming statue in the center of the market district, a sword hanging from one hand and an owl perched on his other. It was haunting in the darkness, shadows slinked across his sharp features to make it appear alive. Made of the same white stone as the palace, it reflected the moonlight and set the image of a ghost. Nekoda had inherited the throne from his father, Kanaan, who nearly collapsed under the weight of civil war, until the young Nekoda showed a strength for diplomacy and aided in reconciling the kingdom. Azrael remembered the news of a possible second civil war as a child, when his father had been called away for the last time. Even if saved, a snake's nature will be to strike.

The palace glowed from its position above the city, so brightly that Azrael wondered how it would look in the sunrise. Surely it wasn't this beautiful as when he was a child. Perhaps the world was opening up to him again, this new chance at life. Azrael scoffed inwardly.

Towers and battlements stretched into the sky, fading into the black. The palace sat on a hill, nestled into the natural curve of the mountainside, facing the east in anticipation of the rising sun. Azrael couldn't take his eyes off, spotting the windows and balconies that dotted the face and the arches that extended between the towers.

Around the Tiras, the constant beat of hooves against stone echoed while the city slowly began to stir. As one, they passed through the palace gates and veered towards the stables. Even those were impressive, more so than he remembered. A long, low building abutted the palace and curved alongside the mountain.

Azrael followed Ahmi while the others filed in behind him. The inside was crafted from birch with each stall bearing an intricate design displaying whose horse lingered within. Stable hands rushed out to guide the beasts in just as the sun began to glow beneath the horizon. Hands took the reins, and Azrael swung off his horse in a swift movement, and untied his bags before those hands carted his horse off.

He was on the edge of a precipice, the fall into a new life equally terrifying and exhilarating, but Azrael couldn't get past the thought that it was a *new* life. This wasn't anything like he had been doing for the past few years. He wouldn't be patrolling estates, keeping ears open for whispers of plans and rebel sympathizers. He would be kept close, kept to protect the king. His life had been a culmination of events to lead him to this.

The Tiras, dismissed by their king, walked stiffly through the stable horses, out to the palace beyond while the king lingered beside the stall his horse shuffled into. Azrael noted how the king's dark eyes trailed the healer as she strode with proud shoulders past the stable doors and through the door at the end of the hall. Once the healer disappeared, the king's eyes turned to Azrael. The stable hands quickly found somewhere else to be.

Azrael looked to his king, wondering if he should say something. The sword at his hip was a sudden weight, pinning him to the moment, and he shifted on his feet, as though to walk past the king.

"You remind me of myself when I was your age," Melech said, his voice quiet but commanding.

"Thank you, my king," Azrael raised his chin, steeling his face as he gazed back at Melech.

"It's an observation, not a compliment."

Azrael ground his teeth together, fighting the heat growing in his chest. He didn't know what to say to that, so he began to tilt his head in dismissal, but Melech shifted to lean against the wooden door.

"I had to see you myself before dragging you to the city. I now see promise in you, a hunger that I know better than anyone else. The night of your...miracle, I felt a calling, so to speak. A call to action," Melech scratched beneath the horse's chin once it moved towards him again, "Believe me, I knew of your name before the attack. I've longed to covet your talents."

"I admit I find myself wanting more, given a second chance to do so."

"As I've said, I see myself in you. Do not fly too close to the sun, lest your wings burn," Melech pushed off the door, turning towards the door leading to the palace, but paused. "I look forward to watching you flourish."

Azrael thanked him again, bowing his head, and watched the king stalk towards the palace. He took a breath before following Melech.

Each footfall was heavy. The lonely soldier boy was back in Vale City after all these years, miraculously healed after an attack that should have left him chair bound. He knew what had happened had spread like wildfire after they were discovered, bloody and broken and on the brink of death. What happened to him in that river, he knew it'd spread faster. Proof of the Greater was few and far between and people grasped at hope and faith with open hands.

Once he passed the threshold into the palace, a sense of familiarity settled into him. Azrael breathed in the scent that still lingered in a faraway memory—rosemary, lavender, and lemon—and noted the worn hall that ended in brilliant yellow light. Suddenly, a head poked out into the light, braid swinging—

"Hi, Azrael?" A soft voice floated towards him, beckoning him towards the light. A promise of mischief glinted in the early morning light as a tall, slender frame silhouetted at the end of the hall.

He stopped short as the morning sun fell onto her freckled face, a shimmer in her emerald eyes that had a smirk twitching at his mouth. It had been so very long since he had found someone that caught his attention. The memories of cold winter night flashed in his head, but the warmth of the girl in front of him melted them away.

"Magdalene," she offered with her hand, delicate tan fingers that were strong in his own. Her mouth mirrored his smile and dimples caved in on either cheek. His gaze snagged on the way her fingers curled to brush back a loose wave of hair. "I'll show you to your home."

"Lead the way," Azrael's voice surprised him, the gravel undertone that had him lifting his chin with the shred of honor he would feign to have. He had admired Hanna in his stay, but they had become friends and she a crutch to his healing. He didn't think it was wise to set sights on the first person he saw in the palace, but the tightening in his hips didn't care. Azrael fought against the blurring thoughts as he followed Magdalene into a bright corridor, her green dress hugging her backside in a distracting way.

He hadn't let himself feel anything beyond the focus and determination in fighting and surviving. He had told himself that he didn't want anything after losing Taya all those years ago, but it was the loss that he didn't want again. Perhaps he was foolish to even think of such a thing the first morning in his new life, so he shifted his attention to the palace bustling around him as they walked.

"So, the Greater healed you? There's a lot of talking, a lot of rumors going around about it. You're almost famous, chosen one," Magdalene said over her shoulder. Her eyes met his and she smirked, the dimples appearing again.

Azrael snorted. "I hope that's not truly what they're calling me and that you're just being a smart ass. It wasn't a god that healed me."

"You don't believe in the Greater?" Her dark blonde eyebrows rose, skepticism obvious in her face. "Then, tell me, chosen one. What was it that gave you the ability to walk again?"

He heard the edge in her words, though they were spoke in a teasing tone, and didn't know how to respond. He hadn't believed in anything in a long time. Nothing had been there the night his mother died, nor when he starved in an attic for days before he was shipped across a vast and empty ocean to the Vale, nor when he found Taya's body in that winter thunderstorm. His history books in school were filled with a long list of gods that had been favored over the millennium.

"Well, no matter what you think, I'm glad to have a miracle in the palace," she continued after it became apparent he wouldn't respond.

They turned a corner that opened to a massive courtyard with lush grass and a giant, intricate fountain in the center of the square bordered by looming trees. An older man knelt beside the stone, scrubbing slowly the base of the bubbling fountain. Gardeners behind the man tended to the tall trees, shaped shrubbery, and the pristine grass. It all looked so very different from the last time Azrael was inside these halls.

The Tiras were said to live in their own quarters in the east wing of the palace, houses built by King Nekoda to keep his most trusted soldiers close to their king. Azrael realized this had been true when the path Magdalene led him along expanded beneath an archway. Two rings of houses were before him; the first held eight homes, surrounding an ashen tree with roots breaking the stones encasing it, and the second ring had twelve houses, none of which were livelier than the tree in their center. Each was painted the same, a light grey with a dark grey trim. A few of the houses had delicate paintings on the doors or windowsills.

Azrael followed Magdalene down the few steps and through the courtyard to the house sitting across from the arch. Two trees bordered a dirt path that was directly beside the house. Magdalene leaned on her toes to graze her fingertips on the top of the windowsill and produced a key. She unlocked the front door, a soft smile on her face.

"Home sweet home," she said as she pushed the door open. She took a step over the threshold and must have put the key down, a resounding *clink* brought the reality of the moment crashing down on Azrael.

A shaky sigh pulled from his lips. He found he could hardly take a step to walk inside, his body roaring at him that this wasn't permanent, that this was not his home, that he did not *have* one. How would it be possible to have his own bed, one that did not fit inside his saddle bags? And was that—a fireplace just beyond the door. Truly a house. Azrael steeled his nerves and followed Magdalene in.

A sitting room was the first thing he walked in to, with a small table imme-diately to his right, beneath the window. To his left was the fireplace where a sofa and a low table sat before it. Beyond that, a tiny kitchen with empty shelves was blanketed in darkness. Azrael had never been good at cooking, but he found himself excited about having a *kitchen* nonetheless.

He walked further into the house, towards a door opposite of the empty fireplace. With fingers he didn't realize were shaking slightly, he twisted the handle and opened the door to a bed positioned in the center of the far wall. A chest sat at the foot of the bed and a low dresser stretched along the wall to his right. The other side of the room opened to a bathroom with a stone tub glinting in the dim light.

This was truly a new life. Maybe he had indeed died at the hands of the rebels, all of his bones smashed, and this was either whatever awaited him in the unlife or he had somehow tricked his way into another man's life. He could hardly wrap his head around it. Years and years—a decade, really—without a stable home. Azrael had been floating, living temporarily wherever his duty required him.

"What do you think?" Magdalene's voice pulled him from his spiral of thoughts.

"It's very nice." Azrael rubbed his face before walking back to where Magdalene still stood beside the front door. He set his bags down, the thud echoing.

"If you need anything, I'll be around." Magdalene smiled, her thin hands folding in front of her. Azrael didn't reply as she stepped outside and closed the door behind her, leaving him alone with his thoughts.

It didn't take long for the silence to ring in his ears and the solitude to feel like a weight over him. He lit a fire, despite the warmth of the summer morning, for the sake of having something other than the enduring stillness. He stood in front of the fireplace for a long while, not knowing what to do. His hands were slack at his sides, fingertips tapping against his thumbs.

The shadows of the room deepened and his thoughts turned over and over in the absence of a second presence. He thought of Hanna, her dark and tender hands trying to fix what had been beyond repair, and Raphael whose chaotic mind somehow saved Azrael's.

He felt foolish, and knew there was an easier way to tell, but he hovered his hand over the growing flames. With a hiss, he retracted his hand and stared at his fingertips. Somehow, he wasn't dreaming. Somehow, he ended up here. Alone, in his very own house, in a Tiras uniform, on two healed legs. He didn't know what he did to deserve any of those things, nor did he know where that left him.

Firewood cracked and Azrael flinched, the sound too close like that of a bone. He rubbed his eyes as he moved away from the fireplace. He ought to take bath, rinse away the smell of horse and death that lingered on him. He ought to stretch, do some training exercises, move his body. He ought to unpack his bags, make some sort of breakfast.

He did none of those things, and instead flopped onto the bed in his dark room and let sleep pull him into her sweet embrace.

# CHAPTER 7

## AZRAEL

An unhurried knock on the front door yanked Azrael from the dreams he couldn't wait to leave; those of late had involved too many ghosts, too many reminders of those he had failed. He rolled out of bed—*his* bed, he was surprised that wasn't also part of the dream—and shuffled to the door.

The Roen Azrael had ridden beside stood in the doorway after he fiddled with the door handle and opened it. He had changed into a loose white shirt and dark pants with a piece of wheat tucked into his black waves. He smiled at Azrael, small and warm, and Azrael racked his brain to remember the man's name.

"Ahmi," the Roen said, his smile turning into a sly smirk, "I know. The king asks for us at daybreak in the armory. It's easiest to get to from the main hall—a right, then a left at the queen's portrait, then a straight shot down the hall and it'll be the last door on the left. I'll see you in the morning."

Ahmi tilted his head in a gesture to excuse himself, his smirk softening before he turned and walked towards the house across from Azrael's. A short, curvy woman stood in the doorway, mirroring Azrael's own stance leaning against the frame, while a small child pulled on the hem of her dress. The woman glowed, cheeks pinker than the dawn, as Ahmi cupped his hands on the sides of her face before disappearing into their home. The woman swung the child with a graceful ease onto her hip before she too stepped into the house.

Azrael's chest tightened, his eyes still stuck on the now closed door across the courtyard. Tiny handprints of dirt covered the lower half of their door. The longing to belong to someone—to belong *somewhere*—cracked like lightning in his chest. He had accepted long ago that a life like that wasn't for him. Some hurts lingered, little but present. He had someone once, a lifetime ago. Taya had been part of his small unit and their ghost, cloaked in shadows, to learn who made their sentiments against the king known. Three years they were a team, the two of them, and one year they were inseparable, hand in hand. Two teenagers hoping for a future that would never arrive, cleaved apart because of a paranoid nobleman. It took Azrael three days to find her body, the feeling of waterlogged flesh and fabric and her cold skin still hanging in the back of his mind, even six years later. The agony had long since subsided but echoed still as a reminder in his heart. Part of him didn't know if he could feel the way he felt for her again, and another part of him didn't want to. He didn't want to lose someone like that again.

He tore his gaze away and instead surveyed the others going about their evening, not at all missing the side eye looks thrown his way. Beyond Ahmi, he didn't recognize any of them from the ride and he met their apprehensive stares with a neutral expression. He didn't feel like he belonged here either, but the unlife be damned if he wasn't going to act otherwise.

A group clothed in the drab grey of servants descended the steps as the sun fell below the horizon. Each carried a small, lit torch and began to light the lanterns. Azrael's gaze followed them without paying attention, until his eyes snagged on a girl on the far end of the courtyard. Wearing all black, stark against the others but half melting into the shadows, it took him longer than it should have to recognize her as the healer from the ride. Lark, he remembered the name she bore. What captivated his full attention was the flicker of white light that jumped from her hand into the lantern in front of her.

Azrael rubbed his eyes, hesitant to tear his gaze from her, but a white haze still hovered in her hands when he looked back. It couldn't have been a trick of the light—not with the color of the flame. He kept watching her as she moved, disappearing into the second circle only to reappear moments later, fingers twitching at her sides. She passed his house, an outstretch of his hand away, without a glance in his direction. He didn't think twice before pulling the door closed behind him and following the healer down the winding stone path. He had been right, then. The Areenian had been injured, shot by the arrow, and both he and Lark had blood on them. Lark had healed him. How was she able to wield magic? Because *that* had most certainly been magic. It had vanished from the world a millennium ago, not even a whisper of what it used to be.

Lark had rejoined the small group as they drifted along the second ring. Azrael kept his distance, appearing to be no more than a restless soldier taking a leisurely stroll, but his eyes bore into her back so he wouldn't miss if she used magic again. The group dispersed in front of the courtyard, momentarily shielding Lark from his view. Her small frame appeared again, dark waves rustling in the breeze down her back like rippling shadows, only to begin to fade into the shadows of dusk. Azrael squinted and sighed. What was he doing? Besides following an unsuspecting woman late at night. He stopped walking.

Magic was dead. Even in Areen, where legend says magic originated, they hadn't been able to conjure anything. This healer, who helped servants and healed soldiers, had to have an explanation—one that he did not need, and did not need to be following her for. A few days out of the infirmary and he was already losing his mind.

Despite knowing better, a tug deep within his bones had Azrael walking still in her general direction. He'd lost sight of her, but he descended the steps and strolled past the guards at their posts at the gate. He nodded to them as they noted the red band on his arm, as though that's all it took to do whatever he pleased.

Azrael walked along the smooth stone path that wound around and up towards the barracks but walked past them, angling his focus to the river that flowed from the waterfall in the west branched throughout the city and snaked along the palace walls. He aligned himself with it until he came to a stone bridge. A white, stone owl sat on each end of the bridge and Azrael decided his eyes very well might have been playing tricks on him. He swore the owl's head swiveled ever so slightly. He leaned against the railing and looked out towards the city, but listened to the river behind him flow and plummet into the raging sea.

The first moon, half full, climbed the sky as stars erupted around it. Darkness rippled in the velvet black, along the horizon, where the second moon would rise soon—as though the black were alive and squirming amongst the stars. Vale City stretched out before him, quiet and twinkling with lanterns. It felt like a lifetime ago that he had been out on the streets, running with friends and drinking stolen Telaanan liquor. He hadn't taken seriously the army, nor the political precipice, nor anything, then. Azrael had lived in a limbo, somewhere between life and death, unable to tether himself to the present. All these years later, and Azrael hardly felt any different.

The in-between feeling had started after his home had been ransacked, the Moor destroyed along with his life there. The weeks after were spent in his aunt's house who consistently forgot his name and that he required food. The island was small, a four day's journey off the coast of Havriel, and the day that his aunt had shipped him to the city had been both the end of his life and the beginning.

Azrael didn't realize how long he stood there, waiting for—waiting for what? Lark? Who no doubt had known he had followed her and shook him off her trail. He had been foolish, feeling even more so once he realized the second moon was well above the tree line now and he had been standing there for far too long. He glared at the owl statues before skulking home.

†

D awn exploded over the horizon as Azrael watched from his rooftop, the brilliant colors touching the Tiras homes gently with a soft summer breeze. A knuckle's rap below him knocked him out of the trance the early morning had put him in. He hadn't slept much, haunted by dreams of magical beings floating around in the dark corners of his mind, and had climbed to the roof long before anyone in the city began to stir.

Azrael scrambled down the side of the house, the metal pipe smooth and cool against his calloused hands. An unamused servant stood at his door with a silver tray in his hands. The servant didn't wait for Azrael to take it, instead set it on the ground in front of the door and walked away muttering. Azrael picked it up hesitantly, unsure what to make of it. Breakfast was delivered? He couldn't remember if courtiers had theirs delivered, or if they had to meet in the dining hall. Although, Melech didn't keep courtiers within the palace, did he? Azrael hadn't seen any of the hideous fashion statements the rich sported, no leering faces as he had wandered.

Either way, he decided, he wouldn't let the food go to waste. He shouldered his door open and set the tray on his little table. Oatcakes, berries, slices of bacon and a small glass of mead. Azrael ate as he dressed in the Tiras uniform—a brigandine, an undershirt, pants, and his boots, all in a black so rich it seemed a night sky awaiting stars. He slung his belt and sword on before heading towards the armory.

A child carrying firewood nearly collided with Azrael, and he stepped aside only to trip over a dog trailing the child. The child snapped a command to the dog who scurried along. Dozens of servants passed Azrael without a glance, and he had to wonder what they all did. The palace was giant, he supposed, so there was no shortage of work to do.

Striding through corridors, and accidentally finding himself in a circle, Azrael eventually made it to the armory. He didn't know how he managed to confuse easy enough directions, but here he was. He walked into a massive room, lit only by torches and lanterns, with bows, swords, and shields lining the walls. A group of soldiers sat around a large table littered with maps, ink wells, and daggers. Not one took note of Azrael's entrance, and he supposed it was for the best. He glanced instead at the paintings that hung on the wall closest to him—the only places weapons weren't pinned to the wall. One caught his eye, taking the time to move closer since he was the first Tiras here.

Of King Nekoda, his face was young and sharp while his gray eyes, though painted, churned with ambition while shadows accumulated like storm clouds behind him. His crown glinted in the light, dark gold, old and worn, but his black armor was shining, with two moons on his breast plate. Azrael wondered if it held to his likeness. He hadn't seen the late king portrayed like this, the warrior he once was.

Azrael shifted on his feet once the door opened and four Tiras, followed by Melech sauntered in. The men at the table jumped to their feet, their boasting of long nights ceasing. Azrael moved beside the others while the king crossed the room to a door half shielded by a rack of bows. Ahmi walked beside Azrael, elbowing him in the ribs in greeting as they followed their king.

The second room was smaller, but cozy with furs laid on the marble floor as well as the chairs with a white wolf's pelt hung on the wall behind Melech. A large table took up the center of the room with the known world's map engraved into the wood, all three kingdoms shining in the fire light as Azrael took a seat. At the head, Melech leaned against the wood, fingertips drumming underneath the table. He wore a crown similar to the one from Nekoda's painting, but his was brighter with milky white and black gems encrusted on the face to mimic the moons. His scruffy jaw was tight, and those bright eyes turned sharp as he settled his stare on the map in front of them.

"Brannon, I trust you've chosen well," Melech said, turning his piercing gaze to the man on his right. "Because this needs to end now."

"I have, though I still am hesitant to send them."

Azrael watched a muscle in the king's jaw feather and his shoulders tense. None of this felt real, more like a fever dream he had conjured up when he thought he would die. The captain, Brannon, cleared his throat, understanding some unspoken threat in the king's face, and nodded to those sitting at the table with him.

"A scout, an archer, two swordsmen," he said, then added with an edge of irritation, "Your Highness."

Turning his attention, Azrael noted the scout sitting at the end of the table, a young Roen man with a piece of wheat tucked within his golden hair. The female archer from the ride sat beside him, with her too far apart eyes and downturned mouth, a ghost of a smile touched her lips as they made eye contact. Azrael couldn't tell what it was, but it wasn't friendliness in her face.

"Westwick is under attack. I won't have our shores look so easily overrun. You four I want there to figure it out, put a stop to it. I trust no one else with this. The port is essential to the Vale, and I won't lose it for a petty squabble." Melech looked to each of his Tiras, their talent earning them that seat at the table with him. Azrael felt out of place until the king met his gaze. Something unspoken laid in his face, and Azrael wondered if this was a test. "Protect your king. You leave in one hour."

Melech turned to his captain, his dismissal clear. Azrael stood with the others and left the king. Ahmi fell into step with him as the archer shouldered past them, twin blonde braids dancing on her shoulders as she strode out.

"Asenneth," Ahmi offered, kindly reminding Azrael of the woman's name.

Before Azrael could reply, a second voice piped, "Nevan."

Azrael glanced over his shoulder at the Roen, his head only reaching Azrael's chest. He stopped walking and offered his hand out. "Azrael."

"We know," Nevan replied. The only surprise that Azrael let show was two blinks before the scout disappeared.

"You have a natural talent that takes years to practice. And don't pretend that we don't know you were the youngest in the army," Ahmi said as they continued walking together. His voice restraining a hint of a laugh, he continued, "Plus, the Greater chose you. Everyone knows who you are."

The weight of his words settled in Azrael, though he couldn't decipher how he meant them. Ahmi smiled and patted him on the shoulder before leaving Azrael alone in the open hall.

# CHAPTER 8

## LARK

S hadows writhed and constricted, holding Lark close as she braced her body and held her breath. This was darkness, absolute and never ending. This is what her end would look like. Her body tried hyperventilating, but she fought to control herself, lest her shadows warp and she end up in the middle of the ocean. The darkness of killers moving in the night—swift, careful, silent—although her mission here in the south was far from death.

She tried talking herself out of it, coming here, but she left the Vale during the moment when she thought this would indeed be a good idea. Her shadows enveloped her then, for only the second time, and she dared the journey across the kingdom. The first time she had travelled this way had been on accident, and she hadn't known entirely what she did, only that one moment she was angry at the king and thinking she needed to do something to cool down, and the next moment she was knee deep in the ocean. Iah, the god of night, had explained what had happened, and how to do it again.

Salt and open air filled her nose and her shadows spun faster, a twisted childhood swing righting itself. Lark braced herself again, bending her knees, and readied for the moment she dreaded.

The black cast her out, spitting her out as if disliking the taste of her, and Lark face planted into the earth, knees digging into the soil. Silence rang around her, and she thanked Iah for it. She didn't know what she would have done if someone had seen this, and she cursed herself for travelling this way. Godsdamn the time restraint she was on—if her plan unfurled before she was ready... Lark pushed the thought away. This was her first big step, and the biggest risk, but it was time.

As she staggered to her feet, a violent wave of sickness hit her. The contents of her stomach emptied onto the ground in front of her and dizziness gripped her head as the retching slowly subsided. It was so much worse this time. Lark braced her hands on her knees then lowered into a squat.

Breathing carefully, slowly, Lark waited until the sickness and pain passed, gritting her teeth against the urge to throw up again. At least she had left early, arriving the night before she met the lord of the south. She glanced up at the sky, judging the second moon's placement, and rested her forehead against her crossed arms. There was plenty of time to rest before she met with the lord, and she tried not to think about the journey home, what Melech would say if he saw her like this. Her heart thundered briefly, as she imagined the fight they would have, before she cast the thoughts away.

Lark pushed to her feet and began walking, the moonlight just bright enough to light the path through the field she had crashed into. She shifted the bag on her back, grateful it had survived the journey. She had studied a map before leaving, and she hoped that her calculations were correct as she headed towards the inn.

$$\dagger$$

S he left the inn early, deciding to walk instead of procuring a horse from the hesitant innkeeper. Even with every inch of her body screaming from the chaotic journey, the early morning and miles she walked felt good on her weary body.

"Lark," Lord Bedivere Tarrae called out from the top of the stairs as she crossed the front yard. His manor sprawled out behind him, dark against the brightness of summer. An equally bright smile stretched across his face that Lark couldn't help but return, her eyes narrow slits from the blinding sun. The lord's long hair was tied in a high knot, strands falling and curling around his warm face. The image of him alone calmed her fraying nerves. "Welcome to the Roe, princess."

Lark's smile wavered, turning sheepish, at the title. She climbed the stairs to him, wood creaking beneath her light step. Bedivere took her hand in both of his as he kissed her knuckles. She was suddenly aware of how the wind had whipped her braid, the strands out of place, and how muddy the hem of her dress had gotten on the walk here.

"My lord," she said as she bowed her head, but he caught her chin with his forefinger.

"You needn't do that before me." His smile was warm still, his wink even more so. "Come, let's go inside."

He turned, offering his arm which she looped hers through, and led them through the open front door. It all felt so relaxed, so carefree. Lark hadn't expected it.

His home was just that—a home. As they passed sitting rooms with worn sofas and one with a grand piano that didn't have a speck of dust, as they strode down the hallway with childlike paintings hanging on the walls, this manor didn't feel as though it belonged to a lord who governed the entire southern tip of the continent. Lark had expected something akin to a palace, or even a large estate like the ones she had seen within the forest. This was a home, cozy and welcoming and warm.

"How was your journey?" Bedivere asked as they turned a corner to another hall. The floorboard creaked beneath them. The entire house felt lived in, rich with history and love. Not at all like the power-hungry lord that Melech had made Bedivere out to be. Lark knew he could easily be deceiving her, but, somehow, she knew within her heart that he wasn't.

"It was rough, at first, but fine overall," she replied, not giving away the *how* she had made the two-week trip here. By the twinkle in his eye as he cast a smile over his shoulder, she wondered if he somehow knew.

Bedivere opened a set of carved doors and gestured for her to walk in first. His study, Lark realized. She noticed first the wall made entirely of glass opposite of her, illuminating the picture of a studious lord. Books were stacked on every surface, spines cracked, pages torn, piled high even beneath his leather chair. Plants in detailed pots were almost as numerous as the books, leafy tendrils creeping towards the glass and the sun outside. A servant remained in the room, setting out tea on a small table in the far corner, her aged face nothing but kind.

Lark followed the lord as he strode across the room to settle in a large chair, plush and forming to his body. She sat in the smaller, equally worn one beside him and noted how his eyes tracked the servant as she flitted about the room, readying a spread of food. Only once she left did he nod to the two cups on the table between them.

"So, daughter of night and storm, how can you do it?" Bedivere asked, elbows on the arms of his chair while one hand stroked his trimmed beard.

Straight to the point.

Lark had been dreading this, even though she had been the one to initiate their meeting. The people in her life had always known she could wield magic, but this was the first step in letting the world know—and letting them know that she was no longer going to hide.

She took a shaky breath and hid the trembling in her hand by raising the cup to her lips. An herbal tea—lavender with oat milk. It soothed her anxious heart. His trust, his support, was more important than her feelings.

"Where would you like me to begin?"

Bedivere leaned back in his chair, not at all reflecting the power he held. It calmed her. Where Melech was everything dark and cold, Bedivere was warmth and light. She settled into her chair, crossing her ankles and letting her shoulders relax.

"The beginning. I know it came from Areen. Texts can hold only so much truth, especially with the Three Oceans between us."

The Three Oceans, named solely because each kingdom, each continent, couldn't decide on a name. Areen, to their northeast. Telaan, to their southeast. Both had magic before their land was discovered and settled. Lark felt the familiar tapping on the back of her mind, at the base of her skull, asking to be let in. The god of night never liked to be shut out, locked out of the head he had been in and out of since she was a little girl. Lark kept her mental walls high and ignored the god.

She was stalling, she couldn't pretend otherwise. She offered the lord a shy smile and tapped her index finger on the rim of her cup. Her ivory light, coiled within her chest, loosened just enough to warm her tea and steady her thoughts.

"Magic was a gift," she started, her voice surprisingly even, "From the goddess of life, for the world. Each of the four gods could grant the gift to a mortal if they wanted."

Maybe she should have written it down instead, the basic history Iah had given her. The truth—hard to find in texts these days.

"It could be anything, whatever the god wanted. Water breathing, teleporting, elemental, animal whispering, it depended on what the god saw in the person's life, if they were truly worthy of magic. A thousand years ago, the three gods decided to cast out the fourth."

Iah's growl reverberated in her bones, shaking the stones of the wall in her mind. She had always been afraid to ask why he had been cast out.

"He is here in exile, to atone. In that, this land had been leeched of magic, and once the first settlers arrived, so did the rest of the world."

Bedivere watched her with an unreadable expression, his eyes tracking each lift and lower of her cup, the shaking in her pinky.

"And how do *you* have it?"

"You knew my father. There was no end he wouldn't reach to have magic for himself. He was convinced he could bring it back. He made a deal with the god of night, but it went wrong—or maybe it went right, I don't know. He had wanted it, but it went to me. Instead of receiving a drop, how the others had given, I received a lake, so to speak."

There it was.

Admitting to the crown's rival that she had one of—if not the biggest—sources of magic in the last few millennia.

*Your powers make you. You cannot shy away from them. The stars do not shy from the moon. An ember does not cower before flames. It becomes them.*

Lark mentally swore at the crack she had let the god slip through. These conversations were one secret she didn't think she could tell anyone, even Harlow, her adoptive mother. Her father hadn't even known the extent of Iah's reach.

"How far have you swam, so to speak?" Bedivere did not seem the least bit fazed as he visibly turned the information over in his head. Lark saw the thoughts stirring in those black eyes of his, the plans and ideas forming.

"I've only just been discovering what I can do. There's a lot I don't know yet; I'm taking it day by day."

Starlight and the darkness that lingered between the stars was the base of her magic—from there she willed different uses for each. The shadows were what she had used to carry herself across the kingdom, reduced herself to a mere wisp and let the wind bring her here. Each experiment, each task she tried to complete that was outside of the things she did daily took its toll. Iah offered his guidance, lessening the effect on her and directing how she could use her magic.

*They could teach you too, if you let them.*

Them—Iah's men. The ones that swam in the stars with him. He had gifted them magic when they walked the earth, and their magic was reflected in Lark's own. This wasn't his first offer of their help, but Lark was reluctant to accept, given the way the air turned to ice whenever they were around—as if life itself didn't want to be in their presence.

"Lark," Bedivere's soft but commanding voice brought her back, his eyes not missing a moment of her inattention. "I don't know if you remember me from the palace all those years ago, but I haven't forgotten the girl I met, so skittish of her own shadows. I can see how long ago that was, but I also see how far you've yet to go before you take your throne."

Her heart stilled. For a moment, she thought even the birds ceased their chirping. The risk she was taking would be worth it. Bedivere's support was more important than the lords of the forest estates, even more than the royals across the ocean.

"So, I have your support?"

"Of course. There are conditions, but nothing I can't see you disagreeing with. I will help teach you diplomacy, guide you on the proper way to care for a kingdom—" The jab at Melech did not go unnoticed, and Lark smiled, small and shy, "—but you must continue to practice your magic. The people want hope, a future, someone they can look to. Melech has had our people torn for too long, and you must repair that tear."

Lark hid her growing smile by taking another sip of her cooling tea, the milk swirling in the cup mirrored her thoughts.

"I will draft my conditions and, tomorrow, before you leave, we will sit and go over them. First lesson," he added with a wink, "get everything written down."

With that, Bedivere stood and smiled down at Lark, gentle and warm, as he slipped his hands into the pockets of his soft linen pants. "I'll have a room prepared for you, and we'll meet for breakfast. Enjoy your night, princess."

Lark watched his tall frame cross the room and disappear past the double doors. As soon as they closed, she jumped to her feet, covering her mouth with both hands so her excitement didn't slip out, and moved to the window to organize the chaotic mess of thoughts pacing in her head. Somehow, she had just sat through the very beginning of a peace treaty between the Vale and the Roe—at least, close enough. She had the Roe's backing for the throne, and that was the single most important thing. She had a very long way to go, a lot of ruffled feathers to smooth, but she breathed a sigh of relief. One step forward, and the throne was one step closer to being hers again.

The view from Bedivere's study was breathtaking. Sitting on the southern end of the house, the window looked out towards the lower part of the city and the docks. Ships with massive sails crowded the wooden docks, but beyond that—uninterrupted blue that blended seamlessly with the sky so it was difficult to tell where the sea ended and the sky began. Maybe she'd go practice magic somewhere by the water—find a secluded beach and try water breathing, or something, anything. She didn't care what; Lark felt like she could do anything with this weightlessness in her chest.

*Birdie can't breathe underwater.*

Lark scowled towards the sky. Somewhere, invisible now but with a presence still weighing heavy, Iah was up there, stuck in the form of the second moon that Havriel was known for. The moon that didn't affect the tide. The moon that no one could explain or account for. No, Havriel never stopped to consider that this phenomenon might be their true god.

*The Greater. Mortals will disregard every bit of truth for the safety of a lie.*

Lark paused, a thought snapping into place. She glanced over her shoulder at the southern lord's study. Bedivere hadn't questioned her. He had taken in everything she said, without contradiction or denial.

*His people worship us. Haven't you noticed?*

Lark didn't know how people worshipped the gods, racking her memory for the books she had read in her schooling about the kingdoms across the ocean. For the Greater, those who believed fasted on chosen days, prayed at noon, and the priests carried gems that reflected the sunlight.

*Would you like to know how my people worship the god of night?*

There was a roughness in Iah's voice, a hunger that rattled Lark and she decided that no, she did not want to know—whether it was all night orgies, ritual lamb slaughter, or something as simple as setting bones on a windowsill. He had never told her how he thrived off mortal's devotion. She rolled the thoughts out of her head and piled her mental wall back up before grabbing her bag from beneath the chair. With the evening before her, she set out to explore what the south offered.

The Roe consisted of this town—the center of their trade—as well as several surrounding towns that blended to be known to the world as the Roe. Lark had learned about the south and its trading empire as a child, and visited a handful of times before her father had cast her away. The eight years that she had been a princess. The eight years her people have forgotten.

Streets of pale stone and dirt wove back and forth, a snake leading down, down, down to the docks and brilliant sapphire water. Brightly colored buildings, in varying shapes and sizes, squished together as if to keep warm during winter. This late in the day, people filed into the street with tired eyes and neutral faces, their long days weighing on their shoulders as a mantle. The people were just as beautiful as their land. Rich shades of tan, brown, russet, olive, and every color between graced their skin and hair. Bright green and amber eyes met hers with kindness as she walked alongside them. It was a stark contrast to the Vale, where not one set of eyes met yours in passing. Even the Roen clothing, simple and practical, was unlike Valen nobles in their mismatching patterns and feathers—this felt welcoming. Lark noted the small bits of wheat tucked in jacket pockets, woven into hair, laced into books, and she didn't understand until she felt the gentle nudge in the back of her mind.

*They worship Banii,* Iah said flatly once Lark lowered the wall. Of course, the goddess of life and creation. They would celebrate her here, where three kingdoms relied on the crops Roen hands harvested.

Winding streets guided Lark while her thoughts traveled, the din of the town a constant buzz around her while the chaos of the docks rose even louder. She continued, walking past Bedivere's manor and the houses that grew more and more spaced, and thought of the vast fields on the other side of the homes. Lark unspooled a thread of shadow from her core, invisible to all but her, and searched for the swiftest way to the water.

Once she tasted the sea breeze, Lark followed the trail through grass taller than her, over small rolling hills, and through a cluster of boulders that looked as though a giant had discarded them like jacks, until she finally came to a bluff.

At the very bottom, a boulder sat in the fading sunshine, beckoning her. Lark summoned her shadows, wrapping herself tightly so that she was no more than a wisp herself. Instead of moving through the world magically, her feet caught together and she pitched herself down the earth. Throwing out a hand, she created a cluster of shadows as a net before she slammed into the rock she had intended to sit on. Her fingers cracked as she rolled, bending backwards at painful angles, and the shadows embraced her as she fell into them. After she calmed her racing heart, a shaky laugh slipped from her. The shadows beneath her dissipated and Lark stood on shaky knees.

No more jumping then, Lark decided. She had hoped she would be able to do it again for the trip home, as she hadn't allotted the time it would take to ride back to the Vale—or even sail. Lark didn't entertain the thought of what it would mean for her if she arrived in two weeks.

She brushed the earth off her dress and fought the rising nausea. Picking the sticks out of her hair was a good distraction as she waded through the faint dizziness that accompanied her attempt at her magic. She wondered what it had been like to use magic before—before it had disappeared. Was it different? Did it take as much from her predecessors, or was the toll solely because the earth fought against the magic?

Lark scrambled onto the boulder, ignoring the roughness that cut into her palms and the blinding ache in her right hand, and savored the smooth top of the rock that had been kissed by the ocean. The water around it was calm, serene. A small pull began to ache in her chest; two ends of a knot trying to come undone. After a few deep breaths, Lark tugged on that knot and focused her power on the sunlight sparkling on the water's surface. Water splashed softly below her as the tide brushed the shore.

Heat had always been easy to work with, whether it was using her light to set fires or warming her tea. Cold had been easy too, summoning the frigid temperatures of the space Iah occupied in the sky with her shadows. She had always longed to master her powers with the peace of the water, its slow push and pull.

*You are not made for peace.*

*What does that mean?* Lark raised her eyes to the sky.

*You are made of star fire and moonlight. You are a storm at sea. You are a force of nature, Lark, not something to sit idle.*

A chill snaked along her bare arms despite the warmth of the day. Lark built, stone by stone, that wall in her mind thicker. Surely she couldn't sit idle if his voice kept erupting in her head. Below her, the water began to churn, tiny waves crashing over one another, and something like thunder broke beneath the surface. The surface bubbled while shadows swelled below. Lark stopped tugging at the knot in her chest and the water calmed, returning to the calmness she envied.

She didn't want to think if Iah was right.

# CHAPTER 9

## AZRAEL

Westwick was a small village on the western coast with a port larger than the town itself and conducted nearly all the Vale's trade with Areen and Telaan across the ocean, and occasionally with the Roe. Inns, taverns, and brothels bordered the coast to accommodate the numerous sailors, merchants, and miscreants that flooded the port daily. Those who lived in Westwick were under the mercy of the travelers—the town itself was wealthy from the trade, but the folk were poor, both in coin and spirit.

Azrael had only been to Westwick a handful of times, each time against his will and under orders, and each time he wondered why he was in fact there. He knew the king did not want to lose the port to the threat currently plaguing it, but he also hadn't expected to be the king's personal errand boy. Azrael supposed, with twenty talented soldiers surrounding him, the king could in fact use them however he wished. Azrael shifted in his saddle, grunting at the fading light.

The edge of the forest was pink when they stopped at the outskirts of town. With the ocean on one side, a thick forest claimed the other side while a long and winding dirt path carved out a place for homes and buildings. Azrael watched as Nevan leapt nimbly off his horse and disappeared into the growing purple twilight. Asenneth did the same, tying their horses to a tree before unstringing her bow from her back, and disappeared between the trees. Azrael narrowed his eyes, straining to differentiate their shapes from the shadows.

As planned, Ahmi and Azrael sat on their horses until a low whistle sounded from Nevan shortly after his disappearance. They dismounted, exchanging a weary glance, before heading along the road.

A heavy, muffled silence descended around them as they passed the first inn, missing horses on the side and any sign of life within. Azrael kept his hand on his sword, the sound of their boots crunching on stones grating his patience. Where was the threat the king had been warned of? The thing that threatened the port's loyalty to the Vale?

Glass sparkled in dirt, the broken windows along the road carrying a breeze laced with fear, sweat, and blood. A ghost town laid bare before them, not even a dog barking or a bird chirping. Smoke billowed into the sky, but there was no crackling of fire, no smell of something ablaze. Azrael's breath caught in his chest, as though his body recognized the threat before his mind did. At the far end of the street, standing amidst rubble, a figure shifted in the growing darkness, hardly visible in the black.

A memory flitted through Azrael, one he long ago buried, and now struggled to push down. A nudge in the back of his head had him taking a step forward. This figure was calling to him, he had to see—

Ahmi grasped his wrist, yanking him backwards. Azrael glanced at Ahmi's hand, then back to the figure and the empty place it had stood. Azrael's head emptied, the silence around him ringing like warning bells. He slowly unsheathed his sword.

Stones skittered across the dirt and both men started at the sound, whirling towards the sound. The small figure of Nevan stumbled from between two houses. Armor ripped to shreds across his chest and face wholly covered in blood, his swollen face turned towards them.

"Run." Blood bubbled from his lips, down his chin, and pooled into the dirt. "*Run.*"

Nevan fell to his knees in a sickening crunch. Ahmi lunged towards him, not before the night twisted in front of him and a figure materialized—taller than the buildings and reeking of blood. Azrael's breath was visible in its presence, the heat of the night leeching from the air. He stumbled backwards, heart beating through his chest. They were so, so much worse up close.

Nevan's eyes were wild as his pleading stare darted between Ahmi and Azrael, both paralyzed where they stood. His broken mouth cracked open and his throat began to distort, bulging like a balloon—

Azrael swung his blade, anything to end this torture. Without turning away from Nevan, a hand of bone gripped the sword with a loud screech and yanked the hilt right from Azrael's hand. The demon tossed the sword into the air, caught the hilt, and swung it toward Azrael's chest. Nevan's body thudded on the ground as Azrael leaned backwards, the tip of his sword grazing beneath his chin. A growl like thunder erupted from within the mass of darkness in front of him. Losing his balance, Azrael reeled backwards and dug his heels into the dirt, pushing himself away from the demon.

The creature dropped the sword as Ahmi lunged at it, his blade passing through smoke instead of a body. The demon was motionless, soundless.

Azrael wasn't healed by some kind of magic only to die here at the hand of a demon. With sweaty hands, he dove for his sword and rolled away from the demon as it turned its attention to Ahmi. Azrael did not spare a look at Nevan's battered body before plunging the blade into the demon's back, twisting and pushing with all his strength.

A scream that rattled the stars exploded from the demon before a crack echoed and the creature turned to stone. Azrael yanked his sword out before it was caught and jumped backwards. The stone body turned to dust and rose into the night sky.

In the remaining purple light, Azrael spared a glance at Nevan, throat splayed open and hand reaching towards him, and vomited. He couldn't hide the shaking in his hands as he sheathed his sword, but he didn't care, not as Ahmi collapsed beside Nevan, silent sobs racking his shoulders.

"What the fuck?" Azrael glanced at Ahmi's sword, discarded uselessly beside him. How did one blade kill the demon while the other passed right through? Why was it here? He swallowed the fear that lingered and wiped his mouth with the back of his hand.

"Find Asenneth," Ahmi said as he glanced over his shoulder. "We're leaving."

Azrael's breath was a cloud in front of him. He swore again and had his sword in his hand in a second. Feet apart, his body screamed at him to run the opposite direction. Two swirling figures cloaked in black stood a few houses down, close enough that Azrael could see their faces—of lack thereof. Jagged bone, teeth covered in blood were framed in pure, unobstructed darkness. His fingers flexed around his hilt, and he raced towards them, yelling louder with each stride. He took one down, he'd do it again—he'd take them both. Sword poised to pierce the one on the right, sweat and fear slick on his face, he realized he had no chance, too late. The figures warped and, within a blink, he was flying backwards and watching his blade skid across the dirt.

He roughly landed, rolling and twisting before he stopped himself. He clambered to his feet, only to stumble forward and drop face first as his balance failed. The figures he had his focus on swirled and flew towards the sky, disappearing amongst the stars.

Ahmi was at his side once he lost sight of the demons, hands around his sore shoulders. Azrael staggered, but Ahmi held tight.

"We're leaving," Ahmi repeated, voice cold, distant, and he spoke through gritted teeth.

Azrael retrieved his sword but didn't sheathe it. He held it ready as he and Ahmi headed back towards the tree line. Squinting through the darkness, he wondered if there were other demons skulking around.

He didn't know how this could be real. Maybe he had never left the infirmary. In the short period of time of his discharge, he found himself thinking that too often. It was all an intricate dream, or nightmare really, that he couldn't escape from.

The first moon was peaking now, finally giving silvery light over the treetops. Azrael was glad to leave the silent town, the occasional groan of wood or crack as weakened buildings started to give made him flinch, but he wondered where everyone had gone. Had they been able to flee before death swept in? There weren't any bodies, no mangled evidence of humanity's demise. He took a deep breath and listened for Asenneth's whistle, or voice, or any movement to guide him. He had to drown out his pounding heartbeat before he finally heard heavy, labored breathing. Between the trees, he couldn't tell where it was coming from. He hoped that wet, shaky sigh wasn't Asenneth; his steps became careful.

Azrael called out her name, hesitant. In response, a sob choked out into the night, followed by his own name.

Her voice had come from near where they had dismounted, the sound of hooves stamping the ground was jarring against the silence. With the moonlight guiding him, Azrael quickly found the archer and, once he did, stopped cold in his tracks. Asenneth sat at the base of the tree with her face turned towards the sky, silver light illuminating her, with a dark branch protruding from her stomach. Her face was white, streaked with scratches, tears, and blood.

Azrael felt useless as he stood before her, hands turned towards her as if to show her he couldn't help. Asenneth's gaze burned strong with pain and fear, but he could see her strength slowly beginning to wane. She couldn't have been like this long, but the black ground beneath her suggested that it didn't matter. He knelt beside her and wiped the tears from her eyes. Ahmi approached from behind them, a gasp choked out of him.

"I'll stay with her. You need to ride like lightning and find a healer," Azrael told Ahmi. There was no question of moving the archer, and the town was deserted without a healer anywhere. Death was crawling for her.

Ahmi swallowed, ran his hand through his hair, and looked away from her. They stood far enough that she couldn't hear their hushed words.

"I don't think she'll have time," Ahmi croaked out, voice broken.

"And she has less the more we stand debating it," Azrael snapped back, only to regret his words at the sight of Ahmi's grief-stricken face. He easily forgot that he was the outsider amongst them; the rest of the Tiras had been together, Ahmi had told him as they rode side by side, for years.

"I need," Asenneth gasped, "Lark."

"Go, Ahmi." Azrael squeezed his shoulder and nodded towards the horses.

Ahmi glanced at Asenneth one more time before he jumped onto his horse, galloping into the night. Azrael moved to Nevan's horse and rifled through his saddlebag, producing a saddle blanket. His body was laying beneath the tree on the opposite side of the horse, and Azrael took care not to look at it. He'd seen so much mutilation and gore in his years, but he was unsettled by the boy's death.

He settled beside Asenneth again, and gently moved her limp fingers away from the branch she tried to hold straight. Overlooking the blood staining his fingers, Azrael shifted the blanket to hold the branch in place. His medical training was limited to basics he learned in his first few years of the army, and his stay in the infirmary, but he had to come up with something before Ahmi rode back with the healer to a dead woman.

"What happened?" he asked her. He knew keeping her quiet would be best, but he wanted her awake too. He couldn't ignore the night they had had and wanted to know what Asenneth had seen.

"Demons," she sighed, her voice hardly louder than a whisper. "It pulled me out of the tree."

Azrael lifted his waterskin to her mouth and let her drink carefully. Some trickled out the side, down her chin and smeared her blood. He didn't know how she had gotten so much all over, how much pain she was in.

"What do you mean?" He sat back on his heels, resting his elbows on his knees, and kept his eyes on her face, studying every flick of her nostrils and every flutter of eyelashes. He couldn't let her die. He wouldn't let her. Her eyes had started to get glossy, and unease settled in his stomach.

"In the street. It waved." A shaky breath slipped through her bloody lips. "I was grabbed, and pulled down."

"I think I killed one," Azrael murmured, partly to himself.

"How?" Asenneth's head tilted to the side, and Azrael lunged to catch her before she toppled over. She smiled sleepily, though it resembled more of a grimace.

"I don't know," he said after a moment. Staring down at his hands, blood stained and shaky fingers, he wanted an answer. He wanted so many answers, but a feeling deep within his chest told him he wouldn't be given one.

Azrael moved to his feet. A fire, he should build a fire. And hope it didn't attract the demons. He sighed, dutifully gathered wood, and settled back beside the archer and set to lighting. Beside her, his eyes constantly darting to her rising and falling chest, he waited.

†

The second moon was on the opposite side of the sky when he heard the faint rumbling of horse hooves against the earth. Azrael jolted up, drawing his sword, and spared a glance to the dying woman. She was unnaturally pale now, but her eyes were open. He hadn't expected her to hang on as long as she had, but he had hoped. As dangerous as the thought was.

Ahmi bounded through the trees, his solemn face illuminated in silver. Petite arms wrapped around his waist, and Azrael recognized the slender hands that dug into Ahmi's ribs. Lark. The healer.

Azrael caught the look in Ahmi's eyes, and he nodded, side stepping to answer the unspoken question. Azrael sheathed his sword as Ahmi swung off his horse and offered a hand to help the healer down. Lark's eyes met his for a split second before moving to Asenneth. If she truly had magic, maybe the archer had a chance to survive. Azrael kicked a log in the fire and watched the sparks fly as Lark knelt in the reddened earth.

With crossed arms, Ahmi moved beside Azrael and breathed a shaky sigh. "I was lucky to find her on the road. I couldn't think about what I'd come back to, if I had to find her in the palace."

Lark's gaze snapped to the men, her grey eyes sharp and alert. "I need a knife."

Ahmi unstrapped a dagger from his thigh and passed it to her. She began to pry bloody and crisp pieces of her shirt away. Her hands were fast, sure, and steady as she gently took away ragged strips of Asenneth's shirt.

"I was pregnant," Asenneth told the healer, her voice hardly more than breath. In the silence of the night, Azrael heard it, and watched as the words settled in the healer. Her hands trembled, and she glanced down at the blood beneath them. Azrael didn't have to look to Ahmi to know tears had fallen down his face. Azrael stared towards the trees.

"I'm sorry," Lark whispered, the trembling in her hands gone as if it were never there. She gingerly touched the branch. "I'm going to need your help guys. I have to cut it and remove it. I'll need water."

"Here?" Azrael asked as Ahmi handed her his waterskin.

"Here," she snapped, "Make yourself useful."

Azrael blinked, surprised that her response had caught him off guard. He grumbled as he stoked the fire with his boot again. He snagged a small, somewhat thick stick before it burned in the fire and shuffled to Asenneth's side. He offered a small, pathetic but consoling smile and she opened her mouth to accept the stick. Tears raced down her face once more, and he wiped them with his thumbs.

The branch was already significantly smaller in the moment he was being useful, the dagger discarded into the bloody grass beside them. He intertwined his fingers with Asenneth's, and her grip tightened as much as her remaining strength would allow. He squeezed her hand.

Injuries he was used to—missing limbs, bones sticking through skin, beheadings, he'd seen everything. It didn't get easier. A memory that refused to stay buried flashed in his head, of Taya's translucent body, but he swatted it away. Ahmi took the archer's other hand with a neutral face.

"Asen, are you ready? I'm so sorry." Lark took a deep breath and, without waiting for a reply, pulled the branch through.

A deafening, heart rending scream echoed through the trees. This was grief, loss, agony, and pain boiling into one unrelenting screech.

Lark immediately replaced the branch with her hands, pushing down, and fumbled for the cloth on her lap. Azrael kept his eyes on her nimble fingers as she shoved the cloth beneath her hands.

"Azrael, catch her head," she snapped at him as Asenneth's eyes rolled back and her head began to slip to the side. He caught it before it slammed into the tree trunk. "I need to bind it, help me lay her down. Watch her, she might vomit."

Azrael carefully lowered her head to the ground as Lark made quick work of cleaning and dressing the front. He and Ahmi turned her ever so gently and Lark worked on the gaping hole in her back, then lifted her so Lark could wrap the cloth around her waist. Ahmi sat down behind her, so that she rested against his body instead of the tree. Azrael stood and took a step back, suddenly feeling out of place as Lark wiped Asenneth's face tenderly and Ahmi hummed a song, a song Azrael recognized as a song for mourning.

B y the time the sun was above them, Asenneth was awake. Eating small bites of berries Lark had scavenged and taking small sips of water, it was as though she hadn't been on the brink of death only hours ago. Azrael dozed, on and off, against the tree opposite of the healing archer, and kept jerking awake to soothe the worry that she had stopped breathing. The fact that the woman meant nothing to him, yet he was still so worried about her survival puzzled him, but he couldn't stop himself from caring.

The three of them—Ahmi, Azrael, and Lark—rotated short watches, naps, and tending to Asenneth. The summer afternoon was heavy with heat and salt drifting in on the ocean breeze, and he struggled to stay awake. Through heavy eyes, he watched Lark stroke Asenneth's hair, plaiting her blonde strands again. He tried not to blatantly stare at the healer, but the sadness in her face softened her features in a way that disappeared when she caught him staring. She had caught him only once since the sun rose, when he was able to see her clearly, and her grey eyes were unsettling, as though smoke had been trapped beneath ice.

Asenneth stirred, her eyes fighting to open, and reached her hand to the healer's once she was fully awake. A tiny smile curled her lips when Lark squeezed her hand.

"We should leave soon," Lark said after she gently untangled herself from Asenneth. She stretched, her bones cracking from sitting for so long.

Azrael stood as well, not hiding his confused stare at Lark. Moving someone who had been impaled seemed counterproductive.

"Thank the Greater," Ahmi said as he strolled into view. "I'm going out of my mind in the quiet. There's still nobody in town. Either everyone sailed out, or..."

"How is she in any condition to ride?" Azrael interrupted, earning a glare from Lark. He wondered how much her magic would be able to heal, how thorough it was.

"She'll be stable enough to ride home, but she needs to be home, where I can properly care for her." Her glare softened, but annoyance reflected in her eyes. "If Westwick had healers or an adequate infirmary, it'd be a different story."

"I'll ready the horses," Ahmi cut in, breaking their stare.

The ride seemed longer, maybe because their pace was slowed for Asenneth who rested against her mare's neck while Lark sat behind her. Or perhaps because Azrael kept glancing over his shoulder at the woman who should be dead and the woman who could hold fire in her hands and heal deadly wounds.

His head was spinning as they rode. A feeling of familiarity had been echoing in his chest since he had seen the demons. What kind of hell was it that he had seen these things twice now? The shadows casted by the memory of his childhood lengthened. The fear the beings from the night his village had burned manifested in his heart beating faster and glancing twice at the passing shadows. Azrael had thought that the habit of glancing behind him had passed, and he didn't know what it meant that he saw the beings again.

Azrael wondered what Raphael would say, what anecdote he would pull from to make this a miracle, proof of the Greater. He looked to Nevan's horse, dutifully riding beside Ahmi's, with his owner's body covered and tied to the horse.

When the group finally reached Vale City, night had already crawled in, and the first moon hung low above them. It seemed it hadn't climbed the sky at all, only passing over them. The makeshift city outside the gate bubbled with activity, loud music, swearing, and jeering. None of the revelers paid them attention as they passed through. A birdcall had the guards opening the gate just enough to let them pass before slamming shut.

Vale City was quiet in the west side and market district. Faint shouting and music floated from the east, but the proximity to the waterfall easily drowned the noise out. Azrael kept his eyes on the palace, glowing in the moonlight, and for once forgot about the two women riding behind him. With the palace so close, a plan formed with the confusion and unexplainable anger churning in his chest. He would get answers from his king tonight.

Ahmi rode beside him, while Lark turned towards the infirmary, but Azrael left him at the stables. Shouldering his way through the stable door, he stopped the first servant he saw and demanded directions to the king's room. He followed the girl's stammered instructions to the fourth floor, and found himself going in circles in endless halls of mirrors. Eventually, he made the right turn and found a guard standing idly by a set of doors. The guard wore the red band around his wrist, but Azrael couldn't recall his name, or if he'd met the man before.

"Open the door," he growled, his emotions tight in his throat. "It's about Westwick."

A call from inside the room made the guard audibly grind his teeth, but he pushed the door open for Azrael.

The king's sitting room was exactly as expected; black walls were adorned with gold filigree on the baseboards. Swords hung on the walls, in between paintings twice the size of Azrael. A rug red as blood sat beneath the king's desk in the center of the room, piled with papers and books. Doors to a balcony were wide open on the right side of the room, and behind the king at his desk, curtains blowing lazily in the warm summer breeze.

"My king," Azrael said as he dropped to his knee. His pride and anger fizzled out as he stared at his reflection in the marble tile. Heat flooded his cheeks, but he controlled his breath and ignored it.

"Son. Stand." King Melech leaned back in his chair, elbows on the arm rests and his hand propping up his chin. Even alone in his room, Azrael couldn't ignore the power he held. "I heard what happened. I'm deeply grieved over

Nevan. Asenneth, though, will be okay, though her emotional wounds will take some time to heal."

Azrael shifted on his feet and glanced to the painting on the wall behind the king, but the king didn't follow his eyes. Melech knew why he was here.

"What are they?" The artist painted them so realistically, Azrael could almost see the smoke billowing from the being. Blood covered its broken teeth and skeletal hands, a mirror image of those he had seen.

"*Daeoan*," Melech said.

Demons. The beings from Areenian folklore, restless spirits who were a bedtime story for children to keep them obedient, and a campfire story for adults who feared what awaited them after death.

"They've come from *Laeseen*, their spirit world. Removed from their posts as...shepherds, so to speak. Are you familiar with Areen's lore?" Melech stood and walked around his desk to stand in front of Azrael, hands clasped behind his back.

The life, or really the *un*life, after death. Where the soul doesn't quite return, but remains as energy—no feeling, no consciousness. Azrael didn't know what he believed in, but he didn't understand how a people could be so happy if they faced that after death. He didn't understand what the king meant as shepherds, but he stayed silent.

"Again, it's lore," Melech said with a condescending wave of his hand, rings glinting in the firelight from the opposite end of the room. "Telaanans would say it's something else. Ask a commoner and who knows what bullshit they'd spout. The point is, it is no coincidence that they appeared during Nekoda's reign. Do you know what happened during his last years?"

"His health steadily declined after Queen Isolde's death. He was sick." Azrael didn't understand. After the young prince's death, then the queen's, the king's health snapped like a twig and sickness took him—burrowing deep within him until his sudden death.

"I thought you were smarter than that." Melech's black gaze blazed with the fire's heat. "Nekoda was starving for power—more power, because a kingdom wasn't enough. He made a bargain with the Greater. He wanted magic, but there's a magic with balance, a give and take, and Nekoda asked for more than what he could give."

Azrael thought of the healer, the freckle on her index finger and how her fingers trembled when she touched Asenneth, and how those hands had healed mortal wounds. If Nekoda had been successful, magic wouldn't be contained to one woman—so how did she have it?

"He got more than he bargained for," Melech said, gesturing to the painting vaguely.

"He brought the *Daeoan*."

A slow nod.

"They destroyed Westwick?"

Another nod as Melech rounded his desk.

"Why?" Azrael's head swam, thoughts and loose ends that didn't make sense and the sound of screaming and the smell of blood and pine.

"I believe they're looking for something, or someone." Melech said, placing his palms on his desk and staring at the paperwork in front of him. "I don't know what, or who. They appear and decimate whatever they find."

"The town is empty." Azrael's chest hollowed. The townsfolk had to have escaped, he wouldn't accept it otherwise. He helped to save one life, but what of the hundreds that were missing?

"I heard. I'm working on it."

"I think I killed one," Azrael murmured, trying not to shudder from the cold pouring from the painting, as though one was in the room with them.

Melech's eyes snapped up, something between surprise and alarm flashing in his face, but as Azrael met his stare, the emotion had disappeared.

"Nekoda had many secrets in his reign, and I was privy to many, but not all. If only I had the answers you're still searching for. The Greater has chosen you, Azrael. Chosen you for something, proving it by healing you, and this isn't something I, nor you, should take lightly. Your destiny is just beginning to unfold."

Silence fell between the two men as the summer breeze ruffled the curtains. Azrael bowed slightly, throat heavy with all things unsaid, and turned to leave.

"Be careful, Azrael." Melech's voice cut through the night before Azrael opened the door.

It felt less like a warning, and more like a threat, and Azrael made his way through the maze of mirrors once more.

# CHAPTER 10

## LARK

"Have you *truly* looked at the new swordsman?" Hadriana trilled from her perch in the doorway, hands stilling from her needlework. Lark ignored the bait in her voice and continued packing her small bag. "He's a bit small for my taste, but I'm sure once we see him training that'll change."

"I'm telling Hollis," Lark chided as she stuffed the last bit of linen into the bag. She tried not to look at the swordsman as much as she could. A living embodiment of rubbing salt in the wound. All the things that Iah could do, and he binds bones together for a lowly soldier who scouted rebel camps. A soldier who couldn't hide his stare and the distrust in his eyes when he looked at her, as if her own magic repulsed him.

Hadriana scoffed, "I'm sure Hollis is thinking the same thing. Maybe they'll become friends and we'll get to see more of him."

Lark lifted her bag over her head, settling the strap across her chest, and needlessly gripped it with both hands. She softly smiled at her friend, one of her first when Lark joined the Tiras six years ago. Hadri was only four years her senior, but acted as though she were four years younger. Seeing Hadri and Hollis together reminded Lark of the lovesick teenagers she used to read about. Reminded her of the naïve seventeen-year-old she had been when she had returned to the palace. She loved her friends dearly, but jealous coiled in her stomach when she would see them in that way. Melech would never allow her to have something like that, nor could she ever have that with him. Lark side stepped Hadri, swatting at the poof of hair she always kept knotted at the very top of her head, and received a pinch in the side in return.

"Don't start that again, you know how it is." Lark laughed, but it sounded hollow even to her.

"I'm just saying." Hadri shrugged, the gold hoops in her ears sparking in the afternoon sun. Hadri was made for sunsets, always glowing. Her face fell as she met Lark's gaze. "Tell me how our girl is doing, okay? And good luck with dinner."

"I will." Lark's smile turned sad, remembering with a sudden sinking feeling that tonight was one of their dinner nights and, with a sigh, "Thanks."

Twice a week, for the last six years, Lark joined the king for dinner, and they were her least favorite nights. Alone in his room, except for the guard who stood at the door inside and one outside. Her presence required the one within the room, and she had never asked if it was for his sake or hers.

Lark pushed away the thoughts and focused solely on the remainder of the day ahead of her: healing a stomach wound that should have killed Asenneth and healing a heart after losing a child. It would be a long few hours.

†

Asenneth sat beside the fireplace, blazing despite the warmth of the afternoon, with her blonde hair knotted in the remnants of a braid, wearing only in an oversized shirt with the sleeves rolled unevenly to bare her freckled arms. Lark knew that Kai, one of her fellow Tiras archers and Asen's husband, was out, working through his own trauma, but Lark's heart turned heavy knowing he wasn't here with her.

Lark set her bag down on the small kitchen table, cluttered with plates and half-finished meals. Asen didn't turn her head, nor give any indication that she knew Lark was there, only tightening her hold on the small, stuffed fox in her lap.

Lark set to clearing the table and heating a kettle for tea, sending her shadows skittering across the floor to push open the window by the front door as she worked. The breeze lazily wafted in, carrying the gentle scent of flowers from the courtyard and pulling away the heat pulsing endlessly from the fire. She didn't have to heat the kettle—the spool of light coiled in her chest capable of completing the task—but she went through the mundane motions for the sake of Asen, letting her come to terms with Lark being there, and preparing herself to talk, if she wished.

Asen said nothing as Lark loosened her braid and worked through the knots in her hair. She unraveled the ivory knot in her chest, letting the healing threads work through her fingers and seep into Asen's hair and burrow within her, evoking a broken sigh from her. Lark kept running her fingers through her hair and let her magic unspool until Asen's shoulders bowed.

Wood creaked, curtains ruffled, stones skittered outside under footsteps, all the while time seemed to slow in the house. The fire slowly died, neither woman speaking still.

Lark rose, gently lifted Asen's shirt up, and gently cleaned her wraps, trying not to jostle her too much. She had healed the deepest wounds when they had found her, stopping the internal bleeding. She tried to reverse the damage, but too much had occurred for it to heal naturally and without trouble. Some wounds were more difficult to heal, and the ones that disrupted organs and cheated death were the trickiest. Once Lark had brought Asen to the infirmary last night, she had stayed with her all night, and cried. She had left her unconscious friend with the city healers and gave explicit instructions on how to move Asenneth to her own house once she woke up, so that Lark could continue her care privately. She knew she could only do so much, but it didn't feel like enough. It still didn't, taking the small amounts of pain that tormented her friend. She took only the physical pain—the sorrow that clouded her heart, Lark couldn't touch that. If, one day, Asen wanted her to, then yes, she would.

She wouldn't be able to forget the amount of blood that had stained the ground beneath her, and the earth-rending scream that had tore through Asen when the branch had come out. Lark hadn't known, and somehow it felt like her fault, that she should have. She would have told Melech to piss off and send another archer.

Lark sighed and wrapped her arms around Asen, and their heads rested against one another. And stayed that way for hours, neither saying a word.

┼

L ark didn't bother changing from her usual Tiras attire, pants and blouse, before heading to the palace. She tried not thinking about what Melech would say, knowing that he liked seeing her like this—in *his* uniform.

She took the back way to his rooms, ducking into one of the closed off corridors, then slipped into the passageway behind it. As a child, she had explored the hundreds of hidden tunnels that lined the palace when her father hadn't needed her. Before he died, before she had left the palace to live with her mother, away from her rightful place. A lifetime ago.

When pushed open the doors to his sitting room, Melech was pacing. His black shirt was unbuttoned but tucked into his pants, his feet were bare, and the sides of his head were still tightly braided while the rest of his hair twisted in waves to his shoulders. His face bore the shadow of not shaving for days, since she had last been here. Under different circumstances, she might have felt differently towards him. Her father's captain who had meant more than the world to him, the captain who received the title of heir. Lark received magic while Melech received her kingdom. In another life, it could have been *theirs*.

"Where have you been?" His voice was rough, a soft growl laced in his words. Melech stopped pacing and turned to face her. His chest struggled to take even breaths, but Lark kept her eyes on his face and pretended not to notice. Melech twitched, as though he wanted to walk closer to her but thought better of it.

"Taking care of Asenneth," Lark said flatly as she walked to the massive desk in the center of the room. It was cluttered with papers and maps, all of it useless and serving only as a decoy if someone were to break in. Lark set her bag down and sat in his chair while she unlaced her boots and let them clatter on the marble floor, purposely missing the expansive rug.

At the mention of his heartbroken archer, the tension slipped, and he sighed. "So, you can understand my worry."

"You have no cause to." A twinge in her temple promised a headache. She reined in her sigh.

"I have all the cause to." His words were tight, clipped. He leaned against the opposite side of the desk, his eyes boring into her. She ground her teeth and avoided that black stare.

"I can handle more than you think."

"You handle more than you have to." His voice turned quiet. Not the voice of a king, but the one of a man who burned for what he couldn't have.

"I can't handle that tonight." Lark couldn't hold the sigh in this time and leaned back in the chair. She rubbed her head beneath her braids, wound too tightly in a faux crown, and regretted letting Hadri do them so tight this morning.

His footsteps were always quiet, but Lark felt him before she heard him. Melech moved to stand behind her, his fingers delicate as he pulled out pin after pin, setting them on the desk. He unraveled each braid carefully. The gentle intimacy of it made her want to run out of the room, but she stayed still and let him continue. She was long past the days of fighting, of arguing; over the vastness that laid between them. Early in their arrangement, she had thought maybe she could grow to care for him, but after all these years later, there was still nothing. Nothing but dinner twice a week and late nights and feeling the moonlight burn her skin when she walked home.

His spidery fingers traced down her neck as he uncoiled her wavy hair. His breathing had turned near silent, as though waiting for her to snap, but he savored each caress.

She could sense him about to say something with the way his fingers lingered on the back of her neck. She untangled herself and stood, away, and said, "Have you eaten yet?"

"No, Freckles, I haven't." Melech sighed and moved away.

Heat flushed Lark's neck. She could never tell how he meant her childhood nickname, but it brought back memories of her sun kissed skin and how the summer heat made each freckle prominent.

And the summer Melech had found out that the healer's name that circulated through the city belonged to the forgotten princess he had helped to bury.

"Come."

Lark let him take her hand and lead her into the dining room. His suite used to overwhelm her, but after years of darkness, the black walls and dark marble floors became a comfort. Melech's rooms were only used by the two of them, and the dining room was accessed only by a handful of kitchen staff. The isolation was even more damning when she would catch Brannon's eyes when he stood within the sitting room. Lark thanked Iah for the small happiness of not having the guard in the room.

The long table, large enough to fit ten people on either side, was empty save for two places: one at the head and on the right-hand side. Massive centerpieces of black and red roses, darkened ferns, and candles in intricate varying shapes that dripped wax took up the rest of the table. Their plates were already set, wine glasses filled to the rim. There was hardly any room for pretense, for regular dinner etiquette, when it was only the two of them. Lark sat down hard in her chair and watched as he circled his, the vulture he was.

"How is she?" He kept his voice low, as though the walls couldn't bear to hear the empathy in his voice.

"We did nothing but sit in front of the fire today." Lark picked at her roasted carrots with her fork. Her throat tightened and she gritted her teeth, her frustration gnawing at her.

"How is her wound healing?"

Her fork clattered on the plate. If Melech was surprised, his face showed no signs of it. Lark leaned back in her chair and finally turned her head to look at him. With his elbows on the table, he had a forkful of mood halfway to his mouth when understanding sparkled in his eyes and he lowered his hand. Lark hardly ever dared to push him, but she couldn't stop herself.

"Which one?"

Melech sighed, ignoring her snap, and lifted his glass of wine.

"Siena, it's not my fault."

His use of her royal name made her blood boil. The name she had been given to rule her kingdom with, stripped as quickly as the bat of an eye. She followed his example and drank her wine, hoping it would quickly go to her head and put out the fire raging in her.

"But it is, Melech, and you know that. Don't pretend to care. You sent her knowing fully well of the dangers she could face, and what she could stand to lose."

Melech didn't respond. He continued to eat, and Lark rubbed her temple. Fine. She stabbed a piece of salmon.

"What do you know of our new swordsman?" he asked after some time. He picked at the grapes in the bowl beside him, and Lark focused on his nimble hands instead of his eyes.

"No more than you. What are you asking?" She took another drink of wine before impaling another carrot. She knew fully well what he was asking, remembering the conversation they had before they had set off to take Azrael from the infirmary.

"I want to know *why*. Why the boy was healed, and what purpose he serves."

"He's hardly a boy." Lark snorted.

"And you're hardly a princess," Melech shot back, his black eyes boring into her. His face changed in an instant, lips parting and eyes softening. Regret darkened his face and he reached his hand to her. "I'm sorry, love, I'm—"

"And whose fault is that, *love*?"

Lark wouldn't back down. Her day had been long and hard, and she wouldn't give into his taunts and torment tonight. Her tongue was sharp, and her heart was guarded. Melech looked at her, a thousand thoughts swirling in his head that reflected in his eyes, and propped his chin with the hand he had extended to her.

"If you would just say yes, you could be so much more than that."

"My crown is not conditional. I am a princess, with or without you."

"You were forgotten by your own father, your own people." His voice drifted to frustration, to spite, to anger. Lark knew exactly where this conversation had turned, and she raised her eyes to his.

"At whose suggestion was I sent away? For a captain, you were a damn good advisor too. I've learned from the best—how to see the bigger picture, how to get what I want."

"And what is it that you want?" Melech purred as he tilted his head back. He took a deep breath as his gaze fell to her mouth. Just like that, the anger in him had evaporated. "Dear Siena, do you know what I want?"

Lark reined her anger in and listened to the quiet hum of a warning Iah whispered in the back of her head. She shifted in her seat and continued eating, the sound of silverware clinking against the plate ringing in her ears.

The remainder of their dinner was silent, the tension taut and tangible. Wind howled through the night, ghosts of the mountainside restless. Low crackling of the fireplace kept Lark company in his room until the even sounds of his breath signaled he was asleep and time to crawl into her own bed.

Lark walked slowly back to the healer's house with the second moon high above her. The echoes of the wind followed her, even long after she slammed the door and curled up beneath her covers.

# CHAPTER 11

## AZRAEL

Azrael stood in the kitchen with a cup of watery coffee in his hands when a knock rapped on the door. He hadn't been able to sleep once he returned from seeing the king. He'd managed to take a cold bath and scrub the night off his skin, but he couldn't shake the feeling of being watched—no matter how many candles he lit or how often he peeked through the curtains covering the window and resolved to see nothing was hiding in the shadows nor in the courtyard outside. His thoughts drifted in circles, but most of the night his head was empty. Devoid of anything productive, except perhaps making the coffee that brought him to his senses.

Setting his cup on the table louder than he intended, Azrael opened the door to a dim light and the girl who had showed him his house—Magdalene, he surprised himself by remembering—stood at the threshold with a bright face and a warm smile. Such a contrast to how he felt. Her smile didn't dim in the moments it took for him to acknowledge her.

"Morning," he finally said.

"Good morning." Magdalene tilted her head, twin braids shifting with the movement. "What would you say to a tour of the palace? I'm sure it's a bit different from the last time you were here."

His first thought was no, but he didn't say it. Instead, he took a breath and decided that he could use a distraction from his thoughts. After another moment, he nodded and said, "Alright."

"Great." Magdalene leaned on her toes and her smile somehow grew.

Azrael stepped aside, motioning for her to step in, before he retrieved his boots from beside the fireplace. He'd been dressed for hours now, had his sword out and lying on the table, utterly prepared for whatever his morning would bring. He hadn't expected her at his door, though.

He laced his boots knowing her eyes kept tracing back to him, and he couldn't help but wonder why. He felt like a shadow compared to his former self, a ghost residing in an empty home. With his time bed-ridden, he had lost the muscle he regularly worked to maintain, and in that, he had grown too skinny. He desperately needed a haircut, his loose curls brushing his shoulders and he hated that too. Once he was settled in his new routine, he made a mental note to find a barber.

Azrael stood, capturing Magdalene's obvious attention now, and secured his sword at his waist. He mustered a small smile for her.

"Ready?"

"As I'll ever be." He grabbed the key from the table and locked the door behind them.

Magdalene offered her arm to him as they began to walk towards the front of the palace. Azrael ignored his hesitation and took it. She was so *warm*. Not only her body heat, but her presence.

"What is it that you do here?" he asked her. He'd never been good at small talk, but he could at least ask questions—have her do all the talking, which she was more than inclined to do.

"I'm a seamstress. My mother used to work for the queen, before she passed—may the earth lay lightly on her—and I've been sewing since I could hold a needle. I mainly do work for the Tiras and the few nobles that the king entertains."

As she spoke, they came to the main courtyard where shouting and rattling exploded. A mass of dark grey uniform stood in front of the palace gates, the ones in the back standing stoically, while the ones in the fray matched the chaos, their voices equally loud as the shouting on the opposite side of the gate.

Magdalene stopped, but Azrael untangled their arms and walked towards the commotion.

"They killed him!"

"Who's to say it won't happen here?"

"It was the Telaanan's fault!"

"The Areenian's!"

"They killed my boy!"

Azrael couldn't understand what the guards were yelling back, until he realized one kept repeating "get back" in all three languages.

"What are you here for if not to protect us?"

Azrael stopped mid-step and glanced over the crowd to find the voice who had said it. Finding a pair of blue eyes already staring at him, the woman repeated the question. One of the guards tried giving her an answer, but she repeated herself again, talking over him, her voice growing louder with each word spoken.

He thought of the empty town, usually so chaotic and crowded. Completely empty. How many lives had disappeared? Would he ever know?

"It's a Tiras!"

"Hey!"

A piercing whistle broke through the noise. Silence fell before another voice behind Azrael spoke.

"It is an attack the king is looking into and will update his valued citizens on once he uncovers the truth of what has happened. Every Havrien is regarded with respect and afforded the king's protection. This problem will be resolved. Until then, disperse. Leave the king's men to find the culprit for the attack." Brannon, the captain, stood in his uniform, complete with a cape floating in the breeze, and looked to be the picture of authority. His face remained neutral through the slew of raised voices again, but he simply repeated himself.

Once the guards began to move away from the gates, and the civilians on the opposite side began to slink away, Brannon turned and disappeared up the palace steps without so much as a glance to Azrael.

"Let's go," Magdalene said as she gripped his forearm. Instinct had him ripping his arm from her and stepping to the side, but she didn't flinch, only blinked. Azrael nodded and slid his hands into his pockets. He kept a small distance between them as they slowly followed Brannon's lead up the stairs.

"Where did you grow up?" Magdalene said as they strolled towards the main hall. Azrael noted how unbothered the guards were by the din outside and wondered how often things like that happened, for it to be smoothed over and ended so quickly.

"The Moor," he replied absently before roping in his attention and turning it back to the girl beside him. "I was sent here when I was eight though."

"Oh, did you have family here?"

"No, I took up space in an orphanage before I joined the army." His own history seemed distorted, moving from point to point, and not really belonging anywhere until he received clearance from a recruiter to enlist him in the army. At age eleven. He could hardly remember his childhood before moving to the Vale, save for the night his village had been attacked. It was as though his life started on that day.

"I'm sorry to hear that. It must have been hard not having anyone for so long." Magdalene drifted closer to Azrael and her hand accidentally brushed against the back of his. She moved it away and toyed with the end of her golden plait.

Azrael wanted to object, that it hadn't been hard. Not really. At first, it felt like drowning; where one's toes are just above the sea floor, but there's no rest to be found. He had worn armor that had been too big, used swords and bows much too heavy for him. He learned, in every lesson he was taught, to not let it get to him and to use his size to the advantage until he grew. Melech's transition to the crown had been difficult for the kingdom and, in turn, Azrael was sent to the field at thirteen. Being declared an heir with no true right for the crown instilled an envy and anger in people that could not be quelled without violence, blood for blood. Azrael fought foreigners on his own shores, fought his neighbors from the Roe, fought lords of estates who deemed wealth was as good as any right to the throne. His first love, Taya, had died in one of those lord's towns after they had been sent to extinguish the rebel flame.

Magdalene didn't press him for an answer as they walked into the main hall, greeted by pillars supporting a circular glass dome displaying the beauty of the twilight. With day receding to the west while night seeps in from the east, the art was on different panes of glass and refracted the sunlight differently. The room was quiet, even as staff walked past them, and Azrael took in the empty throne atop the dais with two tapestries of howling wolves on either side.

"Queen Brae commissioned the art for the glass," Magdalene said as Azrael glanced at it again. "She did most of the art on the walls herself. Neither king had them removed over the years."

Azrael knew this, from a dark and dusty corner of his mind. He had learned in school what Nekoda's first wife had been like, owning a dedicated love and talent for art and all things beautiful. He noted then the halls on either side of the room had paintings lining each wall. Magdalene veered them to the one on the left and he caught a closer look. The royal family, both queens, the deceased child prince, a few of Melech, and the Vale's landscape created a timeline and a messy history. Azrael wondered how many Brae had painted herself before she had died. It was strange to think how some things outlasted oneself, even after when one was no longer part of this world.

The hall ended in an open courtyard lush with grass and greenery and adorned with statues of varying subjects: animals, children, naked women with wings. They walked past it all and turned down another hall, back into the enclosed palace.

"How many floors are there?" Azrael asked her. He knew there were at least four, after going to Melech's room after the demon attack, but he realized how little he remembered of his new home.

"Six, but I hear the king wants to add in a seventh within in the mountainside." Magdalene grinned at him, her emerald eyes shining in the sunlight. Azrael couldn't help but smile back, despite himself. He couldn't place it, but something about her put him at ease.

They continued their tour throughout the day. Magdalene led him around happily, quietly chattering even if he didn't reply. She showed him the easiest way to get to the armory, which he felt foolish not to have realized, and the training grounds that the Tiras used, separate from the barracks. She also showed him an art gallery, a sunroom, an empty infirmary, and a small marketplace in a courtyard further within the palace. It was truly a small city within a large one. Azrael tried recalling the tour he had taken when he was a child, but this was completely different.

The day turned into twilight and Magdalene led him back home. She stopped at the top of the steps and grinned, blush warming her cheeks, before she leaned onto her toes and kissed his cheek. It caught him off guard, his body stilling under the touch of her lips.

"Thank you for today, Azrael." Magdalene giggled quietly before she walked back into the palace.

Still unsure of what had happened, he walked stiffly to his door and fished his key from his pocket when Ahmi caught him. He had stepped out of his house with his hands in his pockets, wearing a loose white shirt, and bare feet.

"Would you like to have dinner with us?"

&dagger;

I sabel was five and insisted on sitting right beside Azrael, her chair touching his and his elbow accidentally jabbing her when he cut his steak. He hadn't hesitated in accepting Ahmi's offer, hadn't even thought about declining, and he was glad for it.

"Darling," Thea, Ahmi's wife, warned as Isabel edged closer to Azrael. "Steal another carrot from his plate and I'll give *him* dessert first."

Azrael looked at the child, surprised to see his own pile of carrots sitting on the scratched table beside their plates. She grinned impishly at him and grabbed a handful before shoving it in her mouth.

"So, Azrael." Thea turned her attention to him; the scolding look in her eyes not quite disappearing. "How have you been settling in?"

"I've yet to see you training in the morning," Ahmi added with a wink.

"Oh hush." Thea swatted at her husband. She was truly kind, Azrael saw it in her face. She was short, curvy, pale as the moon, with russet hair that fell down her back. Her smile was crooked with a small gap between her teeth, and there was not a single flaw about her. "Anyway."

"It's different," Azrael offered. "I feel like I'm living in a dream, and nothing is quite real."

"Ahmi said that you had been injured very badly before they found you, is that correct?"

He noted the soft kick under the table, and pretended not to see Thea's side eye glance.

"That's correct, I was told I wouldn't walk again."

Thea smiled. "I'm glad you're here with us, even if it feels like a dream."

"How did you two meet?" Azrael asked, glancing between them. Their house was full of mementos of their relationship and life together, but he couldn't pinpoint a timeline. They were everything Azrael had missed out on, and what he would continue to miss. He admired the loving glance between Ahmi and Thea.

"I came here when I was sixteen, determined to make something of myself, when I went to the city gardens and saw her underneath the birch trees, drawing a swan with the talent of a toddler holding a pen." Ahmi leaned back in his rickety chair and put his hands behind his head.

Shadows had begun to fall around the room, darkening the mess Isabel had created in the kitchen that she had proudly shown Azrael, and the light from the melting candles on the table warmed Ahmi's face as he spoke.

"I was chicken shit about talking to her, but I saw her there every day, somehow lucky enough to find her again and again. Once I complimented her drawing, we didn't stop talking. I couldn't go a day without hearing her laugh. I couldn't think about anything but her."

"You were so foolish, you never had to *try* to make me laugh." Thea's hand drifted to the side of his face, cupping his cheek in a moment of intimacy Azrael had to glance away from.

"Who's better at fighting?" Isabel squeaked as she stole another bite of vegetables from Azrael's plate. He smiled at her and flicked a pea at her.

"Him."

"Me."

They spoke at the same time. Azrael laughed, from deep within his chest. Ahmi echoed it, shaking his head, while Thea raised her eyebrows.

"Don't worry, you'll catch up to our Tiras training soon," Ahmi said.

"Papa's sword glides through the air so fast, I think he's the best."

"Me too," Azrael agreed, if only to watch Isabel's face light up with pride. Her blue eyes glowed as she looked up at him. She was the perfect mix of her parents, her brown skin and russet hair and eyes full of wonder.

"Can we go for a walk?" Isabel asked between the remaining mouthfuls of vegetables. Azrael's plate was clean with small fingerprints leaving their traces. "And can he come too?"

Azrael helped clear the table, bringing the dishes to the small kitchen and piling them carefully on the counter. It hadn't occurred to him that he had a kitchen now too, and there wasn't anything from stopping him from having dinners like this too. Except company, though he realized that, maybe, that wasn't the case anymore.

Isabel asked quietly and kindly if she could sit on his shoulders, and he retorted that she had wanted to go for a *walk* before letting her climb up his back once they were outside. Night settled in as stars began to shimmer in the deep blue above. Azrael had expected the child to be heavier, given her height she inherited from her father, but she was light as a feather on his shoulders as they strolled slowly along the stone pathway.

Isabel squealed above him and he had to quickly catch her as she scrambled down from him without a worry for her safety. He eased her to the ground before she bounded off into the darkness. He heard a silvery laugh before he finally saw her. Lark emerged from the shadows as though she were a part of them, Isabel sitting on her hip and chattering in her ear. She walked towards the others, oblivious to Azrael standing beside Ahmi.

"Hi, Thea, Ahmi." Her voice was softer than the last time Azrael had seen her. Then she noticed the third figure, and her voice was reserved as she spoke to him. "Azrael."

"Well met," he replied. He observed as Lark turned to Thea and they walked together, quietly talking, light and easy. A knot began to build in Azrael's chest that he couldn't name.

Lark glanced over her shoulder, meeting his eyes, and he didn't shrink from the silver stare. He fell back into step with Ahmi as they followed the women.

"They're very close," he offered to Azrael. "Lark helped deliver Isabel. Thea would be dead, if not for her. So would Asen. You'll get to know her past the whole mysterious outer—" He waved his hand in front of his face in emphasis. "Her whole thing. You'll see past it."

Azrael didn't admit it, but that was what he was afraid of.

# CHAPTER 12

## AZRAEL

A pink and grey dawn carried Azrael to the training field Magdalene had showed him that the Tiras used. He walked along the worn dirt path to a field that was divided into sections by a rope and markings. A house sat on the far-right end, surrounded by boulders covered in splatters and markings. Magdalene had said it was the healer's house; the two Tiras healers lived separate from the others in their own home beside the field.

Before Azrael could relish in his solitude, voices drifted from the path behind him and pierced the quiet of the daybreak.

"There's the legend himself."

"He came to grace us with his *grace*."

He turned to face a few Tiras he hadn't met yet, and quickly realized he had no interest in doing so. He lifted his chin slightly and rolled his shoulders. The sarcasm and disdain were thick in the men's voices and faces. A man with a scruffy beard and two heads taller than Azrael stopped a foot in front of him, crossing his thick arms.

A smaller man poked his head around the big one's muscles, his skin almost translucent in the grey light, and his blond hair made him look sickly, but the leanness of his body told Azrael that he had to be an archer.

"So, this is the one that got Nevan killed?" the sickly man asked.

"I didn't get him killed," Azrael said, swallowing the guilt that threatened to surge. It wasn't his fault. *It wasn't his fault.*

Azrael turned to leave, but a meaty hand locked around his wrist and rooted him to the spot.

"It's too bad Melech doesn't make us fight for our spots like Nekoda did. I'd heard your name before. Death follows you, boy, but not in the way it should. If you were put in that pit, I don't think you'd crawl out." The big man spit at Azrael's feet. "You're here because you're the king's pet. Do not think you are worth your title."

Azrael pulled his wrist free as the familiar Areenian strolled towards him, his vibrant green eyes burning as he took in the way the three of them were standing. Azrael reined in the anger that coaxed him to stay put. He overheard the Areenian threatening the two as he walked to the circle beside the boulders, eyeing the sacks of grain and wooden poles.

He had wrestled with his guilt for the ambush. He wouldn't be buried beneath guilt for something that was out of his control. Nevan's death had nothing to do with Azrael, even if he found it hard to believe that. Still, his chest felt heavy, but he worked to turn it to anger.

Yanking his shirt and sword off, he watched how the others began to trickle in and settle into their routines. Some were running, others standing in the expanding sunshine. Slipping into the daily lives. A life that Azrael had now. As he stretched, he still expected pain in his legs, even a little soreness, but it didn't cease to amaze him that there wasn't a sliver of either as he loosened his muscles.

Footsteps scuffled against dirt, drawing Azrael's attention, just before a fist collided into his ribs. His vision danced with surprise before he took in the scraggly face of his assailant. Surprise had him taking another blow to the stomach. Azrael swore.

Clenching his teeth against the pain humming in his core, he swung and caught the next blow with his forearm. The man's eyes widened with first wonder, then excitement. Azrael, despite his height, was still smaller than his attacker, and he used it to his advantage. Easily ducking the large fists, he slammed his punches to the spots left unguarded. Hit after hit, the large man couldn't dodge Azrael's blows, nor land one of his own.

With an uppercut, blood spurted from the man's mouth along with a slew of curses as he staggered backwards.

"Would you like to try with swords now?" Azrael nodded to his sword resting on his shirt a few feet away. He swallowed his pride as the man flinched before recovering and giving Azrael a glare that promised revenge.

Azrael waited until the man walked towards the healer's house with his small friend at his side before moving back to the poles and grain sacks. Drill after drill, he recalled the same things he had done year after year.

Refining the rush of the fight and the guilt still burdening him, Azrael used it to pinpoint his focus, bringing it far away from the eyes that watched him from across the training field.

&#8224;

**M**agdalene found him in the afternoon at the stables. Azrael had avoided speaking to everyone at the training field, even Ahmi, and gone home quietly once he had finished. He had coffee and eggs in the bath before figuring out what he could do with his day. There had been no summons from the king, no orders or things he had to do, so he wandered until he found himself tending to his horse and ignoring the stable boy's small talk.

"Walk with me?" Magdalene asked with her hands behind her back and her lip caught between her teeth.

Azrael nodded and fed his horse another handful of oats before wiping his hands on his pants and following her outside. She turned to the right and led him along the length of the stables, and followed the palace walls.

"Do you remember your parents?" Her voice was quiet, gentle, as she dove right into the conversation.

"Bits and pieces of them both, memories that feel like dreams." Dreams that more often were nightmares, but he wouldn't tell her that.

The day had proved to be bright, warm, with the air heavy. Fluffy, pristine clouds floated lazily above them, in between the trees that lined either side of the smooth wall.

"My mother is my best friend; I can't imagine a life without her. I'm sorry, Az." She touched the back of his hand and, this time, he didn't move it away. He wanted to correct her—he hardly let anyone call him a nickname—but he didn't have the nerve not to. Not when there was peace between them, a peace that he didn't mind so much now.

He wasn't used to someone trying so hard to win his affection, but he didn't put an end to it either. He knew that, despite his better judgement.

Silence fell again between them like a sheer curtain. A greenhouse loomed ahead of them, surrounded by a multitude of flowers and plants outside the building. Magdalene began telling him that the greenhouse had belonged to Queen Isolde—Nekoda's second wife—so she had a sanctuary from palace life. After she killed herself, the staff had refused to let this piece of her die too. A happy ghost, it seemed, sat before them, with a dozen different aromas filling the air. Gardeners worked in silence in the beds outside, tending to the stalks of flowers and bushes of herbs. Azrael saw her at once, though, even as he pretended not to.

Lark flitted like a hummingbird between the herbs, snipping leaves and dropping them into the satchel swinging at her waist. Wearing an oversized white shirt tucked into pants and muddy knee-high boots, the sight of her recalled the remainder of Azrael's night with Ahmi and his family—how they had all walked together and he hadn't spoken a word to her beyond their awkward greeting. He still didn't know how to speak to her, if he wanted to, but the glare he caught her throwing him a couple of times silenced him anyway.

He couldn't understand her feelings of annoyance towards him, but he understood the other Tiras' lack of friendliness. Though it was frustrating, after that scuffle with the boulder of a man, the ones that he hadn't learned the names of yet kept their distance. The few that didn't despise him—Meir, Kal, Kai, Hollis, and of course Ahmi—had included him in their routine and seemingly drew a line between the Tiras, effectively including and welcoming Azrael as one of them.

He caught Lark's stare as they passed the greenhouse. Magdalene looped her arm around his jealously, inciting a small but knowing smile from Lark.

"Shall we get dinner?" Magdalene asked him, her voice sweeter than honey and loud enough for Lark to hear her, even as they left her behind them.

†

## LARK

L ark pretended not to know what had brought her to Thea's door at sundown and told her friend that she just needed company—company that wasn't sick or dying, in one way or another. And when Lark suggested the sit in front of the window that had a view of the courtyard, including the house beside the pathway, Thea didn't mind. A storm was brewing above them, promising a night of thunder and steady rain. Lark breathed in the smells of her favored lavender tea and the scent of rain on the breeze. Isabel sat behind the two women, chittering away as she colored pictures for Lark.

The real reason Lark had visited Thea was because she was curious. Curious as to why a seamstress had captivated the swordsman's attention, and why the girl had been possessive when she had seen the two walking in the afternoon. A small part of Lark wondered how the remainder of their night would go. The man was healed by a god, only to use his legs to chase common tail.

*Birdie is jealous.* Iah's voice rang in her head, in a sing song tone that insulted her more than she was sure he intended.

*I am not*, she wanted to retort, but instead pushed the god of night from her head. She had nothing to be jealous of. Perhaps, maybe the sense of normalcy in intimacy and relationships, but nothing beyond that.

"Lark, I drew you on Flapjack, but I couldn't get his coloring right," Isabel said from her spot on the floor. Paper rustled before it was shoved into her lap, nearly knocking the mug from her hands. Lark's horse, the one she kept stabled outside the city, with her mother, was a strange peach color with his markings on his nose reflecting accurately.

"Oh, thank you, love. I'll hang it in his stable so he'll think of you when he sees it." Lark kissed Isabel's head and neatly folded the paper to stick in her satchel.

Thunder cracked in the black sky a moment before rain crashed into the window. Lark groaned.

"You're not really thinking of leaving now, are you?" Thea asked, the look on her face reflected the way she looked at Isabel when the girl was about to do something she shouldn't do.

"I should, before it gets worse. Hadri will be wondering where I am." Lark stood and smiled at the exasperated Thea. "Thank you for the company."

Thea took Lark's mug and shooed Isabel into her room. Lark braced herself, willed her shadows to fortify as a cover, and stepped out into the storm.

As long as she kept focus, her shadows would keep her dry on her walk back to her home with Hadri. The lanterns around the courtyard had gone out, drenched by the rain, but the night was still dim enough Lark didn't need a light to walk.

Dim enough that when she made eye contact with Azrael, there was no question that she was using magic to keep the rain off her.

He stood in his doorway, leaning one shoulder against the frame, and Lark hated how she noticed he didn't look as sickly as he did a week ago. Lark heard Magdalene scuttling across the stone, heard her sigh over the rain once she finally reached the cover of the palace. Lark felt a smugness in her stomach that the girl hadn't stayed the night. Perhaps he was nothing special after all.

Azrael shifted, his face flashing with an emotion Lark didn't recognize, before he straightened and looked as though he would say something to her. That's when her focus fizzled out and the rain slammed into her, soaking her white shirt to her bones. He opened his mouth just before she passed his house, but she kept her eyes away from his and hurried along. Even once she was out of his sight, she didn't bother summoning more shadows to cover her, now that she was thoroughly sodden, and ran the rest of the way back to her house.

# CHAPTER 13

## AZRAEL

Azrael's days began to fall into a steady routine. Magdalene finished her work at dusk and ate dinner with him, bringing extra desserts she had swiped from the kitchen on her way to his house. The first night had been uneventful and awkward, but her presence became a welcome distraction. It had been easy to fall into her chatter, and the way her laugh echoed on the stone walls, and she didn't say anything the few times she caught Azrael gazing out the window, wondering if he'd see the mage. Magdalene soothed him, while something about Lark riled and called to him.

Magdalene would fall asleep at his house, which he didn't mind, only to wake up hours later and slip out. He didn't try to sleep with her or get her to stay, and she seemed content in their arrangement.

In the mornings, Azrael created his training schedule and stuck with it. The Tiras had segmented in how they trained—the two spearmen practiced with the swordsmen, and the horsemen trained with the archers. The healers, though, never seemed to sleep. The light in their house flickered on whenever Azrael would sleepily drag himself to the field before the others arrived. He hadn't seen them watching, until today.

"Good morning," Hadriana trilled from her perch in the doorway. Her name he could easily remember, and he had learned it only in a passing conversation with Ahmi. She had golden eyes, skin darker than the earth, and hair she kept piled on top of her head, and a voice that sounded like windchimes. She was married to the Areenian, Hollis. Azrael noticed Hadriana's elbow jam into Lark's side before Lark echoed the greeting.

"Good morning," Azrael said as he moved to his favored section of the field. He eased his shirt off and began his stretches. The two women rustled in the house, hushed angry whispers carried by a breeze.

When Azrael began his run, he wasn't surprised when Lark fell into pace beside him.

"Mind if I join you?"

"If you can keep up." Azrael adjusted his pace, his pride and ego telling him to go faster, and turned out of the palace gates and into the city.

"Aren't you going to say anything about the other night?" Lark's voice was strange, but Azrael couldn't understand why. Reserved, tight. Hesitant.

"Which night?" Azrael smirked. "And what makes you think I haven't?"

"Why wouldn't you?"

Her question caught him off guard, but he tried not to let it show. He didn't know what she meant, by either question, and didn't want to let her see his confusion.

"Why don't you train more often?"

"Why don't you train with the others?" Lark retorted.

"I like my privacy." Azrael winked at her before pushing himself. The strength in his legs still wasn't what it used to be, but he relished in how sturdy they felt beneath him. The two of them flew across a bridge, down a stone path, and towards the east side of the city.

"That's no way to make friends," Lark breathed, her words strained between breathes.

"And you're an expect, are you, mage?"

The city was breathtaking this early—the empty stone streets, the buildings still slumbering, a lazy breeze rustling the flags and leaves. Silence stretched like a blanket, disturbed only by their footfalls and the softs voices drifting through open windows. The deep black of the night began to recede into the light blue of the morning as the stars winked out. Azrael abruptly turned down an alley, earning an exasperated snort from Lark behind him.

"Are you always this pleasant in the mornings?" Lark returned to his side once again, her twin plaits leaping off her shoulder blades with each stride.

"You tell me, I know you watch." Azrael smirked as pink blossomed in Lark's cheeks and across her nose.

"After we heard you fall on your ass in the rain, we started watching." Lark jabbed him in the ribs with nimble fingers and gained speed. He kept his eyes up, on her shoulders, and certainly not letting his gaze drop to notice how tight her pants were. Lark glanced over her shoulder, as if to remark on his view, when an opportunity presented itself.

"Lark?" Azrael had led her around the puddle earlier; she hadn't even noticed how rainwater had pooled in the indent in the street.

She didn't slow her speed, but looked at him for a moment too long and slipped. Azrael caught her elbow, but not before *her* ass landed in the water. Lark let out a train of swears before she wrestled out of his grip and stood, her face glowing with anger. He grinned and her façade cracked. Her lips pursed, trying to hide a smile, before she whacked him upside the head.

"I suppose that's fair. That's not how you make friends, soldier boy."

"I didn't think this was a trial for friendship."

"No? You think I let just anyone knock me on my ass?" Lark put her hands on her hips and tilted her head to the side, her eyes sizing him up.

"You *let* me?" Azrael laughed. He widened his feet and crossed his arms. "I don't think so, mage. Come grapple with me, and we'll see who ends up on the ground."

Lark raised an eyebrow, accepting the challenge, and took off running, her speed increasing until she was sprinting. Azrael kept his steady pace, not minding having her in front of him.

The sun had ample time before rising, despite the world lightening around them, and Azrael couldn't tell if it was a blessing or a curse as he stepped onto the grassy area beyond the healer's house. Lark tightened the yarn at the ends of her braids, grinning like a devil, as Azrael strode to her. There was such a spark in her eyes that he decided this moment was a curse.

Once her hands dropped back to her side, Azrael lunged. She was just able to step away before he stood where she had been. He swung towards her, but she caught his fist, then his elbow with her other hand, and twisted his arm backwards. He grinned as the motion brought their faces closer, even with her behind him. Her eyes flickered to his mouth, and he took the distraction to wrench from her grip and grasp her forearm. Azrael spun around her and knocked the back of her knees with his shin.

He released her arm and stepped around to stand in front of her. Her gaze was piercing as she looked up at him, with lightning in her eyes—

In one swift movement, Lark surged up, wrapping both arms around his waist, and sent them both to the ground. With her weight on top of him, the impact forced the air from his lungs and sent stars into his vision. He tried not thinking about how her body felt on top of his, and ignored the flash of desire that flickered across her face too. He managed to wedge his knee between them and forced her off. Azrael rolled and jumped to his feet, catching her attack with his forearm. His head emptied of whatever distracting emotions he felt towards her in that moment and sent it into his counterattack. Not wanting to test her healing abilities, he pulled back a little as he landed a punch to her jaw, then a jab to her stomach.

"Not so talkative now, are you, Lark?" Azrael laughed as he ducked, her swing losing momentum.

"Talking or not, I can still beat you."

"Do you even train? Or do you simply rely on luck?" Azrael stepped backwards, spun on his heels, and jabbed his fingers into her ribs.

Lark spun, annoyance clear on her face. "What is it you think I do all day? Sit and wait for someone to walk in with a bloody—" Her fist was too fast, he couldn't catch or block it before it collided into his face "—nose. Sorry."

"Precisely." Azrael spit blood into the grass, blinking away the tears that pricked his eyes. Lark's face was a mix of triumph and pity as the blood dripped down his chin.

"I didn't think I'd actually hit you hard enough, sorry. Come on." Lark grabbed his hand and dragged him to the house, where Hadriana had disappeared from.

She gestured for him to sit in the doorway while she disappeared inside. The sun began its ascent, yellow spreading across the horizon. He was sure the Tiras would be arriving soon. Lark returned to him with a handful of linens and a bowl of water.

"There's nothing to be sorry for," Azrael said as she scooted closer to him. "I've had plenty over the years."

"Is that why the bridge of your nose is crooked?"

It was the first moment of softness in her voice and in her face that he had seen. Azrael wanted to blame his lack of breathing to his now swelling nose, but she smiled at him. She had smiled at him, and he forget how to breathe.

Lark gently wiped the blood from his mouth and chin, her fingertips burning through the cloth. She held his jaw with her forefinger and thumb as he began to wipe at the blood beneath his nose. Her touch alone stilled him. She didn't move her fingers as she dunked it in the bowl and returned to his face. Azrael tried looking elsewhere as she focused, but his eyes kept drifting back to hers and the way they flickered between his nose and mouth.

"Hikaim, did you fall on your pretty face?" The spearman he had fought shouted as he strolled up the field with his sickly archer friend on his heels. Lark dropped both of her hands.

"The healer punched me." He stood, their moment of peace gone, and reality shifted back into place.

The spearman laughed, short and ugly. "You deserved it. Are you done? We don't want to interrupt your training, o hallowed one."

Beating the man in a fist fight hadn't been enough to shut him up, but Azrael didn't care. He gestured to the field without saying a word and walked past them. He felt Lark's eyes burning into his back, daring him to turn around.

He kept walking.

# CHAPTER 14

## LARK

Azrael glanced at Lark and Hadri again, not once missing his target as he fought bare chested and bare knuckled with Ahmi. Lark pulled the thread through her canvas, poking her finger with the needle, and blushed when Hadri laughed at her.

"How in the world did you convince the king to throw a solstice party?" Hadri asked from her perch, fanning herself as she watched her also shirtless husband shoot arrow after arrow into his target, splitting each previous arrow straight down the middle. The morning had been slow for the Tiras, a handful out keeping their eyes open for more demon attacks, but the remainder of them were restless, Lark and Hadri included.

She kept working, ignoring the small throb in her finger, without paying attention to the misshapen image she had created. Embroidery was just another way to keep her hands and mind busy, even if her gaze and thoughts tended to wander. Hadri threw her fan at Lark and repeated herself, once Lark met her eyes.

"I can be persuasive when I want something," Lark said, straightening her shoulders in a show of pride. Making up for the lack of pride she had displayed when she had asked Melech for the party. She thought it would be a good idea to meet foreign nobility, ask for support from across the Three Oceans when the time came. She had told Melech it had been long overdue for a party and it would be a good chance to invite people, to become one again. The things it took to finally convince him—Lark shut the memory out.

"Will you come to the seamstress with me later? I want to get something started before she's drowning in work. You probably should too." Hadri smiled and winked. She stretched out her foot and prodded Lark's hip with the toe of her boot. "Will you ask him to go with you?"

"Who?"

Hadri glared in response, her face stating that her question had been obvious.

"For one, when will you stop asking questions like that when you know how it is? For two, he'll have us rotating shifts, you do know that right? It won't be a party for us."

"Oh yes it will. We'll rotate, keep our eyes peeled for *threats* and we'll have fun and dance and drink too." Hadri sighed. "And I know, Lark, but I also know that you two keep making eyes at each other and now you've ruined your stitching—if that even is a flower, I honestly can't tell."

"Making eyes at each other?" Lark dropped her hands in her lap, giving up on her endeavor for now. "I have no idea what you mean, but we should take Thea too."

As though to reinforce Hadri's point, Lark glanced at Azrael and found his eyes already on her. She didn't know what it meant, but since their fight, the feelings of irritation and annoyance had begun to subside. She no longer saw him as an insult from Iah, and she didn't know what that meant. On the opposite side of the stone wall in her mind, keeping the god out, she heard his faint melodic laughter.

"Indeed," Hadri said as she shot Lark a know-it-all look. Closing her eyes, she rested her head against her chair and turned her face to the sun.

Lark looked down at her mess of a canvas and had half a mind to burn it, but she felt Iah's warning rumbling in her head. Instead, she shot to her feet and glared towards the men. She noticed how Azrael stiffened, even without taking his focus away from Ahmi, as he became aware of her again. Lark marched into the house and shut the door.

✝

I t had slipped her mind that the seamstress the Tiras used—or at least Hadri used—was Azrael's girlfriend. With a reluctant Thea, Hadri and Lark walked into the small shop tucked in a corner of the market courtyard. The seamstress that owned the shop apparently let the girl run it nearly by herself. Fabric was strewn everywhere with half-dressed mannequins buried beneath it all. Countless candles lit the room, deepening the shadows. Magdalene sat bent over a desk, only acknowledging them when Hadri moved to stand in her light.

"Oh, my apologies, my ladies." Magdalene scrambled to stand, brushing her fly away hairs from her face and smoothing out her wrinkled dress. "What brings you in?"

Lark stood beside Thea as she thumbed through bolts of fabric, more than happy to let Hadri take the reins. Such was their friendship, the two of them—Lark and Thea—together while Hadri took the lead. Most days, Lark had half a mind to appoint her to her council if—when she took the throne.

"Three dresses for the solstice," Hadri began, then added after a pause, "Will you be attending as well?"

"I do not know yet." Magdalene's voice was caught off guard, even as her face remained neutral. "What sort of dress would you like? I can get them started right away."

"Something gold for her," Hadri said, pointing at Lark, "Slim, revealing, sparkly. For Miss Thea, cream, fitting through the bodice, flowing, something to show off her curves. And for me, I want white, something backless, and with sleeves."

Magdalene nodded, her gaze drifting to Lark's hands. Azrael must have told her why his face was bruised. She curled her fingers into a fist, nails biting in her palms.

"I'll need to take measurements; do you have time now?"

"Of course." Hadri straightened her shoulders and clasped her hands togeth-er. She had a good foot of height over the woman—over all of them, really. Lark had become so used to her that she often forget how tall Hadri was. Magdalene merely looked up then gestured to the opposite corner of the room, where three mirrors stood in sunlight.

Thea and Lark followed the two women through the mountains of tulle, ribbons, and bolts. Hadri stepped onto the platform, only to step off with a sheepish smile toward Magdalene.

"Where is the shop's owner—your mistress?" Hadri asked as the girl began her work while writing down numbers on a small pad of paper.

"In her shop in the market. She only comes to oversee my progress in my work."

"I see, and it's only you that attends this one?"

"There are a few others. Some use the shop while working for others. Sometimes it's nice to have company." Magdalene wrote another number down, and silence settled in the shop for a few minutes while she continued, lining her tape up with Hadri's long legs.

Once she was done, Hadri moved to Lark's side and prodded her to step onto the small platform. She steeled her face as Magdalene's hands flitted around her, resting the tape against her skin. Lark fought the urge to fidget and kept her hands still as the seamstress worked.

"Do you have a husband? A partner?" Hadri asked with a voice that was painfully obvious. Lark met her friend's eyes in the mirror and wondered what had gotten into her friend.

"I'm not at liberties to discuss, my lady. Surely, I can get this done as quickly as you like, if there are no more questions." Magdalene's voice, soft but stern, chafed Lark's ears. She had to know why Hadri was asking, and the thought brought heat to Lark's cheeks.

"Do forgive them," Thea cut in. "By all means, continue."

The room once again fell silent as Magdalene worked around Lark, each touch inciting a flinch that the seamstress didn't note. Thea and Hadri spoke quietly as they wandered around the room.

"I've seen the way he looks at you, my lady. The good will look marvelous on you," Magdalene said quietly enough the other two didn't hear.

Lark's heart thundered. She met the girl's stare in the mirror before them. A ghost of a smile appeared on Magdalene's face.

"I wonder if he will dance with you during your party. I've always wanted to know if the king is a good dancer."

Lark didn't know how Magdalene could have known, but the thought was unnerving. Her heart had gone silent, dropping entirely to her feet. She didn't want to think about how good the king was at dancing and fought against the rising panic that threatened to choke her. Magdalene had to be angry with her for breaking Azrael's nose, and Lark understood that. The blow Magdalene had delivered hurt more than she could possibly know.

"I've heard he is." Lark swallowed the panic and offered a smile, small but with anger burning in her eyes. Magdalene turned as she wrote down Lark's measurements, a clear dismissal. Lark moved to let Thea take her place.

Leaving Thea to recover the seamstress's good graces so she didn't charge the three of them immense amounts, Lark dragged Hadri to the window in the front of the shop and kept her rooted by wrapping her arm around Hadri's. They spoke quietly as the world passed them by outside. Hadri had caught onto Lark's mood change and thankfully remained quiet, not prodding Magdalene with unnecessary questions.

After what seemed to be an eternity, Thea stepped down and Magdalene broke the silence.

"I will get started on these right away, and I'll send word when they're complete."

"Thank you," the three women said at once.

"Now, shall we go find our husbands and some lunch?" Hadri opened the door, flooding the shop with bright sunshine and the commotion of the market. Just before the door clicked closed, she added, "Maybe Azrael will join us."

†

H e did.
       The six of them sat on a patio with an array of food spread across
the table. Tendrils of leaves adorned the posts holding the canopy above them,
casting lazy shadows as the sun hit the greenery. Bread and tea wafted in from the
kitchen on a cool breeze while soft music filled the air from streets over. Azrael
and Lark sat at opposite ends of the table with the other four sitting beside their
partners on either side.

"How's your nose?" Lark asked him. She hadn't been able to take her eyes
off it, or him, once she realized it was setting slightly crooked. The coloring and
swelling were down much more, and he hadn't even realized when she had sent
her ivory threads to him, healing and smoothing out. She couldn't do anything
about the bone, though, without him realizing.

Azrael grinned, as though he didn't care his disappearing pain was her fault.
"It's fine. Though Ahmi didn't care to take it easy, and I think it's staying
crooked."

"Listen, I was just tired of you being prettier than me." Ahmi laughed before
he took a bite of his sandwich.

"You both resemble a horse's ass." Hollis, with his Areenian beauty, spoke
plainly, as though it was the truth.

"Thank you, Lark, for your everlasting devotion to the Tiras," Ahmi said
with a smile brighter than the sun. Lark noticed then the piece of wheat braided
into his curls, behind his ear.

*Are you surprised Birdie? He is of the earth.*

She hadn't heard Iah's voice since the night before and had taken it for
granted. Lark took a sip of her white wine and cut into her chicken. Thea's knee
knocked against hers and gave Lark a soft, supportive smile. Lark always blamed
the mood changes on the toll magic took on her, even if Thea could see through
that lie. She always caught onto Lark's subtleties.

"What have you three been doing this morning? Other than watching us like
hawks?" Hollis asked, sipping his Areenian wine. Lark always admired how he
held onto his roots but remained loyal to Havriel.

"It's our house, we were merely sitting outside," Lark clarified, scrunching her nose at Hollis, and summoned a smile she hoped was convincing.

"Did the embroidery not turn out the way it should have?" Azrael tilted his head as his eyes sized Lark up, ready for a rematch. She met his dark eyes, suddenly so unlike how she had seen them before. He winked at her.

"What have *you* three been doing, if not your duties?" Lark retorted. Even though she knew the answer, she didn't want him to be right.

Ahmi and Hollis laughed, but Azrael simply kept staring at her, as though he could see through the mask she wore, straight through to the thoughts rattling inside her head.

"To be fair," Ahmi said with his hands up, palms out, "We go to our meetings. You should be glad we're here, it means we're not needed."

"Will you have to wear uniforms?" Hadri asked with a note in her voice that pleaded Hollis to say no.

"Of course."

There it was—the lovesick, world ending adoration as they locked eyes. Lark looked away, anywhere but at the table. She didn't hear anything else the two of them said.

It was then she noticed the messenger striding up the ivory stone street, no hesitation in his steps but with his head down. With her back against the wrought iron fence, she knew that he would be stopping beside her. He handed her a small, folded note through the opening in the fence and her friends went quiet. The messenger left just as quickly, just as silently. She knew what the note was for, but unfolded it anyway and ignored five pairs of eyes boring into her. After reading the swooping script, Lark began to regret the wine.

"A patient?" Thea offered before Hadri could say something Lark didn't want her to. Hadri was never cruel, but Lark wasn't sure she thought about what she would say before it snuck out of her mouth.

"Yes." Lark sighed, looking at Thea from beneath her eyelashes. She fished out a few coins that would cover almost everyone's food and plinked them on the table before she rose.

"Do you want us to walk with you?" Thea asked as she reached out to grasp Lark's hand. The simple kindness in the gesture threatened to break Lark's heart. Before Lark could decline, Azrael spoke.

"I will."

"It's fine. It's not far." Her stomach twisted. Her fingers started to twitch.

"I know," Azrael said simply. He stood as well and set coins on the table.

They bid their goodbyes and Lark tried not to catch either woman's stare as they walked through the gate and onto the street. With a good distance between them, the two of them nearly took up the narrow street as they walked in silence. His hands in his pockets, sleeves rolled up, and loose curls ruffling in the breeze, Azrael looked perfectly at ease, while Lark felt like a gremlin laced with anxiety. She was a princess, for gods' sake, and she shouldn't feel anxious with him.

"It's not a patient, is it?" Azrael asked, slicing the silence with the quiet ease of his voice.

"No," Lark admitted. She found herself wanting to admit the truth—at least, partially—to him. She fidgeted with the cuff on her sleeve, suddenly regretting the dress. Even with the slits cut into the sleeves and the different layers patterned to stay cool, she felt too warm. She wondered if she had enough time to go home to change before she went to the king.

"A man?" So carefully posed, but Lark noted the apprehension in Azrael's face as he glanced sideways at her. He stepped closer to avoid walking into a man dressed in vibrant pink head to toe.

"Of a sort." Lark couldn't help but laugh.

"Oh, so a future patient then?" A sly smile stretched on his face. Even with his broken nose and fading black eyes, there was warmth in his face when he looked at her, and Lark couldn't place when that had changed.

"You know me so well." Lark laughed again and surprised herself. When was the last time she laughed this much with someone?

"No, I don't, and that's the problem. I want to." Azrael's smiled faded with reserve, as though he hadn't meant to say it aloud.

The pair walked over the bridge connecting to the outskirts of the market district where it was mainly homes now and empty buildings of businesses that couldn't stay open. Lark had always liked walking through the city, feeling much more a part of it than when Melech kept her in the palace. Even though her people had forgotten her, she had long since stopped holding it against them.

"Do you often come to this side of town?" Azrael asked after a few moments of quiet.

"I don't come to town often, not really." Lark struggled to remember the last time she had walked through the city alone. When she went to her mother's she often had a guard accompany her to the city gate, and if she left the palace gates, a guard would shortly arrive behind her. Lark had never known if the guards were meant to keep her safe or to keep her honest.

"That's a pity. The east has a night life that make priests blush."

Lark had slowed her pace once they reached the palace gates and she wondered if Azrael noticed. His boots scuffed as they stopped.

"Thank you for walking with me," Lark said. Before he had the chance to say anything else, Lark straightened her shoulders and strode towards the palace to find her king.

# CHAPTER 15

## AZRAEL

T he middle of summer brought longer and hotter days. Azrael's life had fallen into predictability: training in the morning, Tiras meetings in the day, and Magdalene in the evening. Their relationship had devolved into an easy friendship, as he still enjoyed her company, and she was better than sitting in silence by himself every night. He saw Lark every morning, but they hardly spoke. She would join him for his runs some mornings, but their conversations were short, much to his disappointment.

The summer solstice approached quickly and that meant parties to honor the extended daylight. Vale City buzzed with excitement in preparation for the king's party—the first official one in years—and rumors had spread that emissaries and nobility were invited from across the Three Oceans, even though invitations were hardly necessary. Nobody would miss a royal party.

Azrael, in his Tiras duties, wandered the grounds for the sake of policing and keeping his eyes and ears open. After Nevan's death, Melech had pulled the Tiras and kept them all within arm's reach. Azrael didn't mind it so much at first, but he could walk the grounds blindfolded and still find his way. The monotony began to take its toll.

He walked with Ahmi, under the blazing blue sky, and relished in the breeze that stirred the heat. Ahmi didn't mind, with his hair trimmed above his shoulders and loose-fitting shirts. Azrael noted to buy some; he had been working to gain his muscle again, and now his clothing hardly fit.

"Is Thea going?" Azrael asked as they roamed together, walking along the eastern allure. The palace walls had become Azrael's preferred place to spend his time. The view of the Three Oceans expanded to the horizon, the vantage point over the city, and the tree line that obscured the southern part of the King's Mountains had become his favorite scene.

"She wants to. I know she had a dress commissioned by your lady friend. Are you going with her?"

"No," Azrael said, and hoped Ahmi wouldn't ask why. Magdalene had brought it up a few nights ago after he had asked how her day had been. She said she'd been working on three dresses for the Tiras women and how much work it was, trying to get him to ask her to go. He was able to see right through it, and steered the conversation, and decided their friendship meant more to her than it did to him.

They neared the curve of the wall and from that point, Azrael had a view of the small harbor that welcomed a handful of ships bearing Telaanan and Areenian flags, the red and green of each, respectively, flashed brightly against the sparkling water.

"So it begins," Ahmi said with his eyes on the ships and the sailors yelling with words lost to the wind.

†

Time slowed as last-minute decorations were set and preparations were finalized. The last of the guest list had arrived, and now to fell to those without an invitation to flood the palace. The halls and floors crowded with nobility, the corridors crammed with those who had already secured a room and those who were determined yet to find one. Banners with large suns had replaced the double moons of their flag and bonfires were lit in every courtyard at sundown. The entire palace felt like a summer sunset.

The guests were easy to pick apart from the Havrien. Areenian aristocrats were taller by at least a foot and cleared the way with their sweeping cloaks, dark eyes, and light hair. Telaanan nobility were dark and walked with a sense of mystery about them, as though waiting for someone to ask about their desert home and the treasure that made them wealthy.

Azrael kept his distance from them, ensuring his routes didn't cross with the guests, but when he heard the beginning of the party and the music floating from the great hall, he couldn't help his excitement. Even though his duties as a Tiras kept him from fully enjoying the night as he desired to, he looked forward to it. So much so, that he consented to sitting in front of Thea's mirror and let her fuss over his appearance before they all went together.

"Honestly, Az, haven't you been to a royal party?" Thea chided as she ran her fingers through his curls after she had trimmed them. A frown line briefly creased her face, but she flattened a stubborn lock and smiled.

"No, Thea, I didn't grow up with noble parents." Azrael laughed. He had attempted to get ready for the night by himself but found he couldn't be happy with how he looked.

Thea had readied Ahmi before Azrael and he lounged on their sofa as Thea flitted around him. She wore a cream dress with a blood red ribbon tied around her waist, accentuating her curves. Azrael had to close his eyes every time she moved to stand in front of him, the deep neckline of her dress revealed freckles Azrael didn't care to note.

"You didn't even grow up with parents," Ahmi offered with a straight face that broke into a shit eating grin once Azrael looked at him.

"Ahmi!" Thea scolded with a look only a mother could perfect, her eyes telling him to shut his mouth before the words came out. In response, Ahmi simply shrugged and slid off the sofa.

Azrael laughed, earning a look with raised eyebrows from the woman before him. Thea rolled her eyes before motioning for Azrael to stand. She dusted his shoulders, flicking off the remaining locks of hair from his trim, and straightened the red sash across his chest. He had felt foolish in the decorative uniform—a black chest piece with two moons on either shoulder with the red sash crossing between them, pants so tight they felt like a second skin, and boots that rose to his knees and silver buckles lined either side, flashing in the firelight. It wasn't much different from his daily attire, but the chest piece was rigid and too formal, and he hated the gaudy sash. Some Old Havrien prayer or another was stitched on the inside.

"Let's go," Ahmi groaned from his place beside the window, "I'm dying to get tonight started."

&#8224;

T he path from their houses to the great hall was bustling with people, some drunk already and shouting, and some slipping away into the shadows together, and it fueled Azrael's excitement, much to his surprise. He had been to many parties while he lived in the city, as well as the makeshift parties in his camps, but none of that prepared him for the magnitude of this. They blended into the crowd, surrounded by vibrancy of color and culture.

Herded as sheep, they eventually made it to the great hall and Azrael felt the heat pouring out of the double doors, propped open to welcome in the masses. The party was in full swing already. Music drifted to him from the band in the corner on their pedestal while banners and tiny suns hung from the vaulted ceilings, fluttering in the stifling air. Two small alcoves on the right side of the hall provided reprieve to couples slow dancing in the dusk on the balconies.

Over the crowd, Azrael noticed his king sitting at the far end of the room on an intricate throne atop a dais, a cup in one hand and his eyes grazing over the heads in front of him. He caught Azrael's stare and turned his head slightly to the side, his eyes never leaving Azrael's.

It took one glance, one look to follow Melech's line of attention, and Azrael felt her hands on his face again, as though it had happened only hours ago, instead of days. Her eyes lifted from Melech's face to his and Azrael's head emptied. He let the guests shoulder past him, ignoring their insults from his lack of movement. He couldn't see much of her from this distance, but he saw blush warm her cheeks and pull the king's attention.

Ahmi gripped his elbow and brought him back to himself. Azrael looked to his friend, recovering his momentary lapse of focus, but Ahmi was grinning from ear to ear.

"Come, let's get a drink. Our rotation doesn't start until two, plenty of time to have some fun," Ahmi said as he began to drag Azrael through the crowd.

Tables with food and wine were set up on the far left of the room and attracted the quiet folk. Azrael took two glasses, ignoring Ahmi's raised eyebrows, and downed both quickly before reaching for a third. It scratched his throat and settled like a stone in his stomach, but he didn't mind. He swiped a sun shaped pastry and munched it while Ahmi searched the crowd for his disappearing wife.

As though the thought of her summoned her, Thea broke through the line of guests, her cheeks red and a smile on her face.

"Will you dance with me?" she asked Azrael. He looked to Ahmi, confused, but Ahmi gestured with a nod for Azrael to go.

"I don't dance," he admitted, a half-lie. He had never been good at it, only learning from drunken soldiers and girls in taverns.

"Nonsense, come." Thea grabbed his hand and yanked him, almost spilling his wine. He hurriedly handed it to Ahmi, who had an amused look in his eyes, before the crowd enclosed around him.

"Why," he shouted at her over the noise. The music had lulled, awaiting a new song, but the din of all the voices was immense.

"Why not?" Thea adjusted her feet and held both of his hands up.

"I don't dance," he repeated, his heart racing in anticipation of embarrassing himself.

"You will," she said as the music began.

Azrael quickly picked up the movements despite himself. What was fighting, if not dancing without music? Thea's face was bright and smug, as though she knew a secret he did not, but he ignored the warning bells pealing in his head. Ignored them until she spun around him and disappeared, only to have Lark step into her place.

His feet tangled together, and he slammed into another dancer before he gathered himself. He fell back into the rhythm with her and the music.

"You're not a very good dancer," Lark shouted over the vibrant strings, a smile on her face.

"You're not a very good partner if you're not going to be supportive," Azrael yelled back. He spun her, and she coiled back to him, her back pressed against his front.

"You're right. You're doing great."

Azrael's head spun faster than she had, and he couldn't tell if it was the wine hitting him, or if it was simply her presence that ignited him. She wore a dress of gold that glowed like sunlight with her hair pulled away from her face, but in her loose waves down her back. His heart grew wings as she moved away from him again and he wondered how her shoulder would feel beneath his lips.

He swallowed, hard, as they kept dancing. The song lasted only a few minutes, but it wasn't enough by the time it ended. Clapping rippled through the hall as the music ended, but Azrael and Lark stayed frozen, chest to chest and eyes locked. Something told him that, if he moved, he wouldn't get another chance like this. He racked his brain for something, but he lost himself in her eyes—a storm at sea, thunder rolling and waves crashing—and he would have given anything to hear her thoughts.

"Will you dance with me again?" Lark asked quietly, unsurely, as though she was prepared for his denial.

"I'd be foolish to deny you. I'm quiet enjoying this peaceful side of yours," Azrael said with a smile. "Though I'm surprised you're not stepping on my feet. Where did you learn to dance?"

"My father taught me," she said as the music picked up again and they fell into rhythm with the other dancers. "I'd ask you, but it's clear nowhere."

His hand on her waist threatened to dismantle the remnants of control he was holding onto.

"Did you mean what you said?" Lark asked him after a spin once she was close to him again. He drank in the smell of her: lavender and sea salt.

"What did I say?"

"The other day when you walked with me. That you wanted to know me."

They had slowed their dancing, and he stopped as he looked at her. He debated telling her the truth, debated running into the crowd. Lark stopped dancing too and looked up at him.

"I did," Azrael answered honestly. There was no point in denying it—not when he searched for her every morning, not when he relished in their short runs.

"Why?" Lark breathed, stepping closer to him. A breath remained between them.

"Why?" he echoed. Her eyes moved from his to his mouth, and back up. He heard the trembling in her breathing, and the small gasp when someone brushed against her and pushed her into him. Instinctively, he wrapped his arm around her. "Why, Lark? I am drawn to you."

Without thinking, his hand reached up to cup the back of her neck. She lifted her chin, eyelashes fluttering, before clarity shot through her eyes and she stepped backwards, ripping away from him. Lark looked anywhere but at him, and he hated for the crushing weight in his chest as he watched her disappear into the crowd.

Midnight passed and Azrael hadn't seen Lark again. The king had disappeared from his throne during the peak of the party, only to return as Azrael and Ahmi began their watch. They had both drank fountains of water to flush out the buzz from the wine and stood dutifully beside the empty throne to await their king. He sauntered in from the corridor, his face dark, and settled back into his chair. Lavender trailed him, and Azrael glanced back to the corridor to find Lark standing in the shadows with Asenneth, who was dressed in a sparkling red gown and not looking like she had been on the brink of death only weeks ago.

The crowd began to thin, guests bid their king goodnight before retiring, while Azrael stood as a statue beside the throne. It was strange to him, standing guard like this, instead of mingling and being active in his role, but he maintained his focus, eyes and ears open to those who approached the king. The only moment he lost that attention was when he watched Lark melt into the crowd again, drink in her hand.

"The attacks are being closely monitored, and I am doing everything in my power to ensure Havriel is safe," Melech said, catching Azrael's attention. An Areenian stood before him, dressed in green robes. The man's stance was casual, his face anything but. Azrael gripped the hilt of his sword,

"If it spreads to our shores due to your lack of control—"

"It will not. It is contained, and will be eliminated," Melech replied, cutting the Areenian off. He leaned forward in his throne, hands gripping the end of the arms. "And if you were about to finish that sentence in a threat, I would suggest you return to your ship instead."

The Areenian clenched his jaw, a muscle feathering in his cheek, and abruptly turned and strode away. Azrael relaxed his grip and glanced at his king. Melech had leaned back into his throne, eyes burning with anger.

Lark reappeared in Azrael's line of sight, her face showing the remnants of a halfhearted smile and exhaustion. Her face shifted once she stepped away from the crowd, and her glare was for the king, and the king alone, as she walked towards the throne.

"My healer," Melech said, disarming her frustration instantly. Lark bowed her head before him. "Come with me. Azrael, walk with us."

Melech stood and descended the steps. Azrael hadn't noticed before that Melech wore his old ceremonial Tiras sash, the proof that the king had been an effective warrior before he was crowned—back when the Tiras fought and killed for their positions.

Heavy silence fell between the three of them as Melech led the way through the corridor, the din of the party fading with each step into the darkness. The king headed through the palace and up the many stairs to his floor. Azrael relished the way his legs felt with each step, how sturdy his body had become, how far he was from the broken man in the mountains.

Melech's floor consisted of the endless mirrors and Azrael took care not to catch either Lark's or the king's eyes in the reflection. The king weaved his way effortlessly through the mirrors to the gilded doors of his rooms. One of the archers—Boaz, Azrael thought his name was—stood outside the doors, his dark face made of stone. Melech paused beside the archer and turned to them.

"Prepare a tonic for my head, and return at once," Melech said to Lark before he shut the door in front of them.

"Boaz," Lark said with a nod. The archer said nothing, his mouth threatening to turn into a sneer, but he refrained. Azrael bristled at the look in the archer's eyes, but he turned and walked down the hall with Lark. His heartstrings tangled as Lark offered her arm once they turned a corner. He looped their arms together and she sagged, a sigh echoing off the mirrors.

"You alright?" Azrael asked hesitantly.

"Fine." Her voice was clipped as she straightened, as if remembering herself. She didn't let go of his arm.

"Is it a lot to make a tonic?"

"No, I make them often enough," Lark said, adding quickly, "Not for him, just in general."

Azrael didn't know what else to say, but he wanted to hear her voice. Instead, neither said anything as they descended the endless stairs and heard the sounds of the party again.

"Good night, Az," Lark said as they stopped beside the entrance to the great hall.

"I could walk with you to the house, if you'd like. So you don't have to walk alone in the dark," he offered, not ready to leave her presence.

Her face was unreadable, but she nodded. "Okay."

She disentangled their arms and they walked side by side, past the great hall. Azrael should be on watch inside, but he knew the others were in there, and he told himself that walking with her was just patrolling the area. Still rightfully within his duties.

"Will you be returning to the party when you're done?" he asked. The corridor was so quiet, away from the loudness of cheering and music.

"Most likely not. It has been a very long day." Lark sighed again. They turned a corner and nearly ran into a couple fervently groping one another. Azrael gritted his teeth as they walked past the moaning couple who took no note that they weren't alone.

"You mean, you don't want to get wasted enough to do that?" Azrael joked, but at the pained expression on her face, illuminated by the torchlight, he apologized, "Sorry, that wasn't appropriate."

"If only it were that easy to let go and pretend I didn't have to worry about someone finding me."

"Wouldn't it?

Lark smiled wistfully at him. "Your nose is looking wonderful, by the way. The bruising is almost entirely gone."

"And I suppose you would like my gratitude?"

"What do you mean?" she asked him. He walked down the steps to the Tiras courtyard first, leaving her confused at the top.

"I've had broken noses before, love, I know they don't heal this quickly."

"That's due to me?"

"Of course, it is." He stopped at the bottom and stared up at her. Head tilted, his brows furrowed. He hadn't felt it, but he had seen her focus both when she initially broke it, and when they were at lunch with the others. A few other times during their runs, his face grew itchy, but he had cast it off as allergies. Truth be told, he was thankful she healed it, he detested the healing process. Even if his eyes were black and blue for a while, it paled in comparison to the full-length process.

In the quiet, leaves rustled.

In the quiet, a bow string was pulled.

In the quiet, a bow string snapped.

# CHAPTER 16

## LARK

*M*ove.

Everything happened at once.

Lark took a step down, and the arrow pierced her thigh. Azrael was on her in a second, his body covering hers. All too warm and heavy. He was yelling, but she couldn't make out the words. She had been shot.

She had been *shot*.

*Birdie.* Iah's voice. Lark couldn't focus enough to build the stone wall to keep him out of her head, but neither could she focus on his words.

Azrael moved to get off her, sword already in his hand, but she grabbed his bicep, her shadows swimming around his arm.

"Don't tell him, please." Lark whimpered. She tried unspooling the ivory threads of light, but they were too tangled. When was the last time she had to heal herself? This *hurt*.

"Who? Lark, let go, I need to find them," Azrael tried breaking her hold, but her shadows tightened, her grip turning iron. His voice was pure ire, but she didn't balk from it.

"The king. Don't tell him."

## AZRAEL

A zrael's voice had gone unheard, and he wrestled with staying with Lark or trailing her shooter. His choice was easy after the woman ripped the arrow from her thigh, her breathing ragged.

"Go," she hissed.

He became rage, the tether broken. He lunged from above her and set off in a sprint.

He knew he should find the guards, find a Tiras, but this was his, and his alone. He passed trampled leaves, a broken fletching, and boot prints.

The archer was slow, impossibly. Azrael had expected a grand chase, not someone hiding in the bushes far behind the Tiras houses and trying to ambush him. The man leaped out, dagger in hand, but Azrael was faster. He swatted the knife away and plunged his blade within the man's belly.

"Why?" Azrael demanded as the man gurgled and sputtered. He wore no notable pieces of clothing, nothing to identify him. The light flickered out in his eyes, and he slumped on Azrael's sword.

"Fuck," Azrael hissed as he let the man fall off, into the bloodied grass. "*Fuck.*"

He wiped his sword clean before sheathing it and ran back to the courtyard.

She was gone. The blood disappeared from the steps. Azrael stood where she had. From there, he could see the training field and gold shimmering in the moonlight. Had she walked home?

He bounded down the steps and across the uneven cobblestones.

"What are you doing?" His voice was hard to control, he tried not yelling at her, but it came out as a harsh whisper once he reached her.

"I made the tonic," Lark said simply, as though nothing had happened. As though she were a child that had been told to stay still and didn't listen. She lifted up the bottle as proof.

"Are you—why are you—are you alright?" He struggled to gather his thoughts coherently. Part of him had grown used to the buzz of an attack, but there was a smaller part of him that blazed with anger—the fact that she was the target ignited him.

"I'm fine," she sniffed. She wasn't putting weight on her leg, but there was no longer a mess of blood and flesh.

"Why?" He didn't even know what to ask, he had so many questions swirling in his head.

"Hadri and Hollis are taking care of it." Lark started walking again, limping slightly, but she hid it well.

"What does that mean?" Azrael asked baffled.

"That means that nothing happened, now walk with me."

"Nothing happened?" He was shouting again.

Lark stopped, turned to him, and sharply exhaled. "No. Nothing happened. You walked with me to my house and walked me back because I did not want to walk alone. Hadri and Hollis were making love, so you waited outside. I made the tonic, and we were on our way again. That is what happened, and what you will say happened. So, let's be on our way again."

"That's it?" Azrael was defeated, confused, and didn't feel like he had much of a choice but to move to her side.

"That's it."

"Fine," he bristled.

"Fine," she repeated. They stood nearly chest to chest again, lightning buzzing across his skin.

"You could have died," he said after a moment of silence.

"You could have, throwing yourself on top of me like that. So desperate to become that couple groping in the shadows, are you?" Lark breathed, her joke not making him laugh.

"Do not tempt me, mage." His voice was strained, his body aching. He stepped closer to her, only the tonic keeping them from touching. He delighted in the shiver that shifted her shoulders, parted her lips. "Come," he said, stepping backwards just before she tilted her head upwards.

Azrael held his breath until they passed his house, tearing his thoughts away from being tucked away in the shadows with her, and finally exhaled with a clearer head.

"I'm walking you back to his floor," Azrael said as they walked up the same steps she had bled on. Lark looked at him but didn't object. "And I can carry you, if you want."

"No," she said too quickly. A pause, then, "Nothing is wrong. I can walk just fine. I'm simply tired."

Azrael offered his arm instead, which she took. She did look tired, a heavy weight he couldn't know resting on her as a mantle. They walked directly from the courtyard to the stairs and up, up, up to Melech's floor. He hesitated on leaving her, but easily saw in the mirrors there was no one hiding behind a corner.

Lark turned to him then, leaned on her toes, and kissed his cheek. Her hand rested on the opposite side of his face, even when she lowered back down. A sad smile flickered on her face, her freckles stark against the paleness in her complexion. He didn't think about it as he lifted his hand and covered hers.

"Thank you," she whispered. She pulled her hand back and straightened her shoulders before walking away.

His head was swimming, his heart was pounding. He needed a cold bath, or a strong drink, or both. Both would have to wait. He waited until her reflection disappeared before he descended the staircases and strode back to the party.

# CHAPTER 17

## LARK

*L**ittle bird.*

Everything hurt.

Lark swatted her hand in the air, as though it would push Iah's voice away, but he only repeated himself. His voice grated against her headache. She had drunk in excess after the party, first after visiting Melech, then more when she got home. She pried open her eyes to a messy room, littered with empty bottles of wine, discarded glasses, cake crumbs, and the bloodied rags she had clean her thigh quickly with. She was grateful that no one besides Azrael, Hollis, and Hadri knew of what happened last night. Melech didn't say anything about her reservations, nor about how much wine she consumed before she left.

Ivory unspooled from her chest, working in her muscles to soothe and un-knot, especially where the arrow had pierced her.

She glanced to Hadri's now empty bed, wondering if they had gone to their home and felt a pang of jealously at that thought. She was grateful that they had been here last night, even if it was awkward walking in on them in the kitchen. They took one look at her and dressed in a second. Lark still couldn't believe what had happened, and it replayed over and over and over in her head. There was no explanation, no motive. It wasn't widely known that she was Nekoda's daughter—not yet—nor that she possessed magic, and Hadri had said the man hadn't been foreign, that he bore Havrien traits.

She had been attacked. Someone wanted her dead.

The idea rattled within her, clanking against her ribs and pitching against her organs.

Lark swung her legs off the bed and shut out the thoughts of last night—especially of Azrael. When had her dislike of him turned into wanting to dance with him, relishing in the way that her body felt beside his? Seeing that rage in his eyes after she had been hurt, she knew that he had left her with the sole intent of avenging her, and she didn't know why that thrilled her so.

A warm bath, that's what she wanted. No, a cold one, to shake off the heat building in her core at the thought of how close they had been to kissing—twice. A cold bath indeed.

Shedding the skimpy dress Hadri had designed for her, Lark shuffled into her bathroom and filled the tub. She thought of leaving it at room temperature, but she sent tendrils of shadows diving into it, cooling it off while she gathered her soaps and oils. She stepped in, gooseflesh rising already, and submerged herself quickly before she changed her mind.

Iah again called to her, but she built the stone wall high and thick in her head, shutting him out. It was too early the cranky bastard and his prophetical bullshit.

It wasn't even moments later when the house creaked in the silence and the air grew cold around her, icy crystals forming on the top of her already cold water. Without announcing itself, Lark knew which spirit had touched down outside her house. It was the kind one, the one who still held onto a shred of its humanity, the healer. This one wasn't a strong as the others, but Lark was acutely aware of its presence, nonetheless.

Once the cold became unbearable, Lark rose from her bath and dried off. She dressed in the plain black uniform, red cuffs on each wrist as usual, and let her hair air dry as she moved to the kitchen to start breakfast. Stone by stone, she let her mental wall lower.

*Her Majesty finally deigns to listen to the cranky bastard, correct? Not the one who has helped you turn into the woman, the mage, the princess you are.*

Lark spread peach preserves on a slice of bread and made a cup of tea, heating the water with her ivory light instead of waiting for the water to boil naturally. All the while, she said nothing to the god of night and listened to him ramble.

*You haven't even made a move yet—*

"It's not time," Lark snapped out loud. She glanced up, making sure Hadri hadn't come home while she was distracted. She sighed and stirred her tea. The frustration from the god was tangible, even at this distance. Lark leaned back into her chair, pinching the bridge of her nose like her father had always done. "There's much to do; I've met with the lord, I met with nobles last night, which possibly could have killed me. One of which, possibly, tried to kill me. Please call back your watch dog. It's summer and my house should not be this cold."

*You know our agreement. You know what the magic demands.*

A give and take. Yes, yes. "What the magic demands, what you demand, it's one and the same. I haven't forgotten."

With that, she felt both the spirit and Iah slip away, dissolving back into the inky blackness of the cosmos they called home. Her head finally felt empty again.

Only for a storm of thoughts to career in after a knock on her door. She opened it to a servant holding a folded note in her hands. Lark watched the girl disappear past the Tiras houses before she opened the note. In beautiful handwriting, *'Have dinner with me tonight.'*

It wasn't their regular scheduled nights, and that realization settled like a stone in her stomach. A hundred things flashed in her head; did he find out about the archer? Was he upset that she danced with Azrael? Had he seen through her plan to invite the other kingdoms? Had someone seen her in the Roe and told him? Yes, she hadn't been secretive when she was there, but she was at least careful. She didn't mind people knowing she was there, the question she wanted to avoid was: how did she make an almost month-long trip, by horse, in days?

"Okay," she breathed. This was fine, everything would be fine. She returned to her seat at the kitchen table and ate silently, trying to avoid the thoughts slamming in her head.

Once she finished, she got to work cleaning the house—every inch, every speck of dust, every herb and salve organized and relabeled. She kept her mental wall high enough to keep Iah out, but thankfully he didn't try to pry. She didn't let herself think of anything except the task at hand. She didn't want to think of anything else, especially not from the last few days.

Hadri still hadn't come home once the sun began to set. Lark bathed again, feeling too many layers of dirt seeping into her skin, and sat naked on her bed deciding what to wear. She wished Hadri had come home—Lark wouldn't mind her strength, her love, when she felt so void of both. Easily enough, that thought helped her choose. Something Melech would both hate and desire: a lilac dress with flowing sleeves that clasped together at the shoulders and wrists with an opening on either arm, a tight bodice that hugged the small curves she had, with a skirt that was thin and layered and swayed with each movement of her hips. She swept half of her hair up, setting it in the back with a silver comb of stars. Lark was dusk incarnate, a calm summer evening compared to his summer rainstorm. She stuck flimsy slippers on, utterly hidden beneath her dress, and took a steadying breath before she strode to the palace.

Lark passed a few Areenians she had invited, dressed as though they were going to another ball, and she smiled and nodded to them. She had met with a few, calmed down one who had been angry with Melech, and met with even few Telaanan. She showed them she was exactly the princess she claimed to be, and each meeting had gone exactly how she had hoped, save for one Telaanan lord who couldn't have cared less who or what she was. The Areenians seemed most helpful, especially one woman whose matriline line had been blessed with flying (though Iah corrected her in Lark's head that it was simply wind magic) and said that she would do anything, support Lark however, for her daughters and granddaughters to touch the skies. Lark had yet to meet the leader of the opposition to Melech's reign, but she allowed herself to be hopeful. For once.

Lark did not shy away from the hall of mirrors as she usually did. Shoulders back and chin up, she didn't care who noted her walking up the stairs, floor after floor, to the halls she had memorized like the back of her hand. Blush touched her chest every time she caught a look at herself and swallowed her pride knowing Melech would like that.

She rounded the last corner, expecting a quip from Brannon who usually waited for her and followed her in, but instead she came face to face with Azrael. His attention snapped to her and suddenly Lark forgot how to walk.

Gods, Melech *had* been jealous that she had danced with Azrael. The king had been jealous. The king, who had her in all the ways he truly cared for.

Azrael's face shifted from surprise to confusion as he noted what she was wearing, the blush on her neckline. His gaze felt like an embrace of thorns, but she bore it.

"Good evening," Lark said, breaking the silence that seemed to stretch on. "You look—"

"Beautiful, doesn't she?" Melech interrupted from the doorway, leaning against the frame. As his usual attire, his shirt was unbuttoned and falling off one shoulder, and he was bare foot. Hair mussed and, if Lark didn't know any better, would have assumed he'd just rolled out of bed with someone. His eyes were set on Lark's face, completely ignoring Azrael beside him. "Ready for dinner?"

It dawned on her then that Melech had requested dinner, hadn't threatened, hadn't demanded. Simply requested, and Lark obliged. She breathed through the anger bubbling in her chest, and strode past both men, into the room. Melech said something to Azrael before the doors shuttered behind him.

"What are you doing?" Lark asked, whirling around on him. He stopped inches from her.

"I've grown to trust him." He cupped the right side of her face, and she stilled so she didn't flinch. Smiling softly, he crooned, "Haven't you?"

His fingers dug into her hair, gently massaging her head. The intimacy of the touch made her sigh.

"Tell me what you want," he breathed, stepping even closer so she had to crane her neck to look at him. "Tell me *who* you want, Siena."

Her kingdom, herself, Azrael. *Azrael*.

"You, my king."

Carefully, he took the comb from her hair and watched her waves tumble down her shoulders. He sighed, his eyes devouring every moment. Carefully, he took each wrist and unlocked the claps. Carefully, he touched his thumbs to the tops of her shoulders and coaxed the fabric.

Lark dove into the lake of her power and threw up a shield of hardened shadows around the room, locking the sound in.

"I wanted to dance with you last night." His voice was rough, restrained in the way Lark knew that it was building. "But I didn't want to upset you."

Still as a statue, her dress fell to the floor in a heap around her feet. Her fingers twitched at her sides.

"Did you want to dance with me?" Melech breathed. His black eyes were on the edge of a precipice, ready to leap. "I couldn't get the thought out of my head—my hands around your waist, and that gold dress."

"Yes, my king." The pieces fell together, each scale of armor that she wore to protect her heart and head.

"Tell me there's nothing between you and him." His lips touched her collarbone and sent her heart into chaos. She took a ragged, deep breath.

"There is nothing, my king."

This close to him, where she felt his desire for her against her body, she saw the change, the tension burrowing within his muscles.

"I saw you two," he whispered against her skin as his mouth moved to touch her jaw, her ear. "The way you danced, the way you looked at each other. Tell me there is *nothing* between you two."

Lark took a second too long to answer. His hand was at her throat as he backed her against the table, the papers that had been stacked on it fluttered to the floor. He cupped his hands around her ass, lifting her onto the table.

"Or should I bring him inside to watch?" Melech growled against her mouth, not quite kissing her, but the threat pierced her.

White hot fire burned in her veins, pure fury. She hated him, hated this man for what he had turned her into, hated him for his games, his manipulations. It was damn time it was her turn.

Lark turned it off, every feeling and every thought, and hoped the shield would hold.

She hooked her legs around his waist and pulled herself against him. Hands no longer bracing herself against the table, she flung his shirt off and unbuttoned his pants. A low sensual laugh rumbled through him, skittered across Lark.

Once she had loosened his pants and freed him, he leaned over her, lowering her against the tabletop, and pushed himself against her. His hands trailed her thighs, applying the slightest of pressure as he anticipated her. His tongue left a trail of gooseflesh as he flicked it across her chest, up the side of her neck. She let out another ragged sigh, and nodded. He took her by the mouth as he buried himself within her, a deep growl of pleasure emanated from him.

Lark dove deep within herself, letting her body play the part as that fire consumed them both.

# CHAPTER 18

## AZRAEL

The warmth of summer began to wane into crisp autumn air. Since the night the king had him outside his door all night, Azrael hadn't been needed for anything specific, other than his continuous patrolling the grounds like a guard. He had seen other Tiras coming and going, whose names he slowly began to learn whenever Ahmi walked with him. He stuck to his schedule and forced himself to spend time with the others in the morning during their workouts, and he'd gotten to know his fellow swordsmen better and didn't mind them.

Lark had kept her distance, no longer perched within the doorway of her house during their workouts, no longer joining him on runs, and Azrael pretended like it didn't ache. He didn't know what had happened with the king, if anything, but her absence only kept him on his toes, his eyes constantly searching for her.

He had returned from a morning of training, like every morning, and bathed in the warmest water he could acquire. Autumnal rain had begun halfway through his session, light but endless, and drenched him to the bone.

Azrael parted the curtains in his sitting room, letting in the dull grey light, before he made breakfast. He'd gotten used to it, going to the market district with Ahmi and Thea, and began to enjoy spending time in his kitchen, even if his meals were simple. For breakfast, he made bacon, warmed bread and spread honey on top, and a bowl of duck eggs seasoned with unlabeled spices he had acquired from a seedy merchant in the market. They had smelled good, and Azrael hadn't given a second thought.

As he settled at his table, a knock rapped on the door. With a mouthful of food, he stood and was met with a face full of mist as he opened the door.

An unhappy, soaked servant stood before him and thrust a note in Azrael's hand before striding away to the next house. He didn't wait to see what other door the boy stopped in front of before he shut the door and returned to his breakfast.

*Midday. Armory. Pack for travel.* The king's handwriting was blotched with rain drops, but still legible. Azrael breathed a sigh of relief. Finally, he had something to do.

†

LARK

"Send Brannon in your stead," Lark said from her place at the small table in the armory. The captain stood in front of the door, arms crossed, visibly irritated. Melech paced across from Lark. Dressed like a soldier, his hair was braided in his usual style on the sides, with everything else gathered at a knot at the base of his neck. He hadn't shaved since he received word of the Roe's insubordination, hadn't focused on anything but Lord Bedivere. It thrilled Lark, but she kept that locked up tightly within herself.

"My king, I would be more than happy to—"

"No," Melech snapped. He glared at Lark, his eyes black with hatred, as though it was her fault the lord hadn't agreed to the heightened trading tax. "I will see this through, and remind our lord that he is only such because I allow him to be."

"It's an unnecessary risk to bring you the entire way down the continent. If we must go, can we not sail?" Brannon asked, gesturing to the map indicating there was a small harbor outside the city for such occasions.

"No," Melech said too quickly, too loudly. Lark sighed, pinching the bridge of her nose. He gave Lark another glare of promised pain, "You of all should understand that."

"I do, my king. I simply do not see the need for you to go." Lark was becoming a wonderful actress in her time with him; he could never see when she was lying, when she told him one thing and meant another.

"This discussion is over. I am leaving, you two are coming with me, and those surely who have arrived already." Melech stopped pacing in front of Brannon, his shoulders back. Lark noted how his pinky twitched, and how quickly he shoved his hands into his pockets to cover it. He was anxious and plotting something. Lark stood and followed her king out.

Azrael and Ahmi sat at the table where the useless soldiers spent their times, Ahmi flipping through a deck of cards someone had left. Lark kept her distance from them, stopping at the opposite end of the table, and kept her eyes on the door. Boaz waltzed in, quiver and bow strapped to his back, his dark skin glistening with rain.

"Now that you're here, we leave. In the south, Bedivere governs his town well. The trade has been excellent, but the lord seems to wish to be free of my rule. He desires his own southern kingdom." Melech struggled to hide his disdain. "We are going to remind him that he is in no place to make orders. If he wishes to discuss politics, then we will. It is a long ride, be prepared for anything. I trust you five to keep me and each other safe as we travel. Prepare your horses. We leave now."

†

The grey clouds gave pause to the rain as the company gathered in the stables, but the sky was heavy, as though the rain were searching for a crack in the cover to slip through and drench the land once more. Lark fastened her bags to her horse, petting his mane before she climbed on. She often missed her own horse, the one she kept at her mother's, but she knew she would be trading his one out at a stable close to the Roe and didn't want to go through the trouble to get hers back. Her mother, no doubt, was giving him all the attention Lark wished she could.

She exhaled as she swung her leg over the horse and settled into her saddle. Melech's fixation since the letter had made Lark uneasy, and had left her wondering how this would affect her plans for taking her throne. If this was another thing Havriel wouldn't accept her for. She had been gone too long already, and was wrapped around the king's middle finger for too long as well, now she was to storm across the continent with him.

"Onward," Melech said, his voice bursting through her gloomy thoughts. Brannon followed him just as fast, leaving the other four to scramble behind them.

As soon as they reached the city gates, the rain started again. They settled into their riding pattern after the city of tents: Melech in the center with Brannon next to him, Boaz and Lark rode in the back, while the two swordsmen rode in the front. Lark ignored everyone, especially Boaz, and focused on the landscape, eyes adjusting to the grey veil of rain and mist.

✝

## AZRAEL

Night closed in all too quickly, and it seemed they had hardly made progress. Azrael knew the path to the Roe, but it seemed as though they kept passing the same landmarks, the same houses, the same estates. Melech had refused, initially, to stop, but the rain held steady, and eventually he relented. Azrael left the company on foot with Boaz, the archer he suddenly found that detested him, so he was quick to find shelter large enough for the horses. Boaz lit a fire while the rest of the group collected dry wood, a feat in itself.

Once the fire was maintained, and obscured from the road, Azrael stretched his damp bedroll out and did not object when the archer offered to take first watch. He had fluffed out his stiff riding blanket when the bedroll beside him was snatched up. Lark's cheek feathered as she scooped her roll and moved paces away from him, leaving him confused and silent. He let it bother him for a moment before he settled down. Azrael was asleep before he laid his head on his arm.

†

The next time they stopped was with the sun falling below the tree line, and Azrael was ready. The clouds had cleared, and stars glinted in the paling sky. Ahmi had managed to find a spot for the night with a small body of water beside him, and Azrael breathed a sigh of relief.

Boaz had shot a deer for dinner on their way into the cove, and sent the newest Tiras to fetch his body. Azrael had expected a clean shot, not a wild deer frantic with pain. He had been foolish—his hunting skills rusted—and ended up thrown into a ditch with mud and deer's blood covering him before he promptly ended the deer's life. He carried the carcass back to the useless archer and dropped it at his feet. Saying nothing, Azrael had set his bedroll out, settled down, before gathering clean clothes and heading off with Ahmi to find the water.

"I wouldn't drink it, but it looks fine enough to rinse off in. If you didn't know any better," Ahmi said when the two of them stood at the edge. A large pond, with algae and reeds and weeds covering the border, but Azrael didn't care.

He removed his boots and belt, setting his sword in the moss, and discarded his shirt. He stripped his pants before sinking into the freezing water, his skin prickling with gooseflesh.

"Don't stay in too long, you wouldn't want to catch something," Ahmi said as he turned to walk away.

Azrael submerged himself, shaking out the mud cakes from his hair, and scrubbed at his arms. He was sure he had rolled in shit too, but he tried not thinking about that. He lifted his head above the surface again and the first thing he noticed was his lack of clothing. The clothing he had in his hand, had set down by his boots—

He groaned.

*Might as well get this over with*, he thought as he scrambled out of the pond. He picked up his boots and blades and walked back to the camp.

At least Lark's back was to him when he approached. Boaz cackled, his dark eyes flickering between Azrael's face and bare ass. Ahmi said beside him, lips pressed into a thin line to hide his guilty smile. Melech leaned against a boulder, face unimpressed as he took in Azrael's naked form. Azrael swiped his clothes from Ahmi just as Lark glanced over her shoulder. Her cheeks flushed red, then scarlet as her gaze dropped. Jaw set, Azrael flashed Ahmi a look that promised revenge, and dressed quickly.

"I'm sorry, my king," Ahmi said, stifling his laughter, after the king had, no doubt, shot the giggling swordsman a withering look.

†

The immense road that stretched from the Vale to the Roe was wet and worn, imprints of passed horse hooves and the wheels of merchant carts pressed into the earth. Low clouds and fog mingled together before their path, obscuring their way, while the sight settled a restlessness in all but the king, who had patience that surprised Lark. He kept her within arm's reach as they rode, day after day, night after night. No one but Azrael had noticed, as the others were accustomed to the king's possessive behavior when it came to her. Still he said nothing, but Lark's cheeks heated whenever she caught his gaze before they settled down at night.

He couldn't understand—none of them could really understand—her and the king, and the thought made her feel even more isolated.

†

R ain began three days outside of the Roe—heavy, relentless, torrential rain. They couldn't ride, couldn't find camp. Brannon had left in search of the inn he had promised that was not too far away, at the edge of the tree line before the landscape gave way to the flat fields of the Roe. The company sat uneasily beneath the cover of the forest while the captain was gone, off bribing the inn keep to stay silent about their stay. Once he returned, they set off as fast as they could, stabling their horses, and rushing inside.

The inn was quiet and warm, nearly empty which Azrael hadn't expected. They all stood, dripping puddles onto the wooden floor, before Brannon brought the king upstairs, keys in hand. The few patrons indulging in the warmth of the fireplace and warm ale didn't look twice at the hooded figures going up the stairs, only at those who still stood at the doorway.

Boaz and Lark floated to the large bar at the side of the room and spoke to the innkeeper's wife, while Ahmi followed his king up the stairs. Azrael hesitated, catching the wide-eyed patrons, and decided his room was the better option.

Each wooden step creaked beneath his weight. The warmth in the air, mixed with the smell of a roast served with ale, was stifling, but a thousand times better than being stuck in the rain. Azrael found Ahmi with the door to the room cracked, and Ahmi waved his hand.

"We're sharing with Boaz," Ahmi said, shuffling cards in his hands. He had shed his wet clothes and sat on one of the two beds.

Azrael dropped his bag, grateful he had brought it in, and pulled out dry clothes. He quickly changed and set out his wet ones to dry.

"A round of cards?" Ahmi asked, raising his shuffled deck.

Azrael shook his head, rain flinging off, and said, "No, but I do need a drink."

He passed Boaz on the way downstairs but paid no attention to the archer. Azrael went straight to the girl behind the bar, a girl not much younger than him with bright eyes and a sly smile that grew as she noted the way his shirt hugged his shoulders. He slid coins to her which she replaced with a pint. She rested her arms on the counter, pushing forward her generous assets, before Azrael winked at her and went to the table beside the window looking out the front of the inn.

Thunder rocked the windowpane as rain plummeted into the earth, significantly harder than when they had been riding and Azrael was glad he was inside for the storm. He couldn't recall the last time he had stayed at an inn—rolling a bedroll in the mountains had always been easier—but it was a rare luxury, even if the rooms were musty, the patrons shady, and the floors sticky. He quite enjoyed eavesdropping on those who still remained seated at their tables, talking loudly about a rogue wolf hunting too close to town and how a soldier had slain it singlehandedly, literally as the man only had one hand. Azrael smiled to himself before Lark sat down across from him.

"This isn't taken, is it?" she asked as she carefully set her glass down, wiping the table with two fingers before she did.

"You wouldn't have liked her anyways," Azrael said, biting his lip to hide his smile. He took a sip of his ale in hopes it would calm his erratic heart, or at least make him funny enough to hear her laugh.

"As if any sane girl would sit in the corner with a brooding man." Lark pulled the fur cloak around her shoulders a fraction tighter, the fur white with bristles of black and looking like it had belonged to a wolf.

"Yet here you are," Azrael replied before he took another sip, keeping his eyes locked with hers. He leaned back in his chair, stretching out his legs and knocking hers out of his way with a crooked smile. "What does that say about you, then?"

"Perhaps that I'm feeling the same as you, only prefer to brood in company."

"What does a healer have to brood over? Not enough wounds to stitch?" He raised an eyebrow as she rolled her eyes.

"What's a soldier to brood over? Not enough skulls to bash?" Lark retorted, eyes narrowed but mouth fighting a smile. She leaned back in her chair and mirrored his posture.

"Darling, there's always more skulls to bash." Azrael laughed. Lark laughed, too, and Azrael found he could never grow tired of it.

After a moment of silence and prolonged eye contact, he broke it by saying, "You've been distant."

"You've noticed?"

"You're doing it on purpose?" he asked incredulously. He hadn't thought of her the one to do something like that. She smiled sadly.

"No," Lark sighed, "No, I'm not, and I apologize if it was taken to heart."

*Taken to heart?* he thought, *You have taken my heart.*

"Can't say I've missed the amount of blood being around you brings." He glanced behind her, eyeing for the king, "How's your leg?"

Lark shuddered, but pretended it was a chill. She tightened her cloak, the fur brushing her cheeks in such a way Azrael wondered how it would feel beneath his fingertips.

"It's fine," she said, "Your nose is crooked."

It must hurt, he realized, if she deflected so quickly. If not physically, then perhaps emotionally—he couldn't imagine being targeted, for whatever reason it had been. He took another drink and traced the circle the glass had left on the table with his index finger.

"It's not too bad," he said, "Every time I look in the mirror, I think of you."

Lark's fingers stalled in bringing her glass to her awaiting lips. She raised her gaze to his, face reminding Azrael of a rabbit caught in the sights of a wolf.

"Don't say that," she whispered. She swallowed, hard, and set her glass down a bit too hard on the table.

"Why? There is truth in it." He finished the last of his drink and set his glass down, sliding it through the circles of water. The storm raging outside had grown so loud, drowning out their voices.

Lark abruptly stood, encasing herself in her cloak so her body was no longer visible beneath it. Using her foot, she pushed the chair in and gave him a small smile.

"Good night, Azrael."

"Good night, Lark."

He watched her small frame tread up the stairs and caught her looking at him once more before she disappeared. He waited until she had surely returned to her room before he stood. The innkeeper's daughter perked from behind the counter at his movement, but he didn't look her way. His feet brought him upstairs, reluctant to share a room, but ready for sleep nonetheless.

Boaz and Ahmi were playing a card game, slapping each other's hands and loudly swearing as one swiped the other's cards, and paid Azrael no heed as he shouldered through the door. He kicked his bedroll out on the creaky floor, snatched a blanket from one of the beds, and curled into a ball before sleep took him.

# CHAPTER 19

## AZRAEL

The vibrant forest thinned and disappeared entirely, opening to the vast land of the Roe. Rich in red earth, sprawling farms, underground bandit camps, and fields that stretched for days, the Roe was a drastic change from the forests and mountains Azrael knew best. The upper section of the Roe was barren middle ground for thieves in search of unsuspecting travelers, but once one passed into the largest section, the land gave way to farms and tiny towns that eventually clustered to form the city that this lord wished to make a kingdom.

With the end of their journey so close, Melech refused to stop. They rode through the day, night, and the following day, taking advantage of their fresh horses acquired from the inn. With the sun rising on their left, the company thundered over small hills, empty fields, and small rivers. This part of Havriel had a rustic charm that Azrael was finally able to notice.

They finally reached the city when the sun touched the western horizon, setting a golden touch to the buildings on the outskirts. Varying in size, color, and shape, it was a stark contrast to Vale City, and it was a breath of fresh air. This was Ahmi's home, Azrael remembered, the land his friend had come from.

The folk they passed were darker than Ahmi, their skin glowing in the sunset, but their eyes followed the company with disdain. Weaving along a dirt road that turned into stone once the homes grew closer together, the company rode slowly as onlookers gathered around.

Ahmi led the way down a small hill, then up another to a large house overlooking the town. Stables abutted the manor on the left, a small building, but a handful of grooms met the company in front. Azrael dismounted, his entire lower half stiff, and stretched his legs a moment before following the king to the front of the house and the staircase that led to the front door.

An older man with white hair opened the door and greeted the king in a small bow that went unacknowledged. They walked in pairs through the entrance. With Lark at his side, Azrael took note of the room, the servant in front of him, anything besides how her hand brushed his. Twice.

The house seemed old, despite the colorful and elegant decorations, with whispers and secrets hiding between the wood panels of the walls. They passed an empty sitting room with two sofas in front of a fireplace. Bouquets of white flowers sat on nearly every surface, filling the rooms with a thick and sweet, but not unpleasant, smell. They passed a second sitting room, or Azrael thought, with a massive piano in the center and a single white flower on the top. He wondered if the lord played, or who it belonged to. The floorboards creaked beneath their feet as they were led through a maze of hallways.

Melech and Brannon exchanged a look as the company stopped in front of a set of doors. Brannon then turned his attention to the four Tiras behind him, his eyes those of a stern father who wanted not a sound from his children. The two men disappeared behind the doors, but not before Azrael caught the stare of Lord Bedivere as he leaned against a desk, hands braced behind him. The doors shut as two guards came around the corner and stood in front of the Tiras, their dark faces blank and uncaring.

Azrael and Ahmi stood with their backs against the wall while Lark settled on the floor beside Azrael. Boaz paced as quietly as he could, stepping over Lark's extended legs with an annoyed look on his face every time he passed her.

A cold night crept in as a heavy quiet fell in the manor. The voices inside the lord's room were hushed so that, even in the newfound quiet, their words couldn't be discerned. A king on the brink of another civil war and a lord who wanted more. Azrael would have enjoyed being a fly on the wall in that room. He knew that Bedivere was a young lord that had inherited his manor and wealth from his father who had been an advisor and emissary for King Nekoda when he had been alive.

Muffled shouting erupted somewhere outside, the many walls of the manor dulling the sound.

Lark shot to her feet, eyebrows furrowing. "Something's wrong."

Just as the words escaped her lips, a crash echoed from the opposite end of the house, followed by wood splitting and more yelling, louder now. The guards before them jumped and jumped again when the doors behind them flew open. Brannon stood on the threshold, mouth agape to point blame, but the lights perched on the walls blew out, drenching the soldiers in darkness.

Boaz unslung his bow from his back, notched an arrow, while Azrael unsheathed his sword. The two young guards scuffled on the floorboards, their swords singing as they withdrew them.

Azrael smelled it then—the stench of rot, overpowering the aroma of flowers. That old fear settled into his bones, reminding him of his childhood home, and watching Nevan die so quickly, so brutally, but he didn't let it paralyze him.

"I'll take care of it," he whispered to the others.

"Like hell you will, what is it?" Boaz snapped as he took a step forward.

"If it's the demon again, then Az is the only one who can help," Ahmi hissed back. Hints of doubt throbbed in the back of Azrael's mind—what if he couldn't help this time?

"Trust me," Azrael said before ignoring the others entirely, pushing his doubts to the side. He moved as silently as he could to the corner and peered around it.

At the end of the hall, a Daeoan towered, bowed slightly under the ceiling. Shadows flickered on it, gently lit by a fire somewhere further down. The crackling and splitting of wood told Azrael a part of the house was on fire. In that light, Azrael could make out the fractured bone of its face, beneath that hood: the long, sharp teeth and the eye sockets empty as a sky without stars. The being stood there, facing partially away from him, as though waiting for something.

Time slowed as Azrael moved towards it, keeping to the shadows as best he could. He wasn't sure if this was a being he could snuck up on, but he was damned if he wouldn't try. Whatever havoc it wreaked before arriving here would stop with Azrael.

The robes the creature wore floated around it on an unfelt breeze and dissipating into the air like ash in the wind. With the dim light, Azrael noted how the being did not float, but didn't possess feet either. It was as though the creature was a sturdy pillar of darkness and smoke and death all formed together to roughly resemble a humanoid.

Wood creaked beneath Azrael's boots, and he froze as the being turned its terrifying head in his direction. The empty eyes seemed to focus on him through the shadows. Azrael flexed his fingers around the hilt of his sword, breathing through the fear that threatened to choke him.

He didn't wait for the being to move. With his sword raised, he sprinted, closing the distance between him and the Daeoan, and buried his sword in the mass of shadow before its bony hand could knock him to the side. As he yanked his blade free, the Daeoan turned to stone, piece by piece, and dissolved into the air as smoke.

"What the fuck was that?" Boaz yelled, his voice wrought with the same terror Azrael felt but pushed down. He glanced behind him at the group and met their wide eyes and tight mouths.

Before he could answer his fellow Tiras, a shout ripped through the night from somewhere still inside the manor. Azrael took off in a sprint again before he could decide otherwise. Heart beating like a hummingbird and head growing dizzy with adrenaline, he passed bloodied but breathing guards. He whistled and yelled out for Lark to help them. He ignored her footfalls behind him, and cursed himself for being able to recognize them out of all the others and how that should be the least of his concerns.

Skidding to a halt, he stumbled into the sitting room closest to the front doors. A Daeoan swirled between the sofas while holding a guard by his throat. The moonlight that pooled into the room reflected off the bony hand, illuminating the blood that dripped down from the guard's nose. In a tight breath,

Azrael launched his sword through the air and into the center of the demon's body. In a piercing clarity, it seemed as though this was what he was meant to do. The quickness that he moved around these beings—it brought mental clarity, despite the fear still swarming inside him.

The demon petrified fast, dropping the gasping guard and his blade. Azrael swooped to pick it up, not even sparing a glance at the guard. He called for Lark again and followed the sound of distant screams.

He didn't know what their purpose was here, or why they had showed up precisely after he did. What he did know was that, from the top of the stairs, he could make out at least two more Daeoan downtown, alit by two buildings smoldering beside them. Death and destruction, it seemed, was their purpose.

His feet carried him down the stairs, down the street, into the midst of chaos faster than he'd moved before. Panic had taken full flight, folk raced from their homes, fleeing for safety away from the demons. Guards, upon finding themselves useless against the beings, herded those running through the alleys, towards shelter further from the destruction.

Azrael ran down an alley, hoping to come up beside the demons, but before he could, one appeared in front of him. Before it finished materializing, he pushed himself faster and positioned just so. His body moved lithely, in the way he had practiced time and time again as a boy, to slide beneath his opponent and slice from front to back. He was coming to enjoy this test of his skills, not so much the threat and ruin they caused, but solely the satisfaction of killing effectively. The Daeoan petrified above him, chunks of stone and ash crumbling on top of him before he slid out of the way.

He raced through the remainder of the alley, cut through another to emerge back on the main road, in front of the burning buildings. The other demon should have been there, but Azrael was only met with heat and ash.

"Azrael!"

Just as he turned to Ahmi's voice, he was flung backwards, white knuckles around his sword to hang onto it, and crashed into a building.

He couldn't see he couldn't see.

Everything was spinning. Everything was ash, smoke, fire, and laughter. There was laughter, his ears rang with it. Rot filled his nose, smothered him, until his lungs were aching with the want for air. He coughed, desperate to rid his body of the smell. His vision returned, spotted and violently circling, but he saw the Daeoan's silhouette coming towards him. Azrael tried getting up, but blinding pain flashed from his neck and shoulders.

"Lark!" Ahmi's voice was so loud, but so far behind the demon.

Azrael slipped again, stones tumbling around him, and failed to rise once more. He rubbed his eyes, refusing to accept a blind death, and saw his friend running towards him, Lark behind him. She was yelling too, her voice loud and furious and terrified, and her hand was outstretched towards Azrael.

No, not towards him.

Towards the Daeoan.

The demon seemed to laugh at Azrael, with its empty eyes and lack of a mouth. Ahmi was suddenly at his side, his hands trying desperately to move his friend away. The being slowed, as though it were heavy.

Lark's face appeared behind the demon, and it gave Azrael enough strength to scramble to his feet. He had somehow been able to hang onto his sword. With a last, lucid breath, he swung his sword, slashing into the demon's face, wiping the dead laughter from its cracking bones. It had been enough—the being petrified and disappeared into the night.

Azrael collapsed into the street, his friend catching him just before his face hit the stone. All he knew was darkness.

†

S oft, white light brought Azrael back to the land of the living. His eyes struggled to open, feeling heavier than they ever had before, but once he managed to blink past the blurriness, he found Lark's face staring at him, brows furrowed in worry. Then, Ahmi's face who mirrored hers.

"He's awake, give him space," Lark's voice was soft but stern. Ahmi took a step back. Azrael tried lifting his head, but the pain radiating from his neck had him dropping his head back into the pillow.

An old fear rising in his chest, he touched each finger to his thumb, then wiggled his toes. A sigh of relief escaped his lips.

"You sprained your neck. Try not to move your head. Nothing's broken, though," Lark said as she scooted closer in her chair, the legs squeaking against the wood floor.

"Nothing except the building," Ahmi joked, Azrael heard the worry in his voice. A thump and a groan ensued, and Azrael didn't have to look to know Lark had whacked him for his response.

He felt it then: a wave of pain washing over everything, letting him know the exact points where his body had collided with the building. His eyes fluttered closed, and he ground his teeth, wading through the wave. Lark touched the back of his hand, her fingers burning at first before her magic pulsed within him and scattered the pain. Her touch alone centered him, while her magic soothed him.

"I'll let the king know he's awake, and I'll bring back some food," Ahmi said before his footsteps receded and disappeared behind a closed door.

After a moment of silence, Lark broke it. "You single handedly killed three demons and the worst you have is a sprain to show for it." Her voice was quiet with an awe that had his heart quickening. The last memory he had before he lost consciousness replayed in his head.

"You helped," he said. He turned his head to fully look at her, wincing through the now dull ache. "You slowed it down. You saved my life."

"I had to." A silent sob stuck in her throat, her brows furrowed even deeper. "You hit the building so hard. I had to do something. I couldn't pull your body out of that rubble."

"Tell me how." Azrael tried to shift to sit up, his dark eyes searching her light ones for answers. Her hand still rested on his, her fingers lowered and wrapped around his. She squeezed once.

"Another time, perhaps." Lark pulled her hand away and straightened her posture. Her jaw tightened as the door opened and heavy footsteps thudded against the floor.

Melech moved to the other side of the bed and peered down at Azrael. He ignored Lark, even as she moved out of her chair for him.

"I've heard stories of you in the field, but seeing you yesterday was another thing entirely. Your bravery and stupidity know no bounds. I am proud to have you as one of my Tiras," Melech said as he moved around the bed and settled into Lark's chair. His black eyes smoldered with vitality as he leaned forward, elbows on his knees. His gaze flickered to Lark, finally acknowledging her presence. "We will be leaving shortly. Will he ride?"

Lark looked to Azrael, then her king. "No. I've done what I can, but he needs rest. I don't want to risk it and he becomes paralyzed."

Melech's jaw tightened. "No. Of course not."

Azrael wondered then if he knew of her magic. He had to; an injury such as his would take weeks to heal, even longer to be able to ride a horse for two weeks straight.

Their king stood. "I'm needed in Vale City. Now that this ridiculous business is over with, I must leave. Azrael, rest easy and ride well when you're able."

With that, he swept out of the room. The door clicked to a close behind him.

"Does he know?" Azrael asked as Lark resumed her seat beside him.

"Are you in pain?" She ignored his question, eyes avoiding him.

The door opened once again, and Ahmi stepped in. Azrael swiveled his head to see his friend holding a bowl stacked with fruit and a pitcher of water. He set both things down on the table beside the door.

"I'll see you two in a couple weeks." Ahmi smiled, winked, and left.

"Are you in pain?" Lark repeated her question, still ignoring Azrael's. She rose and grabbed a peach from the bowl. Removing the dagger from her thigh, she cut the fruit into slices and offered one to Azrael.

"Sore." Every muscle in his body cried out, but he'd faced worse. Much worse. He reluctantly took the peach slice from her and ate it.

"Could you move to your stomach? I know it'll hurt, but I'll be able to reach better." She handed him another slice before setting the peach down and wiping her hands on her pants. Lark flexed her hands.

It was agony turning over, moving his body in that way, but once he stopped moving and rested his forehead against his hands, he was able to breathe easier. Peace washed over him as soon as her fingers were against his skin. Fingertips pressing into his shoulders, gooseflesh remained after her touch had drifted. One by one, his muscles began to loosen and relax.

The feeling reminded him of being in the river, under water; the silence beneath the surface, the push and pull of the water, the slowing of time, and the warmth of being healed. His mind trailed off as her hands pushed and pulled like the river, healing and calming.

Before sleep threatened to take him, a knock sounded at the door and Lark withdrew her hands, but her warmth was still against his skin.

"He's resting, but I will be sure to pass these along. Thank you. Yes, I will tell him."

The door closed and Lark set something on the table, the room instantly smelling of flowers and sea salt.

"I have to check on the others, but I will be back," Lark said quietly in his ear. Her hand made a slow circle motion between his shoulder blades before he fell asleep.

†

Azrael opened his eyes to an empty room, though almost every surface was covered with flowers, herbs, and...rocks? He couldn't tell what time it was, as this room had no windows, but a small amount of light drifted in from beneath the door.

His neck was no longer stiff, no longer harbored pain. Gently, ever so gently, he sat up. He finally took stock of the room he was in, as well as the plate of fruit, bread, and cheese sitting on the chair.

As he devoured the food, he realized he wasn't in the infirmary, but in a guest room. His bed was in the center of the wall with a long table on his right, and a small bedside table on his left with the chair in front of it. Across the room, a bed sat length wise—one side pushed against the far wall—with Lark's bags sitting on top. His own bags sat beneath the long table at his right, sword and daggers on the floor beside it. He couldn't understand why he wasn't stuck in the infirmary but was glad for it when he noticed this room had a bathing room attached. He finished his food and carefully shuffled into it and readied a warm bath.

Azrael couldn't tell how long he'd been unconscious, but it must have not been terribly long, as he was still filthy and covered in dust and ash beneath his clothes. He soaked in the bath for as long as he could before he crawled out and dressed slowly, fighting dizziness. He was able to put his pants on before he had to grip the bed frame to keep himself from falling.

The door opened and Lark gasped, hurrying into the room.

"You're awake. And up! How are you feeling?" To her credit, she kept eye contact as she spoke, ignoring the fact that he was still shirtless and hadn't even tied his pants closed.

"Dizzy, but much better. When are we leaving?" Azrael stood, stepped away from her, and pulled on his clean shirt he had set out. He had noted, as he dug through his bag before his bath, that his clothing had been cleaned, neatly folded, and placed back with his things.

"Tomorrow, since you're still feeling dizzy. Bedivere wants us to dine with him before we leave. You made quite the impression on him, and the people, if you hadn't noticed."

"Walk with me? I'd like to see the town, without a demon attack," Azrael said.

Lark smiled. "I'd like that."

# CHAPTER 20

## AZRAEL

The manor had nearly finished the repairs to the damaged sections. Those working on the repairs had stopped mid-motion when Azrael and Lark walked past, their reverence hard to miss when it was plastered across their faces.

"Demon slayer," one whispered, quietly enough that Azrael almost missed it, and part of him wished he had.

Lark shouldered him, eyebrows wiggling, as they walked by. Azrael scowled, ensuring he looked away from the workers as to not offend them. One reached out to grasp his hand and he flinched, pulling it away. He smiled awkwardly at the woman who had touched him and hurried his steps.

"Did you think I had brought all that into the room for you?" Lark asked as they walked closely together in the narrow hall. Azrael avoided the stares of all that moved past him, the heat of every pair of eyes burning his cheeks.

"No, but I thought—I don't know. That it was somehow exaggerated."

The pair trotted down the front steps and into the bustling street where Azrael could truly appreciate the beauty of this southern domain. Lining the street, the buildings were of various sizes and some seemed to have a different color for every wooden panel. Every door they passed was an equally bright color with small etchings on the corners. Signs hanging over business entrances creaked in the sea breeze, each painted by a delicate hand. What seemed to be the main stretch of road was the market, with homes were spaced between.

The town was built on the edge of a large hill, the stone street winding down and around, snaking lower and lower until it reached the sea. From where Azrael stood, he could make out the longest of the docks and the sails that rose high above salted decks. Sailors shouting, waves lapping, and distant bells drifted up the hill to mingle with the din of the town.

Azrael had very few memories of his home in the Moor, but one consisted of his grandmother displaying a quilt she had patch worked from the later portion of her life, squares not fitting together, but Azrael had been able to see why she had chosen each one. He felt the same way with the Roe. Between the street being cleared of the attack and the happiness in the faces of those he walked past, it felt like home. He felt like an outsider, as though he shouldn't be a part of it, granted the business he and his king had come on. Kids ran past them, holding kites and throwing balls in the air and singing and laughing. Even a supernatural event couldn't dull their joy. It felt exactly like that quilt.

"Oh!" Lark nudged him with her elbow. "There's a seer. Let's go."

She pointed across the road to a sign with a wide eye in front of a sun and two stars, the gold paint glaring in the sunshine. At Azrael's lack of enthusiasm, she turned to him.

"Don't you want to know your future?"

"Can't you tell me?" Azrael kept a neutral face for as long as it took her to realize he was joking. Once she cracked a small smile and rolled her eyes, he laughed.

He offered his hand to her, which she took excitedly, and led him through the small crowd to a door stuck between two dark green buildings, looking as though the city had forgotten about it.

It was exactly as Azrael thought it would be: wide enough for them to stand beside each other—truly only a long hallway—and cluttered with everything from trash to feathers to stones to books. A round table sat at the end of the room, its edges touching each wall, covered in similar clutter and a deck of large cards. A small, old woman was nestled in a massive chair behind the table, her nose stuck in a thick book. Once she heard the door close behind them, she shut the book and watched the pair walk closer through her pair of glasses, much too large for her small face.

"Welcome, sweet birds, to Ilaine's Mysteries. What have you come to seek?" The woman pushed her chair back, squeaking loudly, and stood. She was even shorter when she stood, and a waft of patchouli drifted towards Azrael.

Trying to keep his smile out of his voice, he asked, "You don't know what we seek?"

Lark poked him in the ribs, mouth set in a way that told him to shut it, without her saying anything.

The woman, presumably Ilaine, laughed and simply shook her head. "Young man, but that's not the question. Do *you* know what you seek?"

Answers. A reason as to why he had been healed. Why he had been thrust into a new life.

"That's the question, isn't it?" Azrael mumbled as he took a seat in the chair across from the woman. He felt like a giant compared to her as she scrambled back into her chair.

Ilaine smiled, large and strange that showed many missing teeth and some replaced with silver. This couldn't possibly be someone who knew his future, or anything beyond her own brand of tourism. He leaned back in his chair, but Ilaine reached forward, setting her hand palm up on the table. She looked expectantly at Lark and Azrael for them to do the same. They both obeyed before the woman put a handful of rocks from her pocket into their awaiting palms.

"Close your hands."

They did.

"Flip your hand over, set it carefully against the table, and let go."

Azrael glanced at Lark, surprised to find wariness in her face. Just as he moved his hand away, Ilaine tapped on his wrist, then his knuckles. He hissed in surprise and left his rocks on the table, shoving his hands between his knees. Ilaine peered at Lark's rocks first after she scooted back in her chair and removed her hand.

The woman smiled. "Child, I knew I recognized your eyes. They are the same as your father's. He misses you terribly."

Lark turned to a statue, eyes wide. Azrael wasn't sure she was still breathing. A slow blink let him know she hadn't turned to stone.

"Be mindful of the skies. He isn't what he seems."

Lark's lips parted but she said nothing. Her eyes were still trained on the seer. Her face reminded Azrael of an animal caught beneath a predator it hadn't noticed.

Ilaine took no notice. She moved her attention to Azrael. Lips pursed, brow furrowed, Ilaine tilted her head. Then flinched. Paled. She couldn't move away from the trinkets fast enough, her eyes as wide as her glasses. Her head began shaking slightly, then violently.

"My boy—" Ilaine choked out, her voice hardly above a whisper. "Your story is dark—so full of darkness. I'm sorry."

"What?" After seeing Lark's reaction, he no longer felt like laughing.

"You must leave. This reading is on me, I can no longer perform one for you."

"Can't or won't?"

"Please." She skidded from her chair and moved to stand behind it. "Please, leave."

Azrael stood and looked to Lark, expecting her to have risen with him, but saw a ghost in her place. He gently rested his hand on her shoulder, eliciting a jolt from her and a sudden, but soft pain bloomed in his hand. An anxious smile flickered on her face as she stood, wriggling from beneath Azrael's hand. She hurried out of the room. Azrael was on her heels as she emerged into the crowded street, escaping from whatever shadows she had hide from.

Azrael heard the muffled yelling of the woman through the closed door at his back. Before Lark got too far, he lunged for her hand, anchoring them to one another, but Lark yanked her hand away. It was enough to catch her attention and bring her back to reality. She stopped, turned to him, and sighed.

"You alright?" he asked tentatively. There was still the look of a wild animal in her eyes, the look of something ready to bolt.

"I'd very much like a drink," she said.

Azrael nodded and glanced around the street for a place that could provide one. Once he realized there were none near, he offered his arm to Lark, which she hesitantly took, and the two set off down the road.

# CHAPTER 21

## AZRAEL

A few streets over, the crowd thinning, they found a small tavern nestled between two shops that Azrael wondered if they minded having rowdy neighbors—exactly what the tavern was full of despite its small size. Sailors, pirates, mercenaries, merchants, and all those in between were packed into the room, the barkeep nearly hidden behind the bodies. And the smell—there was the waft of sea breeze and open waters, but the stench of unwashed bodies after many weeks at sea, then the smell of spilled ale—and blood.

Azrael's scowl only deepened as Lark, tiny but pushy, parted the crowd enough for them to reach the bar. He could hardly make out what she said to the barkeep, a haggard older man with an eyepatch, but he nodded and put each coin that Lark passed across the wood in his teeth, testing its quality, before plopping them in his apron pocket. Azrael scanned the faces of those around him while Lark accepted the tankards.

Scarred, pock marked, loud bodies shoved up against one another, and the energy in the room brought Azrael back to the days of his youth; still a teenager and during the more stable moments of Melech's early reign, when he had been able to roam the small northern towns and raise chaos.

This time it was Azrael's turn to part the crowds, and he used his shoulders as a way through the bodies. He weaved through until he came to the back of the room where a large window and a back door was propped open, letting in some air. The tavern had a stunning view over the sea, the rooftops around and below falling away from the view the longer Azrael looked.

He glanced over his shoulder at Lark, her face covered by her tankard as she drank deeply. Azrael positioned himself in the corner beside the window, back to the wall, and took a sip of his drink.

As soon as he did, he moved the tankard into better light, studying the dark liquid inside. Brows raised, he looked to Lark.

"You got us tankards of mead?"

In response, she shrugged and took another swig from hers.

"You want to talk about what happened?" It must have been bad, considering how her soul had briefly left her in the seer's room and how quickly she was consuming her alcohol.

"Nope," she said, her lips popping at the end of the word. At least she was back to her regular self, for the most part.

Azrael heard his name in a rough voice, and his gaze roamed the crowd for its origination, eventually finding a pair of guards with their uniforms wrinkled and worn staring at him.

"To the demon slayer!" one guard boomed over the din of the room, and the phrase was echoed even louder as more realized who was in their midst. Azrael scowled once more and drank deeply.

Lark grinned from her place beside him—a true grin, not her regular shit eating one, but a warm smile that tugged at his heart. He took another drink to avoid looking at her any longer. He began to feel dizzy again, the feeling creeping on him, and he couldn't tell if it was the mead, or the injury, or Lark. He ignored her protests as he stepped around her and slipped out the open door.

A cooling breeze slapped him in the face, bringing him to his senses, as much as it could. He hardly felt like he'd had any sense in the past few weeks. Not when it came to being around the mage, not when it came to throwing down his life for his kingdom against a demon, not when his life didn't make any sense.

He should be dead.

He shouldn't be a Tiras, shouldn't be walking, shouldn't be here drinking in a tavern with a girl who belonged to someone else. He wasn't a fool—maybe he was though. He had seen the way the king watched her, more carefully than a king should look after his healer. Yet, here Azrael was: his heartbeat a hundred horse's thundering across the Roen fields when she touched him, when she stood near.

His dizziness had to be her. Nothing else had affected him as much as her.

Not only was he supposed to be dead, but here he was, for the first time in his life, feeling *alive*.

And that was worth more than anything.

Azrael took another drink, feeling his head clear with each sip, and swirled the tankard.

As darkness began to bleed against the sky, the seer's words began to trickle back into his head. The black that was slowly consuming the twilight sky—what darkness would take over his? What part of his story would have scared the woman so much to have kicked them out? His life hadn't been pretty, especially not now with demons prowling his kingdom, but he shuddered to think of what she could have seen. If she even *saw* anything, if he was being honest with himself. How much truth lived in her statements? She had spooked Lark, but he wondered if she had known more of Lark prior—known the things to say to get her coin.

He decided she didn't know salt from snow and drank the rest of his mead.

Laughter rippled through the night, piercing through the raucous yelling. The sound echoed in Azrael's head, both a melody and warning bells. He rubbed his face before turning towards the still open door and steeled himself before entering the dank room once again.

The first thing he saw was the wonder men's faces as they stared, and the second thing was Lark's fist clenched at her side before she swung, landing square in an old sailor's grungy mouth. Sputtering, he stumbled backwards and crashed into a small table. Wood splintered and groaned as others fell—or perhaps dove—onto the sailor. Louder yelling erupted, incoherently, and Azrael lunged for Lark's bloody hand.

She spun around, preparing for another fight, but grinned when she saw him. She let herself be pulled free from the crowd and into the fresh air.

Lightning was in her eyes, the sparks brilliant, as she spun into the empty street with her arms wide open.

"I punched someone!" Lark laughed, wild and free.

"Yeah, I saw that. Why?"

Lark stopped twirling, her boots skidding in the dirt patch she was standing in. Her brows furrowed. Her hair fell over her shoulder as she tilted her head, her confusion obvious.

"Well, first it started with a lewd compliment I won't repeat. Then, he said it served you right, then he touched my shoulder. And then, I told him where exactly he could go—" Lark hiccupped. "And he slapped me. So, I hit him."

The only surprise Azrael let show was a slow blink. After a moment, staring at her examine her bloody knuckles then wiping them off on her pants, he laughed. She was so unlike everything he'd thought when he first saw her. He laughed so hard his ribs ached, doubling over once Lark began laughing too.

The noise from inside the tavern grew louder, as though some patrons were coming outside. Azrael took her hand again and pulled her along, lest she get insulted again and want to instigate another brawl.

The street was empty and dark now, save for the few lantern posts giving umber light. Below them, the ocean was quiet but persistent as waves lapped against the shoreline. Azrael turned to gaze as the ocean one last time before they followed the street back up and the view became obscured. The two moons now high above, their bright light glittering on the water to create a stark contrast as the horizon was eaten by the black of a sky with no stars. Why weren't there any stars?

"I'm glad we did this," Lark said as she grabbed onto Azrael's arm, pulling his thoughts back to beside her. "I'm glad we were able to stay. I'm glad you're not dead too. I was worried about that."

He snorted. "Thanks, I like not being dead too."

They stumbled in silence then, arm in arm, towards Bedivere's manor. The main street was quiet now too, the late hour took the night owls into the cool embrace of the darkness.

The pair hadn't been quiet as they entered the house. Floorboards creaked beneath their feet as they stumbled, dragging their steps in hopes of being a little quieter. Silence was overpowering and cause for laughter once again.

Azrael was glad Lark now led him—all the doors looked the same, and he hadn't paid much attention when they had left. Lark shouldered the door open, her small grunt was loud in the silence when the latch stuck.

In each step Azrael took inside the room, one boot came off, then the other, then his belt and sword. Lark tried to copy his movement and take her shoes off the same way, only to trip and smack her hand on the wall. She giggled then, a sweet sound that had heat rising in Azrael's blood.

He fell face first onto his bed, savoring the softness he had first mistaken for stiffness when he had woken here. Now, it felt like paradise.

"Azrael—" Lark settled onto the floor beside her cot, legs crossed and hair a dark curtain around her. Candles on the table lit suddenly with a bright white flame that flickered to vibrant orange.

He crawled to the foot of the bed, propping his head on his hands. He thought of asking about the flame, but kept silent, unable to tell if she had fallen asleep or simply wanted to bait his attention. Shadows danced on her eyelashes, hiding the freckles on her cheeks.

"Thank you," she said before sleep tried to take him. His eyes opened again, unaware he had closed them. He squinted at her.

"For what?" His voice was rough, as though he hadn't spoken for a while. Maybe he had fallen asleep.

"For being you."

He moved to lean on his elbows then. A ghost of a smile was on her lips, but she rubbed her eye, catching a tear that glistened in the candlelight before it fell too far.

"What does that mean?"

Lark inhaled through her nose before she sniffled. Azrael slipped off the bed and sat on the floor across from her.

"You're not afraid of me—you don't think I'm strange. For what I can do."

"You *are* strange, mage."

An airy laugh. "You know what I mean. Whenever someone learns about my magic, it's predictable. They can be terrified, or weary, most of the time they're angry. But not you. You haven't treated me poorly because of it."

Azrael bit the side of his cheek, thinking hard through the fog of mead. "It wouldn't be right, if I did. Magic healed me, gave me my old life back. Shit, it made it even better. I don't think I could be angry at it, or you, for that reason."

"I was angry with *you* for that," she said quietly, her eyes avoiding him.

"For being part of the Tiras? Or for being healed?"

"I couldn't figure out why you were healed. I thought that it would make you a rival, especially if you somehow kept a sliver of that magic. I was set on avoiding you, until I found my answer." Lark flexed her fingers, cracked her knuckles, focused on her hands to keep from meeting Azrael's dark eyes.

"What answer did you find?" His voice was rough once more, throat feeling like it was filled with dirt. He inched closer to her.

"That it didn't make you different. That you weren't someone I had to hate. That you're someone I can't stay away from."

Only then did she meet his stare. Without breaking it, he reached for her hand.

"Show me." This woman had healed his broken nose, slowed a demon to save his life, and lit the candles in the room. He wondered how much she could do.

She turned her palm over slowly, hesitantly. Her chest rose with a deep breath before it was lit by a soft white light. His eyes gradually left hers to stare at a small white flame sitting in the palm of her hand.

Azrael gasped softly and raised her hand closer to his face. The flame floated above her skin, not scorching it. He cupped her hand, her skin so warm—not just from the flame. The very edge of the white was a shining gold, so unlike regular fire. It was breathtaking. She was the first person in a thousand years to wield magic, and he was able to witness it like this. He glanced up at her, a soft smile on his face that fell once he saw tears glistening on her cheeks. He let go of her hand and scooted back. The flame guttered and disappeared.

"Why are you crying?" Her tears cracked something in his chest.

"I've never shown someone my magic like this before." She wiped her cheeks with the backs of her hands.

"How can you do it?" Azrael asked after a moment, after she took a few more deep breaths to ease the lines between her brows.

"My father—"

Her father had been the ghost she had faced at the seer's shop earlier. He didn't want her to be buried beneath that pain again.

"It's okay. You don't have to tell me." He shouldn't have asked. A lone tear skidded down her face, and she exhaled harshly, annoyed by the display of emotion. She raised her hand again to wipe it away, but Azrael moved faster. With his thumb, he gently caught it.

He was sinking further and further, too fast to stop himself. He might as well be stuck in the fabled quicksand of Telaan. Accidentally stepping in, until it swallowed him piece by piece. Only now, he accepted his fate. He couldn't keep away. He didn't want to. There was no stopping the swelling in his chest that threatened to break his ribs when he caught her smiling at him, or the whiff of lavender and sea salt, or the storm of her eyes.

He was sinking deeply.

Sighing, he stretched out on the floor, suddenly feeling so heavy. Sleep wrapped him in a warm embrace as his head hit the wood, hardly aware of how Lark curled up at his side.

# CHAPTER 22

## AZRAEL

Bedivere was an older man, about the same age as Melech, with the darkest skin Azrael had seen. Taller than Azrael, he was twice as muscled and wore a white cotton shirt and russet pants. He kept his long hair tied in a knot on the top of his head, and kept his beard trimmed closely to his cheek. Azrael had seen the briefest of glimpses of the lord when he met with the king, but Azrael hadn't been prepared for the full power the lord held.

"Demon Slayer," Bedivere said slowly, savoring the words on his tongue. His mouth curved into a smile, sharp canines peeking out between his teeth.

"It's still strange to hear." Azrael laughed awkwardly. He and Lark stood before the lord in his study, the room perfectly encapsulating a lord with books, ferns, worn chairs, and a wall completely made of glass with an unobstructed view of the back of the manor.

Bedivere gestured to the two chairs on his left before he settled into the one behind him.

"It's still strange to know that your king commands them." Bedivere took a steaming mug from the table beside his chair and lifted it to his mouth. The aroma of coffee filled the air, completing the energy within the study. "But that's beside the point. I am in your debt, Azrael Hikaim, and I will not forget what you've done for me."

Beside him, Lark turned into a statue, her wide eyes stuck to the cup of tea in her hands. Azrael didn't understand what the lord meant regarding Melech, but he let it go, tucking the comment away.

"Of course, my lord. Somehow, it seems I'm the only one who has an effect on them. I'd be a coward to not do anything."

A servant offered Azrael a cup and quietly asked if he preferred coffee or tea. He accepted the first.

"My people will remember you for this for a very long time." Bedivere lifted a finger to call the servant back. She carried a platter of fruit and set it on the table between Bedivere and Lark. "When do you leave?"

"After breakfast," Azrael answered. He scooted his foot closer to Lark's and nudged her boot. She was still lost within her head.

"There's no rush," Bedivere said before he turned to Lark, "Darling, are you alright?"

Something in her snapped then and she looked to the lord. A warm smile spread across her face, but not reaching her eyes, before she nodded.

"Yes, my lord, thank you." She lifted her cup and took a sip, white kissing her knuckles.

"You two have shown kindness in my city, where your fellow Tiras have not. You are both welcome in the Roe whenever you wish. I'd be more than happy to have you here with me. And not just because of the gifts you both have," he added with a knowing smile.

Lark coughed, choking on her tea, but covered it with a gentle laugh. Bedivere looked away and outside to the golden sun still rising in the cerulean sky. Far away, the ocean glimmered in sunlight. Azrael would miss this sight, but he was ready to go back to his mountainous home—his house set beside two trees and a palace that had been chiseled into the mountain side.

†

A fter a quiet breakfast of bread with honey, cheese, fruit, and sausage, Bedivere walked Azrael and Lark to the stables, his dark hands slipped into the pockets of his linen pants. It was strange to think that Melech had thought this man was enough of a threat to ride across the kingdom to deal with him personally. Azrael wondered what lurked beneath the lord's calm demeanor. Lark and the lord spoke beside Azrael about upgrading the infirmary, but he let them drone on as he took in the grounds. The Roe was much more beautiful than he remembered from his last visit, and he couldn't shake the feeling of home, of being welcomed, as though the land itself were grateful for what he'd done for the people by killing the demons. Bedivere had told him over breakfast that no one died—every single person in the infirmary had asked for his name, had instructed for the things that had filled his room to be sent to him.

"I had bags packed for both of you, food and furs and such, as a partial thank you. May the path be clear and the ride smooth." Bedivere smiled at the two stable hands that led their horses from their stalls. "Two fresh horses for you."

"Thank you," Lark said quietly as she petted her chosen horse's nose.

"I hope I'll see you both again," Bedivere said as he held his hand out. Azrael grasped his arm, and he his, and their dark eyes met. Whatever it was that called to Azrael was also in his eyes. Releasing the lord's arm, Azrael nodded before he leapt gracefully onto his horse.

Bedivere kissed Lark's hand, leaned in to whisper in her ear. He smiled at each of them once more before strolling towards his manor. Lark climbed onto her horse, tilted her braided head towards the street, and led the way through the Roe.

Neither had said anything about the night before, about the emotions laid bare between them. Unspoken feelings, thoughts buried deep. He had woken first, on the hard wood floor, a blanket half draped over him, with Lark's leg over his, her head resting on his forearm uncomfortably. He had waited until she woke, shortly after, to wriggle out from beneath her and neither could look the other in the eyes. The room had been silent as they each bathed and readied their bags and parted for Bedivere's study.

Their horses carried them swiftly across the fields, flying through the small town, racing the golden sun. Leaving the events of the past few days behind them.

†

Once the second moon was above them, full and bright, they finally stopped. Both were silent, but an unspoken desire to ride as quickly as they could had them both in agreement. Between only the two of them, they could move faster, move without catching prying eyes or preening gossips, and find more convenient places to sleep.

For their first night, Lark found a spot tucked against massive boulders and a thicket of tall grass. By the time they had dismounted and set a makeshift camp, it was pointless for a fire, even though the night was cool.

Azrael stretched out on his back and gazed up at the night sky. His body was already feeling sore, his hips and lower back aching, but the sight of trees on the horizon, as small as they were, fueled his desire to be home. He hadn't thought that he'd feel that way, as he moved from place to place since he was a child, always moving with the army or changing towns in anticipation of being needed. He never minded being constantly on the move, but for once, he was content to settle back into his routine, his life.

As he snacked on berries, he craned his neck to glance at Lark, to see if she was asleep yet. With the moonlight, he could make out the outline of her face turned to the sky, her eyelashes moving with slow, tired blinks.

He wanted to talk to her, to hear her voice, but he found he hadn't the slightest idea what to say to her now. He wasn't funny, he couldn't joke, and he had no idea how to get inside her head. Popping another berry into his mouth, he listened to the lullaby of the Roe sing him gently into sleep.

†

The ride from the Roe to the Vale was two weeks, if one stopped when the first moon was up and left as the sun rose. They stopped well after the second moon had risen and left at dawn and took short breaks, if only for the horses to have a reprieve. The days bled together: in silence, find an obscure spot to camp, no fire, lay close to each other, eat breakfast and dinner on the road.

They were within five days of Vale City when they approached an inn. Lark shot him a look that said he had no choice before turning into it.

The sun cast a golden hue along the horizon, much earlier than they had stopped before, but Azrael didn't mind. He smelled of sweat, horse, and sweaty horse, and thought only of a bath. They stabled their mounts and walked stiffly into the inn.

An older woman sat behind the bar, talking to three rough looking men, while the only occupied table held a group of wealthy looking merchants laughing and smoking. The merchants paid them no attention, but the men standing at the bar turned as the door closed. Azrael tensed as he noted the change in their faces as they took in his apparel, the red band around his wrists displaying his rank as Tiras like a target. He silently cursed it as the men's hands twitched at their sides. The woman behind the bar sidled to the side, out of Azrael's view.

He ignored the hostile glares of the men and moved to a table away from them, Lark hesitantly following. Her fingers were twitching at her side too, but not towards a weapon.

A girl with one arm stopped at their table, a soft smile on her face.

"What can I get you—"

"Bronagh," one of the gruff men interjected, moving to her side. His red hair was darkened with what looked to be mud, scars crossing on his face like a drunk merchant leaving wheel tracks in dirt. "We don't serve them here."

"Why—" The girl began again, but the man cut her off.

"Don't you know the red bands?" The man tapped his wrist and jerked his chin at Azrael. "This is one of the king's toy soldiers. And this one? Oh wait."

The man laughed, from deep within his extended belly, as he took in Lark. "The king's men are not welcome here, least of all his whore."

The girl backed away as the other two men moved to the first one's side, knuckles cracking as they reached for their weapons.

The words settled like stones.

More slurs fell from the man's mouth, but Azrael heard nothing beyond the last one. The world eddied around him, falling to a pinpoint. The redhaired man reached for Lark, and Azrael erupted.

He lunged from his seat, fist connecting with the redhaired man's jaw before his filthy hands touched her neck. Azrael briefly registered the emotion burning in her eyes but didn't let it settle in his head. His sword at his hip clinked against his chair, but there was too much satisfaction in his knuckles that he ignored the weight.

It happened faster than he had expected.

The first man reeled from Azrael's punch, stumbling into an empty table feet away, and struggled to grab onto something before he fell completely on the ground.

Azrael expected the next swing, though not with a tankard full of ale, and blocked it, only to dump a portion on his arm and chest. A quick jerk of his hand broke the man's elbow and had him howling like an alley cat, skittering away.

The third stared at Azrael for a moment too long, before Lark's arm barred his chest. The touch stilled him, bringing him out of the red haze that clouded his vision. He stepped back, his eyes narrowing but never leaving the last man.

An older man, the innkeeper by the apron around his waist, walked into the room and chortled as he took in the scene. He flicked his hand to the third man, shooing him from the room, and helped the other two to their feet before shooing them as well. Both snarled at Azrael and spit at Lark's feet before walking out the door.

"An impressive display of conduct. Bronagh, bring two ales and plates of roast for the king's soldiers," he boomed across the room to the girl hovering at the end of the bar. She nodded and disappeared into the kitchen.

"I apologize for this unwelcoming behavior, it's not something I tolerate within my inn. Do you two require a room?" The man, despite his size and grey hair, spoke kindly to Azrael and gestured for him to take his seat again.

Azrael breathed, focused on each inhale and exhale, before he settled back into his chair across from Lark. The merchants kept up their laughing and clinking of glasses and smoking behind them as though nothing at all had happened.

Lark looked as though she would say no, but Azrael cut in. "Yes."

"Of course. My girl will take care of that." The inn keep bowed his head, angled towards Lark, before he moved to the merchant's table.

"Why." Lark gritted from beneath her teeth, her jaw was tight as though to hold in the emotion. Azrael leaned back in his chair, feigning nonchalance even if it was the furthest thing he felt.

Azrael didn't answer, biting the side of his cheek to keep back a retort. He wouldn't explain himself, nor should he have to. He shouldn't have taken such offense in the first place, but he ignored that line of thinking. For all the silence that stretched between them, he'd done too much thinking lately and it seemed to be getting him into deeper trouble.

He was saved from a response when the serving girl brought over a tray with two bowls, two glasses, and a key all neatly balanced. She arranged their table, sliding a bowl in front of each of them, ignoring the palpable tension, and pointed at the key.

"Room three. It has a bathing room attached to it." Her voice started out confidently, but withered as she caught Azrael's eyes, her words quiet as though he might take offense. His cheeks heated before he looked away quickly.

"Thank you," Lark said softly. "I appreciate you."

After she had left them, Azrael and Lark dug into their roast, and Azrael drank the ale quickly, appreciating the warmth spreading in his chest.

"I am," Azrael started, only to pause. He took another sip, stabbed at another piece of meat. He wondered how his bowl managed to not leak, despite the crack in it. "I am sorry, Lark."

Her hand froze as she lifted her glass to her lips, eyes boring into him as though she could see every thought churning in his head. She nodded, accepting his apology, and he was grateful that was that.

They finished eating quickly, both declining a second glass and second serving. Azrael followed Lark up the stairs, watching her fingers twitch at her sides instead of the way her hips shifted with each step.

Lark unlocked the door, a loud creak echoing as the wood groaned, and laughed.

"Oh, it's mine." She scurried into the room, dropping her bag, and flopped onto the only bed. Azrael chewed on his lip as the door swung and clicked closed behind him. His bag thudded on the floor.

"Fair enough, then I'm taking the first bath."

The room was small, and the bathing room even smaller, but the wooden tub was all Azrael could ask for.

"But—"

"It's big enough, you can join me," Azrael said over his shoulder as he tugged his boots off. Warm water already filled the tub, candlelight flickering on the surface.

Lark laughed awkwardly, and the sound made his hips ache more than they already did. A thin curtain was in place of a door to the second room, and Azrael carelessly flung it closed before he undressed.

He bathed quickly, and dressed faster, despite having the small reprieve from her presence. Part of him wanted to take his time, move his thoughts away from her for once, but the other part thought of her on the bed, and he cursed having only a curtain between the two rooms.

Azrael rubbed at his face, his eyes tired, as he strode from the bathing room. Lark smiled sheepishly at him before slipping in and yanking the curtain closed.

With the utmost focus, he smoothed out his bedroll on the floor beside the door. He took one of the folded blankets at the foot of the bed and wrapped himself up before lowering onto the ground. His entire body ached, every bone in his body screeched in protest as he stretched out.

Lark hummed quietly, her voice soft as a whisper as she began to sing, the water splashing louder as her hand dropped. He didn't recognize the song, until he realized it was in Areenian. He hadn't thought she knew another language, and realized then he hardly knew anything about her.

He let her voice carry him into a gentle sleep, until the sound of her feet scuffing against the floor had him opening his eyes again. A flash of bare feet, long wet hair, blankets fluffing. The bed creaked. A small grunt.

"Azrael."

A pillow hit him square in the face.

"Azrael," she hissed.

"What," he breathed, not wanting to surface from the edge of sleep.

"*Azrael*," she hissed again.

"*What.*"

"If you promise not to be weird about it, it's big enough to share."

"What?" So much for sleeping.

"Come to bed."

He fully opened his eyes then. She had snuffed out the candles, but his eyes adjusted. She sat up in bed, tucked in the corner. A white flame sprouted in her hand to light her face.

"I'm fine."

The flame dissolved.

"Fine," she snipped. "You can sleep on the floor if you really want to."

The bed creaked again as she shifted. Every instinct was roaring at him to get his sorry ass up and climb into bed with her, but his pride stopped him. He took a deep breath and closed his eyes again.

"Do—do you really want to?"

There was a vulnerability in her voice that made him push himself off the floor. He hadn't heard her like that before. He picked his blanket off the floor and crawled into bed beside her. She scooted over to give him more room as he melted into the soft touch of fresh sheets.

"Spoon me, or *poke* me, and I'm kicking you out. Good night." The vulnerability was gone, a small hint of a laugh in its place.

He stretched out, one arm beneath the pillow and one knee bent, and fell asleep to Lark's soft touches on his exposed bicep.

## LARK

Soft morning light drifted in from space between the door and the floor, alongside the wall. Gentle gold light that held the small dust motes as they floated through the air. Muffled clinks, obscured voices drifted through the floor to their room, stirring Lark's dreams. She had dreamt so sweetly, so peacefully, and woke without anything disturbing her, for once.

Azrael's arm was stretched across her stomach, twitching slightly as he continued to dream. Lark thought for a moment of sending her shadows in, wondering what she would see, but cut the thought down like a weed. That was unacceptable. A talent she never wanted to share; the shadows could pull secrets from the dark places between thoughts. And this—whatever *this* was—she did not want to ruin. Azrael scrunched his nose in her peripheral vision before burying his face further into his pillow. He looked so much younger when he slept, the years of bloodshed and anger evaporating. It was so different than when Melech slept, even in dreams he held onto his pain as though holding onto it with an iron grip could heal his wounds. Lark lifted a finger and, with a touch light as a feather, moved back a loose curl that had fallen across Azrael's brow.

She knew this would never last. In fact, she knew that this would end very badly, with shattered hearts and worse if the king found out, but she couldn't bring herself to stop. Her heart had become a rockslide, and she had told him the truth that night in Bedivere's house. She simply couldn't stay away from him. She was drawn to him, as a moth to flame, even if it would bring her destruction. Pressure built beneath her eyes as she studied the man beside her, his sharp features, his crooked nose she caused, the shadow of facial hair along his angled jaw. The impulsive, short tempered, brave man that had come to mean so much to her in the short time she'd known him.

He stirred, his eyes fluttering as he rose from sleep. As he took in their tangled positions, his hand momentarily grasped her side before he retracted it, his eyes darker than they had been a moment before, the rich brown giving way to the black. He shifted, moving his leg and hips away from her. Her words echoed in her head from last night, about him spooning or poking her, and blush colored her cheeks and chest as she realized he'd been doing both and she hadn't given it a second thought. It had felt so natural intertwined with him, she hadn't remembered she taunted him so.

He didn't move away as fast as she thought he would. It almost seemed as though he had been reluctant to move his arm from her stomach, his fingertips dragging across the folds of her shirt. He rolled over onto his back, folding his hands beneath his head. Bending a knee, the blanket shifted, no longer defining...

Lark closed her eyes, rubbing the corners and pinching the bridge of her nose. That should be the least of her concerns.

"Good morning," she said, a rasp in her throat she promptly cleared before sitting up. Stretching her arms out to touch her toes beneath the blanket, she arched her back and groaned. Sleeping on the ground the past few days had done anything but wonders for her body. She appreciated the softness of the bed, how it hugged her form. As refreshing as it was to be away from the palace, it wasn't worth leaving her own bed.

"Morning," Azrael groaned as he followed suit and stretched. He sat up and leaned against the headboard. "Breakfast?"

Lark nodded, the words difficult to voice when she glanced over her shoulder at him. For a brief moment, she let herself wonder what it would be like if she wasn't already spoken for. How the night would have turned out, how this moment would go.

He swung his legs off the bed, effectively keeping his waist twisted away from her. Her head emptied as she took in the expanse of his shoulders, not quite remembering if he had gone to bed without a shirt, or if he had taken it off during the night. Lark did remember how thin he had been when she first saw him, how much of a ghost he resembled. Now, he had filled out, his skin darker with defined muscles.

"I'll be back," he said as he shrugged on a shirt, then stepped into his boots. A crooked grin warmed his face before he slipped out the door.

Breakfast was taken quietly on the floor of their room. Lark leaned against the bed, across from Azrael who leaned against the opposite wall. Their feet pressed against each other, somehow feeling more intimate than sleeping in the same bed. Spoken words were quiet and secretive glances took place in the silence between. Lark had braided her hair and wrapped it at the base of her neck, reluctantly. The constant wind whipping her loose hair put her in a foul mood all too quickly. She ensured her braids were tight while Azrael had procured their food, giving her hands and mind something to focus on instead of the days they still had left.

F ive days turned into three, then three began a long day and night. Autumn shrouded Vale City in a brilliant array of gold, red, brown, and fading green. The morning was bright in the early sunshine when they finally passed through the city gates and thundered against the cobblestone streets. The palace sparkled from its position over the city, beckoning them home.

# CHAPTER 23

## LARK

Between Melech's frustrating conversation and the quiet, incessant hum of the darkness between the two moons, Lark's mind had begun to melt minutes into their dinner. At least the king had let her sleep through the day before reminding her of what day it was, but a part of her wondered if she would have been more pleasant if she hadn't slept. Being rested, she was in no mood to put up with his shit. Night had settled in while she was tucked away in her gilded cage. She was glad she had chosen a dress—no red cuff at her wrist, nothing to indicate that she belonged to the king, in one way or another. With fistfuls of her skirt to keep her hands from fidgeting, she strode through the palace, down the front steps, and through the gates before her head began to clear. Lark built the stone wall in her head and kept Iah's voice out. No kings, no gods, no thoughts tonight.

With an impulsive thought, she changed her course to the eastern side of the city, her eyes searching each sign hanging in the firelit air for a tavern. The one she did find was perfect, even if her dress would be too much compared to the other patrons. She would have fit in more on the western side, but she no longer felt like walking that far.

Yelling, singing, and laughter burst from the door as she opened it. Perhaps no one would think twice about her here, not with the raucous din constantly tearing one's attention in different ways. Lark squeezed her way past the rowdy men jeering, clanking their tankards together and splashing beer, and past women with their dresses stained and hitched, breasts nearly popping out of their corsets as they danced to musicians Lark didn't immediately see. She thought of the tavern she had visited with Azrael, but cast him from her mind just as quickly as he had popped in. Lark leaned her elbows on the sticky bar counter beside a man face down in his mug. A barmaid passed him by without a second glance, but Lark kicked his stool.

This was the perfectly opposite place for a princess. The perfect place for a distraction. To let go of the king, the god, the plans she had created, the threat on her life that she couldn't forget about.

She ordered the strongest drink the barmaid offered, thankful for the coin purse she had sewn into most of her dresses, and settled onto the stool beside the still sleeping man. With a breath, Lark lifted the tankard to her mouth and drank deeply.

She hadn't noticed how much time had passed when she saw—

Ahmi? What was Ahmi doing here?

Melech? No, he can't—she thought she saw...

Wait, was that Azrael? Oh gods.

Lark stood, fingers trembling around the glass, and tried not to move in the same direction the room did as it spun. Where had that barmaid gone? The glass in her hands was empty. At least the tavern had cleared out, enough to freely walk between the tables and stools without being jostled by elbows and feet. She tried walking in one direction, back towards the counter, but she stepped directly into a broad chest. A deep voice rumbled, but she couldn't make sense of the words. They placed a heavy hand on her shoulder, their thumb under her chin forcing her to look up. Instead, she focused on their hand, sending pinpricks of shadows into their palm. They stepped back, cursing and hissing, only for another hand to grasp Lark's. Dark brown eyes appeared in front of her.

"Lark."

*Lark,* the voice said—not Freckles, not Birdie. Lark. Her name.

"Lech?" she asked anyway, the candlelight casting too many shadows.

*"Lark,"* the voice said again. A slightly crooked nose, loose curls falling on temples came into focus. *Oh.*

"Azrael," she murmured, warmth spreading from her cheeks to her core. The room continued to spin, and she couldn't keep up.

"Walk with me." He interlaced their fingers. Lark's heart thundered so loudly she wondered if he could hear it.

Azrael led them outside, the autumn air a chilled slap in the face. The city was an explosion of orange from the lanterns, the black sky holding no indication of time. Did Melech know she was here? How did Azrael know to find her here? He guided her, hands still tightly together, and a small part of her wanted to yell at him—yell at him and tell him she was fine and did not need his help, but he wasn't Melech. He was helping her because he cared. Right?

Lark stumbled alongside him, her toes catching each other in her slippers, before she stopped him, yanking her fingers from his, and sat on the edge of the river they had walked alongside. She hadn't noticed, hadn't heard its bubbling.

"What are you doing?" Azrael asked, his gaze dropping to her feet. Of course she had chosen the slippers that had the ribbon tied into a knot around her calves. Drunk fingers couldn't handle the silk ribbon quite like sober fingers.

Heat flooded Lark again as Azrael knelt beside her, lithe fingers untying the ribbon. White hot fire surged through her as one hand cupped her calf while his other hand eased her foot out. His touch made her drunk, drunker than whatever she had bought. She wondered what it would feel like if his hands were higher, the dizzying idea burrowed into her chest as he moved to her other foot.

Behind him, the orange of the lanterns blurred together, and Lark wanted to reach her now bare feet into the water, but it was too far down. Autumnal rains hadn't raised the water level yet.

"Are you okay?" Azrael's voice brought her back, centering her. She opened her eyes, unsure when she had closed them. Lark smiled and nodded, making herself dizzy once more with the simple movement.

"I'm fine," she said. She stood, the cobblestones cold against her feet, and reached for the shadows deep within her bones and willed them to steady her.

"I mean," he started, then paused. "I mean, are you okay? Ahmi said he's never seen you like this."

"Like what?" Lark cackled.

"You'll have to ask him, but I'm guessing like *this*." He waved a hand around her face.

"Everything is fine. I'm fine." She hadn't meant for it to come out as curtly as it did, but Azrael wasn't affected by her tone.

Silence fell between them, settling into that comfortability they had. The city—*her* city—was spinning around her, both hers for the taking and not. She felt like a stranger in it, her own crown tucked away and hidden. Melech and her father made it that way when she had been so young, the future of the kingdom and no one knew about her. Frustration boiled in her blood and shadows flickered at the edge of her vision. Her dinner with Melech had reminded her, once again and so painfully, how he had continued to ruin her even after her father's death.

How had she come so far from who she was supposed to be? How had she grown more comfortable out in the city, amongst her people, than inside her palace?

She let Azrael take her hand again and lead her along the river, listening to its soft whisper.

†

AZRAEL

Azrael hadn't expected to find such a sad drunk when Ahmi brought him along to look for her. There was such sadness buried beneath her drunken stupor. Despite their time together, he had seen small glimpses of her melancholy, but nothing like this. There was no hiding it in her eyes.

"Az?" her voice slurred from shadows. He was surprised to hardly be able to see her, so wrapped up in herself that her magic wound itself around her. "Are you happy?"

"This moment, or in general?"

"Both."

"Yes, and mostly."

Azrael took the shortest route he could to minimize extra eyes on them. They were nearly to the bridge outside the palace walls, the one he preferred to take his runs past, when her grip tightened on his hand.

"Lark?"

She mumbled a reply before her head collided with his arm. Wind buffeted around them, a salty chill carried from the ocean, as he held her upright. He swung his free arm beneath her knees and scooped her up like a child. He quickened his pace and kept to the shadows all the way to the healer's house.

Hadriana wasn't in the house when he fumbled with the door. Lark had been awake enough to produce a key for him, but mumbled incoherently as he carried her in.

He set her gently on one of the beds. He tried untangling himself from her, but she wound her fingers in his hair and tried pulling him against her. "Stay with me. The night is so young."

Her lips trailed along his jawline, and he lingered for a moment too long before a layer of guilt enveloped him. He pulled her hands away. She fell back against her pillow, the soft light from a candle she had lit flickered on her furrowed brows.

"You were so keen earlier," Lark said as she fumbled to take her dress off.

"Earlier?" Azrael asked as he set her shoes beneath her bed and pulled the blanket off the other bed.

"You play with me enough, stop. I can still feel your hands on my thigh beneath the table. Hadri says you're ruining me for my future husband, but I tell her it'll be you anyway, that you can't stand to see me with anyone else. Even looking at Azrael makes you mad." Lark groaned. He froze, unsure what she was talking about, *who* she was talking about. Who did she think was here with her, if not him? "Gods, then I shouldn't tell you who I saw tonight."

"Lark," Azrael said, softly but sternly. "Get some sleep."

"Yeah, yeah, good night." She burrowed beneath the blanket. He listened to her heavy breathing a few moments before turning to leave.

Just as his fingers grasped the handle, he heard softly, "He makes me feel alive."

# CHAPTER 24

## AZRAEL

The black of Azrael's clothing was a little too hot, the sun stinging the back of his neck as he walked behind Ahmi. He tried not to glare at Ahmi's head, but the warm autumn weather felt like it was Ahmi's fault. If not the weather, then this excursion. The wooden rod attached to the bag on Azrael's back made him feel like a horse or a pack mule, and when it whacked the back of his calf, the heat boiled his irritation to fury.

"Do you truly enjoy this heat?" Azrael gritted out. Dust from the road drifted up his nose, but he breathed carefully through the building frustration.

"I told you not to wear that," Ahmi said without turning, without faltering, and with amusement in his voice.

Azrael scowled at him and adjusted the bag on his back. He only had the black pants of the Tiras and a loose, thin shirt—still black—with long sleeves. He had thought it would help combat the heat, but he was sorely mistaken and slowly sweltering under the fabric.

"And Thea told you not to wear that too, so don't be grouchy at me for it."

A stifled laugh was in Ahmi's voice and, even though Azrael wanted to laugh too, he settled for another scowl at the wind fluttering in his friend's hair. Ahmi walked as though he had done this trek a thousand times, thumbs hooked on the straps of his back, and a surety in his steps that showed he didn't have to look at his feet. Still, they walked along the main road that stretched from the Vale to the Roe and were an hour outside of the city. And still on the road.

"Where is this lake?" Azrael asked. The only thing that kept him going was the promise of blue water, deep enough to submerge himself in whenever they reached it.

"You've become too accustomed to palace life, my friend," Ahmi said, this time glancing over his shoulder with a smile full of mischief. Azrael crinkled his nose back at him, nothing close to the sneer he had intended. "I forget that you didn't have this growing up. My older brother took me as often as he could. Nothing beats open water fishing, but this spot I found is secluded and no one else ever goes there."

"I think I'd count it as a blessing I didn't have it," Azrael muttered, not entirely a truth, but not quite a lie either. Back when his father was alive, the two of them had gone on as many trips as they could together, before the threat of war called his father away and eventually took his life. They'd done as much as they could, Azrael soaking up every moment as though some small part of him knew, even back then, that it wouldn't last.

Despite the late, lingering heat, he couldn't deny the beauty of the Vale, enduring even as autumn threatened to change the coloring of the landscape. It still held onto the vibrant green, grass half his height still blew in the nearly stagnant breeze between the towering trees. He thought of how the trees in Areen must be, if even these were tall to him—trees large enough to build palaces within and beneath. Birds fluttered around, their constant singing a companion as the pair veered off the road and onto an invisible, rocky path leading up the mountains.

"Where is your brother now?" Azrael asked as he forcefully kicked a rock out of his way. Its collision into another rock was a small but satisfying feeling. Ahmi adjusted their direction and hauled himself up a boulder before answering. Azrael scrambled up after him.

"After my father died, he disappeared to Telaan with some relatives. He inherited the family farm but left everything to my sister. He resented everything that my father had done and worked for. He writes home every now and again, but I haven't heard anything from him since the day he left."

"Is that why you're here?"

"Andir was... He was jealous that I was able to leave—that our father didn't care about me enough to force me to stay. I came here to escape him, but Andir never saw it that way. I wanted something more. I wanted to make something for myself."

And here Ahmi was, a talented swordsman close to the king, a father and a husband. Despite Azrael's rank and title, his home, his place in the world, he felt like he was missing something. He still wasn't who he wanted to be. Ever the wanderer.

Azrael didn't reply as they climbed over another boulder and noted small markings they walked on the indiscreet path. Ahmi must have placed them, stacks of pebbles, branches placed in symbols, to remind him of the way. Once they were nearly level with the trees, the air cooled enough that his irritation was gone.

"Have you taken Isabel fishing?"

Ahmi stopped on a flat rock, chest heaving, and glanced back at Azrael with hands on his hips. It mirrored the exact way Isabel had stood that morning when Azrael had told her that she wasn't going with them. Only when he caved and said he'd bring her back a fish did she clamber up his legs for him to hold her. The child had taken quite a liking to Azrael, and he to her.

"Thea and I brought her here once last summer, and she didn't care for it. She stuck her hands in the water and tried catching fish that way, but she got bored quickly."

"I can't image you two bringing a child on this path." Azrael laughed. He glanced back at the way they had come—how steep the path had grown, how it disappeared almost entirely.

Ahmi laughed, rubbing his temple as the memory no doubt played again in his head. "Yeah, it was not fun. Especially since she refused to be carried for half of the trek."

"I wonder where she gets her stubbornness."

"I'd like to blame her current independence on you."

"But she's always been like that, hasn't she?" Azrael couldn't keep the laugh out of his voice. Ahmi's lack of ownership said enough about stubbornness.

"I have no idea what you mean." Ahmi winked before he turned and continued climbing.

Boulders grew sparse as they walked on, the mountain less rocky. Some rocks gave way to small alcoves and reprieves with grass and brush. The path Ahmi followed levelled out and narrowed to the point where Azrael's steps were one foot directly in front of the other. He kept his left hand grazing the rocks as they passed. He couldn't imagine having a small child on his, either holding her or having her walking in front of him. Ahmi moved with grace, while Azrael tried to mimic it unsuccessfully. A small tree grew out of the path in front of them, thin trunk and bright leaves, and the shade it cast was little, but still a break from the searing morning sun.

His hair was stuck to the back of his neck, plastered to his temples. He hadn't realized that when Ahmi said there was a small hike involved, he didn't think it would involve as much climbing. His side was beginning to feel as though a seam was coming loose, a stitch threatening to spill his insides. Part of his pride wanted to blame his legs for his out-of-shapeness, but he knew that it wasn't true.

Azrael paused beside the small tree, placing his hand on it as he peered over the edge it leaned over. Ahmi paused, turning around at the precise moment the tree ripped from the earth.

Roots, frail but tangled, caught Azrael's feet. His other hand stretched out towards the smooth rock wall. The image of the sheer drop flashed before his eyes, the long way down he'd fall before he'd land, but a brown hand flashed, and fingers dug into his wrist. His arm was yanked with enough force to wrench it from its socket, but the pain didn't register, only the fear pooling in his bones.

Ahmi shoved him against the rock wall with the momentum. Azrael heard the tree crack, splinter, and echo along the mountainside. The bright blue sky stretched out above Azrael, clouds stilling in the air. Chest heaving, he fought to catch his breath and focus his eyes. He'd never minded heights, but he was weary that he had discovered a new fear.

Azrael shifted his shoulder, thankful it wasn't out of its socket, the moment amplifying the feeling.

Shaky breaths slipped out of both men. Azrael looked at his friend who had his hands on his knees, bent over.

Azrael had to laugh, an unhinged, godawful sound ripping out of him. He kept his back firmly against the warm stone. It took a moment, but Ahmi echoed his laugh and finally released Azrael's wrist.

"Shit," Azrael said between breaths of laughter.

"Isabel walked better than you," Ahmi said, the fear and adrenaline slowly ebbing from his face.

"Shit," Azrael repeated once more.

"Don't make me carry you the way back."

"Shut up," he mumbled, throwing his friend a grateful glance. "Let's keep going."

<br>

                                                              †

<br>

T he lake was something out of a picture book. Rocks surrounded the body of water, encasing them in a paradise. The water was so blue, so gentle, that it could have been the sky. Grass surrounded the water with copses of trees for shade. Even the wind was gentle here, rustling the greenery and trailing across the surface of the sapphire water. The scene was so peaceful that Azrael could lay down and never get up. Ahmi left him at the lip of the surrounding wall, climbing over it with grace, and strode down towards the water. The air carried scents of flowers, but Azrael didn't see any amongst the green.

"How did you find this?"

Ahmi turned as he shrugged his bag off his shoulders and untied his pole from the straps. He grinned in response and jerked his head toward the water, Azrael realizing it was a silent gesture meant for him to move his ass. Azrael swung over the rock and trailed down a small hill, each step singing of the perfection of this paradise.

"When I first joined the King's Army, I was shit. I was used to farm labor, not military precision and dedication. For my training and exercise, I studied maps where rebels had camped, and I stayed away from them as I explored. Granted I did what you did a thousand times and almost died. I pushed my body until I eased into my new life."

"You found this on luck?"

"Some." Ahmi shrugged. "I went through a lot of maps and journals of the first explorers. This wasn't marked, but smaller ponds were. I knew what to look for."

"Ahmi the Adventurer," Azrael mused as he slung his bag off his back. He tried ignoring the slickness of his shirt sliding against his skin, tugged by his bag.

"Azrael the Dumbass."

"Can't disagree with you there."

Azrael shucked off his shirt and eased off his boots. "Is anything in there going to eat me?"

"Shouldn't."

"Comforting."

Azrael sprinted towards the water, eyeing the depths, and leapt in before he was able to talk himself out of it. He hardly could ever pass up and opportunity to swim.

Despite the warmth of the autumn air, the water was cold and sent a jolt through his body. He slowly drifted back to the surface, then lazily swam back towards Ahmi. He had rolled his pants up to his knees and sat with his bare feet submerged in the water. With the fishing pole between his knees, Azrael watched as Ahmi attached something to the tip of it.

Azrael hauled himself out and shook himself like a dog to splash his friend before he put on his limp shirt. At least it felt better. Azrael grabbed his pole and sat beside Ahmi.

"So, what do I do?"

"You've never used a fishing pole before?" Ahmi turned his head, face caught between surprise and doubt. A flush of embarrassment before he swallowed the feeling. Azrael shook his head.

"I've set nets, but I've never fished like this before."

"That doesn't surprise me." Ahmi shrugged. "You're not the type."

"And what type am I?" Azrael said as he moved his pole to mirror Ahmi's, feeding the thin line along the wood. Ahmi nudged two small containers closer to Azrael, one full of organized metal hooks and the other with writhing worms.

"The type to set traps because you weren't taught to properly hunt either." Ahmi's words weren't harsh or judgmental. "You've said your parents died when you were young, and if you grew up in the same army I was in, then I know you never had time to learn."

"Hm," Azrael mused. His friend wasn't wrong, or unkind in his words. A soft assessment, a knowing and understanding in his voice.

Ahmi eyed the hook in Azrael's fingers as he feebly tried to attach it to the line. Azrael noticed the stare and offered it to him.

"You never told me how you managed to get into the army at such a young age. I thought fifteen for troubled youth was harsh, I can't imagine the trouble you got into if you went in before that."

Azrael pierced a worm with the hook before he flung it into the water, just as Ahmi had done. It didn't go further than three feet in front of him, but he didn't bother to try casting it again.

"I didn't adjust well when I was dumped in the city. I was stuck in an orphanage and their school, but I didn't take anything seriously. After three years, I was wasted potential."

The memories were faded, as though he were trying to recall a dream from days ago, instead of something that he had lived through. Ahmi's pole bobbed, and he reeled it in. Azrael watched as his friend unhooked the fish's mouth before tossing it back into the water.

"The headmistress practically begged anyone to take me, to teach me a trade so I would be out of her hair. A retired soldier happened to cross us on a field trip and offered to stick me into the program for kids old enough to know they wanted to be in the army, but too young to join. The headmistress was more than happy to pass me off, and I took to it like a bird to flying."

Azrael's pole bobbed, too, then, and before he could reel it in, the fish let go and the pole was still again.

"And the rest is history?"

"The rest is history," Azrael echoed.

"I'm surprised it took Melech this long to find you."

Azrael cast a pointed look at his friend, but his pole jerked before he was able to reply. His hands froze.

"Hold that—no, hold *that,* and wind it. No, Az." He laughed. "Faster than that. The fish is going to wriggle free if you go too slow. There's no fun in that."

The line dragged through the water, closer and closer, until it was right in front of them. Ahmi yelled for him to yank the pole. Obeying, Azrael pulled up a writhing fish—no bigger than his palm. Ahmi laughed and reached forward to grab it. He slid a finger into its tiny mouth and dug out the hook before handing it to Azrael.

"Are we keeping it?" As small as it was, pride radiated Azrael's chest.

"That wouldn't even feed Isabel."

"It would!"

"No, we're not keeping that, Az. Let the poor thing go." Ahmi's smile was small, proud. The men laughed as Azrael dropped the fish back into the water.

"Give me that hook," Azrael said as he plucked a new worm from the container.

The sun faded, leaving them in a purple twilight that rendered their descent nearly impossible. Azrael built a fire while Ahmi gutted the fish he had caught—two twice the size of those Azrael had hooked—and prepared them with a bag of seasoning he dug through his bag for. A chill settled around them, finally feeling like autumn again, but the fire helped to chase it away. They ate, drank Roen liquor Ahmi had brought, and traded stories until the pit they had dug glowed with embers. Azrael fell asleep to the sound of owls hooting far in the distance.

# CHAPTER 25

## AZRAEL

Autumn returned in full force. Bleak gray ocean water crashed like sheets of ice colliding, the sound of breaking bone reverberating too loudly through the quiet kingdom. Azrael flinched each time the cracking echoed, reminding him too much of his own bones shattering. He cursed himself for continuing to walk with Ahmi this way. Sometimes, he was able to bury that pain, that horror and trauma that gave him this new life, but sometimes, it was inescapable. He continued flex his toes in his boots, bending his knee a little more than needed. He walked with focus in each step. Even after all the time that had passed, he still half expected whatever magic—whether it was a curse, spell, or miracle—to wear off and each day that he could still walk took by surprise. The bite of the northern wind hardly affected his bones.

Whispers gathered in the wind with the approaching equinox, stories of ghosts and debts unsettled and secrets buried, and it seemed to set the city on a knife point. A few Tiras had been dispatched to a protest in the mountain town of Einder, some had even been sent to Westwick in place of the king to help rebuild the town, but the remainder of the group was dispersed between the city and the palace. Melech's eyes and ears, Azrael felt more of a conspicuous spy rather than a soldier, but he didn't entirely mind it. He and Ahmi were usually able to perform their duties together, cementing the bond between them.

"There's going to be another war," Ahmi said to the wind as he paused their walk. Azrael moved to his side and looked out to the bleak ocean. "Have you heard the way civilians are talking? I don't like it."

"The rebels have no foothold." Azrael had heard the fervent whispers when he went to the markets, not in uniform. People purchasing in bulk, choosing foods that would last for some time, lingering for a little bit longer before saying goodbye.

"The Roe is just the start." Ahmi's voice was low, as though the wind would carry it if it were louder.

"The Moor has no interest in being its own kingdom." Azrael's birthplace was a tiny island, too dependent on the continent for survival. "Havriel wouldn't last another civil war."

"My point."

Azrael turned away from the ocean and towards the city—with its white walls and stone buildings and proud people. It was the oldest and largest in Havriel and had fought through blood and bone for its position and power, neither of which would be given up easily. The Roe couldn't stand a chance against the Vale.

"The rebels have taken the Falls again and set it as their base. It's growing, and Melech isn't earning loyalty with the strict laws he's passing. The Tiras within the city isn't helping either, Maddox and Caed were caught in an alley with women." Ahmi sighed. The swordsman and spearman, respectively, had been sequestered to their homes after the incident had spread, but he hadn't heard if there had been consequences. It didn't sit right in his stomach.

"The monsters attacks on top of everything, too." Ahmi sighed and turned to face the city too. "You're gaining popularity though, as if you didn't have enough already. What are they calling you?"

"Demon Slayer," Azrael murmured, still not comfortable with the attention he drew. Some of it was kind, some of it was apprehensive, and some was downright suspicious. "They're Daeoan, but same difference."

"What?"

"That's what Melech said they were." Azrael shrugged. One of these days he intended to find the palace library and search through folklore for answers. He just needed to make time for it.

"How does he know what they are?" Unease crept into Ahmi's voice. He crossed his arms.

Azrael shrugged again. Whether they were monsters or demons or lost spirits, it didn't change the fact that they were here, in his world, inciting chaos, killing, and destroying the kingdom.

"Strange how they only recently showed up. I don't like it." Ahmi turned to keep walking and Azrael followed, their boots scuffing the stone. "War is coming, Azrael."

†

R ain fell day after day, the sun struggled to make an appearance between the heavy black clouds, and turned the palace grounds into a swamp. Azrael knew that, far below, in the eastern side of the city, the roads had flooded as well. He used to play in those puddles after training and school, taking the long way home so he could wade through the small rivers running over the cobblestone. From the palace, the city itself was veiled by sheets of rain and he couldn't see anything past the courtyard from his place on the second floor of the palace. On his day off, he found he detested being home by himself and the silence after his indoor workouts haunted him. He trekked through the rain into the palace and wandered there. He'd always loved the rain, so he kept to the open courtyards and balconies, but avoided the staff and guards he passed. He may love the rain, but the dark weather brought out the worst in people.

He had spotted Magdalene in one of the courtyards, drenched fabric in her arms, and a soft ache bloomed in his chest. He missed their late-night talks and having her presence in his house to warm it, but he simply missed having *someone,* he didn't miss *her*—and he didn't know if that made him awful.

In his exploration, he passed a dark doorway, the black space beyond rippling and calling to him. It took Azrael a few foolish steps into the thick darkness to realize that it was a staircase leading down. With the black nearly tangible, a curtain in front of his eyes, he descended carefully and slowly. For a few moments, he thought he ended up somewhere he shouldn't have been, but he continued once he saw the faintest hint of an orange light flickering at the bottom, far below his feet.

A pair of doors, one partially open to let out that firelight, met him at the bottom of the stairs. He didn't know what to expect from this hidden, secret room, but it certainly wasn't a hidden library. He pushed the cracked door open further. He had seen the library, in the east wing of the second floor, with massive windows overlooking the Tiras courtyard and everything beyond it, and shelves taller than he was, but this—this felt personal. The ceiling was low enough that Azrael could lift his arm up and rest his palm against it. The walls were filled with bookcases, some wrapping around in a pattern he couldn't discern.

As he took a few tentative steps in, he noticed a rustic desk with a crude chandelier hanging over it, illuminating an old man hunched over a stack of papers. Azrael half expected the man to jump up and yell at him to leave, but he continued walking in and the man paid him no attention. The first shelf he came to had titles about the Five Princes—the forgotten godlike figures before Nekoda and his father had altered Havriel's religion—and some were about the other kingdoms. He ran his finger along the spines, noting more titles as he walked along the wall. Hardly any books about Nekoda, only some elegies, hardly any about the Greater. Azrael repressed a sigh.

"Are you looking for anything in particular, boy, or have you just come to disrupt my studies?" The old man finally lifted his head, his voice like gravel as though he hadn't spoken in a very long time.

"What is this place?"

"My study. I gave you an answer, now answer me, son." The man's pen hit the table with an exasperated exhale.

"Did Nekoda keep journals? Or is there an accurate representation of his life?" Azrael stopped in front of a title about a deep-sea eel.

The old man laughed, more of a scoff than anything. He twisted in his chair towards Azrael, eyebrows raised. Noting the seriousness on the boy's face, the old man's amused look dissipated into something wicked.

"He did, but I would not part with those for anyone, lest of all you, even with your rank and title. Those on the shelf behind you are some about his life, but I refuse to account for their accuracy for you. Was that all?"

By the tone of his voice, it was all, and Azrael simply blinked at the man before he twisted back to the papers in front of him. He supposed he would be bitter as well, sequestered alone in a secret library with no windows and too much darkness for company. Azrael shifted as to not cast a shadow on the spines as he scoured for something that might hold an answer. He wasn't sure what answer he wanted first, but a deep feeling in his soul told him he needed to ask a single right question and he could receive all his answers.

With careful fingers, he eased a cracked spine out from the shelf, *The Vale and its King*, when a small book clattered to his feet. A slight hum reverberated in the air when Azrael glanced down at it, bringing him back to being beneath the river's surface. That same peace, that same silence, buzzed around the leather-bound book. Azrael replaced the thick book and reached for the smaller one.

"Can I take this?" he asked before he opened it.

"Just bring it back," the old man mumbled, not bothering to turn to see what Azrael held.

A thin leather string was wrapped around it, stiff as though it hadn't been opened for a long time. He carefully undid it and leafed through the pages—drawings of the Daeoan, precious stones, flowers, both moons, birds, and paragraphs beneath each illustration. The latter half of the book was illegible scribbles with two portraits, one of a small girl and the other of an even younger boy. *Siena* and *Kieran* were scrawled under each, respectively, and were the most legible scrawls in the book. Journal, perhaps, was the better term for what he held in slightly shaking hands. He glanced over at the old man, who still did not care for Azrael's presence.

He stuffed the journal into the pocket inside his jacket before slipping back into the shadows and making his ascent.

The trip back up to the light of the palace felt longer than the descent, but as soon as he felt the grey light, he pulled the journal from his jacket and pried it open. The very first page was titled *The Last Years*, with the initials H.A. below it. He wandered through the palace on muscle memory alone, his eyes stuck on the paper. Was it in a different language?

No, it was in *three*.

School had taught him the basic words in sloping Areenian and stacked Telaanan. The few words he was able to recognize made no sense, even with Havrien mixed in. Being unable to read it didn't stop him from trying as he scoured line after line. If it was structured this way, and hidden, he had to know what was captured on the faded yellow pages.

Fog rested in the Tiras courtyard, at last a break from the rain. Still, Azrael closed the book and held it against his chest as he stepped out from beneath the overhang and down the steps. He carefully avoided the slippery stones, the roots of the tree, and the upturned stones near the roots. He fished his key from his pocket before he reached his door. As soon as he opened it, he noticed Lark in his peripherals, striding towards him in her Tiras uniform. He paused at his threshold.

"Hi," she said brightly, a stark contrast to the black clouds above and the grey ones floating around them. Her gaze dropped to his chest, where he still cradled the journal. "What's that?"

"I found a second library, I guess. I don't know what it is, but it looks interesting." Azrael shrugged. "Maybe it'll distract me from the gloom."

She stepped closer to him and leaned against the house, so casual, so heart-breakingly easy, until she noticed what he held. She straightened with wide eyes.

"Can I see that?" She held out shaking fingers, and he placed the journal in her palm. "What have you read?"

"Nothing yet, it's in three languages. I'm not bright enough to translate quickly."

Lark glanced around the foggy courtyard before slipping into his house, her back tense and braid swinging between her shoulder blades. He stepped in after her and shut the door. She lit the fireplace with her white light, flames flickering for a moment with the ivory before changing to orange. Lark stood in front of the fireplace and tossed the book onto the sofa before Azrael sat down on it.

"That should not have been anywhere that someone could find it." She stared pointedly at it, as though she had half a mind to incinerate it.

"What do you know about it?" Azrael looked at it like it was cursed. He settled into the corner of the sofa, one arm draped across the back and the other bent on the arm.

"If I could tell anyone about that book, it would be you. They would have my tongue." Lark bit her lip. "Quite literally," she added after a moment with a breathy laugh.

A seed of doubt sprouted in his head. He didn't like how that sounded, didn't like the look on her face. He wanted to reach out to her, to touch her hand, to do anything to get that haunted look out of her eyes.

"Do you know who H.A. is?" Azrael picked up the journal and left it open to the title page.

Lark reluctantly nodded, her throat bobbing with an anxious swallow.

"And the two other names? Siena and Kieran?"

Lark moved around the table that separated them and dropped onto the sofa beside him, curling her legs up underneath her.

"Kieran," she murmured, "I haven't heard that name in a very long time."

"And the other?" Azrael felt like he was drawing the answers from her, pulling out a string that kept growing without reaching the end. He ground his teeth.

"Siena." Lark sighed and toyed with the end of her braid. "That's, ah. That's a long story."

Irritation built in his chest. This girl he cared for, thought about more than what was good for him, left him in the dark. Refused to give him answers. His eyes flickered between her hands and her mouth, lip tucked between her teeth.

"What will I find in here?" He held the book up and she flinched. Lowering it, guilt reddened the tips of his ears, though he didn't do anything. After the ghost she had seen in the Roe with the seer, he wondered if he would find something like that in the journal. Secrets of her universe she couldn't—or wouldn't—voice. Secrets he wondered if he was truly entitled to.

She met his eyes then, silver lining her lower lashes. "Life. My life."

"This is your journal?" he asked incredulously.

Lark shook her head, furrowed her brows. "Can I try something with you? It's not...it's hard to explain. Do you trust me?"

The question was layered, impossibly so, but Azrael shifted, sitting straighter and moved slightly closer.

"Yes," he breathed, finding himself caught in the storm of her eyes—grey stones beneath an ocean wave.

Lark took his hand then, weaving their fingers together. Her hand was small and cool against his, her nails pressing into the back of his hand.

"I trust you. You cannot breathe a word," she whispered. Azrael nodded, his heartbeat loud in his ears.

A flash, a memory. Something that didn't belong to him flowered in the forefront of his mind, in between his own thoughts. Blurry, but cold, whatever it was.

King Nekoda and Queen Isolde, next to a fireplace, a young woman with dark hair beside the queen.

Azrael pulled away from her, eyes wide as he stared at her. Gooseflesh pricked his arms, unrelated to the chill outside. He swallowed.

"What was that?"

"Do you trust me?" Lark repeated. The question was still heavy, burdened with pain and loneliness. Even if he didn't, he nodded his head all the same.

Another image flashed: Nekoda holding a child's hand at the top of a mountain overlooking the city.

The next one was painful, but he didn't know how: Isolde's perfect face with tears running down her cheeks, sorrow in her blue eyes.

After that, the next one had a voice: "Magic demands balance, a give and take", with a small girl with wide grey eyes in a mirror.

Lark's hand squeezed his for another flash: complete, utter black with a child's crying.

The forest. Precious stones. A fox and flowers. A songbird singing in the leaves, landing on small fingers.

Then Azrael opened his eyes, unaware of when he had closed them. He searched her eyes, her face, for anything to tell him that wasn't what he thought it was. How could she have done that? Shown him those things?

"How." It didn't come out as a question, but it was quiet, tentative, when he didn't mean it to be. He wanted to demand an answer from her, but he couldn't. He couldn't summon anger, or anything beyond the haze swarming his thoughts.

She had shown him a jagged history. The seer in the Roe had known who she was—the princess, daughter of Nekoda and Isolde. The princess who had been given up by her father, handed over to the unknown, to be raised outside of the palace and forgotten by the people.

"My magic has two sides—the light and the dark. The shadows are easier to manipulate. It's hard to explain." Her mouth twitched to the side, and she looked anywhere but at him. Her hands were shaking, her pulse racketing in her wrist.

"The king?" Azrael almost didn't want to ask. After bringing her home from the tavern and listening to her drunken words, he didn't want to hear about the king.

"He knows." Lark inhaling slowly, shakily. "I've been at his side for a very long time now."

"Not just as healer," Azrael said quietly, a small understanding unfolding within him. He rubbed the back of his neck. The fire was suddenly hot, the room too dark, the thunder rumbling above them too loud.

"Not just as a healer," Lark repeated, each word punctuated quietly.

"Why?" he whispered. Sorrow radiated off her, from the set of her mouth to the curve of her arms as she had them crossed, shielding her chest.

Her mouth opened, closed, her brows furrowed, before she answered. "Because I have to. Because I have no choice."

"And what if you did have a choice?"

"I'd choose you."

Azrael's head emptied of every thought, every moment, that he had before. There was only her, only Lark, sitting before him, her mist damp braid on her opposite shoulder to bare the skin on her neck. There was only Lark, sitting tentatively on his sofa as though unsure she should be there with him. There was only Lark.

And they were still holding hands.

He unlaced their fingers, not trusting himself with how his thoughts had turned. He wouldn't put her in a situation like that. He pulled his hand back, but Lark caught his fingers. She blinked, then blinked again. Her other hand lifted to the side of his face, her thumb running over his cheekbone.

"I'd choose you," she whispered before she leaned in.

Her lips on his was everything he'd dreamt. Sea salt, tea, herbs. Her fingers were gentle on his face, neck, and in his hair, while her lips were slow, searching. She moved closer without breaking the kiss, one knee between his legs. His hands grasped her waist, thumbs lifting up the front of her shirt, and roamed, feeling her cool, soft skin beneath his calloused hands.

Lark pulled away, lips slightly swollen in flickering firelight, and breathed heavily. Her head shook in the smallest way before she moved to the other side of the sofa. Azrael ground his teeth and shifted his legs, hiding the evidence of the effect she had on him. He somehow felt responsible for her hesitation, for her impulse to kiss him, and heat warmed his cheeks.

Lark stood on coltish legs and pinched the bridge of her nose, squeezing her eyes shut. She muttered what might have been an apology before she strode for the door. Azrael watched the fire consume the logs, waiting for the door to click shut, but the sound never came.

"Fuck," he heard instead. Then the clattering of boots on the floor, soft pattering of feet hurrying towards him.

Lark was on him again, fervently this time. Her mouth devoured his as she straddled him, her hips settling in his lap with miniscule motions. He wrapped his arms around her, holding her tightly against him, one hand reached up to brace the back of her neck while the other traveled lower to her waist. His tongue danced along her lip, then overtook her mouth with an intense need to taste her. With the hand that was on her neck, he inched it to her braid and untied the string that kept it bound. As it cascaded down her back, he leaned forward, pulling her hard against his waist. He felt her small breasts against his chest, and grasped her right one, his fingers grazing her ribcage.

She reached down, first palming him, his desire hard and yearning for her, then pulled his shirt off, tossing it to the side. Her mouth moved from his to his throat, his collarbone, his chest, her tongue leaving gooseflesh everywhere it touched. His breathing quickened the lower her mouth moved while her hands returned to his pants, untying the string and yanking them down just enough to free him.

Azrael caught her by the chin with his thumb and forefinger before she moved too far. Her eyes met his and he heaved a great sigh as he took in the desire raging in a grey storm. He scooped her smoothly in his arms and moved to his room. She didn't stop kissing him, fingers weaving in his hair, until he set her on the bed.

He'd dreamt of this moment all night when they shared the bed at the inn, over and over, all the different ways he would take her.

With a grace he hardly possessed, he pulled her shirt over her head, her dark hair falling on her bare chest. As he took in the smooth planes of her stomach, the small buds of her breasts, he decided he would take a very, very long time with her. He climbed on top of her and followed the pattern she had kissed him, his tongue slow over the curve of her breast, while his hands slid her pants down her soft legs.

Above them, thunder raged, echoing in his heartbeat as he slowed his tongue, his lips. Rain pounded against the roof, pattered against the window. He moved his mouth slowly down her body, kissing each freckle and line of her body. With his hands, he held hers while his mouth explored, drawing quick, ragged breaths from her once the tip of his tongue found her tender and swollen. He breathed her in, tasting the stars as she peaked, and it sent him over the edge. He moved back to her trembling lips, kissing them gently, and wound one of his hands in her hair, the other waiting. Azrael pressed his nose against hers.

Lark nodded, her eyes locked with his. She inhaled sharply, her head craning into the bed as he slid in until their hips pressed tightly together. Azrael rolled his hips slowly, savoring each movement, and kissed her throat, the tip of his tongue brushing against the chills that enveloped her. Her hands were on his back, nails dragging up and down his shoulders with each motion, not gently, but the sharpness only increased Azrael's speed.

Just before he felt his own peak coming, Lark wrapped her thighs around him and deftly flipped them, burrowing Azrael into the bed. The firelight behind her a brilliant orange, casting her features in shadow, as she rode him. She arched her back, setting her hands on his shins and coaxing a gasp out of both of them. As she rolled her hips, he gently pumped his, burying himself deeper in her. His hands gripped her thighs tightly as he grew closer and—

Thunder drowned out his moan as he tipped over the edge, taking Lark with him as her body quaked over him, wave after wave of ecstasy washing over him. Lark bent forward, pressing herself against his chest, not withdrawing him from her. She breathed shakily onto his skin for a few moments before raising her gaze to his. There was such hunger in her eyes, a challenge that Azrael rose to meet. Without removing himself, he flipped them again, rolling across the bed, and kissed her again, unable to taste enough of her.

The fire dimmed as they devoured each other, body and soul, long after the storm outside quieted and night fell.

# CHAPTER 26

## AZRAEL

A peal of thunder pulled Azrael from dreamless sleep, a warm embrace of shadows that reluctantly brought him to his senses. His eyes struggled to focus on the darkened shape beside him, breathing quietly. He finally discerned the small slope of Lark's shoulders, the scent of lavender and sea salt faintly in the bed, amongst others that caused Azrael to make a mental note to wash his sheets. He was acutely aware of the soft fabric against his bare skin, the coolness of the bed beneath him. His only pillow was beneath Lark's head, so he bent his arm and nestled his head against the muscles of his bicep.

Dull grey light leaked in from the cracked bedroom door, slowly putting an end to the night he hadn't wanted to end. He didn't know how much sleep he had gotten, but between the ache in his body—the good kind—and the heaviness in his eyes, he knew he hadn't slept much at all.

Once his eyes adjusted and the grey illuminated his room enough, he reached over to Lark and carefully, with his middle finger, brushed a stray lock of hair off her face, pushing it onto her bare back. Her mouth was slightly agape, facing him, and it still did not feel real to him. It may as well have been a realistic dream, despite all that they had shared last night, and he wondered how often he would be able to dream this—or if this had been the only time he would experience her in this way.

"I can hear your heartbeat." Her words were whispered, muffled by the pillow, before flame popped in the fireplace and warmth spread into the room. Lark's eyes remained closed, but her hand inched towards him.

"I'd imagine so. You and my heart speak the same language," Azrael mumbled.

A tiny smile cracked her sleepy face, and she opened her eyes. With her smile, he hadn't expected to find sadness residing in her gaze before it turned serious.

"You cannot breathe a word," she murmured, repeating herself from the night before, her hand grasping his. She scooted closer, hooking her leg around his to draw him in. "It's a secret my mother fought to protect and one the king would sooner bury."

He knew she meant the magic she had shown him, the ability that had taken his breath away. He had nearly let it slip his thoughts, how her shadows had worked their way into his head, into the darkness of his mind to plant images and feelings. Unease settled back into his stomach as he thought of it. He didn't like the idea of another person inside his head.

Nonetheless, it was now Azrael's life hanging in the balance with hers. There was no going back, no bowing out gracefully, no keeping his head down any longer. If she was going down, he'd go down with her.

"I still don't understand how it works," he said quietly. He didn't understand how any of her magic worked in a land devoid of it, but his thoughts drifted to the journal on the floor in front of the fireplace, and hoped he would find something in it.

"Read the book," Lark said as though she had followed his line of thinking and it made him uneasy. His brows furrowed, but he said nothing. "Translate it. It's not ciphered, just hard to read and hidden where no one was supposed to find it. It explains more than I could."

"You said your mother?" Spoken with uncertainty, as if she might dodge the question.

"My adoptive mother, you might say. The Queen's favored lady-in-waiting. She raised me from the moment I came into this world. Isolde had been the one

to give me life, but Harlow has shown me what it means to live, and to be loved."
Lark smiled shyly. "Sorry, I didn't mean to get so—"

"I understand," Azrael offered. Lark's legs were still entwined with his, her knee shifting to gently rub against his thigh. He stiffened.

Her hand moved to cup the side of his face before she scooted closer, closing the distance between them. Her lips met his with softness, and he couldn't help but feel like it was a gentle ending.

Her hand slid down his neck, over the curve of his shoulders, down his waist. Fingers gripping the slope of his waist, she waited a moment for taking him in her hand. He groaned into her mouth, her tongue dancing along his as though to absorb the sound.

Before they could move further, a knock cut through the quiet of the morning like a bucket of ice water. Lark stiffened, her hand freezing in its motion. She didn't break their kiss, nor their contact, but her eyes flew open as what looked like fear gripped her. He thought about ignoring whoever stood at his door, especially once her hand continued to move, but the knock sounded again. They both groaned as Azrael withdrew, leaving the blanket to lazily fall in the empty space.

He swiped a pair of undershorts from his drawers and stepped into them, adjusting himself, before he opened the door.

A drenched servant stood before him, face unhappy as ever with a note in his outstretched hand. Azrael snatched it with narrowed eyes before shutting the door.

Before unfolding the damp parchment, he made sure the curtains were still closed. Lark sat up in his bed, blanket clenched in her fist to hide her naked form. His face heated as he took in the mussed hair, the pink in her own cheeks.

In the king's swooping handwriting, *My sitting room. Dusk.*

"He knows," Lark breathed, the color in her face draining. Her freckles were prominent against the paling.

"How? There was no one in the courtyard when you came in, no one saw you with me." He flicked the note into the fire before returning to bed. He crawled in, leaving his shorts on. "Breathe. Don't—"

"Do not presume to give me advice," Lark snapped, the coldness of fear no longer present in her eyes, only a smolder and a tightness in her jaw. "If he knows, I cannot save you."

"Who says I would need saving?" The arrogance in his voice didn't betray the unease he felt. Lark shook her head, slowly.

"The longer I stay—" She broke off as she scurried out from beneath the blanket. The sight of her naked form in the soft light would have aroused him again, if not for the urgency in every movement she made. The hunger for her withered away as he watched her collect the bits of her clothing and hurriedly put them on.

The very thing he had been fighting—the feelings he had buried deeply—was now the thing he was terrified of losing. Though he knew whatever it was that lay between them wasn't permanent, he didn't want to feel the coldness of her absence. He rubbed his face, chasing the tiredness and stress from the planes of his features.

Lark's voice was hardly above a whisper, "When the second moon rises, meet me outside the city. Follow the heather."

Azrael nodded, his eyes not leaving her once. She quickly braided her hair and bent to pick the journal from in front of the fireplace. With a flick of her wrist, she tossed it onto the foot of the bed.

"Try."

Azrael nodded. She peered out the window, the defined edges of her slowly starting to blur.

"Come open the door. Act as though you were admiring the rain."

He obeyed. Standing beside her, the entirety of her began to blur, as though he looked at her through the rain spattered glass. He opened the door, nodding to his fellow swordsman—Piers and Daerin—on their way to the soaked training field. Brows raised in a silent question, Azrael nodded. He'd be there shortly. As thoroughly as his body protested, he'd need to work out the tension and anxiety now burrowing within his muscles.

Lark had disappeared from his side, leaving only a phantom touch bristling his skin with gooseflesh, and he glanced around the courtyard, half expecting to see her materialize. He tried not giving *that* any thought, but he was once again stricken with a mix of unease and awe. Once he was sure she had gone, he closed the door with a finality he didn't enjoy and dressed for his workout.

T he training field was empty, save for Piers, Daerin, Jordie, and himself—only the swordsmen, or women, in Jordie's case. He thought it odd that it was only them but said nothing as he warmed up in the mist. They trained in pairs, working through drills and pushed each other until the rain drenched them. Azrael and Jordie continued until the sheets of rain veiled them from each other, turning the field into a swamp. He thought to keep going, to test himself, but Jordie's protest was drowned out in a peal of thunder and Azrael consented to walk back with her.

The journal tucked beneath his bed called to him anyway.

He bid her goodbye, not that the rain allowed to make it known, as they parted ways at the outer circle. He quickened his pace to his home, ready for a warm bath and dry clothes.

A zrael settled into his sofa in front of the crackling fire, stretching his legs out to rest on the low table, and unbound the leather string of the journal. After dressing in dry clothes, he had attempted to read the book, but found his memory poor in the other two languages. He had begrudgingly returned the large, normal library in the east wing of the palace to grab a book for each language to help him translate the journal.

Now, he sat with the two borrowed books beside him and the journal open and resting in his lap. A quick sliver of doubt pierced his head, telling him that his effort was wasted here, but he shove the thought to the side and cracked open the book for the Telaanan language, the stacking letters and words he had never been able keep straight.

Areenian was easier, as most of the Havrien language came from that kingdom, but it still took him an hour of refreshing his memory in that book.

He slowly began to work through the first few passages of the journal, a few were stories that didn't make sense, and some were observations made by Harlow on Lark as a child; how her magic was growing, expanding, how darkness would descend around their house. A name often appeared near those passages—Iah—but he couldn't find context as to who Iah was, what role they played in Lark's life.

The more he read, the easier it was on his eyes. The words began to shift so he understood them quicker and he worked through the afternoon on passages of their daily life, hoping to find some insight on *something* useful.

He passed a strange poem—at least he thought, or lines from another book, maybe:

*Whispers and starlight,*
*Moonlight dances*
*Shards of bone and stone*
*Darkness spells*

Again, there was no context for it. Azrael wondered if it was simply a piece Harlow had liked, even if it seemed unfinished. The last line had a scribble beside it, as though the next part had been forgotten. He moved onto the next page.

There was hardly any mention of Nekoda or the monsters he somehow brought to Havriel. He came across Melech's name many times, after he realized there was a different word in place of his name, but no mention of his role in Lark's life either. Though Lark had said the journal wasn't ciphered, it proved hard to read, alternate meanings in every sentence, missing context, and plain phrases that held no value—to him, or the passage.

Another story took a few pages, small illustrations drawn in the margins around it, captured his attention. It was about a massive wolf that lived in the mountains and had been followed by a vulture for years. The wolf had grown weak, and the vulture circled closer and closer until the great beast collapsed one night. The vulture landed, finally seeing its opportunity for the meal it had been watching, only to find the wolf resting, very weak but still alive. Impatience had worn down the vulture and it closed in on the wolf, pecking and pushing the wolf towards the edge of a cliff. The wolf tried to fight back, but the vulture was stronger and forced the wolf off the cliffside, onto the rocks below.

Azrael had been so engrossed in the stories, he had lost track of time. The fire in front of him had dwindled with the weak sunlight. Nearly dusk, he stood, his body cracking, and he tucked the journal back beneath his bed, in the bag he always kept lightly packed. Even with his time in his own home, he hadn't been able to break the habit of being able to leave at a moment's notice. He'd lived temporarily for too long to change his ways now.

He pulled on his coat, shoved his boots on, and slipped his belt and sword on before he stepped into the misty twilight.

†

The palace was eerily quiet as he made his way through. The only soul he encountered was the guard standing outside Melech's doors at the end of the mirrored hall. Wright, Azrael thought his name was, gave a smirk as Azrael approached. Wright knocked on the door, waited a moment for a muffled grunt, and opened the door for Azrael.

He kept the confusion he felt off his face as he walked into the king's rooms, his shoulders back and chin up.

Melech leaned against his desk, facing the doorway, with his palms pressed on the wood, fingers curled under the edge. He wore a loose black shirt, half unbuttoned, and black pants, as usual. There was something about the king that unsettled Azrael as their dark stares met. He stopped a few feet in front of the king and bowed.

"My king, you wished to see me?" Azrael spoke to the ground before he straightened.

"Azrael, the Greater has chosen you. You know this." His voice was rough, uncaring, as though their interaction didn't interest him in the slightest. "I sought you out for this. You have been gifted a miracle, a life you wouldn't have had. You can walk, while your fellow soldiers are lying in beds or in their graves."

Azrael reined in his flinch, the only thing he let show was a quick blink.

"I wanted you in the Tiras for your skill with a sword, but, not only that, but you were also handpicked by a god for something far bigger. You are a skilled soldier, yes, nothing to be trifled with." Melech pushed off his desk, so he stood at his full height before Azrael. "Neither am I, and neither is the Greater. We are Lesser men, Azrael. When you flirt with disaster, there is little to expect but disaster itself. Do we understand each other?"

Melech was a king, his presence demanded full attention and respect, but Azrael would be damned if his own did not match the king's. He rolled his shoulders, loosening the anxiety from his muscles. Melech smiled wickedly, his tongue running along the edge of his teeth.

"You don't mean to tell me you've fallen for her? From all the women in my palace, in my city, you find the one that can be your undoing."

"Magdalene is a kind girl," Azrael said smoothly. The king had known who held Azrael's attention, had seen so from the first moment he walked into the palace and she introduced herself. Never mind that they hadn't spoken in weeks, he wasn't going to admit that. He wanted the king to—wanted the king to admit who they were talking about.

Melech threw his head back and laughed, the sound echoing off the black walls. "That she is. I'm sure you've enjoyed your time together. She's taken up much of your time here, indeed."

"Have you called on me to discuss my private life, my king? Surely you wouldn't like to know all the details of our time together." Azrael smiled, equally as bright and wicked as the king's. This, right here, was him flirting with disaster.

"Of course not." Melech's smile had fallen slightly, his words sharply spoken. He took a step forward, the smell of mead and firewood wafting off him. "Do not challenge me. I will send you back to your healer in the mountains without a second thought. See how well she licks your wounds, compared to mine."

Each word the king spoke was aimed to cut, to slice into Azrael's skin and burrow. He took it all, accepting it.

"Understood, my king."

"You may leave," Melech said with a hiss underlying his tone. His black eyes were smoldering beneath his brows, his jaw clenched as though to keep from saying more. Azrael nodded.

Anger bubbled in his chest, but he kept his eyes on Melech as he took steps backward before turning his back on his king. He curled his fingers into fists until his bones cried out and he was well away from the king's rooms.

F og obscured the night and clouds still hid the sky. He returned to his home to grab a thicker coat, lined with fur, before he slipped back into the night. The second moon was still ways off from rising, but he would take the long way through the city to burn through the anger writhing in his chest.

Vale City after darkness fell was a sight to behold. The West lit up with lights, music, and parties with the occasional fireworks. The East was dark, only fools kept their lights on after dark, and the shouts, screams, and groans could be heard throughout the streets. It had been a long time since he spent nights in the east, chasing a feeling he could never hold onto for long enough. Azrael passed the shuttered shops and dark homes, and it brought back the faraway memories of buying liquor that tasted of fire and poison, starting fights in the streets, finding pretty girls and bringing them to the darkest parts of alleys—proving himself in any way he could.

Vale City, capital of Havriel—the city that held the future of the continent—built on money and power and on the backs of those who didn't have either.

Azrael passed through the city faster than he had intended, slipping over the creaking wood bridges, then through the city gates that were still open. He walked through the tents quietly, ignoring the loud invitations to drink, fuck, or partake.

Lark had told him to follow the heather and he cursed her lack of better directions until he cleared the temporary town and found the first shrub. He paused beside it, looking for another amongst the wispy fog. After he found the second, the rest were easy enough to follow. Clouds shifted enough to provide watery moonlight as he walked up a small hill leading to the mountain.

Between the two moons and their dim light, Azrael found his way to a small alcove overlooking the road below. The alcove was empty, Lark nowhere to be seen, and he tried to let that sit with him instead of making him uneasy. A small part of him was thrilled with this small adventure; he felt like a teenager again, sneaking out without anyone else knowing. He pulled his coat tighter around him and settled onto the lip of the alcove, his eyes slowly adjusting to the dark as they scanned the road below for Lark.

He didn't know how long it had been when Lark finally appeared at the first heather. He remained seated as he watched her ascend and finally appear in the alcove.

"Az," she breathed, a small laugh at the end to let him know he had scared her. He smiled and stood. She took a step towards him, as though to hug him, but she wrapped her arms around herself instead, pulling her own coat tighter.

"What did he say?" Her voice seemed as though she knew already, that previous fear creeping into her.

"He didn't say anything outright, but it was strange. He knows something."

Lark took a step back. Azrael wanted to close the distance between them but didn't. His feet stayed planted where they were.

She sighed and walked closer to him, stopping close enough that the clouds of their breath mingled.

"It would be so easy to love you," she whispered into the night. Her coat sleeve fell down her wrist as she lifted her hand to his face. He realized he had forgotten to shave again this morning as her hand rested against the start of a beard. "If only I could."

Though he knew it, that this couldn't go on, a small part of his heart withered. Since the first moment he had seen her, his soul needed to be near hers, even when he tried to fight that feeling. He didn't realize it until then, until she had shared her magic with him, shared her body and heart with him.

"This is the only way I can save you," she murmured. He wanted to retort that, again, he didn't need saving, but he stayed quiet. "We can't go on like this. I cannot let you get hurt because of me."

Lark was his undoing—the very thing that could incite the king to strip his title, his rank, his home, if he wished. Azrael shouldn't be hesitant to walk away. No one is worth that—no one is worth losing his sense of self. But, Lark. There was only Lark.

"And if I don't want to be saved?" He said it, but he hadn't meant to; a thought escaped, vocalized. He lifted his hand to wrap around the back of her neck, fingers burrowing into her braid. "If I let you ruin me?"

Their mouths were merely inches apart, his words settling on her lips.

"You've already ruined me, I suppose it's only fair," she breathed before pressing her lips to his. Her hands moved to his hair, his shoulders. She broke away for a moment. Her voice was shaky, quiet, when she spoke, "This is the last time."

Azrael grunted his agreement and kissed her again. With his hands on either side of her face, he walked her slowly backwards to press her against the cool wall. He grabbed her left thigh and hitched it against his, pushing his hips further into hers, detesting the space their clothing took up.

"The last time," he murmured against her skin. His free hand pulled her other thigh up while her arms wrapped around his neck. He pressed himself against her, achingly slowly rolling his hips.

Lark broke free from his grip on her legs and kicked off her boots, then yanked her pants down. She was instantly on him again, her mouth kissing his jaw and throat as she undid his pants and eased him into her, legs wrapped firmly around his waist.

†

In the darkness of their alcove, clouds of breath were quick, warm, accompanied by a sheen of sweat on both their brows. Outside, rain began to fall, muffling the sounds they made as hearts collided, and stalled their inevitable return to a life where both knew this could have never lasted.

# CHAPTER 27

## LARK

Two days. That was all it had been.

Lark had returned to her home with Harlow after she met Azrael in the mountain, tended to her patients in the city's infirmary, spent the afternoon penning letters to foreign lords, had an awkward dinner with Melech, and repeated it again the following day, save for the dinner. She had avoided thinking of Azrael, trying to keep the healer house's door closed in the mornings, she kept the curtains drawn, but Hadri hadn't listened to her protests so Lark had full view to Azrael as he trained with his men. She even had a flash of jealousy when the female swordsman—sword wielder—had clapped him on the shoulder, laughing with him, after a sparring match.

The jealousy hadn't lasted long, not when he met her eyes through the window, as if knowing she had been watching. They had sworn throughout that night that they wouldn't try to spend time alone again. Lark tried explaining her relationship with the king, but Azrael didn't want to hear it—understandably so. He'd then made her see stars with his tongue—

So it had been two days, then when dawn kissed the world on the third, she had dressed in her running attire and slipped into the crowd of Tiras. She ran beside Asen, chattering until the group split and she followed Azrael, giving her friend a poor excuse that earned her an eyeroll.

He had known she ran behind him and took a way they hadn't gone before. Running down the center of the city, through the heart of the art avenue, by the markets, and along the city wall. Once they curved and were fully on the eastern side of the city, he had slowed, stopped, and turned to catch her. He pressed her against that wall, kissed her until their hands were knotted in each other's hair, and slid in his fingers along the waistline of her leggings, hidden completely by her shadows.

And so the days bled into a week.

A week of a routine she fell into easily, though she was not proud of it when she lay in the king's bed, staring at the black and gold ceiling on his mountain of blankets.

The only thing that interrupted her strange but thrilling days was a letter. Set on her pillow and sealed with a dagger and a ring of heather, Lark's fingers shook when she reached for it, a sinking feeling in her stomach. The seal matched none of the lords or ladies she'd been writing to, and the earthy scent—of moss and rain—emanating from the parchment had her closing her door, bracing her spine as though the letter would hurt her.

Her name, written in four languages, on the flap once she broke the seal. Her royal name, not 'Lark'.

On the paper within, four lines. Four lines that rustled a far-gone memory:

*When moonlight dances,*
*There will be blood in the water.*
*Born a crown of bone and stone,*
*light shall touch the ends of the earth.*

Lark couldn't explain *how* she knew who had written the letter, but a shadow deep within her heart wound around her ribs, probing that hurt she hadn't visited in years. She yanked the paper from the envelope, letting each piece fall separately onto her bed.

*I'll see you soon.* Written below the flap, initially hidden by the letter itself. That sinking feeling went further, settling into her very bones.

*Birdie?* Iah's voice hummed in the back of her head, as though he had sensed her anxiety despite their distance, despite the wall she had thought she kept built.

"Is it him?" she asked aloud. She wanted to hear if the god of night knew, if he had kept this secret from her.

*If it was? What would it change?*

Lark narrowed her eyes at the invisible god's words, as though his response was an answer in itself. She turned her attention to the fallen letter, the wax seal. Unspooling that ivory from her chest, she warmed each tendril, focused on it, and singed the parchment, leaving only ashes and the faint smell of fire and earth.

If it was, it would change everything.

# CHAPTER 28

## AZRAEL

*A* *Daeoan on the eastern shore. Take care of it.*

The note was delivered after Azrael returned from his morning training with the other swordsmen. Eastern shore, a town small enough not to even have a name, as informed by a soldier named Basil who was also delivered after Azrael walked in his front door.

Basil was fresh from his training, longing to gain some experience, and Azrael wondered why he was on babysitting duty, especially if he was the only one capable of bringing the demons down. He tried not thinking about *why* the boy was instructed to go with Azrael, but, as they rode along the main road outside the city, his last private conversation with the king replayed in his head.

True, it'd been a week since he last saw Lark, at least alone—not counting their runs in the mornings and the alley fucks. They had both been careful, watching those who noticed them, staying far away from prying eyes, and Lark's magic shielded them. She never said it, but he had felt its pull, like a moth to a flame. None of the other Tiras had said anything when their runs lasted the longest, not when Azrael trained with a renewed sense of vitality that gave him an edge when he sparred.

Azrael led the young soldier off the main road and into the forest, breathing in the smell of fading leaves and ocean breeze. Once the coast was visible, they tied their horses with enough tether to let them wander and the two men set off down the cliffside.

As strange as their autumn was, it already seemed to fade into winter. The air around them was cold and heavy, humming in the buffeting wind. The light blue water expanded before them, churning with the start of ice formations floating in from the north. Before Havriel knew it, the sea around the northern point of the kingdom would turn into brittle ice sheets. As they descended, their path was slick with mud that had begun to crystalize in the cold. Azrael hoped that, if there was a demon below killing innocents, that he wouldn't be too late as he tried not dying on the way down.

"So, what is down there? He—the King—said you knew what you were doing and to trust you and to watch your back." Basil couldn't have been much older than seventeen, his voice still holding a cadence of youth. His first assignment from the king was to watch Azrael's back as they tracked a powerful demon from a spirit world; even if the boy hadn't been informed of the exact details, Azrael would imagine that would only increase his anxiety.

"Just stay out of the way, behind me, and you'll be fine," Azrael grumbled as he kept moving. He thought of how easily the demons had killed Nevan, trained as a Tiras, whereas this boy was fresh from training and would hardly stand a chance against them.

By the time the two reached the water line, they were both covered in freezing mud and shivering. The sun was just as cold as the air as they walked across the rocky beach to the town atop a boardwalk stretching over the waves. Azrael led the way up the steps to the creaking wood, Basil at his heels.

Calling this a town was generous, and perhaps that was why it didn't have a name on maps. Two rows of buildings on the boardwalk, seemingly divided into shops with signs creaking in the wind on one side while decorated homes sat on the other. Small boats were tied beneath and beside the massive posts the village sat on. All the windows and doors were shut as the two men strolled past. A heavy silence weighed in the air, almost muffled, save the constant lapping of waves below.

No reek, no crystals hanging in the air from the freezing cold the Daeoan brought, no signs of shadows skittering. Azrael wondered if the demon had passed, or if it had even been here.

Azrael paused, his feet shifting on the creaking wood. Faces peered out from behind window slats and curtains, eyeing the sword at his hip, the seriousness in his furrowed brows.

His name echoed then, not muffled by wooden walls or glass windows, but in the breath of a wave, the fading of foam on the rocks. He turned to Basil, but the voice hadn't sounded like his partner's. Basil's face was skittish, unsure. Azrael turned and continued down the walkway. He couldn't tell if he had imagined it, the three syllables lingering in the air like a forgotten spell.

*You are made for so much more.*

The voice again, awkward as though the waves themselves had learned the common tongue. Each word enunciated with a strange accent, followed by a near tangible hum pricking his skin.

"Did you hear that?" He turned to Basil once more, brows lowering further as his ears strained to hear anything else.

"Hear what?" Basil asked quietly with his white knuckled fingers gripping his sword.

Azrael shook his head, as though trying to get the echo of the words out. Further out to sea, the near colorless waves calmed and glimmered in the way moonlight glitters on still water. A small tug in the back of his head, like someone had tugged on the hair that curled on the back of his neck.

*Listen to the bird's song.*

He stopped entirely—walking, breathing, thinking.

Something felt familiar.

Turning to Basil, Azrael nodded and began walking back towards the beach.

"There's nothing here," he said to Basil, then louder to those hiding in their homes, "There is no threat here. You may come out."

The sounds of doors clicking open, hesitant footsteps on the wood, sounded behind Azrael, but he continued, Basil once again on his heels. He answered the boy's questions in a clipped way, not providing many details as the two scrambled back up the muddy slope.

"Azrael, wait—" Basil's protests were drowned by feet sliding in the mud, but Azrael pushed on, feeling only partially bad he had kicked mud into the boy's face.

Azrael pulled himself over the ledge at the crest and held his half-frozen hand out to help Basil over. Once both men were right side up again, they set off for their horses.

"Report in with Melech, I have business to see to," Azrael told the boy, spurring his horse on. Pounding hooves drowned out any reply Basil might have given him.

First, he went to the healer's house. Upon finding it empty, he went to the greenhouse she often clipped herbs, but didn't find her there. Even with his entire body buzzing from the rush of the afternoon, he decided against scouring the city for her, at least in his current state.

Azrael left his horse at the stable, handed over to a groom, and cut through the front courtyard instead of through the palace. He stomped through the second circle and slipped around the corner and in his door. And came face to face with Lark.

Leaning against the arm of the sofa, her grey gaze was trained on the door, then his face.

"What are you—Never mind, I'm glad you're here, because I have questions." Azrael closed and locked the door behind him.

With a grace he only seemed to possess when he was near her, he unhooked his belt and set his sword on the table. In several fluid motions, he undressed, leaving his cold and muddy clothes in a trail to his bedroom.

"No," Lark said as she pushed off the sofa and scuffed her boots on the floor. "Not here. Past the city, my mother has a cabin in the forest."

She strolled in with crossed arms, chin out with her lower lip between her teeth as her gazed track each muscled on his chest, noting the mud that was caked onto his hands and neck. He hadn't realized, in his anxiousness to get down the slope, nor in his determination to get back up it, how many times he'd flung mud at himself and slipped. Lark turned her attention to the tub filling with water, her eyes focused. Azrael noticed the twitch in her fingers once the room began to warm and steam curled from the water.

"Past the tents, it's southeast. There's a handful of cabins, but it's the furthest one. You'll know it when you see it. Meet me there when you're done." She smiled tentatively, but it didn't meet her eyes.

He nodded and climbed into his tub, the water nearly scalding against his cold skin. He inched slowly in as he listened to her boots against the stone, then the door clicking closed.

Azrael rested his head on the rim of the tub, closed his eyes, but a restlessness stirred in his bones. He remained in the hot bathwater for a few minutes before he huffed, stepped out and scurried across the floor, and pulled the journal from his bag. Fingering the leather string that kept it bound, he hesitated before climbing back into the water, holding the book over the edge, in case he dropped it.

He returned to the place he had left off, eyes straining to adjust to the multiple languages again. He was grateful he hadn't let his basic knowledge wither—reading it was one thing, he couldn't hold a conversation in either foreign language to barter, let alone speak fluently.

Page after page, he read about Lark's years, skipping over her first love interest who died suspiciously, Harlow wrote. There was another reiteration of the strange poem, the same words only rearranged differently, a mention of the child prince and his death, a ship bearing a name he couldn't translate, useless after useless entry. He felt foolish for hoping this would provide anything for him, beyond a sense of guilt for prying into Lark's personal history.

Then he caught something.

*Moonlight remains in the trees, however they come in the new moon. They sit with her in silence. Windchimes. His voice, even in the night, cuts deep, never ending.*

Harlow's strange sentences, pieces missing as though it meant more.

*Not what it seems.*

As an afterthought, almost, the line he nearly skipped past, until it tugged on the memory of the seer's shop and those words coming from her mouth. None of it made sense, and Azrael felt stuck in the middle of a puzzle he didn't have all the pieces to, unable to fit the jagged edges together of the ones he did have.

Nothing is what it seems, and he keeps learning that over and over. The demons that appear near him, near the Tiras. Demons that Lark also had an effect on—was she somehow tied to them? Jagged piece after jagged piece laid before him, expanding too far into the darkness.

†

For the second time in his new life, Azrael defied his king and snuck through the city. At least, he avoided drawing attention to himself, which he found easier than he had thought. There wasn't anything special about him unless he held a sword in his hand or displayed the red cuff around his wrists, and he tried not to find offense in the thought. He had hesitantly parted with his sword, swapping it for his daggers he had been practicing with during his early morning training, one in each boot and one on his thigh, glinting in the dying autumn light. He wore his jacket, grateful for the fur lining, instead of opting for the cloak he deemed too dramatic for his trek through the city.

A pull tugged him along the cobblestone streets, towards the city gates, into the twilight slowly falling, growing a deep purple. Stars twinkled to break up the dark, and the silvery light of the first moon streaked across the eastern sky. He trampled through overgrown weeds and shrubs until he found a small dirt path worn in-between and followed it. Passing one cabin, then another, he wondered if they were all abandoned—none so much had a flicker of light nor did the earth around the wooden buildings show signs of being tended to, until he walked up to one with bushes of sage nearly blocking the front door. The windows of this one were barred, as much as the others he had passed, but between the slats, faint orange light filtered out.

He stomped up the few wooden stairs, kicking the remaining mud and dirt from his boots, and knocked. Locks clicked, a chain rattled, before Lark's face appeared in the crack. Grey eyes peered beyond him, then yanked him by the wrist inside.

If the outside of the cabin looked nearing desolate, the inside was alive. A kitchen to his left with a small cooking pit beside it, a table with two chairs on his right. Beyond it, Azrael faced two sofas leaned against either wall to face one another with a thick rug stretched out between them. Across from him, a fireplace sat roaring with crackling wood and floating embers. A rickety staircase in the furthest corner, his gaze followed it up to the second floor, where he guessed the bedrooms resided. Enchanted by this piece of her life, he continued to stare as he shrugged off his coat and tossed it on the table beside him.

Lark held onto his wrist and slipped her fingers down to weave with his. With another gentle tug, she led him to the sofas and sunk into the corner of one after letting go of his hand. Something about her at ease, in her own environment, pulled at his tangled heartstrings.

His attention moved from her home to her, in an oversized light blue shirt, tucked into her usual black leggings. Her hair was loose, tumbling down her shoulders. Perfectly at ease, but her grey eyes were anything but. The eyes that reflected her father—he hadn't realized how much she looked like the late king with the same straight, freckled nose, and the same high cheekbones. The face he had seen countless times in portraits, in his history books. How many people had seen her and connected the dots?

"What happened today?" Lark brought her knees to her chest and set her chin on top.

"Melech sent me to the sea. Sightings of a Daeoan, but I didn't see anything that confirmed that. When I was near the water—I don't know what, but I heard a voice, and it felt like what you did." He wiggled his forefinger at her hands, recalling how her magic had felt mixed in with his own thoughts.

"It said to listen to the bird's song," he continued as he sat down beside her, letting the soft sofa embrace his tired body. Lark paled, freckles stark against the color draining from her face. "What does that mean to you?"

"More than you could know." Lark smiled sadly. "Though, I suppose I should tell you now."

Unease prickled along the back of his neck, anxiety pinching at his stomach.

"I showed you pieces, and I don't know how far you read in the journal, if it even covered it. I don't know even what Harlow wrote about," Lark rambled as she cracked her knuckles, bending her fingers so far back Azrael thought she'd snap them. "Anyway, my father bargained with me as a pawn, hoping to bring magic back to the world. I showed you a frozen moment of when he made that bargain, offered me."

Azrael shifted, pushing himself into the corner to stretch his legs out, unconsciously moving himself further from whatever truth would come from her mouth.

"Whether it's man, magic, or a god, a bargain requires payment, and that's what I was. My father brought magic back, but at a greater price he had thought. And he still wanted it." Lark's lips pursed for a moment. "It was given to me, though, not him. He hated me for it, thought it had been my fault. Our god, right above us for the last thousand years, and no one knew. Do you remember the Princes?"

The Five Princes, though he had never understood why they were called that—each representing an aspect of their world that changed depending on who you'd ask, but never a person, much less an actual prince. Azrael nodded.

"My father rid the world of their worship, the Greater sweeping over Havriel like a fever. My father thought, if we were somehow the ones to bring magic back, it would strengthen his throne and his kingdom."

A few moments of quiet settled between them, as though she didn't want to keep talking. Azrael didn't push her, silently observing each twitch in her left eye, each bend of her fingers.

"I was six when we stood on that balcony and he summoned Iah, who my father thought was the Greater." Lark looked anywhere but at Azrael.

"Iah?" Azrael interrupted, keeping his focus so he didn't lose a piece of her history. The name that had reappeared countless times in that journal, whose context was missing at every mention. He had been able to decipher they were important, but the why had stumped him.

"Our god, that's his name. He took me happily, giving me my magic, teaching me how to use it. My father used me in any way he could, anything he found my power could help with. Isolde killed herself, instead of stopping him. My father only got worse after she died. Harlow brought me here to raise me, but that's a long story. Longer." A wistful smile touched her lips.

"Melech knows. He always has. It's been years, and he still thinks he owns me and my gifts," she continued, voice momentarily devoid of emotion.

Azrael then moved closer to her, leaning against the stiff back of the sofa, and offered his hand out, palm up, on the cushion. Lark slowly slipped her hand in his, locking their fingers. He stayed quiet for the moment, not daring to ask more about the king. He'd seen enough, felt enough in her body the way she tensed whenever she spoke his name.

"So, the Daeoan are truly demons then?" he asked, finally breaking his silence. This new life of his was beginning to crack, an illusion in a mirror with fog obscuring what the truth was.

Two kings he had believed in, had grown up admiring. Two kings he had thought were good enough men, worthy to die for. Doubt seeped into his thoughts, the itch of unease that tore at him whenever he wanted answers to his unfurling questions. He'd never believed in gods, demons, or magic, until that fateful night in the mountains that brought him into this.

"Of a sort," Lark replied. "They're a way to keep balance; another part of a bargain, to pay for sins."

His thoughts drifted to his sword tied to the bag he kept beneath his bed—the physical embodiment of his restlessness hidden away.

"You're not afraid of them." Not a question, but he needed an answer. Not once in the Roe did she balk at the swirling masses of death and darkness. His thoughts trailed back to the journal. Lark softly smiled, almost sadly, and gave the slightest shake of her head.

"Have you noticed how we have two moons, while Areen and Telaan only see one? How the second doesn't seem to affect nature like the first does?" She turned her attention to the boarded-up windows and the faint moonlight slipping in through the gaps.

"What are you saying?" Again, not really a question, not a demand, but delivered with an unnerving calm settling in his chest, in the way a pin drops in a quiet room.

"Our second moon isn't a moon. He's stuck in the sky, living out his eternity above us."

"And you know this—"

"I hear him the same way you did today." Lark flinched, as though her answer physically pained her to say aloud.

"Mm." He wanted to withdraw his hand from hers, suddenly feeling the thrum of her magic on her skin, but gritted his teeth instead. "Melech says the Greater chose me."

Not that he believed it, not for a moment, but there had to be a reason.

"We all have a part to play, Az. Fate, destiny. We're meant to do so much more than this." Lark straightened, finally lifting her head from her knees and dropped them to the side. "And it's time I took my rightful place."

# CHAPTER 29

## AZRAEL

Time slowed, altered by the boarded windows, and settled around them as though the world was there to exist around them. Azrael savored every inch of her skin he touched and tasted after their voices had grown hoarse with speaking, putting their mouths to a different use. There was a finality in their lovemaking, more so than each time that was supposed to be their last, but Azrael chose to ignore that, using that thought as an extra push to savor each thrust, each kiss.

Covered in cooling sweat, they sprawled out on the rug before the fireplace. Lark's head was on his chest while she used the pads of her fingers to draw delicate designs on the planes of his stomach.

"How am I to face Melech, knowing he wears a crown, broken with deceit?" A knot of anxiety and anger writhed in his chest at the thought of seeing his king face to face again. The sense of unknown, uncertainty, in his future curled his stomach.

"You cannot say anything. I am trusting you with my life—"

"I won't," Azrael interrupted, feeling the heat of her own anger. "I won't break your trust."

Lark loosened her muscles again, once more relaxing against him, before she shifted and sat up. "It's nearly dawn."

Azrael groaned. Silently, he began to dress, recovering his clothing from various points in the room. There was nothing more to be said between them, not when the truth of who she was had been laid bare and he still wasn't any closer in finding the truth about his life. Nothing more to be said when she would go back to the king and he would return to his empty home and routine. As he situated his daggers, he watched her as she started making breakfast, wearing only her oversized shirt.

The sight was one he could get used to, even if it was something he had never intended. After Taya died, he had sworn to never care, to never settle. How had Lark phrased it?

It would be so easy to fall in love with her.

With his head at war with his heart, he laced his boots, pulled on his coat, and forced himself to take step after step towards the door. She didn't turn once he opened it, letting in the brisk air, but he did. He turned to see the back of her hand wipe her cheek furiously and the slight shake of her shoulders.

With a sigh, he stepped into the morning and closed the door behind him.

S unlight hadn't yet touched the Tiras courtyard when he turned the foggy corner. He fished his key from his pants and shoved it in the lock, not caring enough to note if anyone was awake and watching him. As he pushed his door, a wisp of fabric fluttered in a slow breeze in the corner of his eye.

The key clattered on the cobblestones.

Magdalene was suspended by the thickest branch of the tree, blood darkening the front of nightgown from a gash along the side of her neck. Azrael's hand gripped the door jamb, wood splintering beneath his fingers. A tearless sob racked his body, threatening to bring him to his knees.

A scream ripped through the fog, doors opened, gasps followed, but Azrael was frozen in his place with guilt. Heavy, leaden guilt.

Her face was peaceful, her emerald eyes closed as though she were simply sleeping. Those eyes that would never open again, never call him by the nickname he had minded coming from her mouth, never sit in the firelight and eat stolen desert.

Wrath coiled around him like a serpent, constricting and narrowing his focus.

Voices around him blurred together, a hand touched his arm, but he elbowed them violently. His feet moved him forward without thinking, only to stop in front of her limp body. Her blood had pooled beneath her. Her death was not quick, it was not painless. That serpent's coils tightened, his grief and guilt and wrath burning him from the inside out.

Then he noticed a crumpled piece of paper within her stiff hand. *Undoing,* was all it said.

He knew this was his fault.

He had given Melech her name, proudly boasted it to hide his intimacy with Lark.

He had done this.

No, *Melech* had done this.

Something halfway between a yell and a roar ripped from his throat as he catapulted towards the palace.

The palace flashed by as he ignored the halls he had walked, ignored his reflection in the hall of mirrors, and punched the Tiras guard in the face before kicking the gilded doors in.

Melech leaned against his desk the same way Azrael had seen him before, the last time the two of them were here. Discussing Lark and Magdalene and Azrael's life. Melech was the picture of calm while Azrael felt like a feral beast, but he held no shame in that.

"This is no way to greet your king." Melech's voice was uncaring, bored, and slightly amused. Azrael clenched his jaw so tightly he could have broken teeth.

"You are not my king," he hissed.

"You did not listen. I did what I had to do. Do I have your attention now?" Punctuated words, straightened shoulders. Melech pushed away from the desk.

Azrael's knuckles screamed at him from the tightness in his fist. He wondered how the crack would echo if his fist collided with Melech's jaw.

"You realize that you are to blame for Maggie's death, don't you? She would have been safe and happy at home, if you have kept your cock in your pants." His amusement, his boredom, his mask slipped. A snarl rippled across his face. Melech moved closer, closing the distance between them. In a flash, his spidery hand was clasped around Azrael's throat.

Before the king could recognize the idea in his eyes, Azrael gripped the king's shoulder with his left hand and, with all his strength, swung his right forearm with enough force to break the king's elbow.

The crack bounded against the black walls, followed by an ungodly growl echoing in the dark.

Melech released his grip and staggered backwards, cradling his broken arm to his chest. He gained his composure faster than Azrael expected, and he couldn't move fast enough to avoid the king's fist. His teeth rattled in his jaw, jarring his vision, but he willed his body to stay upright.

Azrael lunged towards the king, desperate to crack another royal bone, but Melech deflected his blow and used his momentum to send Azrael onto the floor. Skull bouncing on the cool marble, his eyes rolled but he struggled to remain conscious. He wouldn't make it out of the palace alive if he fell prey to the darkness closing in on him.

Melech leaned over him, opening his mouth to say something, but Azrael hit him again with all his strength, sending the king careening backwards. Azrael jumped to his feet, sliding a dagger free from his boot in the same motion.

The king grinned, teeth and beard darker from blood. Silver flashed in the firelight, a dagger to match Azrael's twirled in the king's hand. With years of hatred burning in his eyes, Melech lunged and Azrael had a fraction of a second to step back as the dagger sliced across the base of his throat, along the top of his collarbone. Brilliant, bright pain clouded his mind as warmth spread across his chest.

*Not deep enough not deep enough you're alive you're alive.* His thoughts were a knife grating against stone, too loud, too invasive.

He did the exact same thing to Magdalene, and the tree creaking as her lifeless body hung from it flashed in his head. Azrael had killed her—when he spoke her name to the king, he had doomed her to an early death.

"So she told you everything then?" Melech yelled, his voice suddenly hoarse. He held his dagger up, waiting for Azrael to move. "How her father killed her mother? How she created the demons you so desperately prove yourself against?"

Azrael stilled.

Melech's face lit up with a wicked grin. "Trouble in paradise already? Why would she have told you she singlehandedly created a demon that's nearly unstoppable? It doesn't sound very tragic. Afterall, that's what she was going for. The forgotten princess—abandoned and abused. She didn't have to try hard to win you, did she? Flashed a smile, did a magic trick, and you were taking your clothes off. If you two hadn't been off fucking in the forest, *she'd* be hanging from that tree right now."

Raising his arm to throw the dagger at his king, aiming for the same place he had killed Magdalene, Azrael wasn't fast enough. An arrow pierced his shoulder, yanking him hard to the side. Splintering bone and pain exploded in his head. *Too much, it's too much. Not again. I won't face death again, not like this.*

Panic seized his chest, reliving the moments the bones in his legs had been shattered.

"Azrael Hikaim, you are sentenced to death for attempted regicide."

Boaz strode into the room, his voice a harbinger of fate. Through the swarming pain and darkness, Azrael saw the dark man's fingers flex around his bow. His other hand reached up towards his quiver, ready to kill Azrael then.

For an archer, he wasn't nimble.

And it was Azrael's saving grace.

He skidded around the archer, pain and hate and rage propelled him out of the room, over the still unconscious Tiras guard, and down the hall of mirrors. He avoided his reflection, detesting the beast he glimpsed as he rounded corners.

He ran faster than he had before, slipping on the smooth stone floor, but he didn't stop. Not until he came to the Tiras courtyard and barreled into his house. He grabbed the bag he always had packed, his sword, and anything immediately out he was able to scoop into his bag before he bounded through the second circle and across the front courtyard.

Ahmi held the reins of a horse, sadness in his eyes, and it nearly crushed Azrael. A thought flashed in his head—how Ahmi had known to be here, have his horse ready, but Azrael cast it out. He let his friend help him onto the horse, trying not to meet the gaze of goodbyes. Before anyone would see them together and Ahmi helping him, Azrael spurred his horse on, flying past bewildered guards.

Thunder rolled above him as black clouds gathered on the horizon. Azrael pressed himself against his horse's neck, shifting his arm just so to hide the arrow still protruding from it.

No plan, no destination, but he couldn't gather the energy to care. As the distance grew between him and the palace, his heart only felt lighter.

†

He lost track of time, only collapsing on the ground when his horse wandered amongst trees and all but bucked him off. The ache of the arrow in his shoulder dulled his senses, dulled his thinking. He was almost grateful for it, though he didn't touch it. The pain levelled him, snuffed out his hate.

Night overtook the day, and Azrael wasn't sure how many times he had seen that happen. Only that, once he had fallen off his horse, he tried climbing back on and he knew that happened a few times.

The last time he fell from the horse, pain rattled his consciousness. He turned onto his left side, positioning himself that the fletching didn't touch the earth. He couldn't fall asleep—then he wouldn't wake up. He couldn't fall asleep.

The air hummed quietly around him as the ground opened beneath him and swallowed him whole. He turned his unfocused gaze to the sky. The first moon sat stone cold in the sky as the stars swirled around the celestial being. The second began its ascent. His thoughts grew scrambled as he thought of Lark—what she had told him, and what Melech said. Had he been so foolish to see Lark as she had shown him—a gifted mage who belonged to the crown? Or was he foolish for believing Melech? The thought dawned that he was in fact a fool for both, and for many other things that had brought him here—alone and dying in the middle of the forest.

Thinking of her, and only her, he fell asleep.

# CHAPTER 30

## LARK

Lifeless clouds obscured the sun, leaving the Vale in a grey haze. By the time Lark had finally walked home from Harlow's cabin, it was well into the middle of the day. She had wasted day and night and that morning, painting to distract herself from the fact that she had told Azrael everything. A weight had eased off her shoulders as it felt like something finally clicked into place. As she walked through the city buzzing for equinox preparations, she scattered her shadows to stir the leaves, practicing whenever she could. Her magic was like a muscle, it ached and ached if not used enough, and sang with strings of pain if used too much.

She had felt strange after leaving the cabin—as though her soul was naked, bared to the Vale, and the bleakness of the day rattled her. Few spoke to her as she walked, savoring the cold breeze that gusted in from the ocean. She wondered how often Melech walked through his own streets, spoke to the people he ruled over, wondered how many he knew by name. How many he knew by name in the eastern side.

Since Lark had been cast from the palace as a disgraced pawn, she had become a living, breathing part of the city. She attended lessons in both private and the free one room school were the teacher struggled to maintain control of her students. She had worked jobs in the fish market in the east, tended infirmaries on both sides. Melech hadn't bothered to celebrate holidays until she pushed him. Over and over, year after year, she told herself he didn't care as much as she did. She knew the people, the land, but they didn't remember her. Melech and her father had made that clear. They knew she would be a force of nature—at least, that was what she told herself. She couldn't bear to think of the alternative.

When she reached the healer's house, Hadri sat in the doorway as they always did, a letter twisting in her nimble fingers. Lark noticed the strained look in her friend's eyes, how they wouldn't meet hers. She stopped a foot before Hadri, her boots scuffing in the dirt.

"What happened?" Lark took a breath, trying to calm her racing heart.

"Magdalene is dead," Hadri said without emotion, eyes still downcast and set in the dirt. She took a sharp inhale before continuing, "Az is gone."

A crack so loud, so deep, down the middle of Lark's heart threatened to cave in her in two.

Hadri met Lark's eyes then, as though she had heard the cataclysm inside her chest. "This letter is for you," she said quietly, "No one else has seen it."

Lark couldn't stop the shaking in her hands as she took it from Hadri, nothing the unbroken seal on the back—a wheat stalk. A storm raged inside her head as she wondered what Hadri was thinking, why Lark would receive letters from the Roe.

"Whatever it is you're doing, please think it through." Hadri stood and took Lark's hand. "I love you. Please be safe."

In all their years of friendship, Lark could count the times she heard that softness in her friend's voice on one hand. Hadri let their hands drop before walking past Lark.

A thousand and one thoughts cascaded through her head, some her own, some Iah's, but as she broke the seal and read Luned's note, all those thoughts emptied.

Her feet moved of their own volition, the soft crunch of rock and dirt beneath drowned out everything else. She ignored the bloodstains in the Tiras courtyard, how it had travelled to Azrael's door, and ignored the too-loud whispers that followed her with wide eyes as she strode through the palace. Step by step, she ascended the floors until she came face to face with her reflection in the hall of mirrors.

She stopped at the landing and sent a tendril of shadow down the hall, flinging it against the two guards that stood outside his doors. She waited a moment before continuing. The click of the door echoed. A soft scuffle of feet against marble. A quiet swear.

Then, a hundred reflections of the man who could have been hers, in another life, and a hundred reflections of the girl who was his in this life.

Sinking deeper in the depth of her magic, she wasn't really seeing him as they stared at each other from opposite ends of the hall. No, she knew he was watching her twitching fingertips, pale from the shadows swarming around them.

This man had taken everything from her. *Everything*. Her father, her crown, her *life*.

"It was supposed to be you."

Such sorrow snapped her focus. She truly looked at him, realizing his arm was bound, wrapped, and cradled against his body. She fought the rising instinct to send an ivory thread to him.

"I had wanted it to be you." Melech's voice was pained, a breath away from a sob, but when she took in his face, his eyes, he was torn between wrath and sorrow. His eyes darkened with pain Lark knew she could never heal. That kind of pain festered, growing until it became something else entirely.

"But you saw only what you wanted to," he continued. "And you saw something in that boy that I could never be. Did he truly win you over? Sweep you off your feet? Is this the happily ever after you've wanted? A husband who runs at the sight of consequences? A husband who would merely be a consort, not a king."

He crossed the distance and she let him, planting her feet. There was a war raging within him—his love for her and his hatred for Azrael—and it was as plain as sunshine on his face. His left hand held her face. She didn't cringe from his touch, the way he expected her to.

"When he learned you created the Daeoan, he wasn't happy," he murmured into her hair, his thumb stroking her cheek, "How could he ever trust you now, knowing you made the very thing that set his life into motion? You killed his mother, his father. You killed his plaything. You are the *villain* in his story, Lark."

"That's not true," she gritted out. Even as she said the words, they rang hollowly.

Melech moved so his breath was warm on her neck, his mouth inches from her skin. He could as easily rip her throat out as he could kiss her.

"You killed her," Lark said quietly, feeling his lips against the pulse in her throat.

"It was supposed to be you," Melech repeated just as quietly. The words settled in her as stones on a riverbed. The double meaning. Her spine straightened, but he moved faster, anticipating.

Despite his arm, he pushed her hard against the glass, splintering beneath her. Warm, wetness pooled down the back of her neck. He held his body against her, pinning her arms and legs. A statue against her, Lark looked to the ceiling, avoiding the ravenous eyes that burned into her face every mirror she looked at.

"I don't need you anymore, Freckles," he breathed. His heartbeat thundered against their chests as though his was desperate to break free to reach hers. "Your friends answer to me now, and you've pissed me off a few too many times now."

Melech shifted before she felt the snag of steel against her thigh, then its coldness beneath her shirt. Her head emptied of every bit of training, of every grasp she'd had on her magic. She only thought of the way the blade bit and stung against her skin. Melech moved again, the blade digging in quickly before it flashed and poised above her heart, its tip digging into the fabric of her shirt.

"You've played this game for too long. Sometimes it was hard deciding if I wanted to kiss you here." His lips were slow, delicate, beneath her ear, the tip of his tongue dancing lazily on her skin. "Or if I wanted to drag my blade here."

In emphasis, he pushed.

Further.

The mental wall she kept began to crumble, shake, stones crashing into the churning waters of her magic. Shadows swarmed her vision as her chest grew warm and wet.

Gods, he was killing her—slowly.

She sent a thought—hands grasping in the dark—through any and every part of their bodies that touched.

*I could have loved you.*

Instead of releasing her, he scoffed.

"Six years and you've run into another man's arms. You couldn't have. You didn't *try*," he hissed, digging his dagger in more.

Lark had grown so cold, her blood flowing freely down her front. The dagger inched its way into her chest, so slowly as though he were savoring this. The unlife called to her, the whispers of thousands of souls grasping at her, pulling pulling pulling

Shadows exploded around them.

Melech was thrown from her, glass shattering, but she couldn't see anything. Her hand went to her throat and she unspooled her ivory threads, binding and staunching and stitching.

She tried reeling in the shadows, tried to move her feet, but neither budged. The hall turned a deathly cold. There was nothing beyond the swirling black, beyond the bone chilling cold. She couldn't move from her spot against the cracked mirror. The unlife was taking her.

Her wrist was suddenly crushed in a tight, bony grasp and a thin, vibrating skin of magic enveloped her. She couldn't get a grip on her magic, not when the shadows ensconced her this tightly. Like holding onto an eel, every tendril skidded from reach, the shadows deepening.

These were not just her shadows.

The world shifted, warped, and Melech's cry echoed as she moved through the kingdom, nothing more than smoke in the breeze.

*"I loved you."*

L ark's feet touched the ground at intervals she couldn't keep track of. One hand remained tightly around her wrist and another pressed against her chest, poorly staunching the flow of blood. She couldn't tell whose hand was who's until light ripped through the shroud of shadows and she opened her eyes to a canopy of bare branches, feeling the heat of a fire.

She lurched up, ready to bolt, but her stomach got the best of her, and she hurled its contents up into the dirt beside her.

*Slowly.*

Lark wiped her mouth with the back of her hand as a chill crept over her. She didn't recognize the voice in her head, but a sinking feeling in her wounded chest only confirmed her suspicions. She forced herself to look up to the boulders she had been dropped by, to look at the figure perched on a higher rock. The air around her was cold, but not so much more than the autumn chill easing into winter. The being sat far enough away its coldness didn't touch her.

Why was it here? Her thoughts circled, though kept turning back to Melech. He had been bent on killing her. She never thought he would go so far, not after everything.

Did this Daeoan save her?

*Two of us did. We could have done more, but your boyfriend killing my brothers severely limited their liking to you.*

Lark snorted, almost unsure whether to believe the broken face staring down at her. She hadn't known them to be able to speak this way, but she supposed they were Iah's favorite—why wouldn't they be able to?

"Theirs? Not yours?" Lark hissed as she tried to weave her ivory ribbons into her chest, sewing the tears in her skin.

*I've always liked you, Siena. You need to rest. Your magic needs to rest. You will be on your own again after you've healed. Iah does not approve I'm still here.*

"Then why are you?" she muttered, low enough a human wouldn't have heard, but it had been a very long time since this being was human.

It was then she noticed the bag at her feet, stuffed full of gods knew what and radiating a pulse of cold. She was an exile now, shunned from her home once again, turned away from what was hers. She had known Melech for who he was—what he was. She had been naïve for thinking him anything less.

*You haven't reached as far into your magic as you just had. You are balancing on a knife point, and we cannot let you fall.*

Lark's hands were limp in her lap, so pale they were nearly white—blue veins running black with her shadows in stark contrast. She thought of a flower slowly withering in the frost and how her soul felt that way, curling inwards on itself. Damn magic and its toll.

"Is he still alive?" Her voice was hardly above the brush of her lips together, but the being heard. Her heart weighed heavy with guilt, with unearned loyalty, with fear.

*Yes. Healing.*

Healing. Healing? Had she done something when she had been ensconced in the shadows? Had *they* done something? Her crown wouldn't be bloody—it would not be heavy beneath the burdens of her forebears.

"Where's Azrael?" Lark forced herself to look at the being again. Its empty eye sockets had once terrified her, now they only sickened her. She had been so afraid as a child, thinking them as so much more than simply cursed souls. Lost souls doomed to suffer a fate they had no hand in.

*The Falls. He is wounded but safe. He knows.*

The king was healing, but Azrael was wounded. What had happened with two days for their lives to crumble?

"He knows what?" Lark asked, catching the stiffened tone the being used.

*Of us.*

Oh.

Oh. Lark breathed carefully through her nose, as to not let her rising anxiety choke her. She slowly lowered herself to the ground, positioned away from her puddle of vomit, and stared into the white flames. She must have set the fire, but she didn't remember when. She supposed things like that didn't matter anymore.

Lark had woken up hopeful this morning, despite the ache in her chest after explaining everything to Azrael. Now, she slept in the forest where a demon had dropped her off, and her thoughts were too wild to form a plan.

*Sleep now, child. Think of it tomorrow.*

A single tear slipped off the bridge of her nose and burrowed into the dirt. She lifted a bloody finger to trace a small abstract design in the damp dirt, thinking of her mother and the windchimes she had crafted and the teas she had brewed and the laughs that enriched her childhood. No, she wasn't afraid for her mother if the king would go after her. She hadn't even seen Harlow in weeks and there was solace in that. Her mother had gone to Areen to visit family at the perfect time.

*Stay there, Mama,* she thought, letting the songs of her childhood drift through memories to her. *Stay where it's safe.*

# CHAPTER 31

## AZRAEL

There was no sense in waking up. Drowning halfway between a dream and a nightmare, Azrael couldn't bear the weight of his thoughts and fears as he strained against opening his eyes. Let sleep take him, as fitfully as it was—at least in sleep, he only dreamt, his thoughts evaded.

A lingering echo of someone calling his name haunted the back of his neck, raising the hairs and pricking gooseflesh. He fought his consciousness, even as a voice spoke from somewhere beside him. He wasn't ready to face the consequences of his actions, nor accept whatever change they wrought.

Life won, however, as it always does, and a real hand gripped his wrist—so unlike the phantom touches of those in his sleep. His eyes scoured the canvas ceiling, at first forgetting this wasn't where he had fallen asleep. It wasn't hard earth beneath him, but a creaking cot. His shoulder wasn't jostled with an arrow, only a teeth-grindingly dull ache spreading from his shoulder down his side and his back.

"You're awake." The same deep voice from before spoke again, though it sounded far away, and reminded him of a rockslide. Azrael glanced at the voice's origin—a tall, muscular woman that leaned over him. She was striking with her dark green eyes and the thin but prominent scar that spanned down her forehead, across the bridge of her nose, and ended beneath her right eye. The woman straightened as she noted his studying gaze, her golden head grazing the top of the tent. The woman spoke again, but Azrael wasn't listening, only focusing on her white teeth and the golden canines that poked from between her lips. She sighed and repeated herself.

"How is your shoulder?" she enunciated slowly, as though he were dim witted, but he couldn't fault her for that. His thoughts were sluggish, like dragging his feet through knee high mud.

"Where am I?" he replied as he tried to sit up, only to be forced back down by a dizzy head.

"The Falls," the woman said, her sharp face turned in profile as she gazed out the tent's parted flaps. "We found you in a field, not far from here. I'm surprised you're not dead, boy. Strange to welcome you to my camp when the last time we saw each other, my men chased you and your scouts back to your king."

He couldn't think that far back, all those years ago. He tried to think instead of a map, how far he had ridden. Had it been days? The Falls were only a couple days outside of the infirmary. There was no way he could have ridden almost a week in that state—near delirious from pain with an arrow in his shoulder.

The ache from his wound moved like a wave across his body, pushing and pulling, until it hooked around a thought he hadn't wanted to consider: he didn't have a home. Anymore, again. He was drifting again. Lark was gone, back in the king's arms, and he was content to let her stay there. She had told him so much—filled his head with nonsense of gods and secrets—when she had left out the biggest ones.

The beings that had killed his mother, killed Nevan, nearly killed *him*, had been of her making. Born of her hands, the ones he had studied so dutifully in their time together, the demons only he seemed to be able to kill—

Was there a reason? Was it tied to his miraculous healing? Lark couldn't possibly be—she couldn't have done it on purpose. He couldn't have been placed on this path only to be an obstacle in hers. That line of thinking was off limits; he wouldn't entertain it. It bore a hurt bigger than he wanted to admit.

The woman still stood beside him, her feet shifting and arms crossed, but Azrael turned his face from her, as childish as it was.

"Rook!" A voice from outside captured the woman's attention. She sighed before the canvas rustled and a stillness settled into the tent.

Azrael waited until he was sure no one else would come into the tent before he shakily pushed himself up. Each wave of dizziness he breathed through until he was able to stare through the open tent without wanting to gouge his eyes out.

Pale grass, passing booted feet, trotting paws. He was in the Falls—the rebel camp Melech had never been able to crush. Azrael sighed as he slowly set his feet on the ground, then knitted his brows when he realized he no longer wore his Tiras uniform. At some point, he had been redressed into thicker clothes, brown pants and a warm, green tunic, and socks that kept a chill away from his toes. He wrestled with his boots, forgoing the laces, and hesitantly made his way out into the camp.

Throughout his years, he'd seen many tiny towns and permanent camps that called the mountains home. The Falls was truly a town now. It was positioned near the largest waterfall in the mountain range. The roar of the it was a constant song for these people; just on the other side of the rise, the water fell into the sea beyond.

People slowed as they passed him, still standing in the middle of a pathway between tents. He stood in the midst of a maze of canvas tents and small wooden buildings, feeling so much smaller than he had before.

Azrael lowered his chin to his aching chest and avoided the sharp eyes that followed him as he walked along the path. It curved until he followed it to an opening seemingly in the middle. The structures here faced two large tables in the center of the circle. Each table was laden with a feast. One table was crowded by people standing beside it, the gossip drifting through the air to Azrael, as they nibbled on food. He thought it was strange no one sat, only filling their plate then leaving.

His stomach rumbled then, as he stood on the outskirts, and he swore it was loud enough to be the reason their heads turned. The echo of "king-slayer" and "demon-slayer" burned in his ears, but he gritted his teeth.

The woman—Rook—turned her back to her fellow rebels and strode towards him.

"Hikaim," she said when she stopped in front of him. He had to raise his eyes to meet hers. "You will not die under my care. Return to your tent and rest."

"That's an order?"

Rook cocked her head, unsure if he was joking. Her eyes narrowed. "Would I need medical training for it to be? I can fetch a healer and have her tell you the same thing. Take some food, some ale, and return to your tent. I *advise* you."

Rook turned and walked back to her people with Azrael on her heels. She didn't offer an introduction, neither for him nor the dozen pairs of eyes watching his careful moves. He plucked a peach and what seemed to be jerky from the table before he dunked a mug into the cask in between the tables. The unfriendly stares had him walking back the way he had come.

His poor sense of direction had him lost in the maze, a sense of dread and hopelessness amounting to a pounding in his chest. He knew he would find his tent, but his head was drilled with worry he couldn't fight.

The threads of fate seemed to know what they were doing, however. Azrael nearly missed it—the soft singing that he had woken up to every day for a month and had provided him a small solace in the uncertainty of life before him. He stopped walking and called out her name.

A dark head of untamed hair stuck out of a tent, peeking around. Once Hanna saw him, her eyes lit up as a smile warmed her face. She stepped into the pathway and strode over to him to wrap him in her small embrace, mindful of the bandage on his shoulder.

"I didn't think the rumors were true, but here you are! We heard what happened with the king." Hanna's eyes were sad, but her initial smile didn't fade.

"I woke up here," Azrael said. He wouldn't have come here willingly, but found the idea of leaving just as daunting. "When did you come here? I didn't think—I didn't know you believed in their cause."

Their cause: taking Melech off the throne. Had he inadvertently aligned himself with the rebels he had fought against all those years?

Hanna laughed, a small but genuine sound. "Let's walk."

"Care to help me find my tent? I have no idea how you could keep a sense of direction here."

It felt strange to once again have Hanna as a tether to his life, grounding him in the unfamiliar. She tilted her head towards the way he had come from and they began to walk slowly.

"The day you left," Hanna began, each word careful and slow, "Melech had visited Raphael before you all left. He—Raphael was dead at dawn." A weary glance from the corner of her eye. "He had screamed all night, and no one could get into his room."

"What happened?" Azrael knew in his heart what had happened to his friend but didn't want to think about it. Raphael had spoken nonsense and annoyed Azrael on more than one occasion, but he had been there for Azrael to lean on. He had helped through the agony, the night terrors, and was the reason Azrael could walk again. The reason he was still alive.

"They said he did it himself, but I helped carry his body out. No man could do that to himself." Hanna took a deep breath. "I thought it had been coincidence that the king had seen him before he died, but after I heard what happened in the Roe, I didn't need convincing."

Twilight had wrapped the Falls in hues of purple and black. Braziers were lit periodically along the pathway, deepening the shadows. Hanna stopped walking and gestured to a tent.

"Did you think that it was chance the demons appeared while you met with the Lord? That they terrorized the city the night you arrived?"

A spark, a small memory that had been buried beneath the weight of the past few weeks. Bedivere had said something when they shared breakfast—that Melech had commanded them. Azrael had let it go, but now he felt foolish.

"Rook will tell you more later. Get some rest, Azrael." Hanna held open the flap with a soft smile.

Azrael ducked in and settled on his cot while he listened to her departing footsteps. He ate his food slowly, mindfully drinking his ale so it didn't rush to his head.

A small part of him should have known that things weren't what they seemed. From that first moment with Melech, an itch of doubt had scratched in the back of his head, but he was caught in the whirlwind of a new life.

The glint of metal caught his eye, resting on a small chest in the corner. His sword. His heart flipped in his chest. He hadn't the faintest idea how he had managed to keep ahold of his things, let alone his prized sword, during his feverish travels. He set the peach pit on the bedside table and knelt before the chest—a small bloom of hope curling in him.

His bag had been unpacked neatly and his things organized in the wooden chest. His daggers and the journal that held Lark's secret were tucked at the very bottom. A wave of relief passed over him as he closed the lid. The same way clouds carried the silver lining at their edge, he didn't feel as hopeless or lost as he had before.

Azrael slowly stood, eased off his boots, and settled onto his cot. He was asleep before his head hit the pillow.

┼

An echo of his name haunted his dreams. When Azrael woke, there was nothing but silence around him. His body creaked and protested as he stretched to jostle the stiffness from his muscles. The ache in his shoulder didn't spread as it had before while he dressed then stepped into his boots. He took the daggers from the chest and slid one into each of his boots before greeting the quiet morning outside.

The sky was a gentle mixture of soft pink, blue, and ribbons of yellow as the sun's rays stretched over the forest behind him to touch the mountain top.

Hanna's words had followed him through sleep and echoed in his head as he wandered along the path. Winter's chill caressed his skin, leaving gooseflesh pricking against his warm clothes. The last time he had seen this camp it was half its size—a handful of tents occupying this sprawling field. He had come to scout the camp, report on the growth of the rebel's forces, and to search for its weak points. He and his partner had failed in their stealth. One of the only times Azrael had fled from a fight and it flushed him with shame that Rook remembered that.

Azrael scratched at his throat, momentarily forgetting that the king had tried cutting it open. It felt like a lifetime ago already, the memory so far away. He walked and walked until he came to the edge of the camp.

It was strange to see how strongly these people clung to their hatred of Melech. How much truth did they know? The rebellions were worse, Azrael knew, when the king first took the throne, but even after all these years later, some of his people still rejected him.

Thoughts and the quiet forest wrapped around him like a cocoon until the sound of muffled footsteps had him turning to see Rook.

"How is your shoulder?" she asked, her narrowed eyes glancing between his shoulder and his face. Her face was unreadable. Azrael rubbed at his face, then realized how much his beard had grown. God, it'd been days.

"I've had worse," Azrael replied. True, nothing could compare to his bones shattering. "I have yet to see my healer though. They must have light fingers if they tend to me while I'm asleep."

"Saffron. She's got a mother's touch." The sides of her mouth turned up slightly. "She informed me she's worried about an infection. But," Rook inhaled sharply, "I did not come for a bedside visit."

"Figured as much. Why would you?"

"We have been waiting for something like this—someone like you." Rook turned to him then, arms crossed and brows knit, "Melech will no longer sit on that throne."

"How do you mean?" Azrael kept his gaze on the trees before him, the leaves illuminated in the early morning sunshine.

"We've tried for years to expose him as the man he is, the harm he's done, the deaths he's caused. His followers are loyal. They see no wrong. Havriel is falling to pieces while the other kingdoms laugh at us for failing. He is a disgrace to the kingdom, the people. After what happened in the Roe—"

"You cannot think that's true. The king controls demons?"

Rook opened her mouth, then closed it hard enough Azrael heard her teeth rattle.

"I guess intelligence isn't necessary when you look like that and have a natural talent for fighting," Rook said after a moment.

"What—"

"The demons are the real Tiras, Azrael. He can summon them, control them. He destroyed the Roe because Bedivere pissed him off. He destroyed Westwick because they wanted to work with the Roe's port and lessen the taxes. They've killed more than you've been able to save. Just because you're able to kill them, doesn't mean you're safe. It doesn't mean that there's not more out there waiting for his command to come for *you*."

"How is that possible?" The thought was ridiculous enough that Azrael didn't want to give it credit, but after everything, he found himself believing it.

"I'd like to know. I'd like to know how demons would show up in our kingdom, under control of the king."

Azrael was quiet for a few moments. "What do you want me for?"

"Unseat the king," Rook replied tautly.

"You want me to kill him?"

"Whatever it takes. Force him to step down, face the crimes and damage he's done, or let him meet his maker. I've needed someone with your ambition, your hunger to prove yourself. Everyone wants change, but no one wants to start making changes. We're prepared for whatever the future brings, but we need someone to help guide us there."

*You're wrong,* he wanted to tell her, *There is nothing more for me to prove, there is no hunger within me anymore.*

The words hung hollowly within him.

Instead, he said, "I failed at defending myself against him. What makes you think I could do better a second time?"

"You have someone worth fighting for. You know the cost of losing twice." Rook turned to face her camp. "I have soldiers who could benefit from your expertise. While you're here, while your shoulder is healing, I'd like you to train them. They're in the clearing to the south and will be eager to hear from you."

With that, she cast him a look over her shoulder before striding back to the camp.

Unseat the king, kill the king. Who did they have to replace him?

Azrael missed when he hadn't been anyone, before he had made a name for himself with his sword, with his ambition. He missed simplicity. He missed not being someone's *pawn*.

His life had lost meaning and, here he was, someone pushed their meaning onto him. Slowly, he was falling into another kind of limbo, the in-between that had threatened to claim him before. His thoughts travelled to the journal sitting in a chest, the stories and entries detailing the life of the woman he loved. Part of him wanted to burn the book, but another part of him curled inwards. He could almost feel her phantom touches, hear her laugh. He spat into the dirt and walked back through the camp.

The clearing was a small, near perfect circle with trees packed together like fish on the docks. Ideal for training, as misguided arrows wouldn't go too far. Sacks of grain and hay bales were set up at the end, away from onlookers or those passing by. Men and a few women were hacking away at the grain sacks, some hitting each other with wooden swords.

Azrael sighed. If this is what their training consisted of, it was no wonder how he and the king's army kept the upper hand so long. It proved how pitiful their rebellions had been. The king's army trained constantly, whether it was sparring or endless workout routines, and the initial training lasted a year before they were let go.

None noticed him as he walked up, but all turned once Azrael cleared his throat. Lifting his chin, he assessed each one as they moved towards him.

"I'm Azrael, and I'm here to guide your training. You were all distracted too easily, let that be the first lesson. You, you, and you—" He pointed to the three of those sparring with fake swords who had their backs towards him at first –"would be dead if that were a real sword."

"Azrael Hikaim? Of the Tiras?" A collective gasp sounded from all.

"So it's true you tried to kill the king. Are you really able to kill demons?" The one who spoke was no more than a boy, lanky with patchy facial hair. He held a bow awkwardly in one hand and an arrow in the other.

Pride mixed with shame flooded Azrael's chest. There were still parts of him that was thrilled when someone knew him by name, but the conversations were always one and the same.

"Yes, and yes. But this is about *you*, and what you can learn from me. Put those down and let's begin."

✝

Winter rolled in like a fog, passing the days quickly and coldly. Azrael spent his time in the clearing, working through basic drills to work the rebel's bodies before they picked up another weapon. He had never trained anyone before, let alone a group, but he found it to be easy, exhilarating even, to lead them. His shoulder had grown stiffer with each passing day to the point where he could hardly demonstrate drills to his crowd. He dreaded the thought of Melech sending his demons; Azrael doubted if he could hold his ground. He'd worked on using his left hand and it sufficed for battles with men, but it was hardly good enough to fight an otherworldly being.

Azrael realized he had spent a week with the rebels as he walked into the Meadow, as they called it, to grab something for dinner. The way their camp functioned was still strange to him, but he no longer felt so much as an outsider. Everyone rotated in duties to hunt, they helped cook and clean, and set food out for people to come and go as they pleased.

Rook's eyes tracked him as he grabbed slices of deer, cheese, and a handful of vegetables, dropped onto a plate, and filled a cup of ale. He carried his food and drink carefully, as to not exert his shoulder too much. The woman's stare unsettled him—whether it was the unnatural green of her eyes or the scar that adorned them—but he ignored her. Some diners settled into the still soft grass of the Meadow, but Azrael retreated to his tent.

As soon as the flaps rustled closed behind him, they were pushed open by an older woman. He settled on his cot as she walked in.

"It's nice to see you awake. I'm Saffron," she said in a soft voice that reminded him of home. Her hair was long and grey, while her face and her body were soft with age and a good life. Her apron and dress rustled with her movement as she stepped closer to him. "I'm sorry to have come while you're eating. If it's alright with you, I'd like to take a quick look."

Azrael nodded. She floated to his side, easing his coat off, then pulled his arm from his shirt. With his left hand, he took bites of his dinner. Saffron's fingers were cold as she gently touched, poked, and lifted the bandage, a frown pulling at her mouth.

"What is it?" Azrael said through a mouthful of food. The woman's lips formed a tight line, her gaze avoiding his.

"It's infected, and it's spreading. You'll need to go to the Roe in the morning. You need an infirmary—a real one—before it gets even worse." She set to changing the bandage and cleaning it gently. Azrael repressed the hiss that rose in his throat. From the corner of his eye, he noted the discoloration of his skin, the angry swelling. Saffron continued, "I'll give you something to help you sleep tonight, but you must leave in the morning."

She drew a small handful of leaves from her apron pocket and set it on the bedside table. Once his shirt was back on, the woman cast him a small, pitying look before ducking out of the tent.

His thoughts quieted as he listened to the sounds of the camp beyond, the crackling braziers, the laughter, the soft dinging of metal further away. Each moment of passing quiet seemed to make him shrink, smaller and smaller, until the solitude crushed him, turning his thoughts once again back to Lark. She poisoned his mind, leeching into his muscles and weighing him down like an anchor at sea. She wouldn't leave his heart alone.

To occupy his mind, he reluctantly dug the journal from the chest and flipped through it, looking for one of the many stories instead of the entries about her.

He read again about the wolf and the vulture as the herb his healer had given him began to turn his thoughts softer, more slippery, hard to hold onto. His eyes snagged on something he hadn't noticed before in the story—the last translation of the vulture was different than what had been used in the story, and he had seen it before. He flipped back to another passage, this one about an unpleasant dinner with Melech, but his name was the same word. This was important, but the effect of the herb was drowning his sense of critical thinking. He started to slip into unconsciousness, but the last thing he saw before his eyes closed was Nekoda's crest—a wolf howling to the moon.

# CHAPTER 32

## AZRAEL

W ind tore through the canvas, whipping the flaps open. Azrael jolted awake, his vision darkening with sudden pain, and it took a moment to realize that it was only the wind intruding. He had dreamt over and over of wolves and vultures, and a lone songbird in the top of a tree. Shaking the lingering images of the dream from his head, Azrael dressed slowly, painfully, and sighed at the small flurries that descended. It would be a frozen ride to the Roe.

He packed as quickly as he could, though he didn't have much and it was mostly all together, and tied his sword to his bag, arming himself with his daggers instead. Saffron had stopped by to give him a bag of herbs and helped him into his coat.

The camp was still asleep when he walked to the stables. The sun had brightened the sky but hadn't touched over the treetops yet. He was thankful to leave quietly, even though his entire stay here had been quiet. It quelled the anxiousness in his chest; at least he wouldn't have Rook seeing him off, her uneven stare burning holes into his back. He was relieved, too, when he found his horse readied by a groggy stable boy. Azrael tied his bag and hauled himself onto his horse.

Weaving through the thick trees, he rode slowly and descended the mountainside carefully. He hadn't remembered the camp being this high. As soon as hooves touched flat ground, Azrael set the pace swiftly, but easily. The Roe was four days from the camp, but a small nagging in the back of his head told him that if he took four days, the infection would take him.

The forest was bare, and the road was empty as he flew along. A cold wind nipped at him, but at least snow hadn't fallen here yet. An eerie quiet had dampened the forest, even the horse's hooves sounded muffled as they pummeled the earth. He didn't dare stop, or slow, until he came upon an inn. The second moon—which wasn't a moon, but a god—peaked over the horizon when he stabled his horse and walked in.

The innkeeper's son was falling asleep at the bar and jumped when Azrael closed the door. The boy rubbed his eyes, groggy as they exchanged coin for a key. Azrael headed straight to the room and didn't bother taking his boots off before falling onto the bed.

✝

D awn woke him up, but he burrowed his head back into his pillow. His injury might claim him, but he'd be damned if exhaustion took him first. He slept for another hour before he rose, changed, and accepted breakfast by a homely girl downstairs. Before long, he was once again thundering through the remainder of the forest.

The sprawling fields of the Roe was a welcome sight, even if he still had days to go. Thin but dark wintery clouds rolled over the sky, cooling the air around him, rattling his bones from the inside out. He leaned into his horse's warm neck until the sun made its watery appearance hours later. Farms and massive estates passed him as he pressed on. The first, then second moon rose then fell and were replaced by the light of dawn. He continued to race the sun as it slipped along the vibrant sky, only slowing once he smelled the salt in the air. The town was still a great distance away, but he recognized the colorful speck on the horizon.

He slipped into the outskirts under the cover of night, passing the bright yellow and blue houses without lingering. Focusing on the road ahead, he kept his mind from wandering, from thinking anything other than staying upright in his saddle. He hadn't the faintest idea if the Roe had an infirmary other than Bedivere's house, but he went there anyway. A small part of him craved to see the lord, the same way he had wanted his parent's attention when he had gotten hurt. That sliver of his heart ached for comfort.

As soon as he drew close to the stables, an older woman caught sight of him and gasped, puncturing the quiet night. She followed him into the stables and helped him dismount, lending her body to lean on as they walked inside the manor together. His legs had turned soft and for a moment, his mind played a trick on him, feeling as though his bones were shattered once again. He fought the sob rising in his throat as they stumbled into the silent house.

The woman had her small around wrapped around his waist, his unhurt arm draping over her. He tried ignoring the haste in her steps—he must have looked worse than he felt, but he was grateful for it as she brought him to what looked to be a closet at first. Unhooking herself from him, the woman gestured to a small bed as she lit a fire opposite of him. She eased his coat, then shirt off, before replacing it with a loose cotton shirt he hadn't seen her produce. She removed all his blades, begrudgingly he let her, and covered him with a blanket before slowly pushing him down to lay on the bed. She muttered something he didn't catch before she left him.

Without distractions, everything caught up to him. Shivering and sweating beneath the blanket, a fire he hadn't noticed warmed him, threatening to suffocate him. His eyes itched and ached to the point where he forced his hands between his knees as to keep them from scratching them out.

*Listen to the bird's song*, the moon god had said. Azrael heard it now, in the shadows of this world and that of his dreams. Bodies rustled in front of him, casting violent shadows on the walls, but the little control Azrael still held onto was slipping. He closed his eyes.

&#8224;

B edivere sat in a chair beside the hearth, his ankle on his knee and a knuckle pressed against his mouth. His long hair was tied in his usual high knot atop his head while his beard was longer than their last visit, but still trimmed close. The lord's eyes were unfocused but sharpened when Azrael tried sitting up.

"You're awake," Bedivere mused, the side of his mouth turning up. "How are you feeling?"

"Tired." Azrael rubbed his face, prodding the sleepiness from his skin. He pushed himself up and leaned against the wall.

"It's the herbs. They're meant to keep you relaxed and lethargic. The arrow splintered your bone, I'm sure your previous healer told you. The shards caused quite the impressive infection. The bone itself is taken care of now, but it's up to the herbs to take care of the infection. My healer is the best in the Roe, but it will take some time." Bedivere paused. "I do have another that could help, but I'm under the impression you don't wish to see her."

The lord paused again, gauging Azrael's reaction, but he kept his face neutral.

"She arrived two days ago. I don't like the circumstances that have brought you back, but I am glad to have you both here again. Are you hungry? I'll have some food brought in."

As though on cue, the door opened and a girl carried a tray in, the smell of roast and carrots wafting in the air. She set it on the small table beside his bed, bowed to her lord, and scurried from the room. Azrael's stomach growled loud enough to make Bedivere laugh. He reached over and handed Azrael the bowl of fruit.

"I'll let you rest. I'll check on you soon, in the meantime, my healer will come in to check on you." Bedivere stood, inhaling deeply as he stretched. Azrael wondered how long the lord had been sitting with him, the thought squeezing his chest. "Would you like me to say anything to Lark?"

Azrael flinched at the sound of her name but said nothing. He had nothing to say to her—other than he missed her terribly but also hoped she'd rot wherever the demons had come from. He shook his head in reply before Bedivere offered a small smile and strode out of the room.

The notion of Lark under the same roof as Azrael made him sick to his stomach, the flesh of the pear he had bit into turned to ash in his mouth. Still, he forced himself to swallow. His ribs split, cracking and shifting, to allow room for his swollen heart. He took another bite of the pear, using his tongue to push around the fruit's flesh in his mouth, before he placed the remainder of the fruit back in the bowl.

Shame flooded him as easily as disgust did. Lark had tried warning him of the consequences of being with her, but he had ignored her. *If he knows, I cannot save you,* she had told him. He hadn't needed saving, no, but he should have heeded her words. Should have been prepared.

How far he had fallen.

He curled the fingers of his right hand, his thoughts begging for any feeling other than this shame, this longing, that burrowed into him, but the simple motion didn't bring the usual stinging from his shoulder. The small, cruel part of him craved some kind of physical pain—a manifestation of the internal hurt he couldn't get rid of.

There was something there, though, for in these past months, he'd been injured more than his previous years in the king's army. Alongside the ever present weight of a new life, where his fellow soldiers had hardly made it out of that ambush. His mental state was as tumultuous as his life, constantly turning upside down.

He wondered where his soldiers were now—how many were able to leave that infirmary. He should have kept in touch, shouldn't have locked them out of the same hurt that affected them as well. Guilt warmed his cheeks, constricted his throat.

The door to his room cracked. A man with crooked shoulders and silver hair announced himself as Edhar, the healer, before he shuffled in. Azrael cast his thoughts aside as he studied the man. Despite his slouched and aged appearance, he wasn't old. His face was youthful, though he seemed to be old enough to be Azrael's father, and his eyes were bright, even in the dim light. The room didn't have a window, nor did the corridor beyond provide any natural light to guide Azrael's days.

Neither man said anything as Edhar tended to Azrael's shoulder. He applied a salve extending down his side and bicep. Azrael was curious but didn't ask. Whatever the healer had done since Azrael arrived was working. The salve felt like a breath of winter air, biting but refreshing, as though it emptied his lungs of the stagnant air. Two fingers swiped a glob of salve across the base of his throat, where the cut was slowly turning into a scar, before Edhar resealed the small tin and dropped it in his pocket.

He murmured something too low for Azrael to hear before taking his chin with a slimy forefinger and thumb, staring intently into his eyes. Edhar nodded and let go before shuffling from the room.

The salve relaxed Azrael, letting him breathe easier and think less. He closed his eyes simply to rest them, but he couldn't tell how much time had passed, or if he had fallen asleep, when the door opened again and Bedivere walked in.

"What did Edhar say?" the lord asked as he stoked the dwindling fire. Azrael noticed the lord had changed into loose pants and a loose, half buttoned shirt. He thought it was strange, considering the chill that settled in the house.

"Nothing," Azrael replied. He scooted towards the edge of the bed, figuring his dizziness had long since worn off and the lord was here if he couldn't keep himself up. He stood and stretched carefully.

He paused, wondering if he should ask. "What do you know of Melech? How he became heir?"

Bedivere's face became pensive as he considered. The thought had been nagging Azrael, curling in the corner of his mind. He had to know if he was right.

"My father was one of Nekoda's advisors. Together they maintained a peaceful existence between the north and south. I was often around Melech then. He was Tiras Captain and very capable. I see a lot of him in you, actually," Bedivere said, his face soft as he spoke. He ignored the look Azrael cast him. "He wasn't always as he is now. There were many choices he made that set his fate. One being, growing too close to Nekoda. The two were thick as thieves with twice as many secrets. He was a man who saw what he wanted, and he took it. Nekoda's heirs had disappeared, both assumed dead, and his wives had long since died.

There was no one to continue the Hostien legacy, but Melech always had a plan, always had an idea. You know the answer to your question, Azrael, I just wonder how you found it."

"And I wonder how you know," Azrael muttered, quietly enough the lord could have not heard. Either way, he had his answer.

"Have you thought about where you will go?" Bedivere asked instead, abruptly but not unkindly. A small smile was on his face as he settled into the chair and kicked his legs out, crossing his ankles.

Azrael huffed as he studied the wood panels of the wall. "I have no home. I don't doubt there's a bounty on my head in the Vale."

"If you wish," Bedivere said slowly, "I can arrange for a house for you here. There's a guard position for you too—if you want it."

Azrael turned to him then, still as death. "Why."

Bedivere smiled, and Azrael couldn't find a trace of hidden motives or forbidden secrets in his dark eyes—not in the way Melech had.

"Azrael, do you not see your worth as clearly as I do? Melech treated you as a dog, always waiting for you to prove something, even when he did not know your name. He wanted you the moment you were healed."

"And you're different?"

"I see you," Bedivere said, leaning forward. "I see what you're capable of, beyond a sword in your hands. You don't have to prove anything to me for me to see that. I don't want to collect you, keep you for myself. I'm offering you a home, a future, where you can thrive. No more running, no more temporary situations. A stable, permanent home if you want it."

Tears burned in Azrael's eyes. He looked away from Bedivere, not wanting the lord to know how deeply his words had pierced. While Melech had shattered his life, Bedivere was giving him a new one. Although, Azrael had thought the same thing when Melech had arrived at the infirmary, ready to whisk him away. He didn't want to fall into another ruler's trap, so easy to crush under boot.

"Lark will be staying," Bedivere added quietly.

Disappointment and hope swelled side by side in Azrael's chest. He rubbed his face, pressing against his eyes and the tears that still stung.

"She asks about you. Every time I see her. But don't let her influence your decision. Your future is *yours*, Azrael. It does not rest on the choices of another. Think it over, you have time." Bedivere stood, fixing a button on his shirt, and moved to where Azrael stood, still frozen. The lord rested a hand on his unhurt shoulder, a gentle smile on his face.

"Thank you, my lord," Azrael said as Bedivere walked past him and opened the door.

"I hope you choose your future. There is so much light in you. Rest well, Azrael." The door clicked behind the Lord of the Roe.

†

It felt real. Azrael stood on the northern cliffs of the Moor, looking towards the Vale, though it was closer in the dream. He watched the dark waves rage far below him while a winter wind whipped around him, lashing his hair across his face. Across the water, standing on the plateau on the highest peak of the mountain range, a voice called to him—belonging to a woman, it called, sang, longed for him. The water below ceased its endless crashing, growing still as the voice continued to sing. Azrael could see her then, her shape growing sharper, even the details in her lilac dress. In a blink, the two land masses were close enough to see the gold in the woman's ears, the strands of gold woven into her loose curls. The woman reached a delicate hand out to him, beckoning him to take a closer step. He edged closer, boots sliding in the loose rocks, before clasping his fingers around hers. He reached his foot out, prepared to take the step to bring them together, but the land masses shifted again violently. The woman reached for him, watching as he plummeted down towards the water. She leaned too far, still extending her fair hand, and fell with him.

Once he hit the surface, he jerked awake, his heart in his throat as his body cried out against the sudden movement. Pain cascaded over him in waves, and Azrael breathed through each carefully, not letting the dizziness take hold. He focused on the dying fire, how cold it had gotten in the room, and how the sweat on his skin cooled.

"You look terrible," Edhar said after he opened the door, letting in dull light from the corridor. Azrael wondered why he was still kept here, if the infirmary was full—or if he had been correct about the bounty on his head and was being kept hidden. Edhar eyed him. "Are you resting?"

"I have little else to do."

The healer moved to the side of the bed and began working on Azrael's shoulder, easing his arm from his shirt and poking and prodding again.

"I've done my part. The infection is gone, but you still must let it rest. I'm thinking a sling will help you stop moving it so much."

Azrael snorted. "I don't think so."

"Oh, are you a medical professional? I had no idea."

Azrael exhaled sharply. Boaz knew exactly what he had done when he fired that arrow, knowing it could kill him slowly, but more likely ruin the chances of him using his sword arm again. Knew that would be a pain worse than death.

"If you intend to use this arm again, you'll wear it. Thrashing in your sleep and laying on it isn't helping." Edhar's fingers were cold as he worked. "I'll construct something for you. In the meantime," he paused and looked Azrael dead in the eye, "Rest."

The healer left the room then, leaving the door wide open behind him. Azrael sighed and summoned his strength to get up and cross the room to close it.

Only to find *her* standing just outside it. Loose waves around her shoulders, a black long sleeve with a fur coat over it, she looked exactly as he had left her—only there was a haunted look in her eyes.

Azrael slammed the door with an easy flick of his fingers. He paused, one hand on his temples and the other hovering beside the door handle. A hundred thoughts spurred through his head before his hand twisted the handle enough to unlatch it and he returned to his bed. As soon as he sat down, the door creaked open.

"I love you," Lark said quietly, but decisively as she stepped in. "I never meant to hurt you or lie to you."

"You made them," he replied, his voice cold and even as ice on a pond. "The very demons raging across the kingdom. You may not have lied, but you certainly did not tell me that."

Azrael stood then, unable to bear her looking down at him.

"Az—" She took a step towards him but hesitated and moved back. Blinking back tears, she wiped angrily at her eyes. "I'm not the villain. I didn't want to tell you; I didn't want you thinking that I was. You don't know what he did, why I had to. I don't want to be the monster in your story."

"Why."

"Why what?" Her quiet voice was exasperated.

"Why did you make them?"

Lark tucked her lower lip between her teeth and looked anywhere but his face. She held her hand out. In that simple gesture, his anger fizzled out once he realized what it meant—it hurt too much to speak. He wanted to be a better man, to take her word for what she said, to not take her hand, but he grasped her fingers. A soft, dull pressure he hadn't noticed the last time she did this blossomed in his head before the memory flickered.

*It was dark—pure, terrifying, tangible dark. Lark's cheek stung, her arms wrapped tightly around her small body as it shook violently. So, so cold. Why did he do it? He had hit Mama so hard, her face hit the fireplace. The voices were calling, singing. The stars wanted to play. She reached her delicate hand out, ran her fingers along the jagged stones biting her fingertips. Suddenly it was bright, blinding light, and the stones dug into her as her body pressed against the wall.*

*"Call them." Her father was still angry. His hands were bloody, and his face—she couldn't look at his face. "Call them, Siena, you useless brat."*

*Lark closed her eyes and reached out to the stars, humming the song they had been singing to her for the past few weeks. They sang of home, of trees taller than the palace, taller than the mountains. The back of his hand jarred against her cheek and she tasted blood, but still she called.*

*They heard her. They were moving.*

*The room started to grow cold. Lark hated that they always brought the cold.*

*"Give them bodies. As you practiced. Give them what was promised."*

*"Father..."*

*"Siena, I did not ask you. I am telling you: give them what was promised."*

*She couldn't think of what she had practiced, couldn't think of the human faces she had chosen. No, she could only think of how long she would be here in this darkness, how the stones were sharper and harder to avoid the bigger she grew, how they poked into her back. She thought of how her father only threw her in here when he was furious, how Mama's face cracked as she hit the stone. Magic needed emotion, magic needed to be given something, or else it would take and take and take. Lark wanted the magic to take it all—all the hurt, the fear.*

Lark dropped their hands then, a violent gasp erupting from her. His defenses fell then, and he pulled her against him, wrapping his arms tightly around her. He didn't care that his shoulder screamed at the sudden movement; he squeezed her into his chest as she choked out, "I'm sorry I'm sorry I'm so sorry."

"I love you too," Azrael whispered into her hair, one hand stroking her hair, "I'm sorry."

# CHAPTER 33

## AZRAEL

Lark had been summoned, leaving bleary eyed and quietly. Azrael stood in front of the fire for a long time after she had left, too guilt ridden and numb to move. His head swarmed with things he didn't want to think about, everything buzzing in the forefront of his mind unable to be ignored.

He desperately wanted a bath but didn't want to venture out of his room in search of one. Every footstep outside his door caused him to flinch, part of him hoped it would be Lark coming back, while another part dreaded her return.

He didn't shy away from what she had shown him, didn't think less of her. It only made him think of her more, of her history that he didn't know about. Her history with two men, two kings, that had repeatedly made her less of who she was.

One king his father had devoted and lost his life for, in the name of a wife beater and a piss poor father. Whereas the other king, Azrael almost lost his life countless times for, all for a man who killed his king and lied to the entire kingdom. Did that make him stupid, or blind, for following and believing in those men? For taking Melech's words so easily, so quickly.

The life he lived had taken his parents, taken the women he had cared for, his own life crushed beneath the weight of an ideology he had no idea held merit. The thought made him sick, and shame burrowed deep within him, sinking venom filled teeth into his muscles and sloshing around in his body.

Sudden sickness jolted his body, and he hurled the contents of his stomach into the empty fruit bowl. Once the acid burned in his throat, he slid down, off the bed, and dropped onto the wood floor. He dug his fingers into his temples as though he could push the thoughts out of his head, rubbing small circles. In the motion, he realized his shoulder didn't possess the same ache it did when he had spoken with Bedivere—before he and Lark had spoken. He should have known; of course, she'd work her magic into his body without him knowing. His body tensed, ready to vomit again, but he coughed into his arm instead. He had seen countless horrors, been dealt unimaginable injuries, but thoughts and feelings were what made his stomach turn?

Lark had reached across that rift between them; an offering of forgiveness, of trust, while he flinched at the prospect of her using her godsgiven magic to heal him. His heart had turned traitor, once again falling into her hands.

Once his body calmed, he slowly eased to his feet. He decided he needed to leave the tiny room, and pulled on his coat, yanked his boots on. His thoughts were going nowhere but circles and anything would be better than falling prey to the shadows of his mind. He hesitated at the sight of his bag at the foot of his bed, wondering if he should arm himself. After a moment, he stuck a dagger into each boot and sullenly nudged the bag, and his sword still tied to it, underneath the bed.

Azrael wandered the halls, once more surprised at how large the manor was, but how small compared to the palace. No matter the size of a building, if it had multiple halls and rooms, Azrael was bound to lose himself, his sense of direction always failing.

It was quiet and empty, so unlike the palace with its bustling servants. He saw a few, but none paid him more attention than a furtive glance before continuing on their way. As he walked and the light from passing windows faded, his mind tried tricking him, gooseflesh pricking at his skin faster—as though there were another Daeoan lurking in the manor. His palm suddenly felt too empty without his sword, but he kept his eyes open, taking in every small detail he strolled by. The shadows did not deepen, did not twist, the chill did not fall faster than nature intended. Fire crackled somewhere, giving the illusion of warmth.

Another turn led him down a hall ending in a set of glass doors and a balcony beyond. He eased the door open, instantly greeted by icy wind that chilled him to the marrow in his bones. He tightened his coat around himself as he looked out over the ever-growing town, out towards the massive docks stretching most of the coastline. The sea in the north partially froze during winter, slowing if not halting trade with Areen and, if it had been well that year, Telaan too. There was comfort in seeing the Roe didn't stop—the town and its people kept fighting, kept surviving.

The door creaked behind him, but he didn't turn.

"Feeling better?" Bedivere asked as he moved to Azrael's side.

"Much," Azrael replied as a dark ship encroached the docks. Canvas sails fluttered in the breeze.

"During your time in the Falls, did Rook inform you of their plans?"

"Theirs?" Azrael asked carefully. He was tired of feeling foolish, carefully listening for the unspoken words. The Lord of the Roe had two exiles under his roof, accepted them without fuss, and had already tried writhing from beneath Melech's boot.

"Semantics." Bedivere smiled, his white teeth stark against his dark skin.

"How do you know her?"

"She used to be in the Tiras. I saw her often when my father took me on his trips to the Vale. That is a very old story, and not mine to tell."

Rook, in the Tiras? He thought of the way she carried herself, thought of her beside Nekoda, and the scar across her face.

"How do you fit into her plans?" Azrael asked again, his words soft and careful.

"Support." Bedivere's face and voice were all too casual. "This is where you come in, if you choose to. I wouldn't force you to do anything you don't want to do."

"You think I don't want to kill the king?"

"I didn't say anything about killing. Revenge is yours, if you want that, but I want peace. However, I do not believe the end justifies the means if the kingdom is thrown into chaos. I want peace for my people. The steps to achieve that must be tread carefully, thoughtfully."

"Who takes his place?"

Bedivere turned towards Azrael then, his expression gentle but blank, as though a child had asked a ridiculous question. Azrael bit the inside of his cheek, understanding at once. Lark wasn't accepted here because of her talents—she was here, under the lord's roof, as a piece in the puzzle. The thought of her as queen made him feel small. Made his heart, his feelings, small.

"She has much to learn, but I have faith in a future with her, even more so if you're standing at her side. She has seen the worst of two kings. I know she will rise above both and bring Havriel to a place where we can all be proud of." Bedivere turned to face his town, his hands in his pockets. "Dinner will be served shortly, if you wish to join me."

The Lord of the Roe offered Azrael a soft smile before he left him alone in the winter wind. His words remained with Azrael, hovering in the air. Instead of considering them, he left them on the balcony and followed the lord.

Azrael wasn't sure what to expect, never have dined with a lord beyond his quick breakfast the last time he was here, but it certainly wasn't a homely dining room set with a table and six chairs—two of them occupied. The view outside the glass wall was what Azrael focused on instead of the table's occupants. Stars glinted in the purple sky, past the reflections of candlelight flickering. He admired the cluster of cabinets that took space on the other three walls, then a large mirror interrupting the wood. In the reflective glass, he met the eyes of a woman in white, how striking she was compared to the earthy tones around her. Her eyes were a violent light blue that seemed nearly clear, and her hair was the same color as freshly fallen snow. In the mirror, she smiled before turning her focus.

Azrael hovered where he stood until Bedivere took his seat at the head of the table. He leaned forward to kiss the woman on the top of her head, his dark hand stark against her coloring as he cupped her cheek. Azrael sighed and took his seat at the end of the table, beside Lark.

His heart thundered against his ribs as he raised his gaze to her. She wore a simple dress, a soft grey that matched her eyes, and had her waves swept back and pinned in place with gold detailing, but nothing about her was as beautiful as the smile that overtook her face as Azrael stared at her. His ears warmed at the sight, as if it were only the two of them in the room.

A glass of wine set in front of him, the glass ringing against the wood, brought him back, suddenly aware again that they weren't alone. As the Lord and Lady dove into a conversation, food was brought out and placed.

Once the dishes had been cleared and more wine served, Azrael realized this was a family dinner. The woman—whose name was Luned but went by Lu—tried convincing Bedivere to go ice skating once the ponds were frozen over. The lord had shifted his posture, a smirk on his face, as he spoke.

"I broke *two* ribs and fractured my foot, Lu, or did you forget how horrible your bedside manners were?" Bedivere laughed as he sipped his wine, his black eyes only seeing her.

It was as though Azrael wasn't a true part in the evening, he could have been watching from outside the wall of glass, peering in on this life of theirs. Lark laughed along with the lord, but Azrael wondered if she ever had a family dinner like this. If it had been this easy with her adoptive mother, then if this was what family was supposed to be. Two people obviously, disgustingly in love with each other and laughter, drinks, hot food, and surrounded by warmth and the feeling of home.

He hadn't been silent through dinner, but he had been quiet, and hardly spoke to Lark even when the other two were engrossed in personal stories and jokes no one else understood. A servant carrying a pitcher of wine stopped beside him and lifted it in question. Azrael shook his head and stood.

"Excuse me, my lord, my lady," he said as the chair creaked when he pushed it out. "It's late."

Bedivere and Luned nodded to him, but Lark stood as well.

"I'll walk with you."

Azrael offered his arm to her as they walked out of the room together, leaving the two to fall back into their own world.

"Do you dine with them often?" he asked after a moment of grasping for things to say to her. He hated how it had grown so strange between them.

"Lu, yes, almost every meal. Bedivere only joins us for dinner." Lark paused, then added softly, "I'm glad you come tonight."

He was at a loss for words as they turned a corner and walked even slower. Silence fell like a spool of thread, lengthening the distance between them.

"How's your shoulder?"

"Better. I—uh, thank you for healing it."

He didn't recognize his door until Lark stopped outside of it. Everything looked the same, but he supposed he could note the artwork hanging on the walls to keep himself straight. The painting beside him was a close observation of a wheatfield. He twisted the handle, let the door creak open, but hesitated. Part of him wasn't ready for her to leave.

"Do you want to come in?" he asked with a voice hardly above the rustle of leaves. Lark's lips twitched, pulling up in softness. She opened the door and went straight to the fireplace, a flame leaping from her palm onto the wood.

"How can you do it?" Azrael said after the silence grew too long. Something, anything, to smooth the tension. "How does it work?"

Lark took her slippers off and tucked herself on the bed, leaning against the corner.

"Before it disappeared, magic was given at birth—did you know? When it was given to me, Iah told me he gave me everything he could and that he'd help me to wield it. I told you before I have the light and the shadow, and there's a lot I'm still learning. Think of it as unraveling part of my soul."

"If your father had wanted it so badly, why was it given to you?" he asked as he sat down on the bed as well, as far from her as the bed would allow.

"That's exactly why. The threads of our fate are so tangled, but if my father had received it, there wouldn't be any threads left." Lark looked at her hands, eyes tracing something that Azrael couldn't see.

"I never thought it was real until I met you."

He could have meant magic, he could have meant love, but he meant both, and the look on her face said she knew it.

"I'm proud to have it, even if it's something I have to hide."

They were now talking about two things, her double meaning as glaring as his. Lark inhaled sharply and turned her gaze to the fire.

"Where do you fit in all of this?" Azrael took his boots off, dropping his daggers on the floor and nudging them beneath the bed.

"In too many places." Lark sighed. Her eyelashes cast long shadows on her cheeks. With her attention turned away, he took the opportunity to study her, the straight line of her nose, the gentle curve of her lips. The power that rested in every inch of her. He had tried forgetting her, ignoring the thoughts of her that plagued his waking and dreaming mind.

"Az, I am sorry for how things happened," she said, breaking her unfocused eyes away from the fire, "With Melech, I mean. I tried—"

He cut her off by scooting closer and taking her hand in his. He rubbed his thumb along the back of her hand.

†

## LARK

They sat in silence together for some time, neither brave enough to truly face the other. Lark kept their hands together, but she fought every thought to pull him closer. She hadn't missed the hatred in his eyes when she had first come to his room. True, it had dwindled and disappeared, but that feeling left an echo. An echo that she could see he fought against. She couldn't do anything with it but wait.

His shoulder healed well, she noticed it in the way he held himself, and so did the scar at his throat. She inwardly flinched every time her eyes fell to it, knowing exactly how it had gotten there.

"Az?" she broke the silence, her voice sounding all too loud to her ears.

His black eyes met hers. He looked so tired, as though his soul was weary and cried out for rest.

"I cannot bear it," she whispered. "Be angry with me, fight with me, but I cannot bear this ice between us."

Lark didn't know what that made her—if all the years of heat and hate between her and Melech had twisted her heart into something spiky and black, but the tender ache blossoming like a bruise hurt more than words that cut.

"I have fought so much, been angry so much," he replied, so gently that it didn't seem like her Azrael. "Is a fight what you want?"

"I want you to be open with me, tell me what I can do."

He inhaled and held that breath in his lungs. With his exhale, it seemed whatever wall barricaded his heart had crumbled. Honesty, fear, and sorrow mixed together on his face, darkening the sharp features she had grown to love.

"My mother was murdered in front of me, by the demons you created," Azrael said, pulling his hand away from her. "A bolt of shadow through her throat. I had thought I imagined it, trying to make human nature seem more monstrous. It could have easily been a man with a bow and an arrow splitting her. But I met you and you made me fall in love with you, and those very demons are in my life again."

Lark stayed silent, feeling the ice already beginning to splinter and crack.

"Then the king targets me because he was jealous. You have turned my life around and upside down, and I *know* you will only break my heart again. You will wear that bloody crown, and I will be nothing again, lost in the shadow you cast." His voice slowly grew sharper as his chest began to move rapidly. "I know this will end, and I am fucking terrified for that. I was prepared to kill the king for you, because he intended to kill me for you."

Lark's heart raged in her chest now, seeing the look that darkened his eyes. She unspooled the shadows, unwinding them from the space between her ribs, and arranged them as plates of armor.

"And I would have died with him for you," Lark retorted, her voice sharper than she had meant. Her stomach felt as though she had been hit, and she struggled to keep her voice enough. She sat straighter, then stood. Azrael's hand lunged out to catch her hand, but gripped her wrist, pulling at her sleeve. Revealing the scar she hadn't healed.

Azrael moved to his feet then and pulled at the neckline of her dress. She had let the wound heal on its own, messily and unlike the smooth pale line across his throat.

"Did he—"

"You would have killed for me, and I would have died for you."

Knowing it wasn't a good idea, Lark leaned on her toes and kissed him. She wound her hand in his hair, winding the loose curls around her fingers. His hands moved down to her lower back, then slid up to grasp her waist. He turned them and walked her backwards until she was pressed against the wall, their mouths nor bodies parting.

"I thought I was going to lose you," she hissed against his mouth. A growl within his chest was his response, his hands flicking aside her dress. She hitched her leg around his waist, drawing him closer against her, and made it easier for his cool hand to slide up her thigh.

He rolled his hips against hers and moved his mouth down her jaw, her neck, and stayed there, his lips devouring her. Lark unwound her hands and fumbled with the laces of his pants, giving up and instead sliding her hand down the front. Grasping him, he groaned against her skin and swore.

She hadn't meant for this, but, swept up in the fervor, she realized she needed it—they both did. Needed to let go, be swept up in something other than the wounds they both tended.

With her free hand, she grasped his jaw, lifting him back up and kissed him again. Still working him, he shuddered against her and swore beneath his breath. He reached around and unlaced the back of her dress then pulled it down her shoulders, baring the scar the king had given her.

Azrael kissed it sacredly, slowing his movements, until he moved his mouth down, his tongue tracing the curve of her breast. Lark couldn't suppress the hitched sigh, and certainly not when his mouth kept trailing down until he was on his knees before her, continuing to pull her dress further down. The fabric puddled at her feet while his hands gripped her thighs as his mouth pressed gently to the curves of her hips.

Her hands gripped his unhurt shoulder, the other held his hair. It didn't take long for him to draw the lightning from her, devouring as she exploded into fragments. In a sweeping motion, his tongue left her and she made a noise as though to protest, but he bent her over the foot of the bed and buried himself within her.

Her hands gripped the blanket as she arched her lower back, curving her hips just so. Azrael leaned forward to gather her hair from her back, and held it in one hand, tugging ever so slightly, while the other gripped her waist.

The bedframe groaned beneath their motion, scraping against the wall, but Lark was floating, unable to care or focus on how loud it sounded. She buried her face into the bed, but Azrael tugged on her hair, pulling her head back.

His thrusts slowed as he leaned forward, "I want to hear you, princess."

To make a point, his movements remained slow, but deep, and drew out a low groan from Lark. Azrael swore as his hips moved quicker, and quicker once the motion elicited a gasp. Lark felt the momentum growing, her own stars bracing for the lightning and thunder to burst through her.

"Azrael—" Lark managed to grit his name in a moan before the storm broke through both of them; the moment his began, hers erupted too.

Lark moved forward, letting Azrael withdraw, and flipped to face him.

Chest heaving, his eyes were dark still as he looked at her, but black with heat and passion. She inched forward until their chests were pressed together, sweat slicking on both. She kissed his collarbone, pressing her hand into the back of his neck while her fingers rubbed small circles. Tension slipped off him as he relaxed into her touch. He wrapped his arms around her, pulling her tighter against him, and breathed in the smell of her hair, the smell of her skin. Lark wrapped one leg around his waist, hooking between his thighs, and pulled him over her as she settled backwards onto the bed.

# CHAPTER 34

## AZRAEL

Azrael woke the next morning from a dreamless sleep, limbs tangled with Lark's in the small bed. His shoulder no longer ached as he rolled his neck and stretched his arms, loosening his muscles from the long night.

He managed to procure a bath from a servant who couldn't keep her eyes to herself as the tub filled. He had to stifle a laugh when she asked if he needed assistance, but he had plastered an innocent smile on and declined.

With a weight eased in his chest, as though his heart had shed layers, he decided not to return to his hole in the wall room and wandered the manor grounds in the crisp morning air until he found a small training ring, adjacent to the manor and far from passing staff. Hay bales, grain sacks, a weapon rack of wooden and dull swords. It wasn't much, but he had to quell his excitement to keep from lunging for the sword.

Holding it gingerly in his right hand, he weighed his thoughts and fears, and shoved both aside as he rolled the hilt along his palm, onto the back of his hand, and back into his grip.

Before he dove into his regular drills, he put the sword back and slowly warmed up, despite his body aching for the movements he had honed over the years. A small part of him knew he should still rest, but he knew his body—knew the aches from the pains and knew when to break. His shoulder had healed enough. Once his heartbeat was quick in his chest, he took up the dull sword once again and set himself against the sacks of grain.

Irrelevant in the grand scheme of things, the mess of fate, Azrael slid back to where he was meant to be; a sword in his hand, an extension of his arm, sliding and slicing into the grain. He had heard footsteps growing behind him, a crowd gathering, but he ignored them until he hit the sack too hard, and it crumbled, fabric and grain falling onto the dirt. Behind him, someone groaned, envisioning the guts and gore that would have fallen instead if it had been a real man.

Azrael glanced over his shoulder, noticing first Bedivere at the forefront of the crowd. With a smirk on his face, his arms were crossed, and feet planted as he studied.

"Are you up for a fight?" the lord called out, mischief in his eyes plain as the sun in the sky, even from the distance that separated them.

"Always." Azrael grinned, more than ready to put his body to the test after what seemed like an eternity.

Flexing his fingers around the hilt, he watched Bedivere as he rolled his sleeves up to his elbows and pulled another dull sword from the weapon rack. The pair mirrored their movements, circling around each other, until Bedivere swung his sword overhead and lunged at Azrael.

Catching the lord's blow, fire erupted in Azrael as his focus narrowed to every precise moment. There was nothing beyond the motion in his arms, the way his muscles tensed and loosened as he twisted. Azrael pushed his strength into forcing the lord's blade down, down, until the tip touched the dirt. He stomped his boot on the tip and pulled his sword up to collide broadside into the lord's unguarded ribs. He didn't expect Bedivere to move away so deftly, the calculated move sliding through the air. The lord parried, then caught and held the next swing of Azrael's sword, the steel singing beautifully in the morning air.

Bedivere pushed against Azrael, the lord's dark eyes glinting in the sunlight to match the mischievous smile before he stepped away, leaving Azrael off kilter. He balanced himself quickly and used the awkward motion to skirt around the lord before he lunged. Angling the sword again, the broadside thwacked against Bedivere's bicep. Azrael shifted his weight on his feet, the blade cutting through the cold air, and ducked Bedivere's swing. Time seemed to slow as he brought his blade upwards, effectively cutting through arteries if he hadn't adjusted the line of motion, and if the blade wasn't duller than a river rock.

To Bedivere's credit, he moved quicker than Azrael expected, once again, and didn't forfeit. Azrael realized he hadn't given the lord enough credit—he'd assumed Bedivere was first and foremost a lord, not a skilled soldier who would hold his own against him. Their dance continued as the sun crawled higher into the sky, fighting, slipping in the dirt, stumbling into the hay, mindfully giving the other nothing more than bruises and a slew of curses.

It was only when Azrael's elbow caught the lord's jaw and his other hand pounded into his ribs that Bedivere spit out blood and raised a dark, calloused hand.

Azrael grinned, straightening his posture, and ignored the sting in his cheekbone from the lord's right hook.

"Are you giving up?" Azrael taunted, arms opening in a challenge.

Bedivere laughed, his mouth painted with blood. "You should know," he said, "that I do not bend. I do not yield. I do not *give up*."

The remaining audience they had murmured their approval of their lord. The pair took a few steps away from one another, catching their breath, before beginning the dance once more.

They only stopped when Luned strolled through the sparse audience, a snowflake given life in her white dress that hugged her tall frame with her long, crystal colored hair hanging down her back. Azrael felt a feral beast in her presence, cheek bruised, panting, with a cut on his forearm bleeding through rip in his sleeve. The Lord of the Roe didn't fare much better, his hair knotted and tangled, dirt smudged on his face, and his white shirt now a musty tan, mixed with sweat, blood, and dirt.

Footsteps thudded against the earth as the onlookers departed, leaving Azrael without shame to sit on the cool ground while Luned spoke with Bedivere.

Azrael hadn't noticed how quickly the hours had slipped by while they were sparring. Evening was not far off. They had spent the afternoon fighting, and it had felt *good*. His body was sore, but his shoulder didn't hurt from wielding the sword. For the first time since he had fled the streets of the Vale, he allowed himself to feel a tiny flicker of hope that peace would find his life again.

"Well, Azrael," Bedivere said as he returned to the weapon rack and replaced his sword. "I hate to say you've bested me, but I think that may have been the outcome here. What do you say, darling?"

His arm wrapped around Luned, his dark hand leaving dusty prints on her pristine dress. Her icy stare studied Azrael. She turned and said something to the lord to make him throw his head back and laugh.

Bedivere kissed her cheek before strolling over to where Azrael still sat. The lord offered his hand out and helped Azrael to his feet.

"I'm certainly going to eat my dinner in my bed. I'll have dinner sent to you as well, if you wish."

"Thank you, my lord," Azrael said, hands on his hips to keep his lungs open.

Bedivere smiled before he returned to Luned's side. Before they began walking back towards the manor, Azrael heard the lord, "Come, love, let's get you out of that dress."

Placing his sword back onto the rack, he crumpled the bottom of his shirt in his hand, letting the cold air rush onto the planes of his stomach, freezing the sweat. He followed the lord and lady at a distance, far from ear shot, and thought of nothing but a warm bath.

# CHAPTER 35

## LARK

Bedivere had a small, mostly empty infirmary within the manor, but Lark sought the larger one that sat at the end of town. The one that looked like an old barn overrun with grass and stray wheat stalks on either side of it. The wood itself was the only indication that the building was occupied and taken care of. The front door was ajar to let the last whispers of autumn drift in, and for Lark to squeeze in.

Canvas sectioned off small rooms, illuminated by rustic lanterns hanging from the railing that spanned the ceiling. A rolling ladder sat unused in the corner along a track that inched along the entire platform that sat above the sectioned rooms. Healers walked between the canvas, some with their hands full of bandages and salves, while others simply held journals and a pen. A heavy quiet weighed in the air, and Lark stepped carefully to avoid the crude loudness of her footfalls.

Lark wanted to feel productive, to feel as though her presence in the Roe was as beneficial to the people as it was to her. She had bided her time with Bedivere, ignoring Iah's words of caution and danger in the back of her head, while she had waited for Azrael to eventually arrive. She had been on edge with every loud sound, every lengthening shadow, while coming to terms of being an exile in her own kingdom. Bedivere and Lu, however, made her feel as though she wasn't, as though she were simply there for a visit. Lu had set her up in a small room before Lark figured out something long term. They had helped give Lark a sliver of normalcy.

A pile of her belongings had ended up in a heap in her room, and Lark wasn't sure how it had gotten there, but wasn't about to overlook the small happiness the gesture had given her. Having her things, her clothes, made her feel at home, settling a little bit further into the Roe. Having Azrael here too—

Shame still flushed her cheeks and chest when she thought about the tension and the sex that had dissolved the feelings of mistrust and anger. She hadn't given much thought to how truly damaging being with Melech had been, how she didn't know how to proceed in an argument or tackle the obstacle of the void between them. At least they were past it, Lark reminded herself. She had bared her soul to Azrael, but it didn't make her feel as vulnerable anymore. Melech had known everything about Lark—held those powerful memories and feelings over her head. Azrael cherished knowing her, learning about her, while Melech reveled in it.

"I'll have a bed for you in a moment, dear," a soft voice called to her. Lark had stopped walking, lost in her thoughts in the middle of the barn. A plump older woman passed Lark, arms full of linens, but stopped and did a double take. "What's wrong with you, child?"

Lark glanced down, momentarily forgetting she wore her fur-lined leggings and old Tiras shirt, with the red wrist cuff replaced with lace, and realized she didn't look the part of a healer. If anything, her face held each fragment of exhaustion she had felt these past few days.

"I'm here to help, if I can," Lark said, mustering her confidence as she lifted her chin.

The woman turned her full attention to Lark then, eyeing her suspiciously. Noting Lark's nose, eyes, the change was apparent in the woman's face as recognition alighted the gently wrinkled face.

"Lark, I'd love for you to help, but thankfully we don't have—"

"A woman!"

The door flew open, slamming against the inner wall of the barn. A breathless man stood with one hand on the frame and the other pressed to his stomach as he tried to catch his breath.

"A woman is giving birth on the road. She can't—" a gasping breath "—make it."

Lark looked at the woman with raised eyebrows. A silent question. Lark fingered the strap on her bag as the weight made itself known, digging into her shoulder. The older woman nodded then jerked her head towards a canvas section.

"Take what you need."

"How far?" Larked asked the breathless man who fought to not double over.

"Not far." The man coughed, sounding a breath away from vomiting. "Three fields over."

Lark nodded and hurried towards the supplies, stuffing her bag with linens and extra herbs and liquids. She held a bowl and filled a waterskin as quick as she could before walking to the man.

"Take me to her."

†

A carriage fit for nobility had pulled off the main road, partially obscured by the tall and stiff winter grass. Footmen stood on either side while three guards paced around it. Soft wailing erupted from inside the gilded cab as the man led Lark around horseless front. She had a fraction of a moment to wonder where the horses had gone before one of the guards advanced. Thankfully, the man that led her explained for her as she opened the door.

Inside the carriage was as striking as the outside, colored padded cushions, a small glass chandelier reflecting candlelight, but Lark's focus went straight to the woman hunched on the bench, still wearing a hefty dress and a headpiece that illuminated the beads of sweat budding on her powdered cheeks. Familiarity struck Lark then but couldn't place where she knew the woman. Her heart grew heavy at the sight of the woman entirely alone in the carriage while the men stood outside, their eyes averted.

"Hello there," Lark said gently as she climbed in. She thought of the coolness her shadows could bring and willed them to flicker into the cab, letting them play around the woman's face. Lark kept the door propped open to allow the cool air outside.

The woman grunted something in response, tears running down her face as she looked at Lark. Fingers gripping the edge of the seat hard enough to turn her knuckles white, she let out a scream that had the men scuffling in the dirt outside.

Lark murmured soothing words to her until the contraction had passed, then asked, "What's your name?"

"Aida," she sighed as exhaustion swept over her. The grip she held loosened a fraction as she slumped against the wall. "Raines."

Aida Raines. Daughter of one of the men who sat on Melech's council, a man of a long line of noble blood and one who influenced the way the crown spent money. Lark wondered what she was doing this far from the Vale.

"Is this your first, Aida?" Lark moved closer to the woman, gently removing the headpiece, and pulled pin after pin from the woman's tight hair.

"Yes," Aida breathed. Her neck relaxed as her hair tumbled in ringlets, bright blonde curls. "Will I die? I'm so afraid. I didn't think it'd hurt this much—"

Her words tailored off in a pained, suppressed groan that had her tightening her grip once more. Lark waited until it passed, then moved to ease Aida's shoes off.

"Aida, I need you to breathe through those, okay? Don't hold your breath. How long have you been in labor?"

"Hours."

Lark nodded, her thoughts spinning and spinning. She filled the bowl she had brought with water and soaked a linen before dabbing it on Aida's face, wiping off the makeup that had smeared from sweat and tears.

"Would you help me out of this ridiculous dress?" Aida asked, green eyes flashing with a hundred emotions. Lark nodded, a reassuring smile flickering on her face.

Lark closed the carriage door before undoing the laces on Aida's back, and easing the mass of fabric down her body, mindful of the swollen belly. Once Aida wore only her under dress, she sighed with contentment.

"May I see how far you are?" Lark asked with a soft voice. She rolled up her sleeves and tucked a stray hair behind her ear as she sat on the floor before Aida. The woman nodded and positioned herself enough that Lark was able to glance at a dark head. She swallowed.

"Okay, Aida Raines, I'm going to ask you to push in a moment, and I need you to breathe. Don't let it overtake you. Breath through it." Lark smiled again. "I would like for you to stand, though. It'll make it easier on you, I promise."

Aida nodded before moving slowly to her bare feet. Lark counted the moments before the next contraction and began to unspool the ivory ribbon in her chest, pulling at her ribs. She ignored the twinge it wrought.

"I'm going to feel for the baby's head, alright? Be ready to push, Aida," Lark said as she moved the woman's under-dress to the side. She felt the babe's head just as a contraction took a hold of Aida. She yelled, sobbed, and pushed. Lark felt the smallest movement into her head. Almost.

"That was wonderful, Aida." Her voice was as calm, as soft as she could. Aida rested her head on the padded wall and breathed an airy laugh.

"Do you have any children?" She turned her head just enough to look at Lark, tears running down her pale face.

Lark smiled and shook her head. The question always burned her, a wildfire singeing every heartstring that thrummed in her chest. It reminded her of that night she had received her magic—the way her skin, her veins, her body felt as that lightning ripped through her. Her father hadn't known many things that night, but Lark's womb had been rendered barren, the possibility of bearing her own children torn from her without a choice. She had made her peace, but she wished she had the choice to not have children, instead of being unable to.

She sensed the next contraction at the same moment her counting began to dwindle.

"Aida, this is it. You've done so well, now give me one last push."

Aida took a deep breath, furiously nodding as though talking herself up to it, and screamed as she pushed. A tiny human fell into Lark's awaiting hands, a tiny cry rippling through Aida's. The woman nearly collapsed once she heard the baby, but teetered and caught herself.

With one hand cradling the child, Lark used her other to free the dagger from her bag and cut the cord between mother and child. Aida crumpled onto the bench, twisting to face Lark, and held her arms out with a vacant smile on her face.

Lark quickly studied the babe, a little boy suddenly quiet after the initial cry of life, and wiped him before wrapping him in a linen and handing him to her. Ivory ribbons still drifted towards Aida, gently inspecting and easing the pain. Lark sent another to make sure everything was okay, only then she noticed it.

The drip, drip of blood down her ankle, slowly pooling on the floor. Utter silence cracked Lark's thoughts as the color darkened. Aida's gentle coos to her child were drowned out by the wretched silence of Lark's head.

This had happened only once before, with Thea and Isabel, when the bleeding didn't stop, even with her magic and tools, and Lark had to rely on the sheer willpower of the both of them to save Thea. Lark touched Aida's knees, sending tendril after tendril of healing deep within her. If only she could stop the bleeding, then she could work on the damage—

*I had a child once,* Iah's voice slipped through the cracks in Lark's mind, echoing in the darkness that threatened to drown her. *I don't care,* she wanted to shout back, but only ignored the god instead.

Lark focused her magic on finding the small tears, the source of the damage, and gritted her teeth through her own wounds the magic was creating. Her breath caught in her throat, but she kept pushing, kept unspooling.

Oblivious, Aida kept murmuring to her child, small squeaks in response. Lark refused this to be their last moment together. She would not let Aida die.

Stitch by stitch, moment by moment, sweat beaded along Lark's neck, the palms of her hands, as she sewed this woman up from the inside out. Only when a crack echoed in her head, did Lark stop. Instantly releasing her magic at the pain, she stumbled backwards and clutched at her ribs. She couldn't yet tell if the magic had broken a rib, or if she had merely thought so. *Gods* did it hurt.

The bleeding had stopped, the dark red pool sliding away, slinking along the smooth floor of the carriage. Lark's magic detected no other damage in the young woman, and she breathed a sigh of relief, only to hiss at the pain it wrought.

"How can I thank you?" Aida's voice rang in Lark's ears. "I don't even know your name."

"Siena," she said, quietly enough that Aida may not have heard, then said louder, "Lark. My name is Lark."

"The Tiras healer!" Aida squeaked, her pallid face brighter for a moment. "I'm so glad you were here. Really, how can I thank you?"

Lark smiled, though she felt it may have resembled a grimace instead. "If you would tell your father, Siena sends her regards."

If anything would come of this, Lark would want Aida Raine's father to know the princess saved his daughter's life.

┼

Horses fitted once more and carriage attended to, Lark led the strange entourage towards the infirmary, taking the road instead of cutting through the fields as she had before. She was grateful for the chill suspended in the air as her entire body weighed down with the events of the afternoon, combined with everything that had happened these past weeks. Her head was hardly above the surface, her pain and exhaustion keeping her toes away from the bottom, so she merely floated in the water. So to speak.

Once they reached the infirmary, the footmen paced, the guards snipped until one was allowed inside with Aida, and Lark trailed after them, waiting until the woman and child had been given a bed in the far corner. She lingered to bid farewell and offer a silent prayer for both of them before she was shooed away by the head healer—no longer needed.

*Birdie.*

Lark groaned, realizing too late cracks had appeared in her mind, allowing the seeping darkness of Iah's voice to flood in. He was relentless, even more so when she was on the brink of collapsing from exhaustion. Her feet dragged on the cold earth as she mindlessly stumbled back towards Bedivere's manor.

*You tire too quickly. You are giving too much of yourself for your power. Practice the balance.*

She was too tired to roll her eyes, too tired to throw her hand to the sky in the shape of a vulgar gesture, but she grumbled.

*Keep a steady heart.*

Lark smoothed over the cracks in that wall, blocking him out, and enjoyed the silence in her head as she meandered through the Roe, back up to the manor. She could hardly muster a friendly smile to the staff she passed. As soon as she creaked open the door to the guest room she'd been holed up in, a weight slipped from her shoulders.

Deep breaths still hitched in her chest, nicking at the rib she had sworn broke, but the pain receded, slowly. So slowly. The immensity of her power did not scare her. Lark faced the vast dark water with her chin high and shoulders back. She had accepted it long ago. The pain and payment that vastness demanded took her too quickly, the aftermath of magic adding up faster than she could stop—that frightened her. If she needed to use that expanse of magic, what would be the cost? Would it take her life as payment?

Lark folded the thought, tucking it away, deep inside her heart, and undressed. Only in her underthings, she crawled into bed, curling into a small ball beneath the furs and blankets. She fell into a deep, soundless sleep where no gods walked.

# CHAPTER 36

## AZRAEL

D ays, then weeks passed. Winter was upon the Roe, carrying snow on the frigid wind until the town wielded a thick cover of white. Within a week of Lark and Azrael deciding to stay in the Roe, Bedivere ordered an empty house in town to be cleaned and prepared for either, or both. Azrael debated for days what he wanted, but eventually his heart won, and the two of them moved their few belongings into the house.

Stuck tightly between two brightly colored buildings on either side, their house was a dark shade of red that matched the color of the earth in summer. The front door was a ghastly dark yellow with blue shutters adorning the window on the right, clashing but coming together to feel like home. It was a tall structure, narrow, but small. Azrael had tried protesting, looking at the front of it from the street, until Bedivere led them inside and showed the modesty of it.

Two bedrooms upstairs, one bathing room, a tight kitchen, an open sitting room, and a small backyard currently stacked with snow. It was perfect.

The sitting room took most of the space with its high ceiling with a fireplace on one side of the room. Looking out to the backyard, the wall was made entirely of glass, which Azrael had now learned was a feature of most Roen homes. On clear days, the ocean could be seen over the roofs of the house beyond. The house was unique in its layout, Bedivere had said, because of the staircase that led to the second floor, which seemed to take up only the right side of the house, offering a strange shape. Azrael's room was at the end of this oddity, with Lark's beside it.

As time passed, Azrael fell into learning what he could about Roen life, discovering from an old man on a street corner that there were *four* gods, but Banii was the only one to be praised as she was the goddess of all creation. He learned of bandits that camped out on the barren fields, robbing farmers and merchants who drew too close. He had seen the fluidity the dockworkers held as they managed their days, singing songs of heartbroken women and sailors. Bedivere had also offered Azrael a different job, refusing to allow him stand guard and waste his talent.

"While we bide our time, I don't want you standing at my door waiting for something that may or may not happen," Bedivere had said in his study one day, watching the snow fall. "If you could do anything, what would you do?"

Azrael had shifted on his feet, unsure if he should be honest. He had noted the slack in the guards that were not stationed within the manor. Those that were positioned throughout the town most likely going unnoticed by their captain.

"The Town's Guard needs reform," Azrael said after a pause long enough to nearly have forgotten the question he'd been asked. Snowflakes drifted past the glass, slow and lazy, as though the flecks had all the time in the world to land. Bedivere turned from the window, a knowing smile on his face.

"Sit," the lord had said, gesturing to the chairs. "Tell me."

Azrael had, then was shortly introduced to the Captain of the Town's Guard, a portly man whose eyes drifted too easily towards pretty girls walking by or young men with soft faces. He bore an exceptionally crusted mustache, and Azrael focused on the area surrounding the man, hardly daring a look at him.

The conversation hadn't been pleasant and resulted in the captain losing teeth and yelling the entire way out of the guardhouse, swearing and cursing from a mouthful of blood and gaping holes until his figure had disappeared and the grating voice diminished from distance.

Then finding himself organizing the Town Guard, Azrael accidentally became a reluctant—*temporary*, he stressed with Bedivere, only temporary until someone more suitable is found—captain. Twice now he had risen to above what he believed he deserved and was humbled the moment Bedivere announced it himself in the guardhouse.

"King-slayer!"

"*Sa Tehe Bri!*" Little Death, it meant.

Azrael had scowled at the Telaanan phrase, recalling what the boulder of a man Caed had taunted him with when he had first met the other Tiras— *"Death follows you, boy, but not in the way it should."* He tried to wear it as a mantle, letting it settle on him rather than within him.

Lark spent her days in the manor with Bedivere, learning how to govern, while Azrael spent his amongst men and women who slowly stopped spitting at his boots when they passed him. The fiery anger had subsided into a dull acceptance. He didn't know what changed—surely not the rigorous training in the blizzard that descended, nor the strict schedules he kept them adhered to.

In the evenings, Azrael and Lark were inseparable once more, making a mess in their kitchen and playing a card game to decide who would end up cleaning. Lark would heat the house with her white flames leaping in the fireplace and they would lay on blankets on the floor, shoulder to shoulder, watching the shadows dancing on the sharp contours of the ceiling. They would give those shadows shapes, names, and stories as though watching clouds.

Everything fell away in those moments. The pain both fought, the nightmares that plagued both to the point they stayed up together and made love until the fears had quieted. Azrael let himself feel vulnerable, knowing his own fears were mirrored in Lark, so he did not shirk away from her loving touch or her outbursts when the darkness closed in too tightly.

"Rook will be here tonight," Lark reminded him, three weeks after he had arrived in the Roe, when they were in the kitchen preparing their dinner. Azrael peeled potatoes while Lark tended to the pork, her hair in a mess tied off with a ribbon. He nicked the bottom of his palm as he admired the way she looked in his shirt, all too large for her slight frame, despite her height.

"I remember," he said mindlessly. He had forgot the rebel leader was arriving at some point in the night to call a meeting for the ominous plans of hers.

He dunked his hand into the bowl of water he had rinsed the potatoes in, then continued with his part of preparing, careful not to use his left hand as the blood began to clot and dry already. He glanced at Lark, wondering if she had noticed the small cut and resolved to keep it to himself.

"I still don't like it," he said as he began to cut the potatoes then.

"Well, you're supposed to keep the skin on, love. They taste better that way," Lark said, her fingers rubbing spices into the slabs of meat before her.

"No, I mean—really? You didn't say anything until now?" He continued to cut the potatoes into chunks before dropping them into the pot. "I meant, I don't like that Rook wants Melech dead and she wants me to do it."

"Bedivere won't agree to that."

Azrael said nothing. Once his task was complete, he placed the pot into the fire and let it boil. He poked at the small, angry red line on his palm, avoiding what he wanted to say. He wanted Melech dead, but he didn't think it would benefit the kingdom to remove the man so forcefully. For once, Azrael thought of the consequences of his actions, and it made him dizzy. He moved to the narrow counter he had been working at, bracing one hand against the smooth stone. He poured wine from the pitcher with the other hand, drank it all, then poured another glass. He watched Lark work, placing the pieces of meat onto the pan she had placed beside her, and set it into fire before she sat down at their small table across from him.

"What is it you fear?" she asked as she poured herself a glass, her smooth fingers giving him something to focus on instead of meeting her eyes.

"Failure." A small part of him wasn't afraid to admit that—not to her. "Failure means I die, then you lose everything you've worked for, and it gives motivation for Melech to go to war against Bedivere."

"A big fear."

"A big fear," Azrael echoed. In their late nights filled with anxiety and worry, the two of them sorted their thoughts into big and small. Small: things that had steps outlined to overcome. Big: things that had a path hidden, things that overwhelmed, things that threatened to knock the air from his lungs if he thought about them for too long.

"Bedivere won't agree to regicide. He knows where I stand, and I don't want a crown that's stained with blood. Not if I can help it." Lark bent her elbows on the edge of the table, looking for all the world like an ordinary woman, and Azrael let himself, for a moment, pretend she was. Pretend that he was an ordinary man, their life was ordinary. There was a simple peace in the thought, but it felt wrong, the difference in knowing what is a dream and what is a nightmare. "But, I know that doesn't make you feel any better."

"No," Azrael simply said. He sat down in the other chair, its wood creaking slightly under his weight. He listened to the water boil as he took another sip of wine.

✝

There was irony in each step that Azrael took on the way to their midnight meeting, but he didn't care to acknowledge it. Once his life revolved around fighting the rebels, now he went to join them in their fight against the cruel king. His life had a purpose—a strange, elusive one, and one he certainly wished he had a say in—but a purpose, nonetheless.

He wasn't sure what to expect, though he couldn't keep the scowl from his face as he entered the council room. He picked out Rook instantly, seeing her golden head first, from her place beside Bedivere. Her hair was pulled back into a harsh style, accentuating the tightness in her face and sharpness of her scar. She merely glanced in Azrael's direction, then returned her attention to Bedivere. Lark sat at his left while Azrael settled in beside her, across from Rook. The remaining chairs around the table were occupied by guards, soldiers, and an old man.

"As I was saying," Rook continued, a slightly irritated look flashed on her face as she glanced to Azrael. "I still think we draw him out and make it a statement."

"That would end with innocent lives lost. He'll send the Tiras first. Do you want to slaughter them too?" Bedivere said. The lord was straight in his chair, his long hair loose past his shoulders.

"If it's necessary. A lesser evil, getting rid of them."

"Is it?" Azrael asked. Half a dozen eyes turned to pin him to his chair.

"If it gets him off the throne, breaks up the foundation he has in place, yes." Rook leaned back in her chair. He hadn't dealt with her much, but there was a ferocity in her now that he hadn't seen before. He wondered if it were new, or if he had simply missed it at the Falls.

"And you want me, the disgraced Tiras and attempted king-killer, to take his life." Azrael's voice was even, but his heart threatened to fracture his ribs.

Rook's eyebrows inched higher on her forehead, her scar bunching. "Do you still have loyalty to him?"

"How can you ask that—"

"After he started treating his friends like criminals, letting his dogs run through the city doing whatever they pleased, setting *demons* loose on a town full of innocents for the sake of proving a *point*," Rook leaned forward, her teeth bared, "and you don't want to kill him? He's driving this kingdom into the grave, and his subjects with it."

"You think that won't happen if we forcibly remove the king from the throne? Without an heir, without a thorough plan of action afterwards?" Azrael retorted. "Sending Lark into the palace in a flowing dress and crown will not ally the people to her if we just stuck a sword in the king's chest. Why must his life end so violently, if it's mine on the line too?"

Azrael fought to keep his breath even as he stared across the table at Rook, her jaw so tight he should have heard her teeth cracking. The men beside her began to murmur, then the ones beside Azrael joined, and before too long, half a dozen voices began rising, speaking then yelling over one another. Fingers pointed, palms smacked the wooden table. Rook's heated stare did not waver and Azrael struggled to pinpoint her rage, why it manifested with him. He was first to look away, turning to Bedivere. From the look in the lord's eyes, Azrael saw this wasn't what Bedivere had expected in hosting the meeting.

The lord raised his hand and the room silenced. "Azrael has brought up points I am surprised to find do not have answers yet. I will not send my people to war for revenge, nor send a man to his death merely because he is capable of overcoming it. Melech will answer for his crimes, perhaps with his life, but first with his words."

He shifted his attention to Lark then, his hair gently rustling with the turn of his head. "I understand you have been working on something."

Lark nodded. "I will not end the king's life the way he ended my father's. I will not take the crown with bloody hands." With that, the outline of her body began to disappear, as though she were a ghost, until the sight of her sitting in her chair was gone.

Silence settled in the room. Azrael was convinced no one breathed.

"Great, so we have someone who can become invisible, but refuses to sneak up on the king," Rook groaned, her voice breaking the quiet, heavy with disdain. Lark appeared again, her body coming into focus slowly. An unfocused look lingered in her eyes, but she wiped at her nose and glared at Rook.

"I propose we remove the king from the palace, lock him in a cell until a proper trial can be held. With some help, I can mask him and assist in removing him. I will not kill him," she repeated.

"There will still be blood on that crown, girl. No matter how you take it. Hundreds of years caked onto it. You sure you still want it?" Rook leaned in her chair casually, but Azrael noted the tension in the way she held herself. As though what Lark had done and said didn't surprise the rebel leader at all. "Once it's on your head, there is no stepping back."

"The past kings have made choices and mistakes that ruined countless lives. They've lied and stolen and kept the kingdom in the dark for too long. If you do not have faith in me, say so. I intend to rule as an apology for my father, and his before him. I want to see you as my sister, not as a rebel, a disgrace, who has to hide in her mountains. I have no doubts about the kind of ruler I will be and, if you do, then we are not here for the same reason."

He watched Rook's face as Lark spoke, then glanced at all those sitting around them. There was no hint of jealousy, mistrust in any of them. Rook's mouth twitched up, a small flash of pride in her eyes. Hope swelled in the room, nearly tangible as the murmuring began again, this time in approval of the princess.

"He should stand for what he's done," Azrael added, "If Lark doesn't want blood, Melech needs to stand trial for what he's done and let everyone know who exactly their king was. I'd love to watch him die, but first, I'd like to watch him burn."

†

The meeting bled into the early morning, the endless speaking in circles slowed as the sun's rays began to sketch the sky. Azrael crawled into bed as dawn illuminated his home, leaving Lark with Bedivere to go over their lessons on politics and monarchy. His body wouldn't relax, wouldn't conform to the embrace of his bed, while his mind spun—Melech, Nekoda, the Daeoan, the four gods, Lark as queen... Azrael had to do something, rid himself of these poisoning thoughts by *doing* something. He was drowning.

He dressed into fresh clothes, splashed water on his face from the basin in the bathing room, and adorned his favored daggers and his sword. Tugging on his thick coat, Azrael was out the door and in the cold air with the plaguing thoughts already beginning to eddy from his head.

The sun remained hidden behind Bedivere's manor as he strode up the street to the stables where he still kept his horse. He was glad Bedivere allowed the horse to remain—another kindness Azrael felt he didn't deserve. That, or another debt he owed the lord.

Dogs ran through the stables, their claws clicking on the stone floor and nipping at each other's tails, while the horses chuffed at the noise. Only Azrael's paid him attention as he walked in. The building wasn't as nice as the one at the palace, but this one was quaint, with dark brown wood and hay tucked into every nook and crevice. Only five stalls on either side, Azrael couldn't help but wonder about Bedivere's army, if it were mounted and where they were kept if it was.

A quiet stable boy came to him then, as Azrael was rubbing his horse's nose, and asked a silent question. Azrael nodded and leaned his head against the stall as the stable hand readied his horse. His thoughts began to drift once more, and he found himself wondering why he had never learned what his horse's name was.

After his mare was saddled and given a small square of sugar, Azrael held the reins in one hand while he walked out. In the open air, he breathed deeply before climbing up and bounding towards the sprawling fields.

Bright blue sky and ground of white and brown stretched on forever once he cleared the houses edging the town. The landscape turned flat around him, providing no distractions from his thoughts. Melech killing Nekoda, how and why, if Lark had seen it, where they would be if he hadn't. Was everything meant to be—already planned—or was the world pure chaos? Why was only one god here, in Havriel? Where did gods go?

Azrael waved his hand, shooing away a bug flying in the corner of his eye. He squinted in the bright sunshine, seeing a thin dark shape hurtling towards him. He veered his horse to the side as an arrow buried into the snowy ground beside him. Pulling on the reins, his mare stomped as his eyes grazed the horizon. The angle the arrow had come...

A ditch, sloping strangely, caught his gaze, then the tip of a bow peaked over the lip. Bright red fury burned within Azrael's chest. He stayed his hand, despite the wrath, and kept his eyes on the bow. He'd give the archer the choice—staying where he was, Azrael would be an easier target now. His blood thrummed a song he had missed. A head popped over the lip of the ditch, face indistinguishable from the distance. An arm reached up, back, into the quiver. Azrael gripped his sword and waited until the archer notched the arrow to swing off.

The arrow buzzed by him, close enough that, if Azrael were agile enough, he could have plucked it from the air. Instead, he swiped at it with his sword, cleaving it in half, as he bounded across the distance.

The figure lunged from the ditch, scrambling to right itself before Azrael advanced too closely. He slowed though, once he realized the figure was a gangly boy—no more than sixteen—with a poorly strung bow and a dagger flapping at his hip. Clarity shot through Azrael's anger, and he lowered his sword.

"What are you doing?" he demanded. He didn't move as the boy unsheathed the dagger and moved towards Azrael.

"You can't be that stupid. I'm here for the bounty."

"You're not a bounty hunter," Azrael said evenly. The boy's hand shook enough that sunlight danced off the blade.

"I am," the boy said indignantly, brows furrowing.

Azrael cocked his head. "How much is my life worth?"

"Hundred thousand gold." The boy lifted his chin, pockmarked face proud as he looked at Azrael.

"That's all I'm worth? You must tell the king you deserve more than that." Azrael laughed. "How long have you been out here, waiting for me to pass by?"

The boy shifted on his feet as regret swept over his features, though it didn't last long. Azrael took the moment of hesitation to rock on his heels and smash his knuckles into the boy's nose. Stumbling back, the boy careened into the ditch just as a black figure jumped out, followed by a second. Stark against the landscape, it didn't take long for Azrael to size up both figures advancing, to note only their eyes were visible beneath their dark ensembles. Familiar eyes that spoke of nothing but hate.

With his left hand, Azrael loosened a dagger from his boot and hurled it at the figure advancing on his left, burying the blade deep within their chest. Their body spasmed before falling to their knees. The second figure lunged towards Azrael and drew a sword with a yell that echoed off the cold earth.

He raised his sword to meet the stranger's, steel against steel singing vibrantly in the morning. Azrael tried to ignore the striking familiarity in the blue eyes, but instead on the rage that simmered. He pushed his blade back, back, until the figure slipped, spun on their heels to catch themselves, and launched at Azrael again. A white knuckled fist collided too quickly for Azrael to stop it, right into his cheekbone, hard enough for stars to swirl in his sight. A blur of black lunged again, but Azrael focused on the hatred burning in his chest and plunged his blade through his attacker's stomach, up into their ribs.

They fell into the snow together, rough, dying hands grasping at Azrael before he clambered to his feet. A broken rasp in a familiar voice, a phrase muttered too quietly to make out, but Azrael recognized that voice as Maddox's, one of the Tiras swordsmen. Azrael roughly yanked his sword free from Maddox's ribs, relishing in the crack of bone against steel.

A hundred thousand gold for his life. The thought was so strange to Azrael. That his life had a price, and that his life had changed so drastically that there was a *price* on it.

He hadn't even eaten breakfast yet and he'd killed two men, wounded a boy. He swore before whistling for his horse, who had given the fight a wide berth. Azrael wiped the blood off his sword with Maddox's shirt before letting the dead man rest. Sheathing his sword, he trudged towards his horse before he was close enough to jump on.

Exhaustion crept in as he walked home from the stables. After the long night and longer morning, he was ready to crawl into bed and stay there. He aroused strange stares from the stables all the way to his home, forgetting he had gotten blood on him from Maddox. He rinsed in a half-frozen bath before burrowing into bed, pulling all the blankets over him. Listening to the distant sounds of the docks and the waves crashing, he fell into sleep's tender arms.

†

L ark crashed into the room what seemed like no more than a moment after Azrael closed his eyes. Golden sunset filled the room. He groaned against the brightness, raising his hand to shield his eyes.

"What happened?" Lark flipped the blankets off him, her hands running along his legs, the planes of his stomach and chest, searching for wounds. He would have pulled her against him if he hadn't sensed the desperation to make sure he was unhurt. He remembered the pile of bloody clothes he had left in the bathing room, realizing it was the source of her panic.

"I'm fine." He swatted her hand away. "It was an ambush. I'm worth a hundred thousand gold, did you know?"

She took her hands away and crossed her arms, her mouth tightening in a line. "Is that funny to you?"

"Little bit."

"The farmers are pissed. There's two dead Tiras in their field and an abandoned campsite." Lark uncrossed her arms and sat on the edge of the bed. "Bedivere is out there with them now, smoothing things over."

Azrael leaned on his forearm, quietly watching her. Ink spotted her fingers and he wondered what she had been doing. Her face no longer held the ghosts and shadows it had when he had returned to the Roe.

"You're okay?" she asked, her eyes searching his face for something to indicate otherwise.

"Of course."

"Did you recognize them?" She was quiet, gentle, dreading the answer. Azrael nodded. "They had been my brothers. Maddox—Adrien and I used to hunt for herbs together—" Her words cracked in her voice like a wishbone, and she looked away quickly.

Azrael didn't share that grief with her, only stoking the fire of hate within him. If Melech hadn't sent them, then they had come of their own volition, and Azrael didn't know which was worse. He had followed the king's orders without question since he was a child, inducted and indoctrinated with the lies of the crown.

He had thought he was doing good, keeping the kingdom safe. Melech had slaughtered an innocent girl in her bed to spite Azrael, set a price for his head, and made him an exile in his own home. Somehow—*somehow*—Melech was able to control the demons he had told Azrael plagued Havriel, but killing Nekoda meant certain death.

Azrael steered the conversation from fresh ghosts to those that had lingered. "The kingdom deserves the truth. The people deserve a better leader—someone who truly cares and wants a better future. I will support you in your plan," he said. Shadows dipped from Lark's face as she understood his words.

"I'm terrified people won't see past my father," she replied with a voice hardly above a whisper.

"Your father had been a good king. What he did was for his people—that's what they saw. They didn't know him as you did. They see what Melech has done. For all you know, you are their salvation." Azrael sat up then and inched closer to her. He reached his hand to cup her face. "Darling, you will do *wonders*."

"I'll never know why Iah chose me, but I will not ruin this." Lark shifted so that she sat half in his lap, pressed against him. "I can't."

# CHAPTER 37

## AZRAEL

T he floor was sticky with ale, and the four men had discussed nothing of importance, but the meeting three days later felt productive. Azrael sat with Bedivere, his captain Gideon, and Rook's captain Enos around the table, playing a confusing game of cards and elbowing drinks off the table. Rook had been off doing important groundwork and Lark was out for her queenly lessons. Azrael's meeting had skidded off track too quickly, turning into who could win the most at cards, then who had the strongest arm. Midday passed while Azrael grappled with Enos.

"My lord?" a servant rapped on the doorframe, calling all four men's attention. Enos looked to the servant, but landed the punch he had prepared to Azrael's stomach with an absentminded grin.

"Yes?"

"The King has arrived. He's in your sitting room."

The air in the room constricted and Azrael found he couldn't breathe. His focus narrowed like a single star in a winter sky: Lark. He racked his mind, trying to remember where she had said she'd be today.

Bedivere shook off his drunken haze, discarding it like an old cloak, and looked straight to Azrael. "Find her. Stay out of sight."

Azrael straightened and sorted through the murkiness of his own thoughts to find his own sobriety. Beside him, the two captains exchanged silent looks and disappeared. All signs of laughter and fun from the last few hours had disappeared in the breath of a single sentence.

A thought shot through his mind like a comet, blazing clarity. Lark was at home today, she had said she would read through the books Bedivere had given her. There would be no reason for her to leave; she often stayed holed up in her room for hours reading.

With his fears consoled, Azrael followed the way Bedivere had left, silently as he could. He was beginning to learn the different halls of the manor, and he knew one led beneath the floor his study was on. Azrael followed that path now, and tucked himself in a storage closet that he knew sat below the lord's rooms. Azrael knew better, but he had to learn why the king had come.

"Melech." Bedivere's voice was brisk and held no room to preen that he had been drinking.

"Where's Hikaim?" Melech replied coolly, but Azrael heard the simmering hatred beneath the mask. "Two of my Tiras are dead, and they were hunting him. A boy had seen him outside of your city."

"I had heard what happened. It is unfortunate that it didn't happen within my city, or else I would be able to investigate the situation. I have followed the guidelines you provided to me your last visit in the way to properly govern my people."

Azrael could only imagine the way Melech looked, a feral dog trying to break free from a leash.

"Do not lie to your king. I know you've kept him here as your little *pet*," he spat the word, "so do not play coy with me. I know you wanted him during our last visit. Do not try to fool me into thinking you've given up on your charade."

"Melech," Bedivere's voice was bored, edging on irritated. "You are not my king, as you have made abundantly clear during your last visit."

"Hm. Hikaim said the very same thing before he attacked me. He's spiraling, Bedivere. He's not safe. A true danger to anyone he meets."

"So I hear."

"If he is lurking in your town, I will find him. He is *mine*." The guttural growl in Melech's words reverberated in Azrael, narrowing his vision to seeing only red.

"And you say that I am desperate for him. Melech, are you letting a soldier become your undoing?"

A creak.

"My lord—"

Silence.

Lark's voice hung in the air like a blade at a thief's neck. Everything was silent, everything was too loud. Azrael couldn't hear anything over the thundering of his heartbeat and the closet he was in was suddenly too small, too tight. He didn't know if he should run up there, pound on the walls, or yell—

"Siena." Melech's voice cracked. Azrael wondered what the king looked like; the shock, the surprise on his face as he looked at the woman he almost killed. He must have recovered his composure, for when he spoke again his voice was even. "Where there's one, the other isn't far. Where is he?"

The controlled rage in the king's voice ignited the bloodlust in Azrael. His hands curled into fists, so tightly he thought his knuckles would snap through his skin.

"Melech, I assure you—"

"If," Lark cut Bedivere off. Her footsteps were heavy as she moved across the room. "If I go with you, leave him behind. My king, if I go with you, will you leave Azrael behind?"

"Darling, he committed treason—"

"Will you."

"For you? Yes." Melech was quiet, all hints of rage disappearing from his voice. Azrael's thoughts swirled in his head, threatening to drown him. Melech spoke again, "I'm leaving two Tiras behind to take care of the dead."

"They are not welcome in my home, nor will I object if my people refuse to house them." Bedivere sounded too calm, too collected, for what had just transpired in his room. How could he let this happen? Lark was—everything they had worked for—their plan, their home.

Azrael didn't wait to hear what else was said, what else would damn his heart. He shouldered out of the closet and took off down the hall, past the kitchen, and through the door in the back. A path led around and down the side of the house propelled him away from a crumbling future, the cracking of his heart he thought he could outrun. This side of the manor was empty as he kept to the shadows, his solitude crushing down on him.

Just as he reached the road, he noticed a figure in black standing at the base of the stairs to the manor. Azrael skidded to a stop once he realized he recognized that dark figure, the thatch of black hair. He pushed his back against the house. Ahmi had to have seen him, and Azrael's heart and head battled with what Ahmi would do. Would his friend keep silent, or would his Tiras brother share what he'd seen?

With lungs too tight, Azrael stepped past the house and glanced at Ahmi, but their eyes locked. Ahmi gave the smallest shake of his head before turning to face the street where Azrael had intended to disappear to. Azrael followed his friend's gaze and saw four Tiras, their red cuffs bright around their wrists in the afternoon sun. Azrael slipped back into the shadows of the manor and waited.

It seemed like hours had passed before the Tiras had walked up the street and past Ahmi, but really it had been ten precisely counted breaths. Azrael peered around the corner at his friend once more. Ahmi's shoulders relaxed and he turned so his back was towards Azrael. Silently thanking whatever gods lingered in this world for Ahmi, Azrael sprinted down the street towards his empty house.

It felt too small, too tight. The high ceiling seemed to shrink with the intentions of squashing Azrael like a grape. He vaulted up the staircase in a moment of desperation, as though he had conjured her voice alongside Melech's, but Lark's room was empty, disorganized, as though she had been searching for something before she left. The cluttered desk, bed covered in books, the ink on the wallpaper all made it too real that she was not here where she should be.

His hurt turned to bitterness, his heart refracting the pain back on itself. He spent years avoiding attachment because those in his life seemed to be ripped away without anything he could do. Everyone leaves. Everyone has left. Why did he delude himself into thinking he and Lark could live in this small bubble of happiness forever?

He should know better than to think Lark did it for any other reason than to protect him, to protect what they have been doing here. He should know better, but that small sliver of doubt dug deeper. After all, where would he be after Lark was crowned? Certainly not beside her—a soldier, a killer, trying to unify the people he'd once fought against and the people who now hunted him like a dog for spare gold. He didn't deserve to stand at her side through it. Fuck, he didn't even deserve Lark.

Downstairs, the door shot open. He stumbled into the hall, preparing mentally for a fight, but he wasn't ready for the angry tears on Lark's face as she stormed the stairs.

"Az."

"I know," he said before she could say anything else. His throat was tight.

Lark stopped at the top of the landing, her face softening. The anger in her eyes shifted to sorrow as she launched herself at him, wrapping her arms around his waist. A sob rippled through her as they dropped to their knees together. Azrael's arms tightened around her, gripping her in the way that felt like it would be their last embrace.

"I'm sorry." Lark took a jagged breath, and it sounded like broken glass. "It's the only thing I can do to keep you safe. This will keep us both safe. I—I can be eyes on the inside, this can work. For now."

"For now," Azrael echoed. He couldn't think about the next time he would see her, if it would be at her coronation, in a coup, or at a funeral.

"This isn't our end, Az." Lark recovered and wiped her nose with the back of her hand. Pink rimmed her eyes and red tipped her nose. "You are the center of my heart, and I will find my way back to you."

Lark untangled herself from him, her face lightening as she healed herself. She winced, but it passed so quickly Azrael thought he'd imagined it. After a moment, she sat in front of him as though she'd just woken up—fresh faced and bright.

He felt the pressure behind his eyes, the anger and hurt manifesting in tears that threatened to spill, but he wouldn't cry. He wouldn't make this harder for her. All he could do was watch as she stood and smoothed out the wrinkles in her dress before walking past him into her room. She rooted around in her room, packing a bag heavy enough to make her grunt as she hauled it through the house.

Azrael thought he should help, but he was frozen. Only did he move when a knock sounded on the door. Lurching to his feet, his head eddied of every thought. Lark stepped out of her room, her face a picture of calm, but her eyes burned with the soft fire he knew her to carry. She started down the stairs, but Azrael slipped past her and leaned against the door, peering through the small hole. Two Tiras he recognized stood at the door, the large boulder of a man—Caed—raised his fat fist to pound on the wood again, but Melech, a short distance away, barked an order and Caed's fist lowered.

Azrael's hand went to the handle, a plan unfolding in his mind, the images flashing like a fading dream. It wouldn't take much to disarm and kill the two, and it'd be over quick enough Melech would be caught off guard.

"Don't you dare," Lark hissed as her bag dropped at the base of the stairs. "Go."

"I'm not moving," Azrael protested, leaning away from the door. "If he tries something—"

"Like what? We live in the middle of town. He's not going to kill me right here." Lark trotted up the stairs to produce another bag, seemingly equally as heavy as the first, and placed it by the first. "Put your hands up."

"What?"

"If you insist on standing here when I open that door, you'll be shielded at least. Put your hands up."

He did as she said, raising his palms up and towards her. Tiny shocks of light rippled in front of him, as though he were underwater, and slight pressure rested against his skin like hiding behind a curtain. He didn't know if he had to hold his hands like this, so he remained in the same position as Lark opened the front door, just wide enough for the men to see inside the house.

"Who are you talking to?" Caed asked in his hideous voice. His archer friend, Wright, snickered beside him and said something snarky under his breath.

"My cat," Lark said tonelessly. "Take my bags."

"Why can't you—"

"You heard the princess." Melech cut in. Azrael was glad he couldn't see the king, or else Lark's shield wouldn't be able to hold him back.

Lark's magic guttered, and turned cold, so cold. It started slow, then spread like frost, *burning*. He tried moving his hands, taking them down, but they were stuck, as though fused to the shield. He gritted his teeth from yelling out as time began to slow. An eternity was passing as Caed gruffly shouldered in the house and grabbed Lark's bags, handing one off to his friend. Melech slipped in after Caed had stepped out, his dark eyes searching every shadow for Azrael. Azrael wanted to scream, to yell, to break through and wrap his hands around the king's neck, but he couldn't even open his mouth, the pain in his hands silencing him.

"If you're thinking of breaking our agreement, I will kill you where you stand." Lark's voice was harsh, sharp, as she raised her chin to look at her king.

A grin cracked Melech's cold face. "We're not so different after all."

Azrael tried watching the pair as they left, tried catching Lark's dejected gaze before the door closed, but he couldn't take his eyes off his hands. They were blackening, burning still, with what felt like frostbite. The shadows Lark had used to hide him were as cold as the space between stars and it had seared his skin. Pain took his vision, replacing it with black. He heard snow crunching beneath boots outside, vicious laughter, and a crack as the shield of shadows disintegrated before him.

The world came into focus for a moment before he drowned in the black again.

Azrael couldn't feel his hands, couldn't see, couldn't hear. Melech had to have seen him, sensed him, and killed him where he had stood. Maybe Lark had killed him instead, getting her happy ending with a man who could stand beside her as king. Azrael didn't sleep, didn't dream. Wherever he was, he was stuck.

For too long. It was too long that he remained in the blackness. Perhaps he was wrapped up within his soul, facing each failure, each life he had taken, and this bleakness was the beginning of his penance for how he had lived, blindly swinging his sword without so much as an afterthought to those he had cut down.

"Azrael."

His name pierced through the black as a dagger, cutting to his heart. He flinched, curling tighter within the safety of the black. If this was all there was left to him, he didn't want the temptations of life to call to him anymore.

"Azrael, can you hear me?"

Here in this deathless death, he had no voice to answer with, nor could his tongue curl into the words he'd use. Fingers pried at his face, forcefully opening his eyes, and the light burned so much brighter and hotter than he expected.

Eventually, life and light came into sharp focus, the darkness that had enshrouded him shedding its hold. Edhar, the healer, sat in a chair beside Azrael while Bedivere stood behind him.

Home. Azrael was home, he realized, as he noted the roaring fireplace behind the lord. He tried sitting up, but as soon as his hand touched the sofa, pain exploded, threatening to knock him back into that cold darkness. He choked on it, flustered, and looked at his hands—two stubs of linen bandages.

*What?* He couldn't tell if he had spoken the word, if he regained his vocal chords, or if the thought had echoed loudly in his head, but Edhar's gaze held such pity.

"I've never seen a burn like that. I did what I could."

"Where is she?" Azrael managed to speak this time, his eyes on the lord of the Roe.

"They left hours ago," Bedivere said. "I will have a guard stationed here for the next week while the Tiras are still here—"

"No." Azrael shook his head. He wouldn't consent to being watched like a child.

"Son, you can't pick your nose, let alone hold a sword. If Melech fails to honor his word—"

"Then I die."

"And so does she."

Azrael stilled, letting those words sink like knives into his veins. Edhar moved from his chair so Bedivere could sit. The lord leaned forward on his knees, strands of his hair falling from their place in his high knot.

"You think he won't kill you first, then kill her? If you die, he won't hesitate to kill her too. You are her best chance, and she is ours. This is an order, Azrael. You will rest, my guard will stand outside your house, then once you are healed, you will work, day and night, with us until we walk through those gates and take her back. She will not die for us, and you will not die on us."

"Take these." Edhar scuttled over to Azrael's side and held out his hand. A small ball of herbs rolled in his palm before the healer pinched them between his fingers and shoved it into Azrael's mouth. He then held a glass of water for Azrael and carefully poured some into his mouth. Azrael bristled at the gesture, feeling like a child, but realized holding the glass even for a moment would hurt too much.

"Sleep now. I'll come tomorrow to check on you. If you need anything, my guard Itan will be outside your door." Bedivere glanced at Azrael's hands, then his face, and sympathy spread across the lord's cheeks like blush.

"I'll leave you capsules to take. They act fast, so once you start to feel pain, take one. Eat and drink. I'll return in the morning. Good night, Azrael." Edhar set a handful of capsules on the small table beside the sofa, avoiding Azrael's eyes. The healer tried hiding his pity, the fact settling like a stone in Azrael's heart.

He wondered if Lark knew what she had done, if she could have fixed it before she disappeared if she had known. All too quickly, Azrael was left inside a skeleton of a house. Its looming walls and dark ceiling feeling too much like a ribcage. A house missing a heart.

# CHAPTER 38

## LARK

*I will find my way back to you.*

It felt so far from the truth as Lark rode in silence, Boaz beside her while Melech stayed in front. She didn't pretend to think she was anything other than a prisoner. Boaz had taken her dagger with a smug grin on his face that took all Lark's willpower not to slap off. Though the comforting weight no longer sat on her thigh, the shadows swirling around her fingers brought her more comfort than bits of steel anyway. She could have slaughtered them all if she raised a hand, but Iah's voice hummed in the back of her head, telling her to keep a steady heart. It was exasperating though, when the man who continuously barrels through her life, uprooting everything she cared about, rode mere paces in front of her. And did it all for the sake of possession and power. She didn't doubt a long, drawn out, heartfelt talk awaited them at the palace, but keeping her in his palms, in his bed—beneath him at all times—that's what mattered to him.

Lark focused on what good could come from this as they rode, the days blending together. Boaz didn't move from her side and her hatred bloomed like the first sprout of spring. Someone she had seen as a brother, a friend, was now her jailer and more than happy to be.

She wished every night before she forced the shadows of sleep upon herself that Melech didn't hate water, for her anxiety grew with each hoofbeat beneath her. She dreaded being back within Vale City as a prisoner—all but in name—but nothing was worse than the furtive looks Melech cast her, settling deep within her core and stirring a sense of unease that burrowed into her very bones.

The gates of Vale City rose before them not all too soon, the sight squeezing Lark's throat. Her grip tightened on the reins as she fought the bile rising to her throat. The watch towers, the wall, the guards pacing along the parapet, all of it made her world so much smaller. She turned her face to the black sky and gazed at Iah, the full moon that never faded. The only constant in her life, the one thing Melech couldn't take away from her.

Beneath the god's light, the horses were stabled and Melech strode through the palace, leaving Boaz to tightly grip Lark's arm and half drag her behind the king. Her feet stumbled, caught on each other, but she tried to keep pace with the archer. His sharp profile was harsher now that they were no longer friends—his black brows deeper and furrowed above his green eyes, his mouth set into a permanent frown, and the leanness of his body told Lark that she wouldn't be strong enough to leave him, not with physical force. Even if she tried running, she would hardly make it down the hall before his arrow pierced her heart.

The pair took the most direct path to the king's rooms. The hall of mirrors shot a shard of fear into Lark's heart, until she noticed the missing glass. Three sections had been removed, revealing the dark grey stones beneath, and tiny sparkles of glass glinted on the marble floor, a remnant of their fight. Warmth flooded Lark then, and she held her chin a little higher.

"Leave us," Melech said once Lark and Boaz reached the doors. He stood with his arms crossed, face dark.

Boaz let go of Lark's arm, the feeling akin to letting loose a breath, and she rubbed where he had held. She was sure a bruise had begun to form. Boaz cast her a dark look before storming off down the hall.

Every piece of confidence and pride Lark had summoned disappeared when Melech motioned for her to walk into his rooms first. Faced with the darkness of his rooms, the haunting portraits hanging in the shadows, the memories that burned like wildfire, Lark felt naked, in every way possible. The locks clicked into place behind her, but she steeled herself—straightened her shoulders, steadied her breathing. Shadows tickled her fingertips.

"I could kill you," Melech said finally. He strode past her and unclasped his cloak, letting it settle on the rug before his desk in a dark puddle. He poured a drink, his nimble fingers holding the glass as though he wanted to hurl it at Lark. "But, for once in your *miserable* life, I have a use for you."

Lark blinked at his blatant insult, knowing it wasn't true, no matter how much he told himself it was. She would have to pick her battles with him more carefully now.

"We will be married." Melech turned towards her then, the intensity of his gaze shrinking Lark back down to the girl she had been when he had first pulled her into his rooms. Young, scared, reckless. His mask of her protector, her keeper, fell into place as he looked at her—his face was soft, but his eyes were hard. A small part of his blackened heart didn't want her afraid of this, of him. But the sight of him, with his unkempt hair, unshaven face, dark circles beneath his eyes—her absence had consumed him. *That* scared her. "We will be married. You will be my wife, my consort. You will leave whatever it is you've been planning alone. Let it be forgotten. Let *him* be forgotten."

*Say it. Say his name*, she wanted to say. Melech was threatened by the only person her heart had let in, and she wanted him to admit his weakness. Instead, Lark remained quiet.

"You will put a rest to Bedivere's ridiculous notions of a separate kingdom. You will put all this to rest."

"If I don't?" The words were out of her mouth before she thought better.

"If you don't?" Melech echoed, smiling. Ever the predator, ever the one with an upper hand. "If you don't, Siena, then I will have you locked away, and I will track your boyfriend to the ends of the earth and skin him alive while you watch. Then, I will take your precious lord apart piece by piece and hang those pieces in his tiny kingdom."

Lark's heart raced, a hummingbird in flight, but she kept her voice even. "If I do, if I agree to marry you, will you leave him alone? Let him live in peace, forever? And you won't harm Bedivere?"

"This isn't a negotiation. I have promised already to leave the boy behind."

"It is now. Yes, you promised that, but you will promise to leave him be and never think of him again."

Melech's smile widened. He strode towards her, eyes pinning her in place. With his index finger, he lifted her chin up towards his face. "I do so like when you test me. If it will make you complacent, however, I will not touch him."

"Do not send anyone after him either."

His gaze turned into a lover's. Lark bristled but didn't move. "He will have his peace."

Melech took his hand back, thumb rubbing his finger where it had touched her skin, and took two steps backwards, his eyes never leaving hers, before he turned. Not for the first time in her life, Lark felt displaced. Dropped into something not of her choosing, even if it had been her voice, her stubborn heart, that had offered her life in place of Azrael's. It had been her choice not to send piercing shadows into Melech on the ride back to the city.

*In this, the king does not lie.* Iah had been whispering the entire ride, day after day. He had sung Areenian lullabies, spoken nonsense, and mumbled prophecies Lark didn't deign to pay attention to. She had long forgone trying to make sense of everything he whispered.

Lark made a move to walk towards his rooms, to rinse off the stink of heartbreak and horse, but Melech scoffed. She kept her face neutral as she looked back at him.

"This will not be as it was," he said as she flicked a stack of papers on the desk, "This will not be something you have to do twice a week because I wish it. This is your life now, Siena, and I expect you to act like it. You will be my wife, the consort to my crown. Nothing more, nothing less. You are damaged goods, and we will not go back to thinking otherwise. I will not touch what his hands have touched, but I will allow you to share my room for the sake of being my wife."

For some reason, his words were a thorn in her heart, bristling and poking. With her jaw set, she nodded curtly and turned on her heels, only letting her face fall when she closed the door to his bedroom.

L ark stared at the familiar dark ceiling, the muted sunlight that struggled to get past the thick, dark curtains. Every hoofbeat, every heartbeat, that had taken her away from her life, her future, had followed her into her dreams, plaguing her with nightmares that went in circles. She didn't regret her decision if it kept Azrael alive. If this life with Melech meant Azrael kept his, then she'd make that choice over and over. She only hoped that Melech kept his word.

She rolled off the bed, catching herself in the blankets before she smacked onto the marble floor. She had always hated that he kept them pristine; always able to see every flyaway hair and freckle in her reflection. The thought that this was her life once more, that it would be her life *now*, made her reflection dance as her head began to spin. Gods, they would have to get married, bind their hands in front of nobles and city officials, vowing love and loyalty. Lark braced a hand on the bed. She would be a wife—*Melech's* wife. The crown she wanted, given as a consolation prize. Queen consort to the kingdom rightfully hers. All the planning, the meetings with Rook, Bedivere, and Luned. The conversations with Iah, leading her in the direction she had thought was right.

*Do you doubt me, little bird?*

*No, my lord.* She had grown used to lying in her thoughts, keeping the tone of her words even and hiding the inklings of doubt and deceit far enough within her that Iah wouldn't be able to pluck them out. *Just scared.*

At least that wasn't a lie.

*What if you come to love him?*

Lark laughed—truly laughed, from the depths of her stomach. She was thankful she was alone, hand pressed to the curve of her lower ribs, she leaned into the laughter, the feeling. Six years and she hadn't learned to care for the king. A lifetime couldn't bring her to love him. Azrael, however...

Azrael could have been a good king, for that's what she would have made him. Not a consort, but a rightful king. Her equal, her partner. A man who could lead armies in times of war, serve the people in times of peace. The future she had looked forward to disappeared like smoke in the wind. She had fallen into a quiet comfort living in the Roe with him, in their house, in their own world where they could pretend as though there weren't monsters that targeted him and a king who couldn't check his jealousy, and as though she wasn't a secret Melech tried to bury. They were just Az and Lark, soldier and healer.

Lark dressed slowly, braided her hair slowly. Loneliness threatened to crush her as she sat in his dark bathing room with only a ball of her white light to keep from falling apart. She wondered if Melech would allow her a handmaid, even if only for company. Her thoughts wandered to Hadriana and Thea, so close to her, but so very far away. Did her friends know she was back within the palace? She thought of Magdalene then, who had loved Azrael and ended up dead, when the body hanging from the tree should have been Lark's.

The starlight flickered then went out as the thoughts of Magdalene's body threatened to overtake her, her traitorous mind replacing the women's bodies so the image Lark saw in her head was herself swaying in the breeze. She shut her eyes tight enough to only see black and breathed carefully, focusing on the cold marble beneath her feet and the stone counter her elbows rested on. A thunderstorm roiled in her chest, but calmed once she finally stood and padded back into the bedroom and to the sitting room, where she came face to face with Brannon.

"Morning, Princess," he said around a mouthful of biscuit, the remainder of which slowly began to crumble in his hand. His other hand held a steaming mug of coffee and he raised it in greeting. "Your task today is to write a letter to your partner in a very serious crime to tell him to forget about his kingdom. Then," he paused to sip his coffee, "you get to start planning your wedding."

Lark narrowed her eyes. She'd never liked Brannon. "And he left you to babysit? Seems like a waste of a captain's time."

She moved to sit at Melech's desk, already set up for her with paper, ink, and the king's seal. Biting back a sigh, she dropped into the chair. The emptiness of the paper glared at her as though it were Melech himself, reminding her how powerless she felt.

How powerless she *felt*.

She wasn't truly.

She unspooled a pinch of that light within her, feeling it burn as it loosened from her ribs. She guided it to Brannon's cup, warming the liquid the same way she lit a fire. He now leaned against the other side of the desk, munching on his biscuit, not paying her attention. With a jerk of her hand, the desk jolted, reverberating through Brannon and causing his scalding coffee to splash onto his hand. He yelped and dropped the mug, the shatter echoing off the looming walls.

"You bitch," he snarled, holding his burned hand against his chest. Lark ground her teeth together, keeping her mouth closed, as she met the captain's heated stare. His mind was so open that she watched each emotion flicker in his eyes as he weighed retribution and the consequences it would bring. After a moment, he hurled the remainder of his breakfast biscuit at her and stormed out of the room, yelling incoherently at the guard standing outside the door.

Lark couldn't keep the smirk from her face as she dipped her pen into the ink; even as she dreaded the contents of her letter, her one small victory over Brannon lightened her heart enough that her task no longer pierced her heart.

# CHAPTER 39

## LARK

"All these years later and you've never asked me about your father," Melech said from his side of the sink. The giant mirror that stretched before them provided Lark an uninterrupted side view of Melech as he trimmed his beard. Lark focused on braiding her hair.

"I remember enough," she replied curtly. She remembered enough of her father that she didn't need to hear about him from someone who knew him, someone who had admired him.

"Do you?" His voice held a sharp tone, condescending and playful. He was baiting her. It was enough that he put her on display like a prized deer from a hunt, yet he insisted on making her feel inferior.

"I've tried to forget it. What do you want me to say?"

"You haven't asked about your mother either," he crooned. His eyes never left his reflection; he didn't have to look at her to see what she was feeling, what her face revealed.

"No, because I do not care." She finished her plait and stood from her plush chair. She had nearly succeeded in readying herself in peace before he intruded, clearly asking for a fight before she stood in front of his council, then in front of the city. He wanted her rattled and she didn't want any part of his games.

"Rightfully so. She wasn't your mother."

Lark paused, gripping the back of her chair. That night flickered in her mind, blinding her with the way Isolde had looked before she went over the ledge—her body cracking on the stones echoed in Lark's ears, splintering through her thoughts. She slowly turned to Melech.

"Why." A dull voice, hardly a question. She didn't know how long she could play his games. He hadn't been like this before, though there was comfort in knowing one day she would know all his secrets and there would be nothing to hold against her. One day he would speak to her without a cliffhanger.

"Your father was unfaithful to the queen—"

"Not that. Why tell me now?"

"Today is all about you. Shouldn't you want to know the parentage you're claiming?" He had finished and now ran a small brush down his beard, smoothing it out. His dark eyes found hers in the mirror.

"I've always claimed Harlow was my true mother anyway, this hardly matters. The fault lies with you. You're the reason for this stupid ceremony anyway."

It hit her then. She didn't know how she hadn't seen it before. Melech knew he would snare her somehow, and this was one way to make him likable. Make his reign more legitimate. If it were true, and Lark a bastard, then her grasping for the throne would be meaningless. Melech had been planning this for years, she realized. How had he placed his pieces so perfectly?

"Your father didn't even remember he spawned you at the end," Melech said as he stood, his chair gliding quietly along the floor. "You're just as much a bastard as your—"

Lark loosened her shadows, letting them weave towards the king and curl in his mouth, effectively cutting off the remainder of his sentence. She had never used magic on him like this, only ever healing him before, and the surprise was apparent on his face. One hand went to his throat, while the other grasped for the blade he had been using. He became wrath incarnate, ever the vengeful king. She let go, the breath punched out of her lungs. Before Melech could do anything, Lark whirled out of the room and braced her back with shadows, a hardened armor. She only wished her heart was so easily protected.

†

N either spoke as Melech led Lark down the hall, her dress swishing the only sound. Not even their footsteps echoed. She kept her shoulders back, straight as she could, but the feeling of his knee digging into her back wouldn't disappear. Her face was heavy beneath the extra powder to give her face a hint of color, but at least she had healed before a bruise could set and effectively discoloring her face beyond the powder's capabilities.

The last thing Lark wanted to do was to speak with his council now, but she consoled herself with knowing that this was exactly what his plan had been. He wanted her flustered, broken, and anxious when she appeared. So, she might as well go along with it, with her shoulders back and the coldness vibrant in her eyes. The coldness Melech had planted there, tended dutifully. She wouldn't be the simpering, docile consort he wanted. Those days had long since passed. She was wildfire, burning of shadow and smoke, and she would not be contained.

"Do you understand your role in this?" Melech fell back a step, so he walked beside her. He asked it quietly enough that Brannon, paces behind them, wouldn't hear. Lark murmured a response, earning a stare like daggers.

They walked down, down, down to the first floor, then through more hall-ways. Lark wondered how many of these men would see her as a failure. She had tried to befriend most of them in anticipation of her own rise to the throne, not beside it. Would they see that? Would they condemn her? A shudder passed through her. Would they speak to Melech about it? Melech guessing her intentions and plans was one thing, but hearing from his advisors that she had gone to them behind his back...

Melech offered his arm to her, shattering her downward spiral, as they neared the room. She accepted it and fought the rising bile in her throat at the picture they painted together—the doting couple, soon to be married. No one would believe it for a moment.

The pair stopped before the set of doors, and she set her shoulders proud. His touch burned her arm. Steeling herself with her shadows, she glanced at him, her mind reeling of the hundred ways this could go. He returned her stare with a cold, cruel smile.

If he wanted her to be a princess, she would be no less than an empress. She smiled a deadly smirk back at him as the doors opened.

# CHAPTER 40

## AZRAEL

A week passed. Azrael had to thank the gods—whichever, if any, were still listening—for Edhar's skill. The worst of the damage was his palms, which he tried not to look at when Edhar changed the bandages. Each day, before new linen was wrapped, Azrael bent each finger to his thumb, fighting through the pain that throbbed with a heat that made him wonder if he had thrown his hands into the fire without thinking. After the initial shock and pain had worn off, Azrael returned to the guardhouse and the Town's Guard.

Three weeks passed and his fingers healed much faster once the bandages had come off, regaining the use of his hands. Bedivere had given him a lockpicking kit to redirect his focus and keep his hands working. He worked on it in the pale light of his fireplace, his bedroom too fresh a wound still, and spent his days with the men and women who kept the Roe safe.

News from Vale City passed from mouth to mouth, forming the words Azrael heard over and over in his dreams: King Melech was engaged to Princess Siena, the forgotten daughter of King Nekoda. Azrael found heart in knowing she was still alive—alive but bound to another man. Azrael kept his head in his work, focused on his meetings with Rook and Bedivere, and recounted what had happened with Melech to whoever asked.

Winter was waning. The snow had disappeared, but the air was reluctant to give up its chill. Azrael sat once more before his hearth in the fading sunset's light, feeling the kiss of the flame on his face. His hands had developed a shake, as though the nerves had been frayed at the edges, a side effect of whatever Lark's magic had done to his hands. *Magic demands balance,* he had heard Lark say. He wondered if this was the balance, the payment, demanded for the protection of magic. Most of the time, the shaking was slight, as though he were nervous, but after tedious work, they grew worse.

He kept his hands wrapped, even after they were healed, and avoided looking at them. His fingers, as though dipped in ink, reminded him of the Daeoan and their unearthly presence.

Azrael sighed and stood, setting his kit to the side. Even after a day of drills and training and endless formations he subjected the guards to, his body refused to still. He pulled his boots on and slung another on one of Bedivere's gift—a beautiful sheathe designed to be worn on one's back—before slipping his sword in. He nodded to the guard stationed across the street, exchanging a brief, understanding look. Itan was younger than Azrael, but twice as large and kind. Azrael felt bad for the kid, and his useless post, but didn't mind the company, even if it was at a distance. At least he wasn't entirely alone.

The Roe had picked up in trade again as the seas calmed. The docks bustled with sailors singing or yelling, bells tolling, ropes slapping and heaving. Azrael didn't think he'd grow tired of the way the town was positioned with its weaving roads down to the sea and how, even from his house, had a view of the water and towering ships. He'd always admired the life sailors lived, even if it hadn't seemed enviable when he was on the ship that carried him from the Moor to the Vale, newly orphaned and neglected. Eight years old and the only passenger on the boat, sent away by his mother's sister who hadn't bothered to remember he had a name. She had housed him for two days before deciding another's life was too much too handle. He wondered where she was now.

A faint scream pulled him from the memory. Almost silenced by the roar of the docks, but it sent a chill down his spine. His sword felt cold through its sheathe and his shirt as he followed the sound. No one else moved towards it or seemed to have heard it—perhaps the town itself were too loud.

He strode up the street and past Bedivere's manor before hearing it again, even fainter than the first time. He began to jog, unsure where the sound had come from now. Past the training ring, past a line of willow trees, he came to a small field when the smell hit him like a wall—the decay, the *death*.

A Daeoan materialized in front of him before he could swipe his sword, the being's arms open as though welcoming Azrael. It turned a bony palm towards the sky, raising Azrael from the ground. His feet kicked, trying to touch the earth—suspended in the air. A trap. The being had set a trap and snared him like a senseless rabbit. Paralyzed, he was nothing more than easy prey. The demon floated towards him, raising him up to its level, until its deathless face was inches from his. Bones jaggedly put together, nowhere near resembling a human skull, he noted now that he was this close. Two holes remained where its eyes should have been, a black darker than the night swirled instead. Broken, long, sharp teeth jutted out from the bones like stalactite, meeting not a bottom jaw, but more swirling darkness. He couldn't look away from its face, but from the corner of his eye, he noticed two more demons crept closer.

The Daeoan lifted a finger to the base of his throat. Azrael fought against the hold it had on him, trying to reach his sword, but all he could do was twitch his fingers. He tried screaming out, but the sound was caught in his chest as blood poured from his mouth, down his neck. His body heaved beneath the magic, but there was nothing he could do as his insides violently warped.

*We need him weak, not dead.*

Azrael looked to the other Daeoan, which had moved closer to his side. Within range, if he could just move...

His body was a string strung too tightly, even the breeze rattled him. The being in front of him floated backwards, and the blood stopped. The string loosened a breath.

He didn't hesitate, didn't give himself a moment to think, before reaching for his sword. Slicing his arm out to the side, his blade careened through the closest Daeoan's head and chest until it petrified.

*I don't think we need him at all anymore. Let me kill him.*

Still hanging in the air, Azrael had to force his arm to move how he wanted, as though swimming against the current, but, with the best he could manage, he sent his sword flying into the Daeoan in front of him. As soon as the tip pierced its chest, he dropped to the ground, sliding in the pool of his own blood. He watched the last Daeoan from the corner of his eye as he crawled towards his sword. Unabashed tears ran down his face. He fought to stay awake, fought to dig his fingers into the earth to pull himself closer to his blade.

Laughter echoed in his head, sick and twisted, as the demon glided around him, circling. It grew blurry, the edges of his vision closing in as he gripped the hilt of his sword. He waited, timing it, before he hurled his blade.

A hiss before black swirled and disappeared.

Suddenly alone again, it everything began to rush in. He had heard them talk—the demons talked, and they needed him for, for. For what?

He wanted to disappear beneath the black threatening to take him, to run from the fire searing beneath his skin, run from the tearing inside his chest, but the pain rooted him. His vision shifted, and day turned into night, and night turned into grey. The moon—he could see the moon—full and faint amongst the blue, hiding behind clouds. He turned to his side as he hurled the contents of his stomach, a mix of blood and vomit.

The willows were moving. There were coming to take him home, reaching out their tendrils, welcoming

# CHAPTER 41

## LARK

L ark stared at the dress hanging against the wall, the only color in the room. Melech had wanted it all to be the same: their wedding, announcing her birthright, and what seemed to be a re-coronation for him. She delegated most of her planning to one of his advisors, as she could only think of one of those things at a time, and combining all three stretched her mind and heart more than she could take.

A week had come and gone in a blink, and her entire body held onto exhaustion as though it were water. She had hardly used her magic since she had been shut within the palace, and the lack of use was taking its toll on her—body and soul. It was the rare moments like this that wore on her the most. If she used magic, it took something from her. If she did not use magic, it drained her. There was no winning, and the thought made her want to crawl into bed and never get out.

She stretched a tendril of shadow out, invisible even to her in the dark room. The release it brought had her closing her eyes, falling into the space the pressure had freed—a crack in the dam. Even the small thread curling around her fingers couldn't rid her head of the restlessness she fought day and night. Melech kept her busy that she hardly had time to think, but the moments she did, everything poured in.

He'd made an official announcement of her name, their engagement, and his sitting room began to overflow with flowers, gifts, and letters. The eyes in the palace had begun to shift as well, as though they were seeing her for the first time, or if she had sprouted a second head. Eyes that had passed her day and night suddenly became weary, sketching bows and offering timid smiles. As though she had un-become Lark, Tiras and healer. She supposed there was power in a name. Princess Siena, daughter of King Nekoda, sounded more intimidating than Lark, even if she felt far away from both versions of herself.

Lark scooted off the bed, onto the freezing marble floor, and strolled through Melech's room, out past his desk, and opened the set of doors to the balcony. Snow had fallen for two days, and she wondered if it were a good sign, or a bad one. If it were a sign at all.

Twilight had settled over the city while Lark had been sulking, a dull grey sky turned darker, but the snow was stark against the city. Lanterns and fires shimmered as drifting snow distorted the light. Somewhere out in the streets, kids were building snowmen, throwing snow packed with mud and muck at each other, a chill settling into their bones. She had mentioned to Melech that shovelers should be sent out to clear the streets, but he had laughed at her.

An idea sparked, darkness cooling her fingertips. She glanced behind her, towards the empty rooms that had been her prison. Since she had returned, Melech began to take dinners with a handful of his advisors and Lark knew it was to spend less time around her. Not that she minded, nor did she mind that a guard now stood only on the outside of the suite.

She padded back into their room before her confidence wavered and pulled on her cloak and laced her boots. She dove deeply into the swirling, dark watery depths of her magic and her soul to wrap her shadows around her as a second skin. She went back to the balcony, steeled her heart and nerves, and kept her head clear as she let the shadows carry her.

It was choppy, painful, and not where she had wanted to land, but she made it down to the courtyard. Even with the short distance, she fought to catch her breath, and blinked against the blurriness that sprouted in her vision, threatening to grow worse if she tried something like that again. A wave of nausea rolled through her, bringing the contents of her early dinner earthside, and she wiped her mouth with the back of her hand.

The courtyard had been cleared of snow and the flakes falling hardly dusted the stones enough to leave footprints behind as she made her way across. Her shadows were still wrapped tightly around her, deflecting light and the world around her. Only after she had passed the palace gates, she loosened the shadows, letting them ebb from her with a sigh.

There was a calming difference in walking the streets as Siena. Years and years had passed since the name had followed her. Her name had disappeared one day, and she had never found out how Melech and her father had managed to erase her from history, from life. She had struggled with the fact that no one mourned the disappearance of their princess, not like the way they mourned the loss of her brother. *Apparent loss,* she reminded herself with a cold shard of anxiety piercing through her chest. Back then, she had been content to disappear, to fall through the cracks into a quieter place in the world. Now she wanted to be known. Now she wanted to be loud, here, present. She wanted more.

Lark started in the western side of town, treading quietly as light snowflakes dusted her cloak. Cold air burned her throat, burrowing into her chest, as she breathed in before loosening her magic. The jump had cost her, but this was important—she would give what she needed to. With tendrils of shadows, she carved out pathways in the snow, building the banks lining the street. Staying out of sight, Lark quickly worked through the west, knowing fully well that the rich would only pay those in the east to do their work for them, before she walked carefully across to the opposite side of the city.

Treading silently, she remained a ghost as she passed through the snowed streets. She took great care of the residential streets, leaving the snowmen untouched, only carving through the snow that piled against doorways. Along the half-frozen river, she shoved piles of snow over the edge and listened as it tumbled into the slush of water and ice.

Wetness touched her lips as she finished another street. Red droplets plopped into the dusting of snow at her feet. She touched her mouth with the cold pads of her fingers, drawing them away with blood skidding down her skin. Dizziness threatened to sweep her off her feet, but Lark wiped her nose and mouth on her sleeve and kept walking.

She walked past the tavern Azrael had found her at all those months ago, and felt the shadow of their love creep into her heart, shoving its thorns into her flesh. Her hands curled into fists, nails digging crescents into her palms. The pain, the frustration, the anger, wouldn't stay contained within her, flowing through her magic like white-hot poker. The snow around her melted, pooling across the uneven stones to find a way into the river, as her white starlight burned from deep within her.

Tavern far from view now, Lark breathed easier. A cloud of her breath curled in front of her, but she didn't stop to admire how it looked under the orange light from the lanterns.

The knot in her chest, the stiffness in her bones, began to unravel, ever so slowly. With every street, every snowbank, every chill, she felt closer to the woman she thought she was, and she couldn't find it in her heart to fear what Melech would say if he found her gone.

A thrill rose in her at the thought of Melech finding his rooms empty, only to quiet when she wondered if this was what her life would be. Days blurring together—the only moments that stood out where the ones she stole for herself. If she focused on the people, the small rebellions like this, the small things for herself—maybe she could last this lifetime.

A bone deep cold settled within her as the night wore on. Her hands shook so violently from the cold and the pain radiating through her body from the magic, but she only stopped once she noticed a group of kids shivering as they huddled around a firepit. She moved closer to them, dropping a ball of white light into the burning embers, and watched as it devoured the orange flames, turning a shade to rival the snow. The smallest child, a boy of that hardly reached her hip, scooted closer to her, wrapping his tiny hands in her cloak. She unfastened it and wrapped him up in it.

She wasn't sure how long she sat with them, all tightly sitting on a bench made of discarded wood so their shoulders touched. Only when the two bodies pressed against her stopped twitching did she get up, unspool more of her warm light to embrace them, and continue her walk.

Weaving her way through the streets, Lark aimed back towards the palace. Her fur lined pants and thick sweater did nothing to block the cold from seeping into her, settling alongside her magic. As fragile as glass, Lark struggled to remain on her feet as the wind buffeted against her. She tried remembering if winter was always this bad, but she found her memory blank, nothing beyond this night, as though her thoughts had been siphoned by the night.

*How the bird's song echoes.* Iah's voice was quiet in the midst of her shivering. She'd almost forgotten to keep her mental wall up, but her magic took her strength. She offered one glance behind her, to her city and its people, before she tucked her chin to her chest and stuffed her hands into her arm pits and returned to her palace.

†

"**M**ove it to tomorrow," Melech said from over his book, nimble fingers turning the page with a flick. Lark sat with him in front of the fireplace, a book in one hand and a pen in the other as she doodled in the margins.

She lowered her book slightly to peer over at him, expecting him to continue. He merely gazed back at her, his face blank and passive, but returning to his book.

"Move what?" she grumbled, bending her head back to focus on the scene she had drawn.

"The wedding."

Lark snorted. "What of the plans? The guests?"

"I said moving the wedding to tomorrow. I said nothing of the celebration." Melech's voice was monotone, bored, and the way he spoke to her as though she were a simple child heated her blood. She hated this—hated when he got like this. A grumpy old man who only craved chaos.

"Why?"

"Because I said so." Melech sighed and clapped his book shut, resting it on his outstretched legs. "Don't think I haven't heard of your escapades. Do not think I do not know what you're doing."

Lark matched the emptiness in his tone. "What am I doing?"

His silence was his reply. Melech stood, tossed the book onto his chair, and strode past her. Lark listened as glass clinked, liquid poured, twice. He was abruptly at her side once more, offering a glass of wine.

If he was going to be a stubborn ass, she might as well be on her way to being drunk to deal with it. She took the glass from his cool hands and drank half of it in a sip, savoring the warmth that spread through her chest.

"The people should like at least one of us," Lark muttered into her glass, only to realize her mistake. Her grip tightened as her eyes raised to meet his. Melech bristled as he lowered into his chair, his jaw tightening and hate lighting his eyes.

"Is that so?" he asked before taking a drink, his stare not once breaking with hers. The wine turned to lead in her stomach. "If you freeze to death out there, that will be one less problem for me to deal with?"

"I'm your problem?"

"Of course, you are, darling." Melech flashed a grin at her, one that could be deadly and charming if she didn't know any better. "What else would you be?"

Lark scowled. She should have expected nothing less than his condescending tone and the wrath in his eyes, but a small part of her heart had hoped that her life wouldn't be *entirely* miserable. How naïve of her.

"You're a prick," she said. As childish as she sounded, she didn't care. He was, and she was tired of pretending otherwise.

Melech leaned forward, elbows on his knees, and tapped his forefinger on the rim of his glass. "I'm a prick with the crown," he crooned.

Like a feather falling, a leaf sway gently in the breeze, Lark didn't know she was falling until she hit the ground. The glass splintered on the marble, the wine spilling like blood onto his godsdamned rug. *The wine,* her thoughts were slow, as though wading through mud. She grasped at the threads within her, the fraying ends of her magic, but it was like clutching at clouds, her fingers falling through. Melech watched her with eyes of a predator, his bottom lip tucked between his teeth in a way she'd seen countless times—only this time, it wasn't her body that his gaze devoured.

"What did you do?" she whispered, her voice mangled and tight. She didn't know if she could speak louder than that, or if the poison rendered her quiet. Melech's face warmed, the side of his mouth tilting.

"Taking care of my kingdom, as I've been doing for years now, darling. You and a foot soldier aren't going to change anything." He leaned closer, the scent of firewood and snow drifting towards her. "I'm not going anywhere."

Her fingers scrambled at the shards of glass, as though a splinter could be useful to her when she could hardly creep her hand across the smooth floor. For the first time in her life, Lark was afraid of death. Afraid of it barreling towards her, down the dark tunnel her vision was turning into. Beneath her, it seemed the floor was warping, softening, ready to swallow her whole. The castle, the crown, the kingdom was ready to take her, just as it had taken her parents, and their parents before them.

*Iah.*

*Iah.* The voice inside her head was just as feeble, just as quiet. Silence weighed heavy on the opposite side of the crumbling wall in her mind, not an obstacle for much longer. The god of night ignored her.

Lark reached out with her magic, feeling for anyone or anything that could help, sending shadows skittering sideways and uncoordinated through the walls.

Everything was too far. Azrael was too far.

He wouldn't know how she died. The thought sunk her heart through her chest, her ribs imprinting on the slowing organ. Melech would spin a tale, then kill Azrael. At least there was peace in knowing Azrael wouldn't die without a fight.

So why was she?

She had survived an assassination attempt; healed herself and pretended nothing had happened. She hadn't resolved to bleed out on the cobblestones. So why was she now?

Melech watched the shift in her, the change in her body, and he was on top of her before she could blink. Hands tight around her wrists, she couldn't focus on anything beyond the wild anguish in his eyes.

*It should have been you,* he had said. He had wanted to kill her the way he killed Magdalene, stringing her lifeless body in a tree for the cold morning breeze to stir. Melech wanted her to die beneath him, the same way she had lived. He wanted her kingdom on a silver platter, had taken it so easily from her father. Lark recognized his voice as he spoke to her, but the blood rushing in her ears silenced him.

So Lark dove.

Down.

Down.

So far within herself that she no longer saw his face before hers. Wrapping herself up, she descended into a cavern within her body, as though she had teleported elsewhere. She settled into the dark grey water of her soul, calm despite the storm raging around. Lightning, thunder, hurricane rain, but the water she waded in was still. With the dead air and chilled water, Lark found she wasn't cold. Shadows crept along the mirrored surface, a leviathan snaking at the edge where the rain had stopped. Still no water rippled, even as teeth gnashed—jagged and sharp.

She was aware of her body being touched, fingers pressing against her neck, but so deep within herself, her heart had calmed, her lungs had ceased to hold air. She felt nothing beyond the water against her skin. No fear, no pain.

Only solitude.

Years and years and years of it.

The leviathan slowed, still writhing, and swung a shadowed head towards her. Grey eyes stared back at her before the beast surged.

Lark exploded into shadow and night and starlight, brilliant and burning. New and eternal.

She rose like smoke, swirling and rushing, back towards herself, filling her corporeal body, and expanded outwards. Firelight greeted her as she came alive again.

Melech was thrown off her, but she didn't miss the flash of regret that flickered in his face before his head hit the wall and he crumpled on the floor.

*No no no no*

It wouldn't be this way. Head spinning, Lark crawled towards him, glass burrowing into her hands and knees. The pain didn't hit her, not yet, but she knew it was coming. Lark had to know he was still breathing, even if she could no longer see straight. Only the blood slipping down his neck, down the front of his unbuttoned shirt. With a hand shaking like an earthquake, she gripped his thigh, and collapsed over his shins once she felt the faintness of a pulse. She unspooled the white light from her, weaving it around his bones and sending it to wherever it needed to be.

Behind her, the doors burst open, crashing into the walls. Brannon's voice yelled, loud and angry, but she couldn't understand him. The waves of pain were too close now, the pain she kept at bay was a breath away.

Hands gripped her neck, pulling her roughly to her feet and cutting her breath off at the same time. Glass bit into the bottom of her bare feet. Lark gritted her teeth against the pain, but it threatened to pull her under as the captain's grip tightened.

Brannon shook her, his voice loud in her face. Lark wondered who would be running in now, after hearing the captain's shouting.

Something snapped deep within her, eyes focusing on his. For a moment, she had clarity. Perfect, unyielding clarity as she shot a tendril of shadow through Brannon's throat.

# CHAPTER 42

## LARK

Two things happened at once: Brannon collapsed, eyes glassy with fear and death, and Lark's heart shattered no differently than the wine glass. Her body shook uncontrollably as the captain fell to her feet, his dying fingers grasping at her dress as though she could still save him. Lark stood tall, as tall as she could when her body threatened to topple over.

Grief and guilt replaced Brannon's hands, and Lark suddenly couldn't breathe again. His gasping breaths echoed in her ears, in the room, and the silence of the room rang loudly in her head. She tried listening for footsteps to come running, to see where the captain had gone, what the uproar had been about, but there was nothing beyond a dying man's agony.

Lark stumbled past him, wincing at the glass still embedded in her skin, and stuffed whatever she could find into a bag. There was no escaping this, but she had to try. She knew Azrael wouldn't be safe if she ran to another kingdom, but if she could get to him first, they could hide, then take a boat—

Shouting.

Shouting had erupted in the hall.

Her blood froze. She struggled still with the poison in her veins, her magic slowly working it out of her system. Bracing a hand on the bedframe, she breathed deeply.

A thousand thoughts raced through her head, a thousand ends she didn't want to meet, a thousand lives she didn't live. Lark knew what she had to do, even if she wasn't sure she could. She took a breath, then another. Footfalls slammed onto the marble of the sitting room, more shouting ensuing.

Her name echoed through the room, concerned at first, but turned to wrath once they found their captain. Lark focused all her magic, all her thoughts, all of her soul. Just as the doors to the bedroom wrenched open, she jumped.

Lark would never get used to the sensation of falling between worlds, of being somewhere she wasn't supposed to be. She passed stars, beings that floated in the darkness between each blink, but she kept focus on where she wanted to be. She knew she wouldn't be able to jump to the Roe, not with her blood leaving her body through the wounds in her hands, knees, and feet, and especially not with poison ravaging her body.

She thought of the floor above.

The balcony on the east side.

The walkway that bridged the palace to the mountain.

She thought of the snow lined streets in the east city.

Of the walls circling the life she knew.

Of the

Of the

Lark collapsed, momentarily slipping from consciousness. She collided into a tree and was only aware of birds squawking. Stars clouded her vision as she righted herself, fingers digging into dirt. She heaved whatever lingered in her stomach onto the earth beside her, wave after wave of nausea rolling over her until she dry heaved into a shaking heap beside her sickness. There was no way she would make it. She couldn't even focus her eyes well enough to see where she was, let alone jump—

Everything spun again and she fell through the earth.

Lark was screaming, but there was only silence as the world came into focus. Dim light touched her eyes as a cold breeze fluttered through her dress. Her throat was dry, aching, and she only thought of her white threads of healing, how they seemed so dull within her. Magic couldn't take much more from her without killing her. No more jumping, Lark decided. Not today, not ever. If this was only a short distance, magic would have claimed her life if she had stretched farther.

Lark came to her senses after a while, the feeling akin to waking from a nightmare. She realized then she was in a shallow cave. Smooth walls surrounded her with fallen leaves scattering the cool ground while sunshine warmed the air. Her bag was discarded beside her, the contents spilling onto the ground. She wasn't sure how she had managed to hold onto it for this long, but she was grateful for it. Even more so as she realized what her panicked mind had packed.

She pried her dress off, slowly and with many tears, and tended to her wounds as best she could without her magic and without water, before pulling on her old Tiras uniform. The familiar pants that formed to her body as a second skin, the long-sleeved shirt with lace cuffs replacing the red ones, threads tickling the back of her hands. At the very bottom of the bag, a broken comb rested in three pieces, but she took the largest and raked it through the knotted mess of her hair, eventually using her fingers to work through the thickest tangles.

Lark stuffed the remains of her mangled dress into her bag, noting the coins that littered the pockets. Her magic was still writhing within her, patiently waiting to be used again, but she was so *tired*.

As much as she wanted to lay down, she stood on shaky legs. The glass was no longer embedded in her skin, but the memory of it was still jaggedly stuck. She walked slowly out of the cave, her bag slung on her back, looking like the furthest thing from a princess.

Lord Penerly's estate stretched for miles, which skirted but did not include Westwick, and Lark felt foolish for not recognizing his lands. Only once she saw the wall that enclosed the small town he oversaw, she let out a sigh of relief. She was far enough away from Vale City that it would take time for riders to follow her. She would have time to find food, water, and supplies in Penerly's tiny town and be long gone before the Tiras rode through.

The lord's town was one for mining and the houses that made it were all built of stone, the very same that created the wall and Penerly's home. Lark had been here only a handful of times, but she remembered him for sympathizing with those who stood against the Melech. Somewhere in the back of her exhausted mind, she remembered that Rook had stationed some of her men here.

Lark stopped at the largest building; a general store combined with an inn. An older man sat beside the counter, a book in one hand and a cup of coffee in the other. The room was empty besides him, the shelves stocked full on the left side of the room.

"Child, you're tracking mud on my floor—in the Greater's name, where are your shoes? It's winter, girl. You must be freezing," he said, his book slapped closed and set on the counter. Lark glanced down at her feet, a disgusting mess of mud and blood, but the chill hadn't affected her as much as it should have. She wondered if shock had overruled her senses.

The man, still seated, moved towards her and she realized he was in a chair. Lark's first thought wondered if she could fix him, heal whatever had been damaged, but she dismissed the idea as quick as it came. Not all wanted to be fixed, and not all were broken.

"I'm sorry," she said as he wheeled closer. He waved a hand in dismissal once he stopped, then motioned for her to sit at one of the few tables.

"So, you need boots. Food, a room, what else?"

"I don't need a room, but do you know where I could find a horse?"

Once she sat, and their faces were level, his blue eyes stared back at her studiously. Lark watched as the recognition settled in.

"What happened to yours, my lady?"

"I stopped to make camp when it was spooked and bolted, my supplies with it," she said smoothly, her voice as even as it could be.

"You're sure you don't need a room? I'm sure Lord Penerly wouldn't mind if you stayed—"

"No, I'm quite sure," Lark said all too quickly. She smiled softly. "I don't want to be a burden. I won't be staying long anyway."

"I'll see what I can find for you, my lady." With that, he wheeled away, and Lark was left with only her wild heart for company.

The man didn't take long, much to her delight, and brought with him a waterskin, bundled food, a pair of boots and thick socks, and a cloak. Lark gave him a handful of coin, far more than needed, and he sent her on her way with directions of who may have a horse for her. She offered him a smile that didn't reach her eyes and bid him farewell.

The cold air brought a touch of salt from the water, but it tightened her stomach. If the waters weren't so volatile, she'd happily take a boat, knowing Melech wouldn't send his men after her on the water.

"...soldiers have passed through Westwick. A dozen of them, riding like lightning. They tore through the inns and brothels but didn't stay. I heard they're looking for someone."

"Who would they be looking for?"

Lark caught the women's voices as they walked past her, oblivious. She tucked her chin to her chest and hurried along the path the innkeeper had instructed until she came to the lord's stables.

When she was queen, she'd repay him, gift him ten horses for this one. She kept to the shadows, willing her own—as feeble as they were—to shroud her while she snuck in. She picked the only horse that didn't stiffen once it noticed her. As quick she could, Lark tacked the horse, nearly ready to ride bareback, but she knew she wouldn't last that way, so she worked swiftly, flinching at every footfall, every sound, outside of her shadowed bubble.

Lark raised the hood of her cloak and led the horse out, offering a small cube of sugar to coax it over the threshold of the stables. She rubbed its nose before swinging onto its back and disappearing into the tree line.

She willed a calm, steadiness to the horse, and they were gone—leaving the estate behind.

Towards Azrael.

Towards home.

# CHAPTER 43

## AZRAEL

Azrael jackknifed awake, his body convulsing and heaving the contents of his stomach onto the floor. The force of the jolt nearly flung him off the bed. He grasped at the fraying edges of his dream—Lark in a wedding dress, her hair falling behind her. She had held a single flower, that wilted by the time she had come to him. A shadow given the form of Melech had materialized beside Azrael in the dream, silver shining in the light. The king had thrust the dagger into Azrael's ribs, then took Lark by the mouth, kissing her passionately, roughly, as he ripped the flowers from her hair while Azrael crumpled to the floor. His hand was stained with his blood, tangled in her hair, as he buried the knife into her stomach. The king yelled, louder and louder, blaming Azrael for her death—saying *he* had killed her, not Melech.

Boots scuffed the ground, muffled by doors loudly thrown open. Wherever Azrael was, it was dim, save a single candle on a table beside his head. Three shapes rushed into the room, their faces coming into focus once Azrael sat up in his cot.

No one said anything until after Edhar checked Azrael's vitals, pried his eyes open, and frowned as he put two fingers against Azrael's temple. Edhar's crooked shoulders seemed to bow inwards a little more each time Azrael saw the healer. This time, Edhar sighed and it almost seemed like he'd fold in two.

"How do you feel?" the healer asked, his beady black eyes searching Azrael's face.

"Like I died." His own voice felt detached from his body, feeling for all the world like a ghost.

Ahmi knelt beside the cot and reached out to touch Azrael's hand. "What did it do?"

"I can't be sure," Edhar said. He glanced over his shoulder at Bedivere pacing. "He lost a lot of blood, but there's no wound—"

"I threw it up," Azrael interrupted. The phrase carried him back to being a child, when he was sick and creeping into his mother's room. As he had wished back then, he now wished that something could just take the pain, the sickness away, as he slept. Make him hurt less. A childish wish, but there had been so much coldness in the space between life and death that made him fear returning to that state.

"How?" Ahmi's voice was quiet. It was plain in his friend's face that he was thinking of Nevan, how his body had been so ragged and bloody. It could have been Azrael. Why hadn't it been him? What had stopped them?

"I don't know. It only touched me." Azrael lifted his hand to his throat, where the ghost of the Daeoan's touch remained. Edhar drew a shaky breath.

"Remind me how your hands were burned," Edhar said slowly.

"Lark's magic, when she hid me from Melech."

"It's the same."

Bedivere stopped pacing as silence fell as a curtain around the four men. The lord's long hair was down, tangled around his tense shoulders. Azrael couldn't read the expression on his face. "I'll be back," the lord said before striding out of the infirmary.

Moments passed before Edhar spoke again. "I've prepared these for you. I had a feeling the bleeding was internal. I'm hoping it's slowed by now, but for good measure."

The healer held out his palm with capsules of herbs, while Ahmi produced a glass of water and offered it to Azrael. He took both things.

"Are you in pain?" Edhar asked, watching as a hawk observes a mouse.

The word opened a dam, everything Azrael hadn't been thinking about, avoiding, trying to ignore, all poured in. He had been able to keep his head above the water, keeping the fire of pain at bay. Memories mixed—his bones fracturing, shattering, fire scorching his muscles, darkness swallowing him. His body felt as he had been thrown off a cliff, then eaten by a sea monster. His heart and head didn't feel so different.

"Yes," he mumbled, not daring to admit how much. Edhar dropped another capsule in Azrael's hand before standing. The healer forced a smile before leaving. "Am I dying? I've never seen him smile."

Ahmi laughed dryly, his eyes on Azrael as he swallowed the herbs and chased them with water.

"You and Bedivere look at me as though I'm a ghost. What happened?" Azrael knew enough of what happened for him—he wondered what the others had seen, what they had heard.

"What do you remember?" Ahmi asked, mouth set to the side.

There was so much relief Azrael felt looking at his friend, the familiar and welcome amongst the new and different. His life kept changing directions, but at least he had Ahmi. Even if he couldn't tell his friend of the nightmares he had faced alone in the darkness after the Daeoan had left, before he awoke.

"Being on the ground. The demon left, and everything was black."

"That was three days ago."

Azrael's voice was stuck in his throat as he whispered, "Anything from Lark?"

"It'll be days before we'll know if she's sent anything, if she's heard about this. He won't hurt her."

Azrael shook his head. "The moment I'm dead, he will, and he nearly got that chance."

"What happened with them? You were screaming and yelling. I thought you were going to die," Ahmi's voice equaled Azrael's, caught in his throat halfway between a small sob and a whisper. "Do not go where I cannot."

Azrael squeezed Ahmi's hand before Ahmi rested his forehead against their interwoven hands.

"I heard them speak to me." Azrael said quietly. "They said they needed me weak, Ahmi. They didn't want to kill me, they want me to be weak."

"They're not doing a very good job then, are they?" Ahmi lifted his head to smirk, the sorrow lifted from his eyes.

Azrael had to smile too, even if he felt as though the demons were doing what they intended. His heart felt so heavy, as though a stone had replaced it to weigh him down.

"How are you still here? I figured the rest of the Tiras had left by now."

"Jordie and I stayed. He's convinced you're here." Ahmi let go, untangling his fingers, and stood. "She does know you're here, but she won't say anything. She saw what happened. You're safe."

*For now*, Azrael thought. Safe for now.

It took Azrael two weeks to get back on his feet. He couldn't stand on his own in the days after he had woken up, but slowly, he improved and could manage to walk in a straight line. He attempted the lock picking kit Bedivere had gifted him, but he often forgot what he had been trying to achieve halfway through. It took another week for his mind to catch up to his body. Every time he would ask about Lark, Bedivere or Ahmi—whichever happened to be sitting with him at the time—would say there was no news, and no news was good news, and change the subject.

Bedivere read to Azrael, books ranging from politics to medicine to stories of pirates, while Ahmi's company was easy. Ahmi didn't pry, they worked on puzzles in silence, and helped Azrael shave his face and trim his hair. Tending to his appearance made Azrael realize he was once again a shell of what he had been, and he hated it. He hated every moment of his weakness.

Bedivere talked of their plans, and how they had changed, now they worked towards summer. Which meant they had four months to move—unless something happened to Lark before that. Bedivere had also mentioned Lark had written to him, but refused to elaborate on what the letters were about.

Rook was in and out when she was in the Roe, her visits brief but Azrael counted the moments until she left his presence. She feigned a bedside healer, but Azrael knew better than that.

Spring bloomed while Azrael was stuck inside the infirmary. Edhar finally let him move back into his house, and Azrael couldn't hide the relief. At least something went back to normal.

"Luned has agreed to work with you, to get you back to yourself," Bedivere said as the pair walked together to Azrael's house. "I see the shadows in you, son. Do not let the shadows win."

Azrael nodded, shrugging off the lord's affectionate words. Despite the kind words, all Azrael could feel was those lengthening, rancid shadows the Daeoan had infused into his skin, at the base of his throat—matching to the scars Lark had left on his hands. For all he knew, his heart was blackened all the same.

"She will be here in the morning. Let her help." Bedivere caught Azrael's arm, long brown fingers wrapping smoothly and strongly. Azrael looked to the Lord of the Roe, the dark face he had grown to respect and admire. The dark brows that were often soft, playful, were now drawn together, a crease forming between them. The lord's brown eyes matched Azrael's, though veins of honey woven around the iris, and that was where the worry lay.

Azrael nodded again and Bedivere loosened his fingers, his hand dropping back to his side. With a flicker of a smile, Azrael ducked inside his house, closing the door on his lord.

†

True to the lord's word, Luned was at Azrael's door at dawn. She let herself in, brewed tea, and made breakfast for Azrael before he had dressed. When he met her downstairs, sunshine flooded the sitting room, lighting the silver woman in gold. She wore tight clothing, hugging the slight curves she had, and had her white hair in two long plaits resting down her front. Reflecting the image of a warrior, she was far from the woman who had been dressed pristinely next to the lord, but the sharpness in her face, the fierceness in her crystal eyes, remained.

Luned said nothing to Azrael, merely motioning to the plate of breakfast she had prepared for him. He ate quickly, inhaling the eggs and bacon and mulberry jam, and strapped his blades on, laced his boots, before following the silver woman out of his house.

The two were silent as they strode up the quiet street, towards the manor, and only picked up speed as they passed the house, then the field the Daeoan had nearly claimed Azrael's life. Luned still said nothing when she abruptly stopped, turned, and swung her arm out. Azrael blocked the blow with his forearm, but not the punch with her other hand, straight into his stomach. He began to fold over, but not before her knee jerked up, nearly hitting his jaw.

"Don't let your mind become a battlefield. Don't think about it," Luned finally said, her voice soft in cadence but firm.

"I almost died here, what else am I supposed to think about?" Azrael didn't stop the anger, the pain, that leaked into his voice, not as he threw a fist aiming at her jaw, but Luned moved quickly around him, locking his arm.

"Think about how you survived." A fist to his ribs. "How you refuse to let the demons win." Azrael blocked the next hit, landed one of his own on the edge of her jaw. "Think about how much more you have to offer," she continued, spitting onto the earth.

"To the woman I love as she sits beside a king? What else do I have to offer?" He was nearly shouting now, tears burning the back of his eyes. He didn't want to feel like this, to feel this weakness inside him like a disease, a living organism to plague his waking thoughts.

"You stood your ground against a king, against monsters. You are hope. You give people a fighting chance to stand for what they believe in. Do not tell me these people do not kiss the ground you walk on for saving their sons, their daughters, when those demons came. You fight, you survive, and you do it again and again for what you believe."

Luned's eyes were ice chips as they paused long enough for her to speak, her words sharp as blades.

"You say it like it's so easy," he snapped back. He crouched, preparing for whatever move she would pounce on him with. "As if it hasn't been eating away at me this whole time."

Luned paused, plaits sliding to the side as she tilted her head. Her ice chipped eyes narrowing thoughtfully before she softly sighed.

"I see it. I see the wounds left on your heart, but it doesn't make you any less deserving of what you want. It doesn't discredit anything you've done. Being broken doesn't mean you're weak. Sometimes being broken makes you dangerous."

&#8224;

The two of them grappled for hours, covering one another in purpling bruises. Once the salty breeze shifted with the afternoon sun, Azrael sprawled out in the grass, not minding the sharp stabs of the dead stalks burrowing into his back, and watched as the clouds lazily slid across the blue sky. Luned settled down beside him, her delicate shoulders shuddering with each deep breath she caught.

Bedivere strolled towards them then, looking for all the world like a hero from a storybook romance: white cotton shirt held closed by a single button, flaps ruffling in the breeze, while his long hair billowed behind him. His smile was brighter than the sun as Luned stood and went to him.

Azrael watched the silver woman as she walked back towards the house, her nimble hands flicking her braids over her shoulders. Bedivere didn't follow, hovering near Azrael for a moment before taking Luned's place in the grass. Only he stretched out beside Azrael and faced the clouds.

"Did she behave?" The lord's voice was light, teasing.

"She did. She told me to stop wallowing."

"Sounds like her."

"It felt good to move again, to rely on my body." Azrael sighed. "I'm worried it will always be like this."

What if the Daeoan kept coming back, to keep him in this state? To keep him weak.

"It won't. You will gain your strength, your confidence. You've endured more things in this past year than most would in their entire lives. You'll be back to your pain in the ass self before you know it."

"Thank you, Bedivere. For everything. You have too much faith in me."

The lord sighed. "And you don't have enough."

# CHAPTER 44

## AZRAEL

Azrael's days turned into routine; Luned would wake him at dawn and they'd fight for hours, then he'd train with Ahmi until dinner, which consisted of Bedivere, Luned, and him making small talk and avoiding talking about the king and soon-to-be queen. Two weeks of this brought Azrael back to life. He put on weight, started to build muscle, and the ache of Lark's absence began to fade, even if the shadow of hurt still lingered in his chest.

Rook had scurried off to her mountain town once Azrael had grown better, not failing to remind Azrael she was off to do *productive* work in their cause.

He had finished sparring with Ahmi when the pair began their usual run through the town. Spring was quiet in its arrival, slowly turning everything green and breathing warmth back into the air.

"Melech wants us back in the city." Ahmi kept his gaze forward as the pair kept a steady pace, staying close beside Azrael. "There's unrest and rebellions happening throughout the kingdom. I'm sure you have no idea what that's about."

"None."

"I don't know what you're doing here, Az, or why you stay." Ahmi paused for so long, Azrael thought he had finished. "I'm glad to be leaving. I didn't think I'd ever have to come back home."

Ahmi had grown up here, Azrael remembered. Had grown up and lived on the fields outside of the city. A farmer's son turned into a soldier.

"Thank you," Azrael said, though he wasn't sure what exactly he was thanking his friend for.

"Don't thank me. Make a better future. Make this kingdom something to be proud of."

A hmi and Jordie left at dusk, on a boat boarded with their horses, the latter Azrael had hardly seen in the time she was in the Roe. He'd watched their boat disappear into the horizon before going to Bedivere's study, once again feeling the emptiness weighing at his side. Something in the sight of the ship sailing brought back the memories of Bedivere reading to him, the stories of pirates and assassins living in adventures.

"He's building into the mountainside," Azrael said as he entered the lord's study, interrupting Bedivere as he lowered a book from his face.

The lord's face was patient, not understanding the outburst.

"Someone is adding onto the building plans of the palace, marking out the old passageways, and ways to get through the palace without tracking everything inside."

Bedivere stood abruptly, his book falling forgotten to the floor. "She sent a map."

"What?"

With his middle finger and thumb, the lord rubbed his temples before resting his palm against his face. "I can't believe I was so *dull* to have not seen it before. I thought ink had spilled—"

Now, Azrael stared without understanding at Bedivere, his eyes tracking as the lord crossed the room to a bookshelf. He plucked a piece of parchment from between two books and handed it to Azrael.

"What's this?" He unfolded the paper, his heart pounding at the sight of Lark's handwriting. The words were unassuming, written in a cipher only Bedivere would understand, but it wasn't that capturing the lord's attention—the black lines that intersected beneath the words, strange enough to look like ink had spilled, or a poorly drawn doodle.

"She sent a map," Bedivere repeated.

Azrael turned it this way, and that, unable to see what the lord had, until Bedivere swiped the paper and turned it just so.

A map, outlining the passages of the palace.

"This connects to Melech's floor," Azrael said, his fingertip trailing past a word spelled incorrectly. That brilliant woman, he couldn't keep the admiration out of his heart and off his face. "If we were to get lucky, if we time it right, this would be the way to go."

"Are you prepared for it?" Bedivere's awe struck smile was off his face, replaced by solemnity.

"Without a doubt." The longer Lark was gone, the riskier it got. The sooner Azrael got to the palace, the sooner he could bring her home.

There was something soft, sad, in Bedivere's face before he turned his gaze back to the letter—a wish that it hadn't come to this, that Melech had been a kinder and better king, that Lark hadn't left at all. Azrael felt it all too.

"Rook will be back in three days. You two will ride out, and I'll send soldiers for support. Study this, make your plan, be ready. Let's take our kingdom back."

†

N ight moved in, and Azrael felt impossibly small standing beneath the darkening pink sky. He swirled the warm mead in his glass as he watched as stars began to poke through. Somewhere high above him, there was a god floating amongst those stars. Somewhere far beyond that one, three more existed. Azrael still didn't know if he believed it, any of it, but if his plans went wrong, he'd find out soon enough.

A small part of him didn't know if he was ready to face the king with the crooked crown again. Even hearing his voice beneath floorboards had ignited such a hatred and anger within Azrael, he wasn't sure how he would react when he was face to face with the king again. His heart fractured as his thoughts trailed to Lark. She had been a thing locked tightly within his heart and head, thoughts and feelings kicked beneath shadows as to not recognize nor acknowledge. It was easier that way. When he didn't know the next time he would see her, he thought it better to tuck her away—not forget, never forget.

But now, with the future rising like a tidal wave before him, Azrael couldn't keep the thoughts of her aside. The house behind him truly felt like a skeleton without Lark in it with him. The wooden floors creaked with secrets he'd never know, the windows cold and bare. Lark had been the heart. It'd been two months now since she'd left—willingly, he had to remind himself—and the sting of her absence had turned into a dull ache he was used to. A ghost he had learned to live with. He wondered if she was married to Melech by now, and maybe had her coronation already. The image of her, darkened by time, floated in his memories. Forgiveness and exhaustion numbed him—he was tired of being sad, tired of being tired, and tired of being angry.

*Listen for the birdsong.*

Azrael's gaze snapped back to the sky, to the horizon, awaiting that second full moon to make its appearance. Fingers tightening around the glass, he nearly dropped it as something ancient tapped on the back of his mind. He dumped his drink into the dirt and scrambled through the door. Still dressed, he yanked his boots on, tying them poorly, and swung his sheathe onto his back, before running out his front door.

He'd find her.

Wherever she was, he'd find her.

# CHAPTER 45

## AZRAEL

T he forest was black, as though the sky had bled down, darkness seeping between the trees. The only light was a silvery shaft of moonlight as the second moon wavered overhead, but as hooves pounded into the earth, Azrael realized that it wasn't the moonlight at all.

Their horses passed each other, only for each to send rocks skittering across the path as they stopped. Azrael whipped around, his breath squeezed from his chest as he took in the sight of Lark, wild haired and wide eyed. White light hovered above her horse's head but disappeared in a blink.

"You're alive," she choked out, tears obscuring her voice.

"You're back," Azrael said with a voice that caught in his throat. His blackened hands slacked on the reins as he swung off his horse, unable to keep himself from her. He had half a mind to pull her down from the horse but paused steps away from her, hesitation keeping him at bay.

"I killed Brannon." Lark's voice was hollow and her grey eyes matched. He had adjusted to the darkness now and his gaze roved every inch of her. "I knew about the attack; I thought you had died. Melech, he—he poisoned me after it happened. He lied, he lied, and I had hoped—"

Thunder resembling horse hooves erupting cut Lark off, only for her voice to turn to begging and pleading, but Azrael ignored her and turned to face whatever pounded their way.

Shadows hurtled towards him. Azrael jumped back onto his horse, sliding his sword from its sheathe, and leaned into the horse's neck as he flew towards the soldiers, swords glinting in the torchlight they carried.

Regular soldiers, Azrael realized as he burst through the center of their formation. Both hands on the hilt, Azrael sliced through bodies with raised arms. The sound of bodies hitting the earth only added fuel to the fire burning within him. Anger made him careless, ruthless. He didn't know why she had been pursued, if it was for the death of the captain or an act she'd committed, but her safety, her life, was held higher than the men charging him now.

A small voice began to warn against the rage, but Azrael ignored the warning bells as he jumped off his horse and pulled the closest soldier off his. A blade careened towards him, aiming to sever Azrael's arm from his body, but he moved quicker. His own blade burrowed within his attacker's chest, the crunching of bone and flesh pounding in Azrael's head.

All mindless, he did not let it worry him that he was surrounded by eight men. Didn't think about how easy it was to take their lives, though their blood burned his hands and their eyes etched into his eyelids, to be seen later when he struggled to sleep. Though all of this, Azrael didn't stop, until silence fell, and thick darkness descended before him.

He spun to face Lark, only to meet her bloody knuckles as her fist connected with his nose. The unexpected force of it sent him staggering backwards, the tip of his sword drawing lines in the blood-stained dirt.

Lark yelled and swore, but her words were drowned out, Azrael's heartbeat still loud in his head. Silver light bathed them as Lark stepped closer, but she stopped dead when Azrael lifted his fingers to probe his sore nose.

"What happened to your hands?" Lark's voice was frightened, as though she knew the answer but did not want to be right.

"I had hoped you'd be able to tell me. It's from your magic." Azrael wiped his sword on his pants before sheathing it. "The Daeoan left a mark too."

He pulled down the collar of his shirt enough to see the black stain. All color drained from Lark's face, and the light above them guttered before disappearing.

"What have I done?" Lark stumbled backwards.

His chest cracked. He reached a hand out to her, but she shook her head. "You didn't know."

"And that should make it better? That makes it worse, Az. I didn't—I didn't know. I left and I hurt you, and I know in so many ways. I'm sorry. I know I can't possibly make up for any of it—"

Azrael moved to her then, grabbing her arms and holding her still. Her body shook like a leaf in a storm beneath his hands, her breath hardly passing her lips as though she tried not to breathe at all.

"Lark," he said sharply, bringing her attention to him. Then softly, "Lark." Savoring her name, that she was here with him again.

Hooves against earth brought him back, turning his focus to their horses as they circled Lark and Azrael.

"Let's go home," he whispered, leaning in to press his lips against her forehead. She was sweating, but her skin was cold. He lightly squeezed her arms.

Azrael stood beside her as she climbed onto her horse, swinging her legs over, and he couldn't help but note how thin she'd gotten since he'd last seen her. He hurled himself onto his own horse and they rode away from the bloody forest in a strange silence he hadn't endured with her since they'd met.

"How does it not affect you?" Lark asked eventually, splintering the night and its quiet.

"How does what not affect me?"

"Taking a life."

Now that the rage, the lightning, had calmed, leaving him hollow, the carnage caught up to him. He couldn't recall how many lives he'd claimed tonight, how many nameless ghosts lingered at his back. He thought then to the woman riding beside him, and everything she represented, and chased away the ghosts.

"It doesn't get easier." He knew she was asking for herself, without her having to voice her own hollowness. He wondered how she'd done it, but knew he could never ask her.

"I could have killed him," Lark said, so quietly he had to strain to hear her over the constant hoofbeats. "Many times. It was almost as if he was asking for me to try. After the ceremony—"

*Ceremony?* His head emptied, but he must have said the word aloud.

"I was recognized as Nekoda's daughter, rightful heir to the throne, and he presented our engagement."

Had Bedivere told him that? He couldn't remember what the lord had read to him as he struggled against the wounds the demons had given him.

"It'll be easier for me to take the throne if I'm recognized. It's worth nearly dying for," Lark added, ignoring the silence Azrael maintained. It was easier than crushing down the anger and pain bubbling in his chest. He wanted nothing more than to ride back to Vale City and pull Melech off his gilded throne.

All at once, Azrael could see the lingering damage: the grey at the roots of her hair, the dark circles beneath her eyes, the way her cheeks sunk, how her veins stood out beneath her skin. The faraway look in her eyes burned his soul, whatever was left of it at least. These past two months had taken a larger toll on her, than it had on him.

Neither spoke as they left their horses in the stables at the manor, nor as they walked to their home. Azrael recalled how Iah had spoken to him tonight, how the otherworldly voice had echoed in his head. Iah had wanted him to find Lark, but he couldn't help but wonder why—what would have happened if he hadn't gone? Was the god capable of knowing, of seeing that? Was the god of night so easily able to tug at the threads of their lives?

Lark stepped inside the house and seemed to freeze, shoulders tight and unmoving as if she stopped breathing again. Azrael stepped around her, shedding his bloody clothes and leaving them in the same spot as he had been since they moved in.

"Do you want to go to bed?" he asked her as he moved to stand in front of her.

Lark shook her head.

"Will you start a fire?" Azrael asked as he went into the kitchen, bringing back two glasses and a decanter of whiskey a guard had gifted him. It tasted like the bottom of a waterlogged barrel, but the taste was worth the effect it wrought.

He settled beside Lark on the couch, close enough for their knees to touch but far enough she had her space. Pouring some into a glass, he offered it to her before he poured twice that amount into his.

She was so quiet; his chest seemed to cave in at the sight of her trembling fingers, lips pressed tightly in a soft pink line.

"Tell me what you're thinking," he said quietly, unable to keep the pleading out of his voice. She'd been gone for so long, but even as she sat here with him, it was as though she were nothing more than a ghost. A phantom to break him.

An eternity waited in the breaths she took before she answered him. "He never meant for me to live."

Her words, her voice, were empty. Unthinking. As though she'd been thinking this for so long, it turned to repetition.

"He didn't understand how strong I was, how far I am from the forgotten princess he had known. I was able to work out the poison. I didn't think he'd do it, and I'm so stupid for thinking that. I'm so stupid for thinking I could have saved us both by going with him. If I would have just stopped before going into that room, I could have heard his voice...

"And I hate that I hurt your hands," she continued, "I'll never forgive myself, even if you have. I'll try to fix it tomorrow; I just need to rest before I try."

"You don't have to," Azrael said after he took another drink of the whiskey. "They're healed. They don't hurt."

A half-truth, but he didn't dare tell her. He wanted to reach out, to touch her, but he didn't want his blackened fingers making her feel guilty, more so than he saw in her eyes already.

"I told you what I was thinking, now it's your turn," Lark said, her eyes never leaving the fireplace and the crackling flames within.

How could he tell her? Every thought swirled around her, as though she were the very center of him, the force of her pulling him further and further in.

"I'm tired of hiding. I'm ready to fight, to end this. I'm thinking it's time to end his reign."

✝

A day. A day to themselves before they decided the fate of the kingdom.
The sun was high in the sky, slowly drifting, amongst the few fluffy spring clouds. Lark had packed a bag for food while Azrael had the horses readied before they set off, chasing the coastline.

Her energy improved as they pounded across the expanse of the Roe. Azrael watched from the corner of his eye as the shadows seemed to lift from Lark's shoulders, the ghosts in her eyes disappearing until the grey was as vivid as the storms he knew. At the pace she set, the two of them flew past the ships, farms, and fields, until they reached the plains of the coast. Grass that grew waist high, still crisp and pale from the winter, swayed in sighed in the breeze. Massive trees grew in a small grove just above the cliffside where they dismounted.

Lark began to lay a blanket down, but Azrael undressed, earning a side eye. He grinned, leaving only his undershorts on. His body was once again sculpted, his bones no longer poking through his skin. He placed his hands on his hips, a fire igniting in his blood as he watched Lark fluster under his gaze.

"Let's swim," he said. They had a day before they went back to worrying about the kingdom and their lives. He left his things on the blanket and began walking towards the rocky path leading down the hillside. He paused, glancing over his shoulder, and smiled.

Lark had discarded her dress, wearing now only her shift, a hesitant but mischievous smile on her face as she jogged to his side. He offered his hand out, ignoring the flinch that flickered across her face as she grasped him. *Here and now*, he had to remind himself. He wouldn't worry about anything else.

Hiking down to the beach, Azrael breathed in the smell of the ocean, the sense of peace and insignificance as he stood at the expanse of water. The sand beneath his bare feet was warm, burning only if he stood for too long in the same place, but he quickly waded into the turquoise water, welcoming the coolness.

Behind him, Lark seemingly left her hesitation at their picnic site. Hair unbound, she moved to stand beside him, wrapping her arms around his and resting her head against his shoulder. A soft breeze rustled her hair, strands tickling his bare back. She kissed his skin before untangling herself and easing out of her shift, shucking it behind her and into the sand.

Lark waded further into the water then dove in when it was deep enough. Azrael watched her pale shape below the water, going deeper until the sunlight on the surface masked her. He waited a moment before following her, leaving his undershorts on the beach as well.

Peace came over him the moment he went beneath the surface. There was only this moment, in the silence of the sea. He opened his eyes, spotting Lark's fluid form as she drifted in the water, her hair a web of tendrils around her. As though she knew he watched her, she turned, her gaze finding his. She swam towards him, nuzzling her face into the crook of his shoulder as she wrapped her legs around his waist.

†

## LARK

L ark needed this, more than Azrael could know. Her hands drifted as they slowly moved to the surface, one hand burying beneath his knotted curls and the other one below where her hips rested against his. She felt him tense, both gasping as they broke the surface. The warmth of the sun softened the sharpness of her passion, the sudden urgency she had felt when she'd seen him watching her. She'd noticed the way he looked at her, as though she were nothing more than a fragile bird who'd fallen from a nest, and it angered her, before she had to remind herself he was afraid—the same way she was, and it came from a place of love.

But fragility—that carefulness—was not what she wanted. Not when she needed to put the past months behind her. Not when she needed to forget the way Melech's eyes had devoured her, and his poison had consumed her. Her body tensed, legs tightening around Azrael's waist, as, together, they drifted closer to shore. She knew the moment his feet touched the ocean floor once more, his hands gripping her thighs. Her mouth pressed against his shoulder, his jaw, before finding his, their tongues coming together with the ferocity she craved. Not rescinding that heat, Azrael leaned forward, his arm crushing her against his chest as his fingers explored down her back, beneath her, then finally burrowing within her. She followed his example, reaching further down to grasp him, drawing curses from beneath his breath as his shoulders twitched. His fingers paused, only to quicken to match his breath.

Lark tightened her grip, savoring the feeling of him in her hand, before his fingers withdrew and he leaned back just enough to adjust the way she was pressed against him, allowing room for her hips to shift downwards slightly. His teeth caught her bottom lip as he angled his hips and buried himself within her. Lark groaned, closing her eyes at the feeling, and rolled her hips before he began thrusting, slowly at first, but his pace quickened. His right arm grasped her shoulders, fingers splaying on her left collarbone, while his left wrapped around her waist, keeping her in place.

The ocean rocked against her back as Lark tipped her head back, letting both the water and the feeling wash over her. Her tangled hair stuck to her bare back, knotting around Azrael's arms, and she breathed in the salt of the air and the scent of firewood and moss that he always somehow carried. With each thrust, he pulled her back into herself, as though her shadows and her light had spooled far out from her, fraying her like a forgotten blanket. His mouth pressed against the column of her throat, his tongue lightly grazing her skin as he moved upwards, until the hand he had on her shoulder moved to the back of her neck, pushing her face down to meet his.

Her tongue explored his mouth, the way he tasted, as he moved, without withdrawing himself, towards the shore, the sandy beach. With a tenderness she couldn't chide him for, he let go of her to smooth out her shift and his undershorts before settling her on them. Warm sand pressed against her, cradling her as the earth welcomed her, as he moved over her. Lark ran her nails down his back, feeling the heat that radiated off him as the sun beat down, but he shivered nonetheless before lifting her hands above her head and pinning them down together in his. His salty kiss like echoes on her mouth, on her jaw, before he devoured her again.

Summoned for dinner, Lark led Azrael through Bedivere's manor, their hands tightly pressed together. She had dressed in one of her cool chiffon dresses, enjoying the soft breeze that ruffled the fabric during their walk to the house, and she was glad she chose the one without sleeves, the light pink fabric clasped together with silver moons on her shoulders.

After their day together, Lark felt lighter than she had in months, the shadow within her heart shortened. The two of them had lay beneath the grove of trees until the sun began to fall in the sky, as though nothing beyond them had mattered. Relishing in nothing other than their company. Azrael hadn't asked her about her time in Vale City, nor about her journey back, and she wondered if he knew the phantoms that had followed her.

As she opened the doors to the dining room, Bedivere and Lu turned from their place at the glass wall, looking like king and queen. Bedivere wore a silver tunic, threaded with white detailing that stood stark against his skin, with white pants that hugged his long legs, pooling at his bare feet. Lu was striking too, a sapphire dress that fit like a second skin, with slits cut at her waist to reveal her porcelain skin. Her long, pin straight hair was crowned with delicate silver prongs, barely protruding from her head. Lark's heart warmed at the sight they struck together—the powerful couple she had grown to love in her time with them.

"Princess," Lu crooned, her icy smile genuine as she reached out a hand to Lark. Letting go of Azrael's hand, Lark went to her friend and embraced her.

"Rook arrived earlier than expected," Bedivere said as Azrael moved to his side. Lark disentangled herself from Lu and looked to the lord as he gestured to the table. "She may very well invite herself, looking like the disheveled devil she is."

As though commanded, the doors opened with a forceful push to alit Rook on the threshold—looking very near to Bedivere's description. Wearing riding clothes—clean at least—but with a mass of golden, knotted hair, Rook grinned, her scar tugging slightly with the motion. She crossed the room, leaving dusty footprints in her wake, before settling at the table.

"Rook," Bedivere said, a small, warm grin on his face, "Welcome. How was your ride?"

"Exhausting. Bashing heads and spreading the gospel is hard work, you know." Rook sighed, leaning back in her chair with a breathless smile on her face as she met Lark's stare. The rebel leader winked.

"So, that's what you've been doing?" Azrael asked as he sat down, in his preferred seat at the end of the table, opposite of Bedivere. Lark followed the others as they also took their seats. She sat at Azrael's right. She'd much rather look out the window than have her back to it, but she didn't want to sit beside the rebel leader.

"Yes, and it's more than what you've been doing. Which is what, exactly? I see you found our princess again, but wasn't it your fault we lost in her the first place?" Rook's voice was light, but there was a serrated edge in her voice that straightened Lark's shoulders, calling her attention to the golden-haired woman across the table.

Before Lark could snap back at her, Azrael shifted, quick and forceful, and Rook grunted, forced forward with the exhale. Rook straightened in her chair, boots scuffing on the floor, as Azrael's knees bumped into Lark's. Down the table, Bedivere's glare was heated. Lark hid her smirk, finally understanding Azrael had kicked Rook. It was a childish reaction, but she warmed nonetheless that he had defended her.

"Now that you're here, when will we leave?" Lark asked the rebel leader after food had been placed before them. Seasoned lamb with glazed carrots shining in the firelight, slices of tomato with powder sprinkled over it. Her stomach turned leaden. Instead of picking up her utensils, she grabbed the glass of water in front of her, beside the glass of wine tormenting her. She still felt like talons of the poison laced within the wine, coiling within her. Repressing a shudder, she forced herself to look at Rook.

"Right now, if you want, princess." Rook shrugged, violently cutting into her food. All elbows.

Bedivere sighed, cutting through the conversation. Tiredness was in his eyes, but Lark knew better. He looked to everyone at the table, his gaze resting on hers for a moment to long before settling on Lu's. It was sadness in his eyes, and Lark wondered why, but crushed her curiosity.

"Daybreak," the Lord of the Roe said before he took a sip of his wine. With another sigh, he repeated it. "Daybreak."

# CHAPTER 46

## AZRAEL

Neither slept. Held hands, but Azrael and Lark lay shoulder to shoulder, listening to each other's breathing and the way their hearts fluttered in harmony. Dawn crept in too quickly as Azrael packed his bags before light touched the earth. The hollowness in Lark's face was sudden and tender. The only solace Azrael could find in their departure was that if they went to meet death, he was dragging Melech with him. If taking the king's life meant forfeiting Azrael's own, he'd do it, over and over. For her. For the numbness, the fear, the hatred that swam in her eyes when she didn't think he was looking.

Azrael slid his daggers into place, strapped his sword to his back, and laced his boots only to watch as Lark fretfully paced the house for the few things she still had.

He wondered if they would see this house again, the tall ceilings, the fireplace with missing stones, the precarious drop from the landing if he leaned over the railing. If their plan failed, they would have to run, unable to come back to Havriel. If it worked, however...

Lark stopped walking in his line of sight, her hair piled on top of her head the way Bedivere kept his, with her own daggers strapped to her. She offered a smile that didn't meet her eyes as she stepped closer to him. He took her chin with his forefinger and thumb, angling her face up.

"You will sit on that throne, Lark. You will survive this," he said as he moved his hand to hold her face, his thumb stroking her cheek. Her eyes closed, but not before he noticed the silver lining her grey eyes. "I'll be with you, at your side."

Eyes still closed, Lark opened her mouth to say something, but behind him, the door opened, and Rook popped in.

"Time to go, Your Majesties." A wicked grin stretched on the woman's face, wild eyes brighter than the first ray of sunlight touching a forest, before she disappeared into the street.

Together, the three of them—Azrael, Lark, and Rook—boarded a boat, to Lark's chagrin and Azrael's excitement, which surprised even him. He was simply glad they weren't spending two weeks on horseback, and he knew that Lark felt the same way, even if she gripped his hand too tight as they set off.

Azrael didn't know what to expect on the boat ride, but he was thankful for the spring weather that kept the waters calm. Bedivere had charted the boat for them, so they were the only ones on board, besides the skeleton crew that had been paid too much to keep silent about their passengers. In that, there was no need to hide in the cabin the three of them shared, so Azrael remained on the deck, watching the men and women work, pulling various ropes and remarking about the water.

Rook befriended the captain, an older man with one eye who kept to himself, and Azrael had to wonder if they bonded over their shared facial injuries, if that was something that brought people together.

Lark appeared at Azrael's elbow, her head resting against his shoulder as they looked out over the water. He'd chosen this spot as a reprieve from the noise, from Rook, and for the fading view of the Roe, the fields far behind them now.

"I always wanted to travel by boat, and now I regret not taking my horse," Lark said, her voice quiet over the hum of the water.

"It reminds me of coming here for the first time as a child. I don't care for it, but I find I do like it more than horseback," he replied. He rested his head against hers.

"I'm scared, Az." Her voice was so quiet, he wouldn't have heard her if he wasn't also thinking the same thing.

"A big fear." Something smaller steps couldn't ease the strain of, nor prepare him for.

She said nothing to this, only wrapped her arms around his, holding onto his bicep. He wondered how big her fear was, how the thorns of it embedded into her, if they stuck her the same way as they stuck him.

"Would you be my king?"

The words settled like stones in him. He stilled, as though the world around him would shift as it did in dreams. Lark was just as still beside him, as though the words had escaped her when she hadn't meant it. Had she meant it?

"Is that what you want?" he asked hesitantly.

"Is that what you want?" Lark echoed, picking her head up and turning to face him. She had loosened her hair, letting the breeze play with it.

"A consort, you mean."

"I don't. I mean a king."

Azrael laughed, strange to even his own ears. Lark hadn't made him nervous in a long time, but she was making him nervous now.

"Why do you laugh?"

He looked at her, his wonderful, incredible princess, and the determined look in her face. She was serious—asking him to be a king.

"How? I don't think a commoner would be allowed to wed a princess, let alone a queen."

"Do you think I would let you go so easily once I gain a crown? That I would so deftly move you to the side once I have what I want?" Lark's shoulders moved back as anger sparked in her eyes. "You're a king in your own right, marrying me wouldn't take that away, nor add it. Hasn't this—" she gestured to the space now between them "—been for that? I can't imagine falling in love with someone, only to prepare to give them up."

He opened his mouth, but snapped it shut. Hadn't that been what his heart had told him all this time? That this time with her was more important than anything? A moment with her was worth more than a thousand without, and that was what he had known. What Melech and Bedivere had known, what Ahmi knew any time they were together.

"You are not less than me because you were born to a solider, and I to a king," Lark huffed, her eyebrows knitting together. The anger had fizzled out of her as she turned to face the water once more. "And if this is how you feel—"

"It's not," his voice spoke without his mind thinking. "You have given me a higher purpose in this life. If I were either, consort or king, as long as it was by your side, I would die a happy man."

"You truly mean it? I do not want to face a new life without you in it." The corner of Lark's mouth twitched, curving upwards into a hesitant smile.

Azrael leaned his forearms against the railing, following Lark's gaze. The sun began its descent behind the mountain range, the sky a brilliant orange against the black outline. The word rattled around in his head, echoing endlessly.

*king king king*

"Are you prepared for what the kingdom will think?" Azrael couldn't imagine what he would have thought a year ago, if he had heard Melech took a commoner for a wife.

"What they *think* does not matter, and I know you'll prove their preconceived notions of you wrong. What you do is what will make our marriage worth everything to the kingdom." Lark turned her head towards him, but her eyes were on his clasped hands. "For the sake of the four gods, why can't you see yourself the way I do?"

A ghost of a smile touched his lips then as he remembered the similar words Bedivere had spoken to him, even the small speech Luned had given to him as they trained together.

"I'll give you time to think about it. You don't need to give me an answer right now." Slowly, Lark raised her eyes from his hands to his gaze. So determined. He admired the set of her mouth, the steel in her eyes, before she turned and left him alone at the railing.

## LARK

L ark climbed into the net turned bed, settling into the mass of cloth and blanket, feeling all the world like an animal burrowing into a nest. Below her, Azrael lazily swung his hammock side to side, the creaking of the rope nearly unnerving if not for Rook's occasional chatter with him. She hadn't expected him to give her push back about their marriage, though, the more she thought about it, she should have seen it coming. He hadn't known palace life as she had, hidden as she was in recent years. He'd spent his life in the world, exploring and fighting and *living*. Here she was, asking the bird to willingly come into the cage simply because she refused to let it go.

Was that what he wanted? No, the thought was foolish itself.

*Soldier king. Little bird, it will be as it should be.* Iah's voice was muffled, as though he shouted the words against the wall she kept in her mind. She had scarcely heard the god of night lately, and she wondered if the god felt shame for leaving her on her own as she battled the poison out of her body. His silence had weighed so heavy on her afterwards, as he had been a near constant companion after these long years.

She wanted to ask him what he meant by this, why he spoke to her now, but her trail of thoughts was interrupted by the words spoken below her.

"The army is outside of Westwick, in the woods waiting for our arrival."

"Army?" Lark piped out, leaning carefully over the edge of her bed. Rook looked up at the princess, her usual cocky attitude nowhere in sight. Only the calm, battle ready gleam in the woman's eyes.

"Aye, princess. If needed. Once we dock, they march silently behind us and await my signal if they're needed."

"If I fail," Azrael offered, smoothly and without emotion, but Lark knew better than to believe that coolness he spoke with.

"If you fail," Rook echoed as she turned her attention to her slim hands, the redness around her nails.

# CHAPTER 47

## AZRAEL

The boat docked in the black of night and three shadows slipped off it and into the thick shadows of the forest. Neither moon dared show its face, not as heavy footfalls followed the three shadows. Moss and leaves absorbed the impact as though the earth itself were of the same mind as those looking for secrecy.

Azrael left Lark and Rook far from the city walls, feeling the darkness whisper at his back as he tread across the forest floor, his eyes set on the white city—bright even in this heavy blackness. The daggers strapped to each thigh, each arm, inside both boots allowed him to breathe easy as he thought over and over of the hundred possibilities of this night. In the days they had been stuck aboard the boat, Lark had gone over the map she had sent Bedivere with Azrael, describing the passageways he would take to sneak through the palace in such thorough detail he saw them in his dreams.

The tents outside the city walls were alive with hedonism. Merchants, drunks, soldiers, and vagrants paid Azrael no mind as he weaved through their tiny city to where the wall met the mountainside. He adjusted his walk, adding a lilt when the glazed over stares lingered a moment too long, before he was able to disappear into the shadows. Above him, the first moon—the *only* moon—had just enough light for him to find the gap between the wall and rock. He scrambled over it, the smoothness of rock cold on his hand.

*Soldier, killer, king.* Iah's voice was just as cold as the rock as it rang inside Azrael's head. The god's voice had been a hum in the back of his mind since they docked, easy to ignore at first, but growing louder with each step, each breath Azrael took. Azrael couldn't tell if the god was looking out for him, or merely watching—mortal lives ever the constant entertainment. The god of night continued, *No, not consort, not Azrael. King Azrael.*

While expecting guards, women in jewels prowling the streets in search of the noblemen drunkenly walking home, Azrael was met with a quiet street and the sounds of a party not too far away. He kept moving, lest someone walk by, and kept his guard up as he wove his way towards the market square—which was also empty, save for the second floors of the buildings where laugher, singing, and conversation floated down from the families reveling in their night. He had taken this way to build an easier lie if he were caught, though the thought didn't bring him peace until he could hardly hear the waterfall, its cascade turned into a quiet hum. The babble of the river flowing from it echoed in his heartbeat once he realized how close he getting to the palace walls.

He had found the crack in the wall on one of his endless rounds of patrol in the time after Westwick. He'd noticed then how a guard stood always near it on the opposite side, but it was left unguarded on the palace side. This would be his way in.

The guard standing beside the gap was the picture of boredom as he paced back and forth before the wall, one hand holding a torch and the other limply resting on the hilt of his sword. Azrael tracked the guard's movement, each scuff of the standard boots, each dance of shadows from the fire. Azrael had one chance to do this—or risk being caught and Rook sending the soldiers in. He wouldn't kill tonight, not if he could help it. He was a soldier, not an assassin. If these people were going to be Lark's, and therefore his one day, he very well couldn't execute this plan and sacrifice them to do it.

He lingered in the shadows beside a tree and waited. The guard eventually slowed his pacing, before turning to face the city, his back to the gap. Azrael, without taking his eyes off the man, felt the ground for a rock, his fingers curling unearthing the stone gently, before he sent it skittering down the cobblestone street. The guard jumped, the hand atop the sword tightening before he took steps towards the light.

Azrael took the opportunity, slipping from his hiding place, and quickly and silently moved to the crack. Angling his body, he took a deep breath, compressing himself as much as he could, and squeezed through. The only sound was a whisper of a blade against the stone, but the guard didn't turn.

He lingered a moment on the opposite side, eyes devouring everything he could. He'd have to move quickly, stay alert, and stay focused. The palace was well-lit, even the wall had lanterns placed along it to make the shadows in between harder to hide in. To his right was the greenhouse, lights and shadows flickering inside, and to his left was the path towards the stables. With his weight carefully distributed on his feet, he walked silently along the path, grateful for his time endlessly circling the grounds for he knew which parts to avoid, where the stableboys lingered after dark drinking their ale and playing their card games.

The night was still, as though the world had taken a breath—waiting, watching. Even the horses were quiet when Azrael finally snuck into the building. His fingers were already shaking with nerves as he pulled out the lockpicks Bedivere had gifted him. He pressed his ear against the door first, straining to hear how far the distorted voices were. At the bottom of the door, light filtered through, but no shadows to indicate someone was on the other side. He took a breath before angling the picks in the lock.

One try.

Two.

Three tries.

Azrael took a breath, narrowing his focus. Relief dropped through him as the door clicked on the fourth, all his anxious thoughts eddied from him. The door creaked as he slipped in, but its quiet raised no alarm. He thought of the crudely drawn maps Lark had went over with him, and remembered when Magdalene had walked him through the palace—now, he felt like a stranger lurking in these halls.

He turned over each step of his part in his mind as he carefully moved forward, towards the main hall of the palace. Find the wolf, follow the right wall, get into the king's room, the signal—hoping Rook was where she was supposed to be—and capture Melech. The rest was up to Lark. Azrael still detested relying on Rook, but he knew that Lark was in the city as well, watching the palace. Ready to move if something wasn't right.

Just as he edged the corner, a servant walked past, her back rigid and eyes forward, completely missing Azrael. He pitched himself against the wall, unsure if his heart would burst through his chest right here in the palace, and gave himself five even breaths before glancing around the corner. Now that it was empty again, he inched up the incline, towards the circular throne room.

Azrael had grumbled and protested that this was the easy way in when Lark reviewed the passages with him. If the main hall was the most used and accessed, how would this be easy?

The voices he had heard before, distorted from the distance in the stable, were clear now. One on each end of the hall. Azrael snapped against the pillars that lined the floor just before the guard on the eastern side turned towards him.

This he was prepared for, but he much preferred outright battle to stealth. He had nothing to throw, as he had before, instead he curled his hand into a fist and pounded twice on the pillar he leaned against. The voices stilled.

If he had to be stealthy, he would at least work it to his advantage.

Footsteps grew closer to him, the guard's annoyed breathing sounded just on the other side of the pillar. Azrael waited another moment—

The guard was at his shoulder, the irritated look lasting only a fraction of a moment before shifting into surprise. Azrael's hand flew out, careening straight into the guard's neck. He crumpled without a word, though his body thudded against the floor.

The second guard called out, unsteady footfalls crept closer. Azrael thanked the god of night for Melech's incompetent guards as the second unsheathed his sword, the hiss of steel revealing to Azrael the distance of the second man. Swiftly, he turned, planting his right foot over the unconscious body, and caught the guard's wrist with one hand while his other collided in the same spot on the man's neck. Just as quickly as the first, the second guard was unconscious, suspended still by Azrael's hold on his wrist.

He debated, as he sheathed the guard's sword to leave the men there or to move them and risk being caught. Only giving himself a moment to weigh both options, he hastened to move both bodies back to where they had stood, positioning them just so as to imitate they had fallen asleep. Azrael lingered, listening for hurried footsteps or concerned voices, but heard nothing before he moved to the throne.

The tapestry of the wolf billowed softly in the air from the windows far above him, though it seemed the wolf called to him. He touched a fingertip to the threaded image before slipping behind it, pushing against the wall. As Lark had described, it gave way beneath his hands, and he stumbled into pure black.

He may as well have stepped into the mountain itself. The dampness in the passage, the spiderwebs clinging to his face, the eerie quiet unsettled Azrael as he kept his right hand pressed against the cold stone. He walked carefully, despite Lark telling him the walkway would be smooth and that he didn't have to worry about tripping or falling. The black was so pure, he couldn't make out his left hand as he held it to his face, never mind his darkened fingers.

An eternity, hundreds of steps, hundreds of tumultuous heartbeats later, Azrael's fingertips ran along a seam in the stone, a perfectly straight crack. Melech's sitting room. He emptied his head of every thought, every worry, and narrowed his focus to this. The king would leave this palace, dead or alive, and Azrael would be with him. He pressed against the door, heard a click, and shifted to open it before he stepped down onto the red carpeted floor.

The king's rooms were silent—deathly silent. Azrael hovered near the door, straining to hear the king, but only heard the sounds of the city. He crept forward, towards the king's empty desk, and glanced to either side as he stopped before it. Behind the desk, Azrael noticed the double doors to the balcony were open, inviting the warm air. Moonlight danced on the stone and a shadow shifted, stretching across the ground.

Azrael moved as a ghost, half hidden by the shadows in the room, to see Melech leaning against the railing, looking out over the courtyard. Even from his cloaked place, Azrael could see the lights in the streets, the fires by the tents, but no sign of the army that waited out in the darkness.

"I knew you would come for me again."

Melech's voice was different than the last time Azrael had heard him. Calm. The king wore his usual clothes: his shirt partly unbuttoned and fluttering in the breeze while parts remained tucked into his slim pants, and no weapons Azrael could see. His fingers grazed the dagger on his right thigh.

The king turned once Azrael made no reply, his face a lethal calm. Rage burned in his eyes clear as the day, while the shadows accentuated the sharp lines of his cheekbones. If Azrael hadn't seen a true demon, he would have thought the king looked like one now. Every nerve in his body screamed that something was wrong; that his plan would not work.

"Sorry to keep you waiting," he said, mustering as much venom as he could, but he knew his voice fell flat. As angry as he was with the king, he couldn't shake the unsettling chill that spread across his back, as though someone was watching him from the shadows.

"Where is she?" The words were clipped, spit through clenched teeth, as the king's jaw feathered.

"Is she not here?" If he couldn't be angry, he would be daring. "Weren't you two supposed to get married—so you could be a rightful king?"

Melech's face warped into something even darker, something hardly human. "You are *nothing,* boy. Did she tell you you'd be king? You thought you could be something more, something *greater,* but you are fated for nothing. You are nothing, and you will not be remembered for anything. A better swordsman will come along, a better fuck for your woman, and you will be forgotten in the past. You are nothing," he hissed, each word like a dagger.

The king had moved closer as he spoke, his face a breath away from Azrael's. Spitting and seething, Melech's eyes were black with rage and hatred. Azrael's chill deepened as he realized the king was trying to push him back into the room, away from the balcony.

He rooted his feet, raised his chin, and kept his eyes locked with the king's. He was only a hand taller than Azrael, but he seemed to tower. Azrael waited, the groan of wood hardly more than a whisper, before he darted to the side. An arrow embedded itself in Melech's arm.

He howled in pain as Azrael ripped the arrow from the king's arm and hurled it back through the room. A grunt, sputtering, a thud.

Azrael pulled a dagger from its sheathe and walked over to the archer. Boaz trembled, fingers weakly grasping at the arrow in his throat. Azrael swiped the sword from his side, kicking the archer in the ribs as he did, and ignored the swearing and the blood quickly pooling around him. The archer's eyes flickered to the side, and Azrael had a moment to turn before another Tiras leapt from the darkness. Their blades met, steel against steel singing in the night. The spearman—the boulder of a man, Caed, grinned horribly in the silvery light as his free hand lunged for Azrael's throat.

Using that force, Azrael shifted, letting Caed stumble forward as he withdrew his own sword. In a swift downwards swing, Caed's sword clattered to the ground and Azrael's cut through the spearman's wrist, severing his giant hand. Caed's yell was unearthly as he whirled towards Azrael, the bloody stump of what had been his hand raised in the air as though he might still try to strangle Azrael.

The steadiness of Azrael's anger returned, as though now his body had come to terms with the sudden, violent threat and rose to meet it. He flipped his sword in his hand before sliced through Caed's other wrist, the dull thud drowned out by his howling.

"Death follows you," Caed spit as he lowered to his knees, nearly eye level with Azrael now.

"No," Azrael said, stepping closer as he angled his blade, "I *am* death."

And buried his sword in Caed's neck.

A bow groaned in the night, a bowstring snapped, but Azrael dropped to the floor, using Caed's body as a shield. With his free hand, Azrael loosened a dagger and hurled it towards the archer. A string of curses told Azrael it had found its mark, and he slid his sword free.

"I thought you were trouble," Daerin, his training partner and fellow swordsman, hissed as he appeared before Azrael, blade in hand. His pale skin and crystal eyes made Azrael think of Luned, and how he was here for a purpose bigger than revenge.

"I'm here for him," Azrael said, swinging the tip of his sword towards Melech, who stood by the balcony cupping his bleeding arm as he watched the melee. "To answer for crimes against the kingdom, and to step down as king."

"Ah," Daerin said, as though it were a misunderstanding. "For your witch bitch to climb onto that throne? I don't think so."

A dagger clattered to the marble floor as the archer behind Daerin yanked the blade from his body, from wherever it had found its mark.

"Drop the bow," a female voice growled, rupturing the tension in the king's rooms as it called both dueling men to attention. Azrael glanced towards the doors, lit faintly by a lantern outside, to Jordie, chin high as her sword lifted to the archer's neck. Her eyes did not leave Wright, but Azrael realized the red cuff around her wrist on her uniform had been removed, replaced by lace.

Behind her, more bodies filled the space in the entrance to the king's room. For once, Azrael thought only of how to save the lives remaining in the room, instead of his usual thought process of how to easily kill them.

"Kill them," Melech's voice pierced the moment.

Daerin whirled on Azrael, but he knew how the swordsman fought, having trained with him often. Daerin moved too fast and without thinking, trying to gain the upper hand quickly through overwhelming attacks. Azrael matched his ferocity, but pushed back, slowing Daerin's next hit.

Fighting din roared by the doors, as boots scuffled and blood dripped onto the tile, but Azrael didn't dare take his eyes off the swordsman before him.

Daerin advanced, his footwork pushing Azrael backwards, into the shadows untouched by the fighting and the light. Azrael let him, adjusting his own pattern as their fight turned to a deadly dance. Time slowed as Azrael neared the wall, a plan forming quickly and messily in his head. He turned from Daerin, using the natural curve of the wall to his advantage and propelled himself upwards, turning with his sword posed to cut down his once-partner.

But Daerin was quicker, his own blade not raised to meet Azrael's, but to cut through his abdomen.

# CHAPTER 48

## AZRAEL

Azrael didn't know what happened, not as Daerin disappeared in a flash of red and black, until a string of swearing caught his attention as he dropped to the floor. Ahmi had taken Daerin to the ground, the latter's sword skidding across the floor. Azrael glanced over to where Jordie had been, where she stood once more, only now she was covered in blood and holding Wright's hands while he kneeled before her. With both his assailants detained, Azrael turned his attention back to the king.

Melech stood once more on the balcony, his body relaxed as though a man hadn't been murdered in his sitting room moments before.

"Face me, you demon," Azrael hissed as he slammed the balcony doors shut.

"Says death himself." Melech's arm bled slowly now, a steady *drip drip drip* onto the smooth stones of the balcony.

Azrael circled his wrist, the sword in his hand arcing, itching to bury it within the king, but forced himself to remember the plan—bringing the king down alive. *Alive.*

Melech turned fast while Azrael reminded himself of the plan, that fury once again bright in his body, with a sword in his weakened grip. The tip slashed along Azrael's chest—shallow enough to make him stumble, but not deep enough to stop him. The plan he was supposed to stick to was slipping from his blackened fingers. Azrael lunged at the king.

Melech sidestepped before Azrael's blade collided with the railing, the reverberation echoing through the palace and courtyard. Yelling below the two men erupted, warning bells pealed in the dead of the night, and Azrael knew his lack of a signal had brought this upon the city. Angry with himself and his part in the plan, he lunged for the king again, aiming for the man's ribs as he thought about the splintering of bone as the blade burrowed within, but Melech put his feeble strength into deflecting the blow. Melech moved too quick for a man wounded, knocking Azrael's sword from his hands and kicking it off the balcony.

Azrael laughed without humor, seeing it as nothing more than a challenge. He kneed the king between his legs then. As the king buckled, Azrael caught where the arrow had embedded itself in Melech's arm, grasping his bicep and tightening his grip. Melech dropped to the ground, spitting and swearing. His grip had loosened enough that Azrael nudged the sword from the king's hand and sent it over the edge, following his own sword.

Leaning over the king, Azrael tightened the pressure on Melech's wound, inciting an inhuman sound from deep within him. Melech thrashed forward, his head colliding with Azrael's nose. Blinding pain fractured across his vision as the bone broke, but Azrael stumbled away from the king.

He pulled the dagger from his left thigh and leapt at the king again, who wielded no weapon now. Melech lifted his forearm to block the blow and howled as the blade ripped through his flesh. With a sudden and iron grip, Melech wrapped his hand around Azrael's arm and yanked him closer, close enough they shared the same breath. The king wrenched the dagger from Azrael then, just before Azrael skidded backwards.

His lungs were *burning* and his face *fucking hurt,* but he knew that there was no taking the king alive. Melech would fight until his very last breath, and would not let Azrael live long enough to rejoice in that victory. He dared a glance towards the city, seeing the shadows of an army advancing through the streets. His heart sunk, knowing the months of planning and ideas of stealth had dissipated in the matter of a few moments that last too long.

With a yell that ripped from his burning core, he unsheathed a knife from his arm and hurled it at the king.

Melech lifted the dagger he had stolen, and swatted the flying blade away. Before Melech could do the same, Azrael leapt forward, gripping the weakened wrist in one hand and the king's shoulder in the other, yanking it over the railing. With a swift movement, he broke the king's elbow, nearly the same way he had broken it months ago.

The king fell to the ground then, yelling in rage and pain as he coddled his arm against his chest.

"Surrender!" Azrael yelled, his voice hoarse and hardly recognizable.

"Death first!" Melech lifted his head towards Azrael, his black eyes a challenge Azrael couldn't ignore.

Azrael leapt on the king again, unable to quell the rage and pain he had felt all these months that rose to redden his vision. Hit after hit, Azrael didn't stop until his knuckles screamed, red and bloodied, and Melech's knee jammed into his stomach. His spin hunching, the king's knee hit again, rattling Azrael's ribs. His aching knuckles hit the king's jaw again, before Melech hurled Azrael off of him.

In a swift movement, Melech was on his feet and had Azrael by his throat with his unhurt hand. He pushed Azrael against the railing, forcefully enough that the air slipped from his lungs and he couldn't catch his breath.

His spine would break, he thought. He would break in half as the king wrenched the air out of his lungs.

Azrael tried prying the king's fingers away, but his grip was deadly.

His head was going to explode.

His lungs would burst within him.

He'd fall over the railing, into whatever battle raged below, and Lark would scrap him off the stones.

Far below and all too close, he heard his name in the darkness, in the wind. Was she here? She couldn't be.

Azrael pushed his foot against Melech's thigh, trying to kick him away, but his grip broke too soon, and he flipped himself over the railing. Azrael desperately gripped for the metal, everything slowing down around him as his knuckles turned white.

He couldn't die like this.

He wrapped his feet around the posts, trying to find support. Melech pounded on his fingers, trying to lift them, prying them one by one, to loosen him.

Coward. *Bastard.*

"Azrael, you will die a traitor's death tonight."

Whatever had happened below stopped. Silence.

Dead silence ripped through the palace.

Azrael hurled himself up, knocking Melech's legs out from under him. The king crashed on top of him and pummeled his fists anywhere he could land a blow. Melech dug his unbroken elbow into Azrael's chest, where he had sliced his sword, and once more emptied Azrael's lungs.

He had another dagger in his boots, if only he could—

Melech noticed what he was trying, and removed the blade himself, and sunk it in Azrael's ribs.

He didn't realize he was yelling, even as his body convulsed beneath the king, until Melech twisted the blade, and everything went black. Focused. Black again. Focused again.

Melech yanked the dagger out—Azrael's breath, his life, his *soul* with it. The king lifted him to the railing once more, as though Azrael were nothing but a doll.

"Siena!" Melech roared, his voice growing hoarse as the syllables dragged on.

The sound of blood dripping on stone.

Breathing.

Whispers.

Far, far away laughter.

"Here is your king."

It was the whispers that guided Azrael back. Back from the darkness that threatened to take him. As though a hand were guiding him, he pushed away from the railing. He swiped the dagger from the ground, and whirled on Melech, his arm wrapping around the king's neck, the blade kissing the skin below his left ear. Every muscle, every single nerve, in Azrael's body screamed in agony, but anger and that pinpoint focus kept him on his feet.

"Tell them!" Azrael screeched. "Tell them what a monster you've become!"

The crowd below had grown—nobles and soldiers alike converged in the palace courtyard. Azrael knew Lark was amongst them, knew her soul amongst all the others.

"Tell them who controls the Daeoan," Azrael said, loud enough each word drifted down to the crowd with deadly precision.

"I do," Melech hissed.

The blade bit a little deeper into the king's neck.

"Tell them how you killed Nekoda—how you took the throne from his bloodline. Tell them!" he roared. Azrael hardly recognized his own voice.

"I did it—for Havriel—"

"The Greater doesn't watch over Havriel. Who does, Melech? What's the god's name you erased?" The whispers erupted within him, burning and swirling in the darkness.

"Iah."

"Who should be on that throne?" Azrael pushed the blade harder, its tip biting further into the king.

"Siena—"

Hissing, gurgling, and Azrael's hand burned as the king's body shuddered beneath his hold. Azrael let go, the dagger clattering on the stone before sliding off the balcony's edge. Melech tried turning, to face Azrael, eyes unfocused and black as the night with such *hatred* burning within them. The king took a step backward.

Over the rail.

Melech landed with a crack.

# CHAPTER 49

## LARK

Lark stumbled forward, pushing past the sweaty, bloody bodies that kept shoving into her, hand thrown out before her as shadows lurched forward from her, invisible even to her in the mess of the courtyard. The lanterns deepened the black pools of night, casting a decisive orange light on the falling body. Her name lingered in the air, singling her out as a spotlight, but she had ignored the pairs of eyes that had turned to her. Once he had bent over that railing, Lark was moving, not fast enough through the din that had erupted after Ahmi and Jordie had led the way out of the palace with two Tiras tied up and bloody, followed by Hollis and Kai, their bows at the ready.

Her shadows wrapped around the king's body just as it shattered on the stone, the crack of his spine piercing through her like lightning.

She fell to her hands and knees as noise exploded behind her—shouting, screaming, the hiss of steel. It may as well have been all in her head, for as loud as it was, until wetness touched her lips, and she realized she was crying. Everything stopped then.

The darkness covering his body quivered before it disappeared, reveling the broken man she had spent the last six years beside. Those black eyes, unfocused and unseeing, with bruises and blood nearly obscuring. The unnatural jut of his neck and collarbones. The blood pooled beneath him, slipping across the stones to her as though he wanted to touch her one last time.

It was too much.

All too much.

Her mother, her father, and now Melech—the kingdom had taken their lives as though Havriel itself was hungry for their blood.

Arms scooped beneath her, trying to pull her up and away, but she swatted them away. This was her doing—this death was on her hands.

She hadn't wanted him to die, hadn't wanted this to be the ending for him. She hadn't wanted Azrael to hold this death within him, blackening his heart the way he denied, but Lark knew it did anyway. A hole had been ripped in her own heart, jagged and tender, the day Melech had turned against her, but it felt fresh and brutal seeing his body in this way.

Lark looked up to the balcony where Melech and Azrael had fought, but the latter was nowhere to be seen. She wiped at her face, mixing her tears with his blood that had found its way to her, but hands grabbed her once again—more this time—and dragged her back, away from the king. Her eyes didn't leave him, until soldiers and nobles alike crowded around her, obscuring his body and making Lark painfully aware of all those who watched her.

Her body came to attention, and she caught her feet, wrenching herself free from those who dragged her along. Her mind fell quiet, ignoring the violence quieting around her and the chorus of names floating above the city. Straightening her shoulders, she walked alongside, who she now noticed, Hadri and Asenneth with her chin high, cheeks streaked red and white.

In a night of death and darkness, Lark was queen, and acutely aware of the world watching.

# CHAPTER 50

## AZRAEL

Something had carried Azrael back from the unlife, whatever it had been that awaited beyond death. He had caught a glimpse of that shimmering world, only to be whisked back to the one where his body *ached* and his soul felt like a weight within his chest.

The world around him went on in silence, the only thing that seemed to move was the sun as its light shifted across the floor in the room. He was stuck somewhere between sleeplessness and fitful bouts of sleep, even after the darkness that had taken him nearly as soon as he walked back into Melech's rooms. He'd collapsed onto the bloodstained rug and departed from Havriel, drifting in the stars.

He hadn't seen Lark since Melech fell, but he knew that she had been carried off by lords and nobles and officials to sit through a meeting to stitch Havriel back together.

Pressure began to build within his head, spreading from the back of his neck as though someone pressed against his spine. He groaned, covering his sore eyes with his hands, wishing he could fall back into that blackness that he lingered in when he fell asleep. Not exactly peaceful, but easier than this.

A knock interrupted his thoughts, piercing the air before the creak of wood echoed. Boots scuffed against the marble floor, coming up beside the bed.

"You're awake." The voice sounded far away, despite the footsteps at his side.

Azrael moved his hands from his eyes and blinked against the dull brightness. Ahmi stood at his side, his wavy hair longer than the last time Azrael had seen him. His friend's face was bright, but his eyes were dark.

"The coronation is at dusk, and Lark wonders if you can make it."

His heart sank. A small part of him had hoped he could be there once he didn't feel death breathing down his neck. He must have said it aloud, as Ahmi sighed.

"She said that too, but she can't put it off. It has to be done. It's been three days," Ahmi said as he settled down on the edge of the bed. *Bed*—Azrael was in a room.

He sat up, quicker than he meant to, and his body barked in protest.

"You don't look great, but no one will be looking at you anyway," Ahmi said, his head tilting as he studied his friend. Azrael wondered what it was that Ahmi saw.

*Demon slayer. King killer.*

"Though, I suppose that's not true. You'll be the reason everyone is there, and the city loves good gossip—"

Azrael glared at his friend, but the annoyance he felt dissipated when Ahmi smiled, his shit eating grin that told Azrael he'd be fine.

"We'll get you wine, and I'm sure Hadri has some kind of herb in her stockpile that will make you feel like you're in the clouds. I'll find you the cleanest clothes I can and—" Ahmi stopped, still studying Azrael's face. "Enough saw what happened, Az. It wasn't in cold blood. They know that."

He wasn't sure if he believed Ahmi. Even if he did, Azrael knew that the dark part of him, the one that thrived and had made him the skilled soldier he was, had wanted to kill the king in cold blood, for all he'd done. The kingdom's opinion didn't matter if Azrael thought the worst of himself.

The fear of hanging off the edge, as Melech tried to pry his fingers from the railing, still lingered in his stomach, his feet, his hands. The sound of Melech's bones breaking echoed over and *over again,* the memories thorns burrowing into his heart. If the kingdom hadn't seen it, Azrael didn't know where he would be.

Ahmi slid off the bed, his smile warming his eyes. "Come on, I'll help you get ready. The kingdom of wolves awaits."

†

## LARK

Lark's hands were slick with sweat as she stood before her people, all packed into the room as tightly as they could. She had asked Ahmi to bring Azrael, hoping that he was well enough to be on his feet, but she couldn't hope any longer. Not when the two city officials beside her, covered from shoulder to floor in black, flowing robes with silver glinting in their ears and hands, stared her down when she had taken her time walking up the dais. Nothing about this moment could be postponed.

Dusty purple light filtered in from the domed ceiling window above her, and she breathed a little easier, knowing at least if her nerves were unravelling, she knew she looked the part of queen. She'd had Magdalene's mother sew one of the most extravagant gowns she'd ever worn, with thin layers of lavender, pink, and silver flowing together to resemble dusk incarnate. The sleeves were cuffed at her wrists, but she hid them amongst the folds of her dress, hoping the twitching and beads of sweat wouldn't be as noticeable as she thought.

In Havrien custom, the two city officials began speaking—a tale of becoming, a tale of parts molding to be one, a tale of two kingdoms turning into three. Lark listened to her kingdom's history without focus while her eyes roved over the crowd, soaking in each breath, each flicker of eyes.

All her life was built around this point—this *becoming*.

Shadows flickered around her fingertips, aching to be let loose. She hadn't used her magic since Melech fell, other than to stabilize Azrael and keep him from death's embrace, and the toll of not using it threatened to overwhelm her.

*The pieces come together,* Iah's voice floated around Lark's head, curling like a cat might before it settles down. The god of night had been unusually quiet since she'd taken residence in the palace again, hardly a whisper or a hum of a lullaby. *Now you cannot fall.*

"Sienna Hostien, daughter of late King Nekoda Hostien, princess of the Vale, eyes of the Roe, and protector of Havriel."

Lark's attention snapped to the officials beside her, away from the mystery manifesting in the form of the god of night and towards the two mortal men beside her. She offered one of the small, polite smiles she'd been perfecting for this moment, and nodded.

"Swear your oath," the two men said, once again, together.

She looked away from them, back towards the sea of people before her, all awaiting the promise her family had made them. Lark could see the shadow of hope lingering in their faces—hope that she would be different than those who had come before her. Better.

"With my life, I protect and serve Havriel and her people. I will honor her and lead her into a bright future, out of the shadow of tragedy. From this day until my very last, I swear this."

Once the words were out, peace settled within Lark. The pieces of her life came together, finally creating the image she had been working towards. The official at her right lifted the crown from the pedestal behind her and moved close enough his breath was hot on the back of her neck. With steady hands, he rested the crown on her head, its weight a welcome feeling.

"Sienna Hostien, born of the Vale, heart of the Roe, Queen of Havriel," the officials spoke in unison, voices booming over the crowd, echoing off the stone walls.

A tear skidded down her cheek, slicing a line in the powder on her face, as cheering erupted—her people finally welcoming her home.

# CHAPTER 51

## AZRAEL

Two weeks of planning passed by in a frenzy. Preparation for their hand-fasting, new ships docked every day in Westwick while horses carried lords and commonfolk, and everyone in between, into the city. Azrael watched them all from the view on his balcony, sitting with his legs dangling over the edge and his forehead pressed against the bottom of the railing. The part of him that had feared heights had died. Many parts of him had died since that night. Darkness had made its home within him, swirling and churning like the storms he had always seen within Lark's eyes.

After her coronation, which Azrael watched with a painful dizziness, she had made an announcement, first in appointing him as commander of Havriel's armies, then as her soon-to-be husband and king. Both had been a struggle for the people to come to terms with, but he had known why she did it, and so soon. The kingdom needed stability, and having two on the throne would do just that.

Within his rooms, the door opened, a servant announced his celebration attire was ready and on the bed, and the door closed.

He didn't move, only kept watching as the palace gates opened and a brightly colored crowd passed through. Glancing down at his shaking hands, he imagined the way they would look tied to Lark's, intertwined with leaves and string. His heart still meant what he had told her—as long as he was at her side, he could die a happy man. He would be at her side, forever and always, even if the notion of commanding armies and ruling a kingdom terrified him. A big fear, one that Lark would know and understand.

Azrael gave himself a few more moments of numbness before he pushed his melancholy, miserable thoughts aside and welcomed the joys of the celebration to come. He pulled himself up, hands tight on the railing, and ambled back into his rooms.

He'd commissioned an intricate shirt and detailed pants from Magdalene's mother and overpaid her. Once he looked at the final design of it, laid on his untouched bedsheets, his heart swelled. He knew the design was a compliment to Lark's dress, and he could only imagine how she looked as she was getting ready with Hadriana and Thea in the next suite. With the Vale's custom, he hadn't seen Lark since the morning before.

Within the threads, Azrael picked apart a story in the detailing—the one of him and Lark, his life in tangible form, colored richly in ornate threading. He hadn't realized that the seamstress had known so much or been privy her queen's life. On the section of cloth that would rest against his heart, the coloring changed from silver into lavender to the very gray of Lark's eyes. He ran his black fingertip over this, shaking ever so slightly.

The moment didn't feel real, even as he dressed and smoothed out the mess of curls in his hair. It still didn't feel real as he made the trek through the palace, up to the top floor, and set out onto the pathway that led up the mountain's face to the small plateau that overlooked the Vale.

Dusk began to fall, but enough light led his way along the dirt path. Each nerve, each muscle, was on fire within Azrael. He pulled and picked at the edges of his sleeves, rubbing the pads of his fingers along the threading, searching, not for the strength to bind himself to Lark, but for the knowledge that this was the right thing for the kingdom—not just themselves.

At the end of the path, there was a small ledge he hauled himself up, dirt dusting his knees, and, as he straightened, took in the sight of everyone—his family. Bedivere stood with Luned, her right arm wrapped around his waist as he spoke to Ahmi. Thea and Isabel were crouched beside the edge, pointing out towards the ocean. Hadriana and Hollis stood with Jordie and the other

Tiras, the ones who remained devoted to Lark and Azrael. At the far edge of the plateau, Lark, a woman he could only assume was her mother Harlow, and the official to guide their handfasting.

As he took in the sight of Lark, dressed in the lavender hues daring to match her eyes and the same detailing that wove on his shirt front, his heart thundered against his ribs, desperate to burst. Her hair was down, perfect waves down her straight back, and a smile that threatened to knock the air from his lungs as she turned her head towards him.

Harlow squeezed her daughter's arm before stepping away, joining the awaiting crowd. Azrael paid them no heed, not after his eyes settled on Lark, and he walked straight to her. How foolish he was to be frightened of this, weary of these next moments. How dull he was to think that, together, they wouldn't build Havriel stronger, better. The darkness writhing within his heart seemed to shrink in the purple light of her.

"Darling Az," she murmured, her hands now slack at her side. She extended her fingers just enough to graze his.

The official before them, a wiry old man whom Azrael was sure also had been present during her coronation, nodded in a silent question.

"My queen," he whispered back. He straightened his shoulders as he reluctantly turned his attention to the official and the length of cord he held in both out-stretched hands.

"We are brought together to bind these souls as one. Bound by mulberry, for ever will there be sweetness." The official paused, awaiting their hands. Together, they intertwined their hands and offered them to the official. As he spoke, he began to wrap the cord. "Bound by rosemary, for there will be remembrance of this moment and all those before that brought you here. Bound by nettle, for ever will you protect one another, and the kingdom borne forth from your union."

The official lowered his head in reverence as he tied the final knot, whispering a prayer in Old Havrien.

Azrael turned then to Lark, their joined hands in-between them. He lifted his free hand to cup her cheek, studying each miniscule detail of her face—the glint of the rising moonlight bouncing off the gems encrusted into the delicate crown she wore embedded in her hair, the brightness in her grey eyes, the way her gentle lips curved into a smile once she noticed his intense attention.

"I am yours, and you are mine," Azrael began. Lark began to speak the same words, their voices overlapping. "The center of my heart, the light in my darkness. I am bound to you in life until the unlife, where I will find you again."

At the end of their voices coming together, their friends and family burst into the beginning of night.

"To you, the kingdom of Havriel, and to the god above us," the official's voice rose against the din, "I present: Queen Siena Hikaim, and her husband, Azrael Hikaim, future king of Havriel."

# EPILOGUE

## JAKIAH

*G* *o now.*
        *Take our kingdom.*

Jakiah obeyed his god, swimming down from his place amongst the stars, shifting and swirling. He relished in the faint kiss of freedom, even as he dove willingly into a cage. He would become mortal again, thrive once more amongst humanity. A thousand years amongst the black of night, wading in the cosmos the same way as mortals drifted in their oceans. He laughed as he fell, the light from both moon and god shining on him.

## AZRAEL

Azrael leaned against the railing, overlooking the sleeping city. He still wore no clothes, the warmth of the night still burning within him. He was certain he was still drunk, despite his coronation celebration having been over for hours now.

*King Azrael* sounded strange to him, and would for some time. Lark hadn't been shy of using his new title though, and the sound of her gasping it as they molded together echoed in his ears.

He glanced behind him, through the open doors, at the sleeping form of his wife, a thin sheet strewn over her as she slept. He couldn't help the smile that stretched his lips at the sight. So long he had dreaded this, so long had he feared this position. So long had he hidden in the shadows.

Turning back to the city, Azrael noticed a shadow flickering before him, as though darkness had solidified. From within that black, a growl erupted, sending a shiver down Azrael's spine, before the smell hit him—death and decay. His hand flew to his side, where his sword rested, and his heart sunk. Before he could shout to Lark, a phantom hand wrapped around his throat.

The Daeoan closed the distance between them, its smell choking the air from his lungs. The demon grabbed the back of Azrael's head and placed its other on his bare chest. A coldness spread within his chest, as though he'd been out in the cold for too long, moving throughout his body. It quickly turned to a haunting emptiness that made him feel entirely hollow. Azrael could do nothing but stare into the black, barely making out the details of the broken face that devoured him.

The demon began to distort then, darkness flashing like bolts of lightning. Every bone in Azrael's ribcage began to crack and splinter, every wound Melech had given him opened again. He tried to cry out, only for his collarbone to snap.

Suddenly, a stillness fell over him, and the Daeoan had disappeared. Everything stopped, his breath, his heart, the sounds of merriment and fire crackling within the city.

*King.*

The thought erupted from the base of his skull, as though it had been spoken from behind him. A deep growl reverberated along his bones, setting his heart and lungs back into motion, though neither were of his own accord. He was paralyzed.

Azrael tried lifting his finger, tried turning towards Lark, still sleeping, but he could not. His body would not obey.

The Vale grew dark, sheer curtains dragged over the view he beheld. Familiar darkness pooled within him, stretched along his consciousness like a cat—making itself at home within him, burrowing into the nooks and crannies of his soul as though it had known them. With a sudden jolt of cold, Azrael knew no more.

# PRONUNCIATION GUIDE

in order of appearance

**Azrael Hikaim** – AZ-re-el HEH-kame

**Nekoda Hostien** – Neh-kod-ah Hoe-sti-en

**Melech avi-Predae** – Meh-leck ah-vee Preh-day

**Havriel** - Have-ree-el

**The Roe** – Roh

**Tiras** – Tier-az

**Lark Areeta** – Lark Ah-ri-tah

**Brannon** – BRAN-nin

**Kal** – Cahl

**Ahmi** – AH-me

**Meir** – Mare

**Asenneth**- ASS-en-eth / **Asen** – ASS-en

**Hollis** -Hall-ess

**Hadri** – HAD-ree / **Hadriana** – HAD-ree-ah-nah

**Kanaan** – CAN-ahn

**Magdalene** – Mag-dah-lane

**Taya** – Tay-ah

**Areen** – AH-reen

**Nevan** – NEV-ahn

**Bedivere Tarrae** – BED-eh-veer Tah-ray

**Telaan** – TELL-ahn

**Iah** – EE-ah

**Banii** – BAH-knee

**Daeoan** – DAY-oh-en

**Laeseen** – Lay-scene

**Isabel** – Ee-sah-bell

**Thea** – Thay-uh

**Boaz** – Bow-az

**Ilaine** – EYE-lane

**Siena** – See-en-ah

**Kieran** – Keer-en

**Luned** – Loo- NED

**Piers** - Peers

**Daerin** – Day-rin

**Edhar** – Edd-HAR

**Jakiah** – YAH-kih-ah

# Acknowledgements

Where to begin?

I wrote a book!

A book that started as a short story that kept expanding, demanding that Azrael and Lark's stories be told.

I cannot possibly thank those who believed in this book enough. From those in my everyday life to the incredible friendships I've made through bookstagram.

Thank you Michelle, for seeing what my book is worth and providing me invaluable feedback.

Thank you Renee, for answering a million questions and never tiring of answering them.

Thank you Lindsey, for endlessly cheering me on and hyping me up.

Thank you Edwin, for being one of my biggest supporters of my book and my characters. Your support means the world.

Thank you to my partner for allowing me to work through plot holes, character arcs, and timelines with a straight face and willing to help through every step. Thank you for believing in me and supporting me in this dream.

The biggest thank you to you, dear reader, who has given life to this world I've created. I can't thank you enough for even picking up this book.

Now onto book two...

# About the Author

From the point where she could create stories, Cait always knew she would be a writer. From poetry, short stories, to full length novels, she is happiest when she's lost in a world she's created.

After earning a degree in arts, Cait decided that the world of writing was where her heart belonged. After life was uprooted during the pandemic, Cait decided to dedicate her time to writing and honing her craft—through reading, writing endless stories, and creating too many Pinterest boards.

When not in front of a blank document debating on a story, she's working on various projects, including a small bookstore, or spinning fantasy stories with her spawn.

Made in the USA
Middletown, DE
05 November 2023

41907584R00243